Dark Ave

❦

"I have been keeping an eye on Bunin's brilliant
talent. He really is the enemy."
Andrei Bely

"Your influence is truly beyond words… I do not know any
other writer whose external world is so closely tied
to another, whose sensations are more exact and
indispensable, and whose world is more genuine and
also more unexpected than yours."
André Gide

"He was a great stylist who wrote very suggestively.
He didn't spray us with ideologies or worries.
His writing is pure poetry."
Andrei Makine

"A most powerful 'connoisseur of colours'. One could write
an entire dissertation on his colour schemes."
Vladimir Nabokov

"You have, Mr Bunin, thoroughly explored the
soul of vanished Russia, and in doing so you have
most deservedly continued the glorious traditions
of the great Russian literature."
Professor Wilhelm Nordenson,
at the 1933 Nobel Prize banquet

ONEWORLD CLASSICS

Dark Avenues

Ivan Bunin

Translated by Hugh Aplin

ONEWORLD
CLASSICS

ONEWORLD CLASSICS LTD
London House
243-253 Lower Mortlake Road
Richmond
Surrey TW9 2LL
United Kingdom
www.oneworldclassics.com

Dark Avenues first published in 1946; the two stories 'In Spring, in Judaea'
and 'A Place for ther Night' in the Appendix first published in 1953
This edition first published by Oneworld Classics Limited in 2008
© Ivan Bunin, 1946, 1953
English Translation and Notes © Hugh Aplin, 2008
Extra material © Andrei Rogatchevski, 2008

Printed in Great Britain by CPI Cox & Wyman Ltd, Reading, Berkshire

ISBN: 978-1-84749-047-6

Contents

Ivan Bunin (1870–1953)

Dark Avenues

Part One

Dark Avenues

IN THE COLD, FOUL WEATHER of autumn, on one of Tula's highways, flooded by rains and indented with many black ruts, up to a long hut with a government posting station in one wing and private living quarters where one could rest or spend the night, have dinner or ask for the samovar in the other, there drove a tarantass,* bespattered with mud and with its top half-raised, pulled by three quite ordinary horses with their tails tied up out of the slush. On the box of the tarantass sat a sturdy peasant in a tightly belted, heavy cloth coat, serious and dark-faced, with a sparse, jet-black beard, looking like a robber of old, and inside the tarantass sat a svelte old military man in a large peaked cap and a grey greatcoat with an upright beaver collar of Nicholas I's time, still black-browed, but with white whiskers which joined up with similar sideburns; his chin was shaved, and his appearance as a whole bore that resemblance to Alexander II* which was so prevalent among military men at the time of his reign; his gaze was both enquiring, stern and at the same time weary.

When the horses came to a halt, he threw a leg in a level-topped military boot out of the tarantass and, holding back the skirts of the greatcoat with suede-gloved hands, ran up onto the porch of the hut.

"To the left, Your Excellency," the coachman cried out rudely from the box and, stooping slightly on the threshold because of his height, the man went into the little entrance hall, then to the left into the living quarters.

The living quarters were warm, dry and tidy: there was a new, gold-coloured icon in the left-hand corner, beneath it a table covered with a clean, unbleached tablecloth, and at the table there were benches, scrubbed clean; the kitchen stove, occupying the far right-hand corner, was newly white with chalk; nearer stood something like an ottoman, covered with mottled rugs, with its folding end resting against the side of the stove; from behind the stove door came the sweet smell of cabbage soup – cabbage boiled down until soft, beef and bay leaves.

The new arrival threw his greatcoat down on a bench and proved to be still more svelte in just his dress uniform and long boots; then he took off the gloves and cap, and with a weary air ran a pale, thin hand over his head – his grey hair, combed down on his temples towards the corners of his eyes, was slightly curling; his attractive, elongated face with dark eyes retained here and there minor traces of smallpox. There was nobody in the living quarters and, opening the door into the entrance hall a little, he cried out in an unfriendly way:

"Hey, anybody there?"

Immediately thereafter into the living quarters came a dark-haired woman, also black-browed and also still unusually attractive for her age, looking like an elderly gypsy, with dark down on her upper lip and alongside her cheeks, light on her feet, but plump, with large breasts under her red blouse and a triangular stomach like a goose's under her black woollen skirt.

"Welcome, Your Excellency," she said. "Would you be wanting to eat, or would you like the samovar?"

The new arrival threw a cursory glance at her rounded shoulders and light feet in worn, red Tatar slippers, and curtly, inattentively replied:

"The samovar. Are you the mistress here or a servant?"

"The mistress, Your Excellency."

"The place is yours then?"

"Yes, sir. Mine."

"How's that, then? A widow, are you, that you run things yourself?"

"Not a widow, Your Excellency, but you do have to make a living. And I like being in charge."

"Right, right. That's good. And how clean and pleasant you have it."

The woman was all the time looking at him searchingly, with her eyes slightly narrowed.

"I like cleanliness too," she replied. "I grew up with gentlefolk, after all, so how could I fail to know how to keep myself respectable, Nikolai Alexeyevich?"

He straightened up quickly, opened his eyes wide and blushed.

"Nadezhda! Is it you?" he said hurriedly.

"It's me, Nikolai Alexeyevich," she replied.

"My God, my God!" he said, sitting down on a bench and staring straight at her. "Who could have thought it! How many years since we last saw one another? About thirty-five?"

Thirty, Nikolai Alexeyevich. I'm forty-eight now, and you're getting on for sixty, I think."

"Something like that... My God, how strange!"

"What's strange, sir?"

"But everything, everything... How can you not understand!"

His weariness and absent-mindedness had vanished; he stood up and began walking decisively around the room, gazing at the floor. Then he stopped and, blushing through his grey hair, began to speak:

"I know nothing about you from that time on. How did you end up here? Why didn't you stay with your owners?"

"Soon after you, my owners gave me my freedom."

"And where did you live afterwards?"

"It's a long story, sir."

"You weren't married, you say?"

"No, I wasn't."

"Why? With the sort of beauty that you had?"

"I couldn't do it."

"Why not? What do you mean?"

"What is there to explain? You probably remember how I loved you."

He blushed to the point of tears and, with a frown, again began his pacing.

"Everything passes, my friend," he began mumbling. "Love, youth – everything, everything. The ordinary, vulgar story. Everything passes with the years. How does the Book of Job put it? 'Thou shalt remember it as waters that pass away'."*

"God treats people differently, Nikolai Alexeyevich. Youth passes for everyone, but love's a different matter."

He raised his head and, stopping, gave a painful grin:

"But I mean, you couldn't have loved me all your life!"

"But I could. However much time passed, I kept on living for the one thing. I knew the former you was long gone, that for you it was as if there had never even been anything, but then... It's too late for reproaches now, but you know, it's true, you did abandon me ever so heartlessly – how many times did I want to lay hands upon myself out of hurt alone, not even to mention everything else. There was a time, after all, Nikolai Alexeyevich, when I called you Nikolenka, and you called me – do you remember what? And you were good enough to keep on reciting me poetry about various 'dark avenues'," she added with an unfriendly smile.

"Ah, how good-looking you were!" he said, shaking his head. "How ardent, how beautiful! What a figure, what eyes! Do you remember how everyone used to stare at you?"

"I do, sir. You were extremely good-looking too. And you know, it was you I gave my beauty to, my ardour. How on earth can such a thing be forgotten?"

"Ah! Everything passes. Everything gets forgotten."

"Everything passes, but not everything gets forgotten."

"Go away," he said, turning and going up to the window. "Please, go away."

And taking out a handkerchief and pressing it to his eyes, speaking rapidly he added:

"If only God can forgive me. For you, evidently, have forgiven me."

She went up to the door and paused:

"No, Nikolai Alexeyevich, I haven't. Since our conversation has touched upon our feelings, I'll tell you straight: I never could forgive you. Just as there was nothing on earth dearer to me at that time than you, so was there nothing afterwards either. And that's why I can't forgive you. Well, but what sense is there in remembering, the dead don't get brought back from the graveyard."

"No, that's right, there's no point, order the horses to be brought up," he replied, moving away from the window with a face already stern. "I'll tell you one thing: I've never been happy in life, please don't think that. I'm sorry that I may be wounding your pride, but I'll tell you frankly – I was madly in love with my wife. But she was unfaithful, and abandoned me even more insultingly than I did you. I adored my son – while he was growing, what hopes did I not place on him! But he turned out a good-for-nothing, a spendthrift, insolent, without a heart, without honour, without a conscience... However, all that is the most ordinary, vulgar story too. Keep well, dear friend. I think I too lost in you the dearest thing I had in life."

She went up to him and kissed his hand, and he kissed hers.

"Order the horses..."

When they had set off on their way, he thought gloomily: "Yes, how delightful she was! Magically beautiful!" He remembered with shame his final words and the fact that he had kissed her hand, and was immediately ashamed of his shame. "Isn't it the truth, then, that she gave me the best moments of my life?"

Close to setting, a pale sun had peeped out. The coachman drove at a trot, ever shifting from one black rut to another, choosing the less muddy ones, and thinking about something too. Finally he said with serious rudeness:

"She kept on looking out of the window, Your Excellency, as we were leaving. You've probably been good enough to know her a long time?"

"A long time, Klim."

"That woman's got her head on her shoulders. And they say she keeps on getting richer. She lends money on interest."

"That doesn't mean anything."

"What do you mean, it doesn't! Who doesn't want to live a bit better! If you lend with a conscience, there's nothing much wrong with that. And they say she's fair on that score. But she's a harsh one! If you haven't repaid on time, you've only yourself to blame."

"Yes, that's right, you've only yourself to blame… Keep driving on, please, I'm afraid we might miss the train…"

The low sun shone yellow on the empty fields, the horses splashed steadily through the puddles. He gazed at the fleetingly glimpsed horseshoes, his black brows knitted, and thought:

"Yes, you've only yourself to blame. Yes, of course they were the best moments. And not merely the best, but truly magical! 'All round the scarlet dog rose bloomed, the avenues of dark limes stood…'* But my God, what would have happened later on? What if I hadn't abandoned her? What nonsense! This Nadezhda, not the keeper of a lodging house, but my wife, the mistress of my house in St Petersburg, the mother of my children?"

And closing his eyes, he shook his head.

20th October 1938

The Caucasus

ON ARRIVING IN MOSCOW, I put up furtively at inconspicuous rooms in a side street near the Arbat and led the tiresome life of a recluse – from meeting to meeting with her. During those days she visited me just three times, and each time she came in hurriedly with the words:

"I've only come for a minute..."

She was pale with the beautiful pallor of an excited woman in love, her voice would break, and the way that, after tossing her umbrella down anywhere, she would hurry to raise her veil and embrace me struck me with pity and delight.

"It seems to me," she would say, "he suspects something, that he even knows something – perhaps he's read one of your letters, found a key to open my desk... I believe he's capable of anything with his cruel, proud character. Once he said to me outright: 'I won't stop at anything in defending my honour, the honour of a husband and an officer!' Now for some reason he's watching literally my every move, and for our plan to succeed I have to be terribly careful. He's already agreed to let me go, so vehemently did I suggest to him I'd die if I didn't see the south, the sea, but for God's sake be patient!"

Our plan was audacious: to leave for the coast of the Caucasus by one and the same train and to live there in some completely wild place for three or four weeks. I knew that coast, I had once lived for some time near Sochi – when young and single – I had those autumn evenings amidst black cypresses by the cold, grey waves committed to memory for the rest of my life... And she would turn pale when I said: "And now I'll be there with you, in mountainous jungle, by the tropical sea..." We did not believe in the realization of our plan until the last minute – too great a happiness did it seem to us.

* * *

It was cold and wet in Moscow, it looked as if the summer was already over and would not return, it was dirty, murky, the crows were cawing, the streets glistened wet and black with the opened umbrellas of passers-by and the raised tops of cab men's droshkies, shaking as they sped along. And it was a dark, repulsive evening as I drove to the station, and everything inside me was freezing from anxiety and the cold. I ran through the station and along the platform with my hat pulled down towards my eyes and my face buried in the collar of my coat.

In the small first-class compartment which I had booked in advance, the rain was pouring noisily over the roof. I lowered the window blind at once and, as soon as the porter, wiping his wet hand on his white apron, had taken his tip and gone, I locked the door. Then I opened the blind a little and froze, my eyes fixed upon the heterogeneous crowds, scurrying back and forth beside the carriage with their things in the dark light of the station lamps. We had agreed that I would arrive at the station as early as possible and she as late as possible, so that I should not somehow bump into her and him on the platform. It was now already time they were here. I looked ever more tensely – still they weren't here. The second bell rang – I turned cold in fright: she was late, or suddenly at the last minute he had not let her go! But immediately after that I was struck by his tall figure, officer's peaked cap, tight greatcoat and the suede-gloved hand with which he held her by the arm as he strode out briskly. I recoiled from the window and fell into the corner of the couch. The second-class carriage was next door – in my mind I saw him getting into it with her masterfully, looking around to see if the porter had arranged things for her well, taking off his glove, taking off his cap, kissing her, making the sign of the cross over her... The third bell deafened me, the train moving off plunged me into a state of numbness... The train gathered pace, knocking, rocking, then began moving evenly at full speed... With an icy hand I slipped a ten-rouble note to the conductor who brought her to me and carried her things...

* * *

Coming in, she did not even kiss me, only smiled pitifully as she sat down on the couch and took off her hat, unfastening it from her hair.

"I couldn't eat dinner at all," she said. "I didn't think I could sustain this dreadful role through to the end. And I'm terribly thirsty. Give me some Narzan,* dear," she said, addressing me intimately for the first

12

time. "I'm convinced he'll come after me. I gave him two addresses, Gelendzhik and Gagry. Well, and in three or four days he'll be in Gelendzhik... But who cares, better death than this torment..."

* * *

In the morning, when I went out into the corridor, it was sunny and stuffy; from the toilets came the smell of soap, eau de cologne and everything a carriage full of people smells of in the morning. Passing outside the windows, heated up and dull with dust, was the level, scorched steppe, dusty wide roads could be seen, and carts drawn by bullocks, there were glimpses of trackmen's huts with the canary-yellow circles of sunflowers and scarlet hollyhocks in the front gardens... Further on there began the boundless expanse of bare plains with barrows and burial grounds, the unendurable dry sun, the sky resembling a dusty cloud, then the spectres of the first mountains on the horizon...

* * *

From both Gelendzhik and Gagry she sent him a postcard and wrote that she did not yet know where she would stay.

Then we went down along the coast towards the south.

* * *

We found a primeval place, overgrown with forests of plane trees, flowering shrubs, mahogany, magnolias and pomegranate trees, among which there rose fan palms and the cypresses showed black...

I would wake up early and, while she slept, before tea, which we drank around seven o'clock, walk over the hills to the woodland thickets. The hot sun was already strong, clear and joyous. In the woods the fragrant azure mist was shining, dispersing and melting away, beyond the distant wooded summits gleamed the everlasting whiteness of the snowy mountains... I would go back through our village's sultry marketplace with its smell of pressed dung burning from the chimneys; trade was seething there, it was crowded with people, saddle horses and donkeys – a multitude of mountaineers of different races assembled there at the market in the mornings – Circassian girls floated about in long, black

13

clothes down to the ground and red slippers, with their heads enfolded in something black, and with quick, birdlike glances flashing at times from that funereal enfoldment.

Later we would leave for the seashore, always completely deserted, bathe and lie in the sun right up until lunch. After lunch – always pan-fried fish, white wine, nuts and fruit – in the sultry twilight of our hut, under its tiled roof, hot, gay strips of light reached through the slatted shutters.

When the heat abated and we opened the window, the part of the sea that was visible from it between the cypresses standing on the slope below us had the colour of violets and lay so flat and peaceful that it seemed there would never be an end to this tranquillity, to this beauty.

At sunset, amazing clouds often piled up beyond the sea; their glow was so magnificent that at times she would lie down on the ottoman, cover her face with a gauze scarf and cry: another two or three weeks – and Moscow again!

The nights were warm and impenetrable, in the black darkness fireflies floated, twinkled, shone with a topaz light, tree frogs clanked like little glass bells. When the eye grew accustomed to the dark, the stars and the crests of the mountains stood out on high, and above the village were the outlines of trees that we did not notice in the daytime. And all night, from there, from the inn, could be heard the muffled banging of a drum and the throaty, doleful, hopelessly happy wailing of what always seemed to be one and the same endless song.

Not far from us, in a coastal ravine descending out of the wood to the sea, a shallow, limpid little river leapt quickly along its stony bed. How wonderfully its lustre rippled, seethed, at that mysterious hour when, like some marvellous creature, the late moon looked out intently from behind the mountains and the woods.

Sometimes during the night, terrifying clouds would approach from the mountains; there would be an angry storm; in the noisy, sepulchral blackness of the woods, magical green abysses were continually gaping open, and cracking out in the heavenly heights there were antediluvian claps of thunder. Then in the woods eaglets would wake up and mew, the snow leopard would roar, the jackals would yelp... Once a whole pack of them came running to our lighted window – on such nights they always congregate around dwellings – we opened the window and looked at them from above, and they stood in the gleaming torrent of rain and yelped, asking to come in... She cried for joy, looking at them.

* * *

He searched for her in Gelendzhik, in Gagry, in Sochi. The day after his arrival in Sochi, he bathed in the sea in the morning, then shaved, put on clean linen, a snow-white tunic, had lunch at his hotel on the terrace of the restaurant, drank a bottle of champagne, had coffee with chartreuse, unhurriedly smoked a cigar. Returning to his room, he lay down on the couch and shot himself in the temples with two revolvers.

12th November 1937

A Ballad

O N THE EVE OF the big winter holidays the country house was always heated up like a bathhouse and presented a strange picture, for it consisted of spacious and low rooms, the doors of which were all wide open throughout – from the entrance hall to the divan room, situated at the very end of the house – and its red corners* gleamed with wax candles and lamps in front of the icons.

On the eve of those holidays, they washed the smooth oak floors – which soon dried out from the heating – everywhere in the house, and then carpeted them with clean rugs; they set out in their places in the very best order the furnishings that had been moved aside for the period of work, and in the corners, in front of the gilded and silver settings of the icons, they lit the lamps and the candles and extinguished all other lights. By this time the winter night was already darkly blue outside the windows and everyone dispersed to their own sleeping quarters. Complete quiet was then established in the house, a peace that was reverential and seemingly waiting for something, and which could not have been more in keeping with the sacred nocturnal appearance of the mournfully and touchingly illumined icons.

In the winter the wandering pilgrim Mashenka was sometimes a guest on the estate, grey-haired, withered and tiny, like a little girl. And it was just she alone in all the house who did not sleep on such nights: arriving in the hallway from the servants' quarters after supper and removing the felt boots from her little, woollen-stockinged feet, she would go noiselessly over the soft rugs through all those hot, mysteriously lit rooms, kneel down everywhere, cross herself, bow down before the icons, and then go back to the hallway, sit down on the black chest that had stood in it from time immemorial, and in a low voice recite prayers, psalms, or else simply talk to herself. It was thus I found out one day about this "beast of God, the Lord's wolf': I heard Mashenka praying to him.

I could not sleep, and I went out late at night into the reception hall to go through to the divan room and there get something to read from the bookcases. Mashenka did not hear me. She was sitting saying something in the dark hallway. Pausing, I listened closely. She was reciting psalms from memory.

"Hear my prayer, O Lord, and give ear unto my cry," she said, without any expression. "Hold not thy peace at my tears, for I am a stranger with thee, and a sojourner on the earth, like all my fathers were...*

"Say unto God: how terrible art thou in thy works!*

"He that dwelleth in the secret place of the most High shall abide under the shadow of the Almighty... Thou shalt tread upon the lion and adder, the young lion and the dragon shalt thou trample under foot..."*

At the last words she quietly but firmly raised her voice and pronounced them with conviction: trample upon the lion and the dragon. Then she paused and, after slowly sighing, spoke thus, as if conversing with somebody:

"For every beast of the forest is his, and the cattle upon a thousand hills..."*

I peeped into the hallway: she was sitting on the chest with her little, woollen-stockinged feet hanging down from it evenly and holding her arms crossed at her breast. She was looking straight ahead, not seeing me. Then she raised her eyes to the ceiling and uttered distinctly:

"And thou, beast of God, the Lord's wolf, pray for us to the Queen of Heaven."

I approached and said softly:

"Mashenka, don't be afraid, it's me."

She let her arms drop, stood up, gave a low bow:

"Hello, sir. No, sir, I'm not afraid. What have I got to be afraid of now? It was in my youth I was silly, afraid of everything. The dark-eyed demon troubled me."

"Please sit down," I said.

"No, sir," she replied. "I'll stand, sir."

I put my hand on her bony little shoulder with its big collarbone, made her sit down, and then sat down next to her:

"Sit still, or else I'll leave. Tell me, who was it you were praying to? Is there really such a holy one – the Lord's wolf?"

Again she tried to get up. Again I restrained her:

"Ah, just look at you! And there you are, saying you're not afraid of anything! I'm asking you: is it true that there's such a holy one?"

She had a think. Then she replied seriously:

"There must be, sir. There is the beast Tiger-Euphrates,* after all. And if it's painted in a church, there must be. I saw it myself, sir."

"How do you mean, you saw it? Where? When?"

"Long ago, sir, in a time beyond memory. And where – I can't even say: I remember one thing – we were travelling there three days. There was a village there, Krutiye Gory. I'm from far away myself – perhaps you're so good as to have heard of the place: Ryazan – and those parts would be even further down, beyond the Don, and what a rough place it is there, you couldn't even find the words. It was there our prince had his main village, his grandfather's favourite – maybe a full thousand clay huts on bare mounds and slopes, and on the very highest hill, on its crown, above the Kamennaya River, the masters' house, all bare too, three-tiered, and a yellow church with columns, and in that church this here God's wolf: in the middle, then, there's a cast-iron slab over the tomb of the prince it slaughtered, and on the right-hand pillar – the creature itself, this wolf, painted at its full height and size: it sits in a grey fur coat on a thick tail, and its whole body's reaching up, with its front paws resting on the ground – and its eyes just boring into yours: a grey fur collar, long-haired and thick, a large head, sharp-eared, its fangs bared, furious, bloodshot eyes, and around its head a gold aureole, like saints and holy men have. It's terrible just remembering such a wondrous marvel! It's so lifelike sitting there, looking as if it'll rush upon you at any moment!"

"Wait, Mashenka," I said, "I don't understand a thing: who painted this terrible wolf in the church and why? You say it slaughtered a prince – so then why is it holy, and why should it be over the prince's tomb? And how did you find yourself there, in that dreadful village? Tell me everything clearly."

And Mashenka began telling her story:

"I found myself there, sir, for the reason that I was then a serf girl, serving in our prince's house. I was an orphan, my father, so they had it, was some sort of man passing through – a runaway, most likely – he seduced my mother unlawfully and disappeared God knows where, and mother, soon after giving birth to me, she passed away. Well, so the master took pity on me, took me from the menials into the house as soon as I hit thirteen, and put me at the beck and call of the young mistress, and for some reason I so took her fancy she wouldn't let me out of her favour for any time at all. And it was she that took me on the voyage with her when the young prince got the idea of taking a trip with her to his grandfather's legacy, to that there main village, to Krutiye Gory. That estate had been long neglected, deserted – the house had just stood boarded up, desolate, ever since the grandfather's death – well, and our young master and mistress thought they'd like to visit it. But what a terrible death the grandfather had died, we all knew about that from legend…"

In the reception hall something gave a slight crack, then fell with a little thud. Mashenka threw her legs down from the chest and ran into the hall: there was already a smell of burning there from the fallen candle. She put out the still-smoking candlewick, stamped out the smouldering that had started on the nap of a rug and, jumping up onto a chair, relit the candle from the other burning candles stuck into silver sockets beneath the icon, and fitted it into the one from which it had fallen: she turned the bright flame downwards, dripped the wax, which ran like hot honey, into the socket, then inserted it; deftly, with slender figures, she removed the burnt deposit from the other candles, and jumped back down onto the floor.

"My, how cheerfully it's started gleaming," she said, crossing herself and gazing at the revived gold of the candle lights. "And what a smell of the church there is now!"

There was the smell of sweet fumes, the little lights trembled, from behind them the ancient face of the icon gazed from a blank circle in its silver setting. In the upper, clear panes of the windows, which were frosted over at the bottom with thick, grey rime, the night was black, and white nearby in the front garden were the ends of boughs burdened with layers of snow. Mashenka looked at them too, crossed herself once more and came back into the hallway.

"It's time for you to sleep, sir," she said, sitting down on the chest and stifling her yawns, covering her mouth with her withered little hand. "The night's grown menacing now."

"Why menacing?"

"Because it's mysterious, when only the chanticleer, the cockerel, as we call it, and the night crow, the owl, can stay awake. Then the Lord Himself listens to the earth, the most important stars begin to twinkle, the ice holes freeze in seas and rivers."

"And why is it you yourself don't sleep at night?"

"I sleep as much as is needed as well, sir. Is an old person meant to have a lot of sleep? Like a bird on a branch."

"Well, go to bed, only finish telling me about that wolf."

"But you know, it's a dark business, long ago, sir – perhaps a ballad."

"What's that you said?"

"A ballad, sir. That's what all our masters used to say, they liked reading those ballads. Sometimes I'd be listening and there'd be a tingling on my head:

> Howls the cold wind o'er the mountain,
> Whirls in white the pasture,
> Comes foul weather and the blizzard,
> Buried deep's the highway*

"How beautiful, Lord!"

"What's beautiful about it, Mashenka?"

"What's beautiful about it, sir, is you don't know what it is that's beautiful. It's scary."

"In the old days, Mashenka, everything was scary."

"How can I put it, sir? Perhaps it's true that it was scary, but it all seems dear to me now. I mean, when was it? Just so long ago – all the kingdoms have gone, all the oaks have crumbled from old age, all the graves are level with the earth. Now this story too – among the menials it used to be told word for word, but is it the truth? The story was supposed to have happened still in the time of the great Tsarina,* and the reason why the prince was sitting in Krutiye Gory was supposed to be that she'd grown angry with him over something, had shut him up a long way away from her, and he'd become really fierce – most of all in the punishment of his serfs and in fornication. He was still very much in his prime, and as for his appearance, wonderfully handsome, and both among his menials and throughout his villages there wasn't supposed to be a single girl he hadn't demanded come to him, to his seraglio, for her wedding night. So he went and fell into the most terrible sin: he was even tempted by his own son's new bride. The son was in St Petersburg in the military service of the Tsarina, and when he'd found himself his intended, he got permission for the marriage from his father and married, and so then he came with his new bride to pay his respects to him, to that there Krutiye Gory. And the father goes and falls for her. Not for nothing, sir, is it sung about love:

> Love's fires rage in ev'ry kingdom,
> People love all round the globe…*

And however can it be a sin, when even an old man's thinking about his beloved, sighing over her? But here, after all, it was a completely different matter, here it was like it was his own daughter, and he'd stretched his grasping intentions to fornication."

"And so what happened?"

"Well, sir, the young prince, remarking this parental design, decided to flee in secret. He put the stablemen up to it, gave them all sorts of presents, ordered them to harness up a good quick troika for midnight, stole out from his own family home as soon as the old prince had fallen asleep, led out his young wife – and he was off. Only the old prince wasn't even thinking of sleeping: he'd already found everything out that evening from his informers and straight away gave chase. Night-time, an unspeakable frost, so there's even rings lying round the moon, snows in the steppe deeper than the height of a man, but it's all nothing to him: he flies along on his steed, sabres and pistols hanging all over him, beside his favourite whipper-in, and already he can see the troika with his son up ahead. He cries out like an eagle: stop, or I'll shoot! But they don't pay any heed there, they drive the troika on at full blazing speed. Then the old prince began shooting at the horses, and killed as he rode first the one outrunner, the right-hand one, as it ran, then the other, the left-hand one, and already he meant to lay low the shaft horse, but he glanced to the side and sees rushing at him across the snow, beneath the moon, a great, fantastic wolf with eyes red like fire and with an aureole around its head! The prince set about firing at it too, but it didn't even bat an eyelid: rushed at the prince like a whirlwind, jumped onto his chest – and in a single instant slashed through his Adam's apple with its fang."

"Ah, what horrors, Mashenka," I said. "Truly, a ballad!"

"It's a sin to mock, sir," she replied. "God's world is full of wonders."

"I don't disagree, Mashenka. Only it's strange, nonetheless, that this wolf has been painted right beside the tomb of the prince it slaughtered."

"It was painted, sir, as the prince himself wished; he was brought home still alive, and he had the time before dying to make his confession and take communion, and in his final moment he ordered that wolf to be painted in the church above his tomb – as a lesson, then, for all the prince's descendants. Who could possibly have disobeyed him in those days? And the church was his domestic one too, built by him himself."

3rd February 1938

Styopa

J UST BEFORE EVENING on the road to Chern the young merchant
Krasilschikov was caught by a thunderstorm and torrential rain.
In a knee-length jacket with raised collar and a peaked cap pulled
well down with streams running off it, he was riding quickly in a racing
droshky, sitting astride right up against the dashboard with his feet in
high boots pressed hard against the front axle, jerking with wet, frozen
hands on the wet, slippery, leather reins, hurrying along a horse that
was full of life anyway; to his left, beside the front wheel, which spun
in a whole fountain of liquid mud, a brown pointer ran steadily with
his long tongue hanging out.

At first Krasilschikov drove along the black-earth track beside the
highway, then, when it turned into an unbroken grey, bubbling torrent,
he turned onto the highway and began crunching over its little broken
stones. Neither the surrounding fields nor the sky had been visible for
a long time now through this flood, which smelt of the freshness of
cucumbers and of phosphorus; before his eyes, like a sign of the end
of the world, in blinding ruby fire, a sharp, nakedly branching flash
of lightning kept searing sinuously down from above across a great
wall of clouds, and with a crack above his head there would fly the
sizzling tail, which then exploded in thunderclaps, extraordinary
in their shattering power. Each time the horse would jerk its whole
body forwards, pressing back its ears, and the dog was already at a
gallop... Krasilschikov had grown up and studied in Moscow, had
graduated from university there, but in the summer, when he came to
his Tula estate, which resembled a rich dacha, he liked to feel himself a
landowning merchant of peasant origin, he drank Lafitte and smoked
from a gold cigarette case, yet wore blacked boots, a *kosovorotka* and
poddyovka,* and was proud of his Russian character – and now, in the
torrential rain and thunder, feeling the coldness of the water pouring
from the peak of his cap and his nose, he was full of the energetic
pleasure of rural life. This summer he often recalled the summer of the
previous year, when, because of a liaison with a well-known actress,

he had moped the time away in Moscow right up until July, until her departure for Kislovodsk: idleness, the heat, the hot stench and green smoke from the asphalt glowing in iron vats in the upturned streets, lunches in the Troitsky basement tavern with actors from the Maly Theatre who were preparing to leave for the Caucasus too, then sitting in the Tremblé coffee house, and waiting for her in the evening at his apartment with the furniture under covers, with the chandeliers and pictures in muslin, with the smell of mothballs... The summer evenings in Moscow are unending, it gets dark only towards eleven, and there you are, waiting, waiting – and still she's not there. Then finally the bell – and it's her, in all her summer smartness, and her breathless voice: "Please do forgive me, I've been flat on my back all day with a headache, your tea rose has completely wilted, I was in such a hurry I took a fast cab, I'm terribly hungry..."

When the torrential rain and the shaking peals of thunder began to die down and move away and it began clearing up all around, up ahead, to the left of the highway, the familiar coaching inn of an old widower, the petty bourgeois Pronin, appeared. There were still twenty kilometres to go to town – I should wait a little, thought Krasilschikov, the horse is all in a lather, and there's still no knowing what might happen again, look how black it is in that direction, and it's still lighting up... At the crossing point to the inn he turned at a trot and reined the horse in beside the wooden porch.

"Granddad!" he gave a loud cry. "You've got a guest!"

But the windows in the log building under its rusty iron roof were dark, nobody responded to the cry. Krasilschikov wound the reins onto the dashboard, went up onto the porch after the wet and dirty dog which had leapt up onto it – it had a mad look, its eyes shone brightly and senselessly – pushed the cap back from his sweaty forehead, took off his jacket, heavy with water, threw it onto the handrail of the porch, and, remaining in just a *poddyovka* with a leather belt decorated in silver, he wiped his face, mottled with muddy splashes, and began cleaning the mud from the tops of his boots with his whip handle. The door into the lobby was open, but there was a feeling of the building being empty. Probably bringing in the livestock, he thought, and, straightening up, he looked into the fields: should he drive on? The evening air was still and damp, in different directions in the distance quails were making a cheerful noise in corn crops heavy with moisture, the rain had stopped, but night was coming on, the sky and earth were darkening morosely, and a cloud beyond the highway, behind a low, inky ridge of woodland, was a still more dense and gloomy black, and a red flame was flaring up, widespread and ominous – and Krasilschikov strode into the lobby and groped in the darkness for the door into the living quarters. But they were dark and quiet, only somewhere on a wall was there a one-rouble clock ticking away. He slammed the door, turned to the left, groped for and opened another one, into the rest of the hut: again nobody, in the hot darkness the flies alone began a sleepy and discontented buzzing on the ceiling.

"As if they'd snuffed it!" he said out loud – and immediately heard the quick and melodious half-childish voice of Styopa, the owner's daughter, who had slipped down from the plank bed in the darkness.

"Is that you, Vasil Lixeyich? I'm here by meself, the cook had a row with Daddy and went home, and Daddy took the workman and went away into town on business, and he's unlikely to get back today... I was frightened to death by the storm, and then I hear someun's driven up, got even more frightened... Hello, please forgive me..."

Krasilschikov struck a match and illuminated her black eyes and swarthy little face:

"Hello, you little idiot. I'm going into town as well, but you can see what's happening, I dropped in to wait it out... And so you thought it was robbers that had driven up?"

The match had begun to burn out, but it was still possible to see that little face smiling in embarrassment, the coral necklace on the little neck, the small breasts under the yellow cotton dress. She was hardly more than half his height and seemed just a little girl.

"I'll light the lamp straight away," she began hurriedly, made even more embarrassed by Krasilschikov's penetrating gaze, and rushed to the lamp above the table. "God Himself sent you, what would I have done here alone?" she said melodiously, rising onto tiptoe and awkwardly pulling the glass out of the indented grille of the lamp, out of its tin ring.

Krasilschikov lit another match, gazing at her stretching and curved little figure.

"Wait, don't bother," he suddenly said, throwing the match away, and took her by the waist. "Hang on, just turn around to me for a minute..."

27

She glanced at him over her shoulder in terror, dropped her arms and turned around. He drew her towards him – she did not try to break away, only threw her head back wildly in surprise. From above, he looked directly and firmly into her eyes through the twilight and laughed:

"Got even more frightened?"

"Vasil Lixeyich…" she mumbled imploringly, and pulled herself out of his arms.

"Wait. Don't you like me, then? I mean, I know you're always pleased when I drop in."

"There's no one on earth better than you," she pronounced quietly and ardently.

"Well, you see…"

He gave her a long kiss on the lips, and his hands slid lower down.

"Vasil Lixeyich… for Christ's sake… You've forgotten, your horse is still where it was by the porch… Daddy will be coming… Oh, don't!"

Half an hour later he went out of the hut, led the horse off into the yard, stood it underneath an awning, took the bridle off, gave it some wet, mown grass from a cart standing in the middle of the yard, and returned, gazing at the tranquil stars in the clear sky. Weak, distant flashes of summer lightning were still glancing from different directions into the hot darkness of the quiet hut. She lay on the plank bed all coiled up, her head buried in her breast, having cried her fill of hot tears from horror, rapture and the suddenness of what had happened. He kissed her cheek, wet and salty with tears, lay down on his back and placed her head on his shoulder, holding a cigarette in his right hand. She lay quiet, silent, and with his left hand, as he smoked, he gently and absent-mindedly stroked her hair, which was tickling his chin… Then she immediately fell asleep. He lay gazing into the darkness, and grinned in self-satisfaction: "Daddy went away into town…" So much for going away! It's not good, he'll understand everything at once – such a dried-up and quick little old man in a little grey *poddyovka*, a snow-white beard, but whose thick eyebrows are still completely black, an extraordinarily lively gaze, talks incessantly when drunk, but sees straight through everything.

He lay sleepless until the time when the darkness of the hut began to lighten weakly in the middle, between the ceiling and the floor. Turning his head, he saw the east whitening with a greenish tinge outside the windows, and in the twilight of the corner above the table he could already make out a large icon of a holy man in ecclesiastical vestments, with his hand raised in blessing and an inexorably dread gaze. He looked at her: she still lay curled up in the same way, her legs drawn up, everything forgotten in sleep! A sweet and pitiful little girl.

When it became fully light in the hut, and a cockerel began yelling in various different voices on the other side of the wall, he made a move to rise. She leapt up and, half-seated, sideways on, unbuttoned at the breast and with tangled hair, she stared at him with eyes that understood nothing.

"Styopa," he said cautiously. "It's time I was off."

"You're going already?" she whispered senselessly.

And suddenly she came to and, arms crossed, struck herself on the breast with her hands:

"And where are you going? How will I get along without you now? What am I to do now?"

"Styopa, I'll come back again soon..."

"But Daddy will be at home, won't he? – how ever will I see you? I'd come to the wood on the other side of the highway, but how can I get out of the house?"

Clenching his teeth, he toppled her onto her back. She threw her arms out wide and exclaimed in sweet despair, as though about to die: "Ah!"

Afterwards he stood before the plank bed, already wearing his *poddyovka* and his cap, with his knout in his hand and with his back to the windows, to the dense lustre of the sun, which had just appeared, while she knelt on the bed and, sobbing and opening her mouth wide in a childish and unattractive way, articulated jerkily:

"Vasil Lixeyich... for Christ's sake... for the sake of the King of Heaven Himself, take me in marriage! I'll be your very meanest slave! I'll sleep by your doorstep – take me! I'd leave and come to you as I am, but who'll let me do it like this! Vasil Lixeyich..."

"Be quiet," Krásilschikov said sternly. "In a few days' time I'll come and see your father and tell him I'm marrying you. Do you hear?"

She sat down on her legs, breaking off her sobbing immediately, and obtusely opened wide her wet, radiant eyes:

"Is that true?"

"Of course it's true."

"I already turned sixteen at Epiphany," she said hurriedly.

"Well then, so in six months' time you can get married too…"

On returning home, he began preparations at once, and towards evening left for the railway in a troika. Two days later he was already in Kislovodsk.

5th October 1938

Muza

I WAS THEN NO LONGER in the first flush of youth, but came up with the idea of studying painting – I had always had a passion for it – and, abandoning my estate in the Tambov Province, I spent the winter in Moscow: I took lessons from a talentless, but quite well-known artist, an untidy, fat man who had made a very good job of adopting for himself all that is expected: long hair thrown back in big, greasy curls, a pipe in his teeth, a garnet-coloured velvet jacket, dirty grey gaiters on his shoes – I particularly hated them – a careless manner, condescending glances at a pupil's work through narrowed eyes and, muttering, as if to himself:

"Amusing, amusing... Undoubted progress..."

I lived on the Arbat, by the Prague restaurant, in the Capital rooms. I worked at the artist's and at home in the daytime, and not infrequently spent the evenings in cheap restaurants with various new acquaintances from Bohemia, both young and worn, but all equally attached to billiards and crayfish with beer... I had an unpleasant and boring life! That effeminate, slovenly artist, his "artistically" neglected studio, crammed with all kinds of dusty props, that gloomy Capital... What remains in my memory is snow falling continually outside the window, the muffled rumbling and ringing of horse-drawn trams down the Arbat, in the evening the sour stench of beer and gas in a dimly lit restaurant... I don't understand why I led such a wretched existence – I was far from poor at the time.

But then one day in March, when I was sitting working with pencils at home, and through the open transoms of the double glazing there was no longer the reek of the wintry damp of sleet and rain, the horseshoes were clattering along the roadway no longer in a wintry way, and the trams seemed to be ringing more musically, someone knocked at the door of my entrance hall. I called out: "Who's there?" but no reply ensued. I waited, called out again – again silence, then a fresh knock. I got up and opened the door: by the threshold stands a tall girl in a grey winter hat, in a straight, grey coat, in grey overshoes, looking fixedly, her eyes the colour of acorns, and on her long lashes, on her face and hair beneath the hat shine drops of rain and snow. She looks and says:

"I'm a Conservatoire student, Muza Graf. I heard you were an interesting person and I've come to meet you. Do you have any objection?"

Quite surprised, I replied, of course, with a courteous phrase:

"I'm most flattered, you're very welcome. Only I must warn you that the rumours that have reached you are scarcely true: I don't think there's anything interesting about me."

"In any event, do let me come in, don't keep me at the door," she said, still looking at me in the same direct way. "If you're flattered, then let me come in."

And having entered, quite at home, she began taking off her hat in front of my greyly silver and in places blackened mirror, and adjusting her rust-coloured hair; she threw off her coat and tossed it onto a chair, remaining in a checked flannel dress, sat down on the couch, sniffing her nose, wet with snow and rain, and ordered:

"Take my overshoes off and give me my handkerchief from my coat."

I gave her the handkerchief, she wiped her nose, and stretched out her legs to me:

"I saw you yesterday at Shor's concert,"* she said indifferently.

Restraining a silly smile of pleasure and bewilderment – what a strange guest! – I obediently took off the overshoes, one after the other. She still smelt freshly of the air, and I was excited by that scent, excited by the combination of her masculinity with all that was femininely youthful in her face, in her direct eyes, in her large and beautiful hand – in everything that I looked over and felt, while pulling the high overshoes off from under her dress, beneath which lay her knees, rounded and weighty, and seeing her swelling calves in fine, grey stockings and her elongated feet in open, patent-leather shoes.

Next she settled down comfortably on the couch, evidently not intending to be leaving soon. Not knowing what to say, I began asking questions about what she had heard of me and from whom, and who she was, where and with whom she lived. She replied:

"What I've heard and from whom is unimportant. I came more because I saw you at the concert. You're quite handsome. And I'm a doctor's daughter, I live not far from you, on Prechistensky Boulevard."

She spoke abruptly somehow, and concisely. Again not knowing what to say, I asked:

"Do you want some tea?"

"Yes," she said. "And if you have the money, order some rennet apples to be bought at Belov's – here on the Arbat. Only hurry the boots along, I'm impatient."

"Yet you seem so calm."

"I may seem a lot of things…"

When the boots brought the samovar and a bag of apples, she brewed the tea and wiped the cups and teaspoons… And after eating an apple and drinking a cup of tea, she moved further back on the couch and slapped the place beside her with her hand:

"Now come and sit with me."

I sat down and she put her arms around me, unhurriedly kissed me on the lips, pulled away, had a look and, as though satisfied that I was worthy of it, closed her eyes and kissed me again – assiduously, at length.

"There," she said, as if relieved. "Nothing more for now. The day after tomorrow."

The room was already completely dark – there was just the sad half-light from the lamps in the street. What I was feeling is easy to imagine. Where had such happiness suddenly come from! Young, strong, the taste and shape of her lips extraordinary… I heard as if in a dream the monotonous ringing of trams, the clatter of hooves…

"The day after tomorrow I want to have dinner with you at the Prague," she said. "I've never been there, and I'm very inexperienced in general. I can imagine what you think of me. But in actual fact, you're my first love."

"Love?"

"Well, what else do you call it?"

Of course, I soon abandoned my studies, she somehow or other continued hers. We were never apart, lived like newly-weds, went to picture galleries, to exhibitions, attended concerts and even, for some reason, public lectures. In May I moved, at her wish, to an old country estate outside Moscow, where a number of small dachas had been built and were to let, and she began to come and visit me, returning to Moscow at one in the morning. I had not expected this at all either – a dacha outside Moscow: I had never before lived the life of a

33

dacha-dweller, with nothing to do, on an estate so unlike our estates in the steppe, and in such a climate.

Rain all the time, pinewoods all around. In the bright blue above them, white clouds keep piling up, there is a roll of thunder on high, then gleaming rain begins to pour through the sunshine, quickly turning in the sultriness into fragrant pine vapour... All is wet, lush, mirror-like... In the estate park the trees were so great that the dachas built there in places seemed tiny beneath them, like dwellings under trees in tropical countries. The pond was a huge, black mirror, and half of it was covered in green duckweed... I lived on the edge of the park, in woodland. My log-built dacha was not quite finished – the walls not caulked, the floors not planed, the stoves without doors, hardly any furniture. And from the constant damp, my long boots, lying about under the bed, soon grew a velvety covering of mould.

It got dark in the evenings only towards midnight: the half-light in the west lay and lay over the motionless, quiet woods. On moonlit nights this half-light mixed strangely with the moonlight, motionless and enchanted too. And from the tranquillity that reigned everywhere, from the clarity of the sky and air, it forever seemed that now there would be no more rain. But there I would be, falling asleep after seeing her to the station – and suddenly I would hear it: torrential rain crashing down again onto the roof with peals of thunder, darkness all around and vertical flashes of lightning. In the morning, on the lilac earth in the damp avenues of trees there was the play of shadows and blinding patches of sunlight, the birds called flycatchers would be clucking, the thrushes would be chattering hoarsely. By midday it would be sultry again, the clouds would gather and the rain would start to pour. Just before sunset it would become clear and, falling into the windows through the foliage, on my log walls there would tremble the crystalline golden grid of the low sun. At this point I would go to the station to meet her. The train would arrive, innumerable dacha-dwellers would tumble out onto the platform, there was the smell of the steam engine's coal and the damp freshness of the wood, she would appear in the crowd with a string bag, laden with packets of hors d'œuvres, fruits, a bottle of Madeira... We dined amicably, alone. Before her late departure we would wander through the park. She would become somnambulistic and walk with her head leaning on my shoulder... The black pond, the age-old trees, receding into the starry sky... The enchanted light night, endlessly silent, with the endlessly long shadows of trees on the silvery lakes of the glades...

In June she went away with me to my village – without our having married, she began living with me as a wife, began keeping house. She spent the long autumn without getting bored, with everyday cares, reading. Of the neighbours, a certain Zavistovsky visited us most often, a solitary poor landowner who lived a couple of kilometres from us, puny, gingery, not bold, not bright – and not a bad musician. In the winter he began appearing at our house almost every evening. I had known him since childhood, but now I grew so used to him that an evening without him was strange for me. He and I played draughts, or else he played piano duets with her.

Just before Christmas I happened to go into town. I returned when the moon was already up. And going into the house, I could find her nowhere. I sat down at the samovar alone.

"And where's the mistress, Dunya? Has she gone out for a walk?"

"I don't know, sir. She's been out ever since breakfast."

"Got dressed and went," said my old nanny gloomily, passing through the dining room without raising her head.

"She probably went to see Zavistovsky," I thought. "She'll probably be here with him soon – it's already seven o'clock..." And I went and lay down for a while in the study, and suddenly fell asleep – I had been frozen all day in the sledge on the road. And I came to just as suddenly an hour later – with a clear and wild idea: "She's abandoned me, hasn't she! She's hired a peasant in the village and left for the station, for Moscow – anything's possible with her! But perhaps she's come back?" I walked through the house – no, she hadn't come back. The humiliation in front of the servants...

At about ten o'clock, not knowing what to do, I put on my sheepskin coat, took a rifle for some reason, and set off down the main road to see Zavistovsky, thinking: "As if on purpose, he hasn't come today either, and I still have a whole terrible night ahead! Is it really true that she's left, abandoned me? Of course not, it can't be!" I walk, crunching along the well-trodden path amidst the snows, and the snowy fields are gleaming on the left beneath the low, meagre moon... I turned off the main road and went towards Zavistovsky's estate: an avenue of bare trees leading towards it across a field, then the entrance to the yard, to the left the old, beggarly house; the house is dark... I went up onto the ice-covered porch, with difficulty opened the heavy door, its upholstery all in shreds – in the entrance hall is the red of the open, burning stove, warmth and darkness... But the reception hall is dark as well.

"Vikenty Vikentich!"

And noiselessly, in felt boots, he appeared on the threshold of the study, lit too only by the moon through the triple window.

"Ah, it's you... Come in, please, come in... As you see, I'm sitting in the dusk, whiling the evening away without light..."

I went and sat on a lumpy couch.

"Just imagine, Muza's disappeared somewhere..."

He remained silent. Then in an almost inaudible voice:

"Yes, yes, I understand you..."

"That is, what do you understand?"

And at once, also noiselessly, also in felt boots, with a shawl on her shoulders, from the bedroom adjoining the study came Muza.

"You've got a rifle," she said. "If you want to shoot, shoot not at him, but at me."

And she sat down on the other couch opposite.

I looked at her felt boots, at the knees under the grey skirt – everything was easily visible in the golden light falling from the window – and I wanted to shout out: "Better you kill me, I can't live without you, for those knees alone, for the skirt, for the felt boots, I'm prepared to give my life!"

"The matter's clear and done with," she said. "Scenes are no use."

"You're monstrously cruel," I articulated with difficulty.

"Give me a cigarette, dear," she said to Zavistovsky.

He strained timorously towards her, reached out a cigarette case, started rummaging through his pockets for matches...

"You're already speaking formally to me," I said, gasping for breath, "you might at least not be so intimate with him in front of me."

"Why?" she asked, raising her eyebrows, holding a cigarette with outstretched hand.

My heart was already pounding right up in my throat, my temples were thumping. I rose and, reeling, went away.

17th October 1938

A Late Hour

AH, WHAT A LONG TIME it was since I'd been there, I said to myself. Not since I was nineteen. I had once lived in Russia, felt it to be mine, had complete freedom to travel anywhere I wanted, and it was no great trouble to go some three hundred kilometres. Yet I kept on not going, kept putting it off. And the years came and went, the decades. But now it's no longer possible to put it off any more: either now or never. The one final opportunity must be taken, for the hour is late and nobody will come upon me.

And I set off across the bridge over the river, seeing everything all around a long way off in the moonlight of the July night.

The bridge was so familiar, as before, it was as though I'd seen it yesterday: crudely ancient, humped and as if not even of stone but sort of petrified by time into eternal indestructibility – as a schoolboy I thought it had already been there in Baty's time.* The town's antiquity, however, is spoken of only by a few traces of the town walls on the precipice below the cathedral and by this bridge. Everything else is simply old, provincial, no more. One thing was strange, one thing indicated that something had, after all, changed in the world since the time when I had been a boy, a youth: previously the river had not been navigable, but now it had probably been deepened, cleared out; the moon was to my left, quite a long way above the river, and in its uneven light, and in the flickering, trembling gleam of the water was the whiteness of a paddle steamer which seemed empty – so silent was it – although all its portholes were lit up, looking like open but sleeping golden eyes, and were all reflected in the water as rippling gold columns: it was as if the steamer were actually standing on them. It had been like this in Yaroslavl, and in the Suez Canal, and on the Nile. In Paris the nights are damp, dark, there is a pinkish, hazy glow in the impenetrable sky. The Seine flows under the bridges like black pitch, but under them there also hang the rippling columns of reflections from the lamps on the bridges, only they are three-coloured: white, blue and red – Russian national flags. Here there are no lamps on the bridge, and it is dry and dusty. But up ahead on the hillside is the darkness of the town's gardens, and protruding above the gardens is the fire-observation tower. My God, what ineffable happiness it was! It was during a fire at night that I kissed your hand for the first time, and you gave mine a squeeze in reply – I shall never forget that secret accord. The whole street was black with people in ominous, abnormal illumination. I was visiting your house when the alarm was suddenly sounded, and everyone rushed to the windows and then out of the gate. The burning was a long way off, beyond the river, but it was terribly fervent, greedy, urgent. Thick clouds of smoke were belching out there like a crimson-black fleece, bursting out from them on high were red calico sheets of flame, and near to us, trembling, they were reflected in copper in the cupola of the Archangel Michael. And in the crush, in the crowd, amidst the alarmed, now compassionate, now joyous voices of the common people, who were flocking together from everywhere and not taking their widened eyes off the fire, I smelt the scent of your maidenly hair, neck, gingham dress – then suddenly made up my mind and, turning quite cold, took your hand…

On the other side of the bridge I climbed up the hillside and went into the town along the paved road.

There was not a solitary light anywhere in the town, not a single living soul. All was mute and spacious, tranquil and sad – with the sadness of night in the Russian steppe, of a sleeping town in the steppe. The gardens alone had their foliage quivering, scarcely audibly, cautiously, from the even flow of the light July wind, wafting in from somewhere in the fields, blowing on me gently, giving me a feeling of youth and lightness. I was moving, and the large moon was moving too, its mirror-like disc rolling and visible in the blackness of branches; the wide streets lay in shadow – only in the houses on the right, to which the shadow did not reach, were the white walls lit up and was a funereal lustre twinkling on the black window panes – but I walked in the shade, treading along the dappled pavement – it was transparently paved with black silk lace. She had an evening dress like that, very smart, long and elegant. It was extraordinarily suited to her slender figure and black, young eyes. She was mysterious in it and insultingly paid me no attention. Where was that? Visiting whom?

My objective was to spend some time on Staraya Street. And I could have got there by another, quicker route. But the reason I turned into these spacious streets with gardens was that I wanted to take a look at the grammar school. And reaching it, I marvelled again: here too everything had remained as half a century before; the stone boundary wall, the stone yard, the big stone building in the yard – everything just as conventional, boring as it had been before, in my time. I lingered by the gates, wanting to provoke in myself the sorrow, the pity of memories – and couldn't. Yes, I had first entered these gates as a first-year with close-cropped hair in a nice, new blue cap with silver palms over the peak, and in a new little greatcoat with silver buttons, then as a thin youth in a grey jacket and foppish trousers with straps under the feet – but is that really me?

Staraya Street seemed to me just a little narrower and longer than it had before. Everything else was unchanging, like everywhere. The potholed roadway, not a single little tree, on both sides the white, dusty houses of provincial merchants, the pavements potholed as well, such that it would be better to walk down the middle of the street in the full light of the moon… And the night was almost the same as that one. Only that one had been at the end of August, when the whole town smells of the apples which lie in mountains at the markets, and was so warm that it was a delight to be wearing just a *kosovorotka* with a Caucasian belt around it… Is it possible to remember that night somewhere up there, as if in the sky?

I could not make up my mind to go as far as your house after all. It too had probably not changed, but all the more terrible to see it. Some new people, strangers, live in it now. Your father, your mother, your brother – they all outlived young you, but also died when their time came. And every one of mine has died too, and not only my relatives, but also many, many with whom I began life in friendship or comradeship; was it so long ago that they too began, certain in their hearts there would be simply no end to it, but everything has begun, elapsed and come to an end before my eyes – so quickly, and before my eyes! And I sat down on a bollard beside some merchant's house, impregnable behind its locks and gates, and started thinking about what she was like in those distant times of ours: simply dressed dark hair, a clear gaze, the light tan of a youthful face, a light summer dress, beneath which were the chastity, strength and freedom of a young body… That was the start of our love, a time of happiness as yet unclouded by anything, of intimacy, trustfulness, enraptured tenderness, joy…

There is something utterly special about the warm and bright nights of Russian provincial towns at the end of summer. What peace, what well-being! An old man wanders through the cheerful nocturnal town with a watchman's rattle, but solely for his own pleasure: there's no need to keep watch, sleep peacefully, good people; you are watched over by God's goodwill, by this lofty, radiant sky, at which the old man casts the odd carefree glance as he wanders down the roadway, heated up in the course of the day, just occasionally, for fun, letting go a dancing shake of the rattle. And it was on such a night, at that late hour when just he alone in the town was not asleep, you were waiting for me in your family's garden, already a little dried up towards autumn, and I slipped into it by stealth: I quietly opened the gate, unlocked in advance by you, quietly and quickly ran through the yard and, behind the shed in the depths of the yard, entered the dappled twilight of the garden where, in the distance, on the bench under the apple trees, the whiteness of your dress was faintly visible, and approaching quickly, with joyous fright, I met the lustre of your waiting eyes.

And we sat, sat in a sort of bewilderment of happiness. With one hand I embraced you, sensing the beating of your heart, in the other I held your hand, feeling through it the whole of you. And it was already so late that even the rattle was not to be heard – the old man had laid down on a bench somewhere and dozed off with his pipe in his teeth, warming himself in the light of the moon. When I looked to the right, I could see the moon shining high and sinless above the yard, and the roof of the house gleaming with piscine lustre. When I looked to the left, I saw a path, overgrown with dry grasses, disappearing under more apple trees, and beyond them, peeping out low from behind some other garden, a solitary green star, glimmering impassively, and at the same time expectantly, and soundlessly saying something. But both the yard and the star I saw only in glimpses – there was one thing in the world: the delicate twilight and the radiant twinkling in the twilight of your eyes.

And then you accompanied me as far as the gate, and I said:

"If there is a future life and we meet in it, I shall kneel down there and kiss your feet for all that you gave me on earth."

I went out into the middle of the bright street and set off for my town-house lodgings. Turning back, I saw there was still whiteness in the gateway.

Now, rising from the bollard, I set off back by the same route by which I had come. No, I had, apart from Staraya Street, another objective too, one which I was afraid to acknowledge to myself, but the fulfilment of which was, I knew, unavoidable. And I set off – to take a look and leave, this time for ever.

The road was again familiar. Always straight ahead, then to the left, through the market, and from the market – along Monastyrskaya – towards the exit from town.

The market is like another town within the town. Very strong-smelling rows of stalls. In the refreshments row, under awnings above long tables and benches, it is gloomy. In the hardware row, on a chain over the middle of the passage hangs an icon of a big-eyed Saviour in a rusty setting. In the flour row in the mornings there was always a whole flock of pigeons running about and pecking along the roadway. You're on your way to school – what a lot of them! And all fat, with iridescent craws – they peck and run, waggling their tails in a feminine way, swinging from side to side, twitching their heads monotonously, not seeming to notice you: they fly up, their wings whistling, only when you almost step on one of them. And here in the night-time large, dark rats, foul and ugly, rushed around quickly, preoccupied.

Monastyrskaya Street juts out into the fields, and is then a road: for some, out of town towards home, to the village, for others – to the town of the dead. In Paris, house number such-and-such in such-and-such a street is marked out from all other houses for two days by the pestilential stage properties of the porch, of its coal-black and silver frame, for two days a sheet of paper in a coal-black border lies in the porch on the coal-black shroud of a little table – polite visitors sign their names on it as a mark of sympathy; then, at a certain final time, by the porch stops a huge chariot with a coal-black canopy, the wood of which is black, resinous, like a plague coffin, the rounded cut-outs of the skirts of the canopy bear witness to the heavens with large white stars, while the corners of the top are crowned with curly, coal-black plumes – the feathers of an ostrich from the underworld; harnessed to the chariot are strapping monsters in coal-black horned horse cloths with white-ringed eye sockets; on the interminably high coach box sits an old drunkard waiting for the bearing-out, symbolically dressed up too in a theatrical burial uniform and a similar three-cornered hat, probably forever smirking inwardly at those solemn words: "*Requiem* *æternam dona eis, Domine, et lux perpetua luceat eis."** Here everything is different. A breeze blows down Monastyrskaya from the fields, and the open coffin is carried into it on towels, while the rice-coloured face with a vivid ribbon on the forehead above the closed, bulging eyes rocks from side to side. She too was carried thus.

At the exit, to the left of the highway, is a monastery from the times of Alexei Mikhailovich,* fortress gates, always closed, and fortress walls, from behind which gleam the gilded turnips of the cathedral. Further on, quite out in the fields, is a very extensive square of more walls, but low ones: confined within them is an entire grove of trees, broken up by long, intersecting prospects, down the sides of which, beneath old elms, limes and birches, all is sown with diverse crosses and memorials. Here the gates were open wide, and I saw the main prospect, regular, endless. I tentatively took off my hat and entered. How late and how mute! The moon was already low behind the trees, but all around was still clearly visible as far as the eye could see. The entire expanse of this grove of dead men, its crosses and memorials, was decorated with dappled patterns in the transparent shade. The wind had died down towards the hour before dawn – the light and dark patches that made everything under the trees dappled were sleeping. In a distant part of the grove, from behind the graveyard church, there was a sudden glimpse of something, and it rushed at me in a dark ball at a furious pace – beside myself, I staggered aside, my entire head immediately turned to ice and tightened up, my heart gave a leap and froze. What was it? It rushed by and disappeared. But still my heart remained standing still in my breast. And thus, with my heart stopped, carrying it within me like a burdensome chalice, I moved on. I knew where I had to go, I kept walking straight ahead down the prospect – and at its very end, just a few paces from the rear wall, I stopped: before me, in a level spot, among dry grasses, there lay in solitude an elongated and quite narrow stone, its head towards the wall. And from behind the wall, like a wondrous gem, gazed a low, green star, radiant, like that previous one, but mute and motionless.

19th October 1938

Part Two

Rusya

AFTER TEN O'CLOCK in the evening, the Moscow-Sebastopol fast train stopped at a small station beyond Podolsk where it was not due to make a stop, waiting for something on the second track. On the train, a gentleman and a lady went up to a lowered window of the first-class carriage. A conductor with a red lamp in his dangling hand was crossing the rails, and the lady asked:

"Listen. Why are we standing still?"

The conductor replied that the oncoming express train was late.

The station was dark and sad. Twilight had fallen long before, but in the west, behind the station, beyond the blackening, wooded fields, the long summer Moscow sunset still gave off a deathly glow. Through the window came the damp smell of marshland. Audible from somewhere in the silence was the steady – and as though damp too – screeching of a corncrake.

He leant on the window, she on his shoulder.

"I stayed in this area during the holidays once," he said. "I was a tutor on a dacha estate about five kilometres from here. It's a boring area. Scrubland, magpies, mosquitoes and dragonflies. No view anywhere. On the estate you could only admire the horizon from the mezzanine. The house was in the Russian dacha style, of course, and very neglected – the owners were impoverished people – behind the house was some semblance of a garden, beyond the garden not exactly a lake, not exactly a marsh, overgrown with sedge and water lilies, and the inevitable flat-bottomed boat beside the swampy bank."

"And, of course, a bored dacha maiden whom you took out boating around the marsh."

"Yes, everything as it's meant to be. Only the maiden wasn't at all bored. I took her out boating at night mostly, and it was even poetic, as it turned out. All night in the west the sky's greenish, pellucid, and there, on the horizon, just like now, there's something forever smouldering and smouldering... There was only one oar to be found, and that like a spade, and I paddled with it like a savage – first to the

45

right, then to the left. The opposite bank was dark from the scrubland, but beyond it there was this strange half-light all night long. And everywhere unimaginable quietness – only the mosquitoes whining and the dragonflies flying around. I never thought they flew at night – it turned out that for some reason they do. Really terrifying."

At last there was the noise of the oncoming train, it flew upon them with a clattering and wind, merging into a single golden strip of lighted windows, and rushed on by. The carriage immediately moved off. The carriage attendant entered the compartment, put the light on and began preparing the beds.

"Well, and what was there between you and this maiden? A real romance? You've never told me about her for some reason. What was she like?"

"Thin, tall. She wore a yellow cotton sarafan and peasants' shoes woven from some multicoloured wool on bare feet."

"In the Russian style as well then?"

"Most of all in the style of poverty, I think. Nothing to put on, hence the sarafan. Apart from that, she was an artist, she studied at the Stroganov School of Painting.* And she was like a painting herself, like an icon even. A long, black plait on her back, a swarthy face with little dark moles, a narrow, regular nose, black eyes, black brows... Dry and wiry hair which was slightly curly. With the yellow sarafan and the white muslin sleeves of her blouse, it all stood out very prettily. The ankle bones and the beginning of the foot in the woollen shoes – all wiry, with bones sticking out under the thin, swarthy skin."

"I know the type. I had a friend like that at college. Probably hysterical."

"It's possible. Especially as she resembled her mother facially, and the mother, some sort of princess by birth, with oriental blood, suffered from something like manic depression. She'd emerge only to come to the table. She'd emerge, sit down and say nothing, cough a bit, without raising her eyes, and keep on moving first her knife, then her fork. And if she did suddenly start talking, then it was so unexpected and loud that it gave you a start."

"And her father?"

"Taciturn and dry as well, tall: a retired military man. Only their boy, whom I was tutoring, was straightforward and nice."

46

The carriage attendant left the compartment, said that the beds were ready, and wished us a good night.

"And what was her name?"

"Rusya."

"What sort of name is that?"

"A very simple one – Marusya."

"Well, and so were you very much in love with her?"

"Of course, terribly, so it seemed."

"And she?"

He paused and replied drily:

"It probably seemed so to her as well. But let's go to bed. I'm terribly tired after today."

"Very nice! Just got me interested for nothing. Well, tell me, if only in two words, what brought your romance to an end and how."

"Nothing at all. I left, and that was the end of the matter."

"Why ever didn't you marry her?"

"I evidently had a premonition that I'd meet you."

"No, seriously."

"Well, because I shot myself, and she stabbed herself with a dagger…"

And after washing and cleaning their teeth, they shut themselves into the tight space formed by the compartment, undressed, and with the delight of travellers lay down beneath the fresh, shiny linen of the sheets, onto similar pillows that kept slipping from the slightly raised bedhead.

The bluish lilac peephole above the door gazed quietly into the darkness. She soon dropped off, but he did not sleep, he lay smoking, and in his thoughts looked back at that summer…

She also had a lot of little dark moles on her body – that peculiarity was charming. Because she went about in soft footwear, without heels, her entire body undulated beneath the yellow sarafan. The sarafan was loose, light, and her long, girlish body was so free in it. One day she got her feet wet in the rain, ran into the drawing room from the garden, and he rushed to take off her shoes and kiss her wet, narrow soles – in the whole of his life there had not been such happiness. The fresh, fragrant rain rattled ever faster and heavier beyond the doors, open onto the balcony, in the darkened house everyone was sleeping after dinner – and how dreadfully he and she were frightened by some black and metallic-green-tinted cockerel, wearing a big, fiery crown, which ran in suddenly from the garden too, with a tapping of talons across the floor, at that most ardent of moments when they had forgotten any kind of caution. Seeing how they leapt up from the couch, it ran back into the rain, hastily and bending down, as though out of tactfulness, with its gleaming tail lowered...

At first she kept on scrutinizing him; whenever he began talking to her she blushed heavily and replied with sarcastic mutterings; at table she often annoyed him, addressing her father loudly:

"Don't give him food to no purpose, Papa, he doesn't like fruit dumplings. And he doesn't like kvas soup either, nor does he like noodles, and he despises yoghurt, and hates curd cheese."

In the mornings he was busy with the boy, she with housekeeping – the whole house was down to her. They had dinner at one, and after dinner she would go off to her room on the mezzanine or, if there was no rain, into the garden, where her easel stood under a birch tree, and, waving away the mosquitoes, she would paint from nature. Later she began going out onto the balcony, where he sat in a crooked cane armchair with a book after dinner, standing with her hands behind her back and casting glances at him with an indefinite grin:

"Might one learn what subtleties you're so good as to be studying?"

"The history of the French Revolution."

"Oh my God! I didn't even know we had a revolutionary in the house!"

"But why ever have you given up your painting?"

"I'll be giving it up completely at any time. I've become convinced of my lack of talent."

"Show me something of your paintings."

"And do you think you understand anything about painting?"

"You're terribly proud."

"I do have that fault..."

Finally one day she proposed going boating on the lake to him, and suddenly said decisively:

"The rainy season in our tropical parts seems to have ended. Let's enjoy ourselves. True, our dugout's quite rotten and the bottom has holes in it, but Petya and I have stopped up all the holes with sedge..."

The day was hot, it was sultry, the grasses on the bank, speckled with little yellow buttercup flowers had been stiflingly heated up by the moist warmth, and low above them circled countless pale-green butterflies.

He had adopted her constant mocking tone for himself and, approaching the boat, said:

"At long last you've deigned to speak to me!"

"At long last you've collected your thoughts and answered me!" she replied briskly, and jumped onto the bow of the boat, scaring away the frogs, which plopped into the water from all directions, but suddenly she gave a wild shriek and caught her sarafan right up to her knees, stamping her feet:

"A grass snake! A grass snake!"

He glimpsed the gleaming swarthiness of her bare legs, grabbed the oar from the bow, hit the grass snake wriggling along the bottom of the boat with it and, hooking the snake up, threw it far away into the water.

She was pale with an Indian sort of pallor, the moles on her face had become darker, the blackness of her hair and eyes seemingly even blacker. She drew breath in relief:

"Oh, how disgusting! Not for nothing is a snake in the grass named after the grass snake. We have them everywhere here, in the garden and under the house... And Petya, just imagine, picks them up in his hands!"

For the first time she had begun speaking to him unaffectedly, and for the first time they glanced directly into one another's eyes.

"But what a good fellow you are! What a good whack you gave it!"

She had recovered herself completely, she smiled and, running back from the bow to the stern, sat down cheerfully. She had struck him with her beauty in her fright, and now he thought with tenderness: but she's still quite a little girl! Yet putting on an indifferent air, he took a preoccupied step across into the boat and, leaning the oar against the jelly-like lakebed, turned its bow forwards and pulled it across the tangled thicket of underwater weeds towards the green brushes of sedge and the flowering water lilies which covered everything ahead with an unbroken layer of their thick, round foliage, brought the boat out into the water and sat down on the thwart in the middle, paddling to the right and to the left.

"Nice, isn't it?" she cried.

"Very!" he replied, taking off his cap, and turned round towards her:

"Be so kind as to drop this down beside you, or else I'll knock it off into this here tub, which, forgive me, does after all leak, and is full of leeches."

She put the cap on her knees.

"Oh, don't worry, drop it down anywhere."

She pressed the cap to her breast:

"No, I'm going to take care of it!"

Again his heart stirred tenderly, but again he turned away and began intensifying his thrusting of the oar into the water that shone between the sedge and the water lilies. Mosquitoes stuck to his face and hands, the warm silver of everything all around was dazzling: the sultry air, the undulating sunlight, the curly whiteness of the clouds shining softly in the sky and in the clear patches of water between islands of sedge and water lilies; it was so shallow everywhere that the lakebed with its underwater weeds was visible, but somehow that did not preclude that bottomless depth into which the reflected sky and clouds receded. Suddenly she shrieked again – and the boat toppled sideways: she had put her hand into the water from the stern and, catching a water-lily stalk, had jerked it towards her so hard that she had tipped over along with the boat – he was scarcely in time to leap up and catch her by the armpits. She began roaring with laughter and, falling onto her back in the stern, she splashed water right into his eyes with her wet hand. Then he grabbed her again and, without understanding what he was doing, kissed her laughing lips. She quickly clasped her arms around his neck and kissed him clumsily on the cheek...

From then on they began boating at night. The next day she called him out into the garden after dinner and asked:

"Do you love me?"

He replied ardently, remembering the kisses of the day before in the boat:

"Since the first day we met!"

"Me too," she said. "No, at first I hated you – I didn't think you noticed me at all. But all that's already in the past, thank God! This evening, as soon as everyone goes to bed, go there again and wait for me. Only leave the house as cautiously as possible – Mama watches my every step, she's madly jealous."

In the night she came to the shore with a plaid on her arm. In joy he greeted her confusedly, only asking:

"And why the plaid?"

"How silly you are! We'll be cold. Well, get in quickly and paddle to the other bank..."

They were silent all the way. When they floated up to the wood on the other side, she said:

"There we are. Now come here to me. Where's the plaid? Ah, it's underneath me. Cover me up, I'm cold, and sit down. That's right... No, wait, yesterday we kissed awkwardly somehow, now I'll kiss you myself to begin with, only gently, gently. And you put your arms around me... everywhere..."

She had only a petticoat on under the sarafan. Tenderly, scarcely touching, she kissed the edges of his lips. He, with his head in a spin, threw her onto the stern. She embraced him frenziedly...

After lying for a while in exhaustion, she raised herself a little and, with a smile of happy tiredness and pain that had not yet abated, said:

"Now we're husband and wife. Mama says she won't survive my getting married, but I don't want to think about that for the moment... You know, I want to bathe, I'm terribly fond of bathing at night..."

She pulled her clothes off over her head, the whole of her long body showed up white in the twilight, and she began tying a braid around her head, lifting her arms and showing her dark armpits and her raised breasts, unashamed of her nakedness and the little dark prominence below her belly. When she had finished, she quickly kissed him, leapt to her feet, fell flat into the water with her head tossed back and began thrashing noisily with her legs.

Afterwards, hurrying, he helped her to dress and wrap herself up in the plaid. In the twilight her black eyes and black hair, tied up in a braid, were fabulously visible. He did not dare touch her any more, he only kissed her hands and stayed silent out of unendurable happiness. All the time it seemed that there was someone there in the darkness of the wood on the shore, which glimmered in places with glow-worms, someone standing and listening. At times something would give out a cautious rustling there. She would raise her head:

"Hold on, what's that?"

"Don't be afraid, it's probably a frog crawling out onto the bank. Or a hedgehog in the wood..."

"And what if it's a wild goat?"

"What wild goat's that?"

"I don't know. But just think: some wild goat comes out of the wood, stands and looks... I feel so good, I feel like talking dreadful nonsense!"

And again he would press her hands to his lips, sometimes he would kiss her cold breast like something sacred. What a completely new creature she had become for him! And the greenish half-light hung beyond the blackness of the low wood and did not go out, it was weakly reflected in the flat whiteness of the water in the distance, and the dewy plants on the shore had a strong smell like celery, while mysteriously, pleadingly, the invisible mosquitoes whined and terrible, sleepless dragonflies flew, flew with a quiet crackling above the boat and further off, above that nocturnally shining water. And all the time, somewhere something was rustling, crawling, making its way along...

A week later, stunned by the horror of the utterly sudden parting, he was disgracefully, shamefully expelled from the house.

One day after dinner they were sitting in the drawing room with their heads touching, and looking at the pictures in old editions of *The Cornfield*.*

"You haven't stopped loving me yet?" he asked quietly, pretending to be looking attentively.

"Silly. Terribly silly!" she whispered.

Suddenly, softly running footsteps could be heard – and on the threshold in a tattered black silk dressing gown and worn morocco slippers stood her crazy mother. Her black eyes were gleaming tragically. She ran in, as though onto a stage, and cried:

"I understand everything! I sensed it, I watched! Scoundrel, she shall not be yours!"

And throwing up her arm in its long sleeve, she fired a deafening shot from the ancient pistol with which Petya, loading it just with powder, scared the sparrows. In the smoke he rushed towards her, grabbed her tenacious arm. She broke free, struck him on the forehead with the pistol, cutting his brow open and drawing blood, flung it at him and, hearing people running through the house in response to the shouting and the shot, began crying out even more theatrically with foam on her blue-grey lips:

"Only over my dead body will she take the step to you! If she runs away with you, that same day I shall hang myself, throw myself from

52

the roof! Scoundrel, out of my house! Maria Viktorovna, choose: your mother or him!"

She whispered:

"You, you, Mama…"

He came to, opened his eyes – still just as unwavering, enigmatic, funereal, the bluish-lilac peephole above the door looked at him from the black darkness, and still with the same unwavering, onward-straining speed, springing and rocking, the carriage tore on. That sad halt had already been left far, far behind. And all that there had been already fully twenty years ago – coppices, magpies, marshes, water lilies, grass snakes, cranes… Yes, there had been cranes as well, hadn't there – how on earth had he forgotten about them! Everything had been strange in that amazing summer, strange too the pair of cranes of some sort which from time to time had flown in from somewhere to the shore of the marsh, and the fact that they had allowed just her alone near them and, arching their slender, long necks, with very stern but gracious curiosity, had looked at her from above when she, having run up to them softly and lightly in her multicoloured woollen shoes, had suddenly squatted down in front of them, spreading out her yellow sarafan on the moist and warm greenery of the shore, and peeped with childish fervour into their beautiful and menacing black pupils, tightly gripped by a ring of dark-grey iris. He had looked at her and at them from a distance through binoculars, and seen distinctly their small, shiny heads – even their bony nostrils, the slits of their strong, large beaks, which they used to killed grass snakes with a single blow. Their stumpy bodies with the fluffy bunches of their tails had been tightly covered with steel-grey plumage, the scaly canes of their legs disproportionately long and slender – those of one completely black, of the other greenish. Sometimes they had both stood on one leg for hours at a time in incomprehensible immobility, sometimes quite out of the blue they had jumped up and down, opening wide their enormous wings; or otherwise they had strolled about grandly, stepping out slowly, steadily, lifting their feet, squeezing their three talons into a little ball and putting them down flat, spreading the talons – like a predator's – apart, and all the time nodding their little heads… Though when she was running up to them, he had no longer been thinking of anything or seeing anything – he had seen only her outspread sarafan, and shaken with morbid languor at the thought of, beneath it, her swarthy body and the dark moles upon it. And on that their final day, on that their final time sitting together on the couch in the drawing room, over the old volume of *The Cornfield*, she had held his cap in her hands as well, pressed it to her breast, like that time in the boat, and had said, flashing her joyful black-mirrored eyes into his:

"I love you so much now, there's nothing dearer to me than even this smell here inside the cap, the smell of your head and your disgusting eau de Cologne!"

* * *

Beyond Kursk, in the restaurant car, when he was drinking coffee and brandy after lunch, his wife said to him:

"Why is it you're drinking so much? I believe that's your fifth glass already. Are you still pining, remembering your dacha maiden with the bony feet?"

"Pining, pining," he replied with an unpleasant grin. "The dacha maiden... *Amata nobis quantum amabitur nulla*!"*

"Is that Latin? What does it mean?"

"You don't need to know that."

"How rude you are," she said with an offhand sigh, and started looking out of the sunny window.

27th September 1940

A Beauty

AN OFFICIAL FROM THE provincial revenue department, a widower, elderly, married a young thing, a beauty, the daughter of the local military commander. He was taciturn and modest, while she was self-assured. He was thin, tall, of consumptive build, wore glasses the colour of iodine, spoke rather hoarsely and if he wanted to say anything a little louder would break into a falsetto. And she was short, splendidly and strongly built, always well dressed, very attentive and organized around the house, and had a sharpness in the gaze of her wonderful blue eyes. He seemed just as uninteresting in all respects as a multitude of provincial officials, but had been wed to a beauty, in his first marriage too – and everyone simply spread their hands: why and wherefore did such women marry him?

And so the second beauty calmly came to hate his seven-year-old boy by the first one, and pretended not to notice him at all. Then the father too, out of fear of her, also pretended that he did not have, and never had had a son. And the boy, by nature lively and affectionate, became frightened of saying a word in their presence, and then hid himself away completely, made himself as though non-existent in the house.

Immediately after the wedding he was moved out of his father's bedroom to sleep on a little couch in the drawing room, a small room next to the dining room, furnished with blue velvet furniture. But his sleep was restless, and every night he knocked his sheet and blanket off onto the floor, and soon the beauty said to the maid:

"It's scandalous, he'll wear out all the velvet on the couch. Make his bed up on the floor, Nastya, on that little mattress I ordered you to hide away in the late mistress's big trunk in the corridor."

And the boy, in his utter solitude in all the world, began leading a completely independent life, completely isolated from the whole house – inaudible, inconspicuous, identical from day to day, he sits meekly in a corner of the drawing room, draws little houses on a slate or reads in a halting whisper always one and the same little picture book, bought still in his late mother's time, builds a railway out of matchboxes, looks out of the windows... He sleeps on the floor between the couch and a potted palm. He makes up his little bed himself in the evening, and diligently clears it away, rolls it up himself in the morning, and carries it off into the corridor to his mother's trunk. All the rest of his bits of belongings are hidden away there too.

28th September 1940

The Simpleton

THE DEACON'S SON, a seminarist who had come to the village to stay with his parents for the holidays, was woken up one dark hot night by cruel bodily arousal and, lying there for a while, he inflamed himself still more with his imagination: in the afternoon, before dinner, he had been spying from a willow bush on the shore above a creek in the river on the lasses who had come there from work and, throwing their petticoats over their heads from their sweaty white bodies, with noise and guffawing, tilting their faces up and bending their backs, had flung themselves into the hotly gleaming water; then, unable to control himself, he got up, stole in the darkness through the lobby into the kitchen, where it was black and hot as in a heated stove, and groped, stretching his arms forwards, for the plank bed on which slept the cook, a beggarly lass without kith or kin and reputed to be a simpleton, and she, in terror, did not even cry out. After that he slept with her the whole summer and fathered a boy, who duly began growing up with his mother in the kitchen. The deacon, the deacon's wife, the priest himself and the whole of his house, the whole of the shopkeeper's family and the village constable and his wife, they all knew whose this boy was – and the seminarist, coming to stay for the holidays, could not see him for bad-tempered shame over his own past: he had slept with the simpleton!

When he graduated – "brilliantly!" as the deacon told everyone – and again came to stay with his parents for the summer before entering the academy, they invited guests for tea on the very first holy day to show off before them their pride in the future academy student. The guests also spoke of his brilliant future, drank tea, ate various jams, and in the midst of their animated conversation the happy deacon wound up a gramophone that began to hiss and then shout loudly. All had fallen silent and started listening with smiles of pleasure to the rousing sounds of 'Along the Roadway',* when suddenly into the room, beginning to dance and stamp, clumsily and out of time, there flew the cook's boy, to whom his mother, thinking to touch everyone with him, had stupidly whispered: "Run and have a dance, little one."

The unexpectedness bewildered everyone, but the deacon's son, turning crimson, threw himself upon him like a tiger and flung him out of the room with such force that the boy rolled into the entrance hall like a peg top.

The next day, at his demand, the deacon and the deacon's wife gave the cook the sack. They were kind and compassionate people and had grown very accustomed to her, had grown to love her for her meekness and obedience, and they asked their son in all sorts of ways to be charitable. But he remained adamant, and they did not dare disobey him. Towards evening, quietly crying and holding in one hand her bundle and in the other the little hand of the boy, the cook left the yard.

All summer after that she went around the villages and hamlets with him, begging for alms. She wore out her clothes, grew shabby, was baked in the wind and sun, became nothing but skin and bone, but was tireless. She walked bare-footed, with a sackcloth bag over her shoulder, propping herself up with a tall stick, and in the villages and hamlets bowed silently before every hut. The boy walked behind her with a bag over his little shoulder too, wearing her old shoes, battered and hardened like the down-at-heel things that lie about somewhere in a gully.

He was ugly. The crown of his head was large, flat and covered with the red hair of a boar, his little nose was squashed flat and had wide nostrils, his eyes were nut brown and very shiny. But when he smiled he was very sweet.

28th September 1940

Antigone

I N JUNE, A STUDENT SET OFF from his mother's estate for his uncle and aunt's – he needed to pay them a visit, find out how they were, about the health of his uncle, a general who had lost the use of his legs. The student performed this service every summer and was travelling now with submissive serenity, unhurriedly reading a new book by Averchenko* in a second-class carriage, with a young, rounded thigh set on the edge of the couch, absent-mindedly watching through the window as the telegraph poles dipped and rose with their white porcelain cups in the shape of lilies-of-the-valley. He looked like a young officer – only his white peaked cap with a blue band was a student's, everything else was to the military model: a white tunic, greenish breeches, boots with patent-leather tops, a cigarette case with an orange lighting wick.

His uncle and aunt were rich. When he came home from Moscow, a heavy tarantass was sent out to the station for him, a pair of draught horses and not a coachman but a workman. But at his uncle's station he always stepped for a certain time into a completely different life, into the pleasure of great prosperity, he began feeling handsome, jaunty, affected. So it was now too. With involuntary foppishness he got into a light carriage on rubber wheels with three lively dark-bay horses in harness, driven by a young coachman in a blue, sleeveless *poddyovka* and a yellow silk shirt.

A quarter of an hour later, with a sprinkling of little bells softly playing and its tyres hissing across the sand around the flower bed, the troika flew into the round yard of an extensive country estate towards the perron of a spacious new house of two storeys. Onto the perron to take his things emerged a strapping servant wearing half-whiskers, a red-and-black striped waistcoat and gaiters. The student took an agile and improbably big leap out of the carriage: smiling and rocking as she walked, on the threshold of the vestibule there appeared his aunt – a loose, shapeless, tussore day coat on a big, flaccid body, a large, drooping face, a nose like an anchor and yellow bags beneath brown eyes. She kissed him on the cheeks in a familiar way, with feigned joy he pressed his lips against her soft, dark hand, quickly thinking: lying like this for three whole days, and not knowing what to do with myself in my free time! Feignedly and hurriedly replying to her feignedly solicitous questions about his mother, he followed her into the large vestibule, glanced with cheerful hatred at the somewhat bent, stuffed brown bear with gleaming glass eyes standing clumsily at full height by the entrance to the wide staircase to the upper floor and obligingly holding a bronze dish for calling cards in its sharp-clawed front paws, and suddenly even came to a halt in gratifying surprise: the wheelchair with the plump, pale, blue-eyed General, was being wheeled steadily towards him by a tall, stately beauty with big grey eyes in a grey gingham dress, a white pinafore and a white headscarf, all aglow with youth, strength, cleanliness, the lustre of her well-groomed hands and the matt whiteness of her face. Kissing his uncle's hand, he managed to glance at the extraordinary elegance of her dress and feet. The General joked:

"And this is my Antigone, my good guide, although I'm not even blind, like Oedipus* was, and especially not to good-looking women. Make one another's acquaintance, youngsters."

She smiled faintly and replied with only a bow to the bow of the student.

The strapping servant with the half-whiskers and the red waistcoat led him past the bear and up the staircase with its gleaming dark-yellow wood and a red runner down the middle and along a similar corridor, took him into a large bedroom with a marble bathroom alongside – on this occasion a different one to before, and with windows looking onto the park, and not into the yard. But he walked without seeing anything. Spinning around in his head there was still the cheerful nonsense with which he had driven onto the estate – "my uncle, the most honest fellow"* – but already there was something else too: there's a woman for you!

Humming, he began to shave, wash and get changed, and he put on trousers with straps under the feet, thinking:

"Such women really do exist! And what would you give for the love of such a woman! And how with such beauty can you possibly be pushing old men and women around in wheelchairs!"

And absurd ideas came into his head: to go on and stay here for a month, for two, to enter in secret from everyone into friendship with her, intimacy, to arouse her love, then say: be my wife, I'm all yours and for ever. Mama, Aunt, Uncle, their amazement when I declare to them our love and our decision to unite our lives, their indignation, then persuasion, cries, tears, curses, disinheritance – it all means nothing to me for your sake...

Running down the stairs to his aunt and uncle – their rooms were downstairs – he thought:

"What rubbish does enter my head, though! It stands to reason, you can stay here on some pretext or other... you can start unobtrusively paying court, pretend to be madly in love... But will you achieve anything? And even if you do, what next? How do you finish the story off? Really get married, do you?"

For about an hour he sat with his aunt and uncle in the latter's huge study, with a huge writing desk, with a huge ottoman, covered with fabrics from Turkestan, with a rug on the wall above with crossed oriental weapons hanging all over it, with inlaid tables for smoking, and with a large photographic portrait in a rosewood frame under a little gold crown on the mantelpiece, on which was the free flourish, made with his own hand: Alexander.*

"How glad I am, Uncle and Aunt, to be with you again," he said towards the end, thinking of the nurse. "And how wonderful it is here at your place! It'll be a dreadful shame to leave."

"And who is it driving you out?" replied his uncle. "Where are you hurrying off to? Stay on till you're sick of it."

"It goes without saying," said his aunt absent-mindedly.

Sitting and chatting, he was continually expecting her to come in at any moment – a maid would announce that tea was ready in the dining room, and she would come to wheel his uncle through. But tea was served in the study – a table was wheeled in with a silver teapot on a spirit lamp, and his aunt herself poured. Then he kept on hoping she would bring some medicine or other for his uncle... But she simply did not come.

"Well, to hell with her," he thought, leaving the study, and went into the dining room, where the servants were lowering the blinds on the tall, sunny windows, glanced for some reason to the right, through the doors of the reception hall, where in the late afternoon light the glass cups on the feet of the grand piano were reflected in the parquet, then passed to the left, into the drawing room, beyond which was the divan room; from the drawing room he went out onto the balcony, descended to the brightly multicoloured flower bed, walked around it, and wandered off down a shady avenue lined by tall trees... It was still hot in the sunshine, and there were still two hours left until dinner.

At half-seven a gong began howling in the vestibule. He was the first to enter the dining room, with its festively glittering chandelier, where beside a table by the wall there already stood a fat, clean-shaven cook all in starched white, a lean-cheeked footman in a frock coat and white, knitted gloves, and a little maid, delicate in a French way. A minute later, his aunt came in unsteadily like a milky-grey queen, in a straw-coloured silk dress with cream lace, her ankles swelling above tight silk shoes, and, at long last, her. But after wheeling his uncle up to the table, she immediately, without turning round, glided out – the student only had time to notice a peculiarity of her eyes: they did not blink. His uncle made little signs of the cross over his light-grey, double-breasted general's jacket, the student and his aunt devoutly crossed themselves standing up, then sat down ceremoniously and opened out their gleaming napkins. Washed, pale, with combed, wet, straggly hair, his uncle displayed his hopeless illness particularly obviously, but he spoke and ate a lot and with gusto, and shrugged his shoulders, talking about the war – it was the time of the Russo-Japanese War:* what the devil had we started it for! The footman waited with insulting apathy, the maid, assisting him, minced around on her elegant little feet, the cook served the dishes with the pomposity of a statue. They ate burbot soup, hot as fire, rare roast beef, new potatoes sprinkled with dill. They drank the white and red wines of Prince Golitsyn,* the uncle's old friend. The student talked, replied, gave his agreement with cheerful smiles, but like a parrot, and with the nonsense with which he had got changed a little while before in his head, thinking: and where is *she* having dinner, surely not with the servants? And he waited for the moment when she would come again, take his uncle away, and then meet with him somewhere, and he would at least exchange a few words with her. But she came, pushed the wheelchair away, and again disappeared somewhere.

In the night, the nightingales sang cautiously and assiduously in the park, into the open windows of the bedroom came the freshness of the air, the dew and the watered flowers in the flower beds, and the bedclothes of Dutch linen were cooling. The student lay for a while in the darkness and had already decided to turn his face to the wall and go to sleep, but suddenly he lifted his head and half-rose: while getting undressed, he had seen a small door in the wall by the head of the bed, had turned the key in it out of curiosity, had found behind it a second door and had tried it, but it had proved to be locked from the other side – now someone was walking about softly behind those doors, was doing something mysterious – and he held his breath, slipped off the bed, opened the first door, listened intently: something made a quiet ringing noise on the floor behind the second door... He turned cold: could it really be her room? He pressed up against the keyhole – fortunately there was no key in it – and saw light, the edge of a woman's dressing table, then something white which suddenly rose and covered everything up... There was no doubt that it was her room – who ever else's? They wouldn't put the maid here, and Maria Ilyinishna, his aunt's old maidservant, slept downstairs next to his aunt's bedroom. And it was as though he were immediately taken ill with her nocturnal proximity, here, behind the wall, and her inaccessibility. He did not sleep for a long time, woke up late and immediately sensed again, mentally pictured, imagined to himself her transparent nightdress, bare feet in slippers...

"This very day would be the time to leave!" he thought, lighting a cigarette.

In the morning they all had coffee in their own rooms. He drank, sitting in his uncle's loose-fitting nightshirt, in his silk dressing gown, and with the dressing gown thrown open he examined himself with the sorrow of uselessness.

Lunch in the dining room was gloomy and dull. He had lunch only with his aunt, the weather was bad – outside the windows the trees were rocking in the wind, above them the clouds both light and dark were thickening...

"Well, my dear, I'm abandoning you," said his aunt, getting up and crossing herself. "Entertain yourself as best you can, and do excuse your uncle and me with our illnesses, we sit in our own corners until tea. There'll probably be rain, otherwise you could have gone out riding..."

He replied brightly:

"Don't worry, Aunt, I'll do some reading..."

And he set off for the divan room, where every wall was covered with shelves of books.

On his way there through the drawing room, he thought perhaps he should have a horse saddled after all. But visible through the windows were various rain clouds and an unpleasant metallic azure amidst the purplish storm clouds above the swaying treetops. He went into the divan room, cosy and smelling of cigar smoke – where, beneath shelves of books, leather couches occupied three whole walls – looked at the spines of some wonderfully bound books, and sat down helplessly, sank into a couch. Yes, hellish boredom. If only he could simply see her, chat with her... find out what sort of voice she had, what sort of character, whether she was stupid or, on the contrary, very canny, performing her role modestly until some propitious time. Probably a self-assured bitch who looks after herself very well... And most likely stupid... But how good-looking she is! And to spend the night alongside her again! He got up, opened the glass door onto the stone steps into the park, and heard the trilling of the nightingales through its rustling, but at that point there was such a rush of chill wind through some young trees on the left that he leapt back into the room. The room had gone dark, the wind was flying through those trees, bending their fresh foliage, and the panes of glass in the door and windows began sparkling with the sharp splashes of light rain.

"And it all means nothing to them!" he said loudly, listening to the trilling of the nightingales, now distant, now nearby, which reached him from all directions because of the wind. And at the same moment he heard an even voice:

"Good day."

He threw a glance and was dumbstruck: *she* was standing in the room.

"I've come to change a book," she said, cordially impassive. "It's the only pleasure I have, books," she added with an easy smile, and went up to the shelves.

He mumbled:

"Good day. I didn't even hear you come in..."

"Very soft carpets," she replied and, turning round, now gave him a lengthy look with her unblinking grey eyes.

"And what do you like reading?" he asked, meeting her gaze a little more boldly.

"I'm reading Maupassant now, Octave Mirbeau..."*

"Well yes, that's understandable. All women like Maupassant. Everything in him is about love."

"But then what can be better than love?"

Her voice was modest, her eyes smiled quietly.

"Love, love!" he said, sighing. "There can be some amazing encounters, but... Your name, nurse?"

"Katerina Nikolayevna. And yours?"

"Call me simply Pavlik," he replied, becoming ever bolder. "Do you think *I'll* do as an aunt for you as well?"

"I'd give a lot to have such an aunt! For the time being I'm only your unfortunate neighbour."

"Is it really a misfortune?"

"I could hear you last night. Your room turns out to be next to mine."

She laughed indifferently:

"And I could hear you. It's wrong to eavesdrop and spy."

"How impermissibly beautiful you are!" he said, fixedly examining the variegated grey of her eyes, the matt whiteness of her face and the sheen of the dark hair beneath her white headscarf.

"Do you think so? And do you want *not* to permit me to be so?"

"Yes. Your hands alone could drive anyone mad..."

And with cheerful audacity he seized her right hand with his left. She, standing with her back to the shelves, glanced over his shoulder into the drawing room and did not remove the hand, gazing at him with a strange grin, as though waiting: well, and what next? He, not releasing her hand, squeezed it tightly, pulling it away downwards, and he gripped her waist with his right arm. She again glanced over his shoulder and threw her head back slightly, as though protecting her face from a kiss, but she pressed her curving torso against him. He, catching his breath with difficulty, stretched towards her half-open lips and moved her towards the couch. She, frowning, began shaking her head, whispering: "No, no, we mustn't, lying down we'll see and hear nothing..." and with eyes grown dim she slowly parted her legs... A minute later his face fell onto her shoulder. She stood for a little longer with clenched teeth, then quietly freed herself from him and set off elegantly through the drawing room, saying loudly and indifferently to the noise of the rain:

"Oh, what rain! And all the windows are open upstairs..."

The next morning he woke up in her bed – she had turned onto her back in bed linen rucked up and warmed in the course of the night, with her bare arm thrown up behind her head. He opened his eyes and joyfully met her unblinking gaze, and with the giddiness of a fainting fit sensed the pungent smell of her armpit...

Someone knocked hastily at the door.

"Who's there?" she asked calmly, without pushing him aside. "Is it you, Maria Ilyinishna?"

"Me, Katerina Nikolayevna."

"What's the matter?"

"Let me come in, I'm afraid someone will hear me and they'll run and frighten the General's wife..."

When he had slipped out into his room, she unhurriedly turned the key in the lock.

"There's something wrong with His Excellency, I think an injection needs to be given," Maria Ilyinishna started whispering as she came in. "The General's wife is still asleep, thank God, go quickly..."

Maria Ilyinishna's eyes were already becoming rounded like a snake's: while speaking, she had suddenly seen a man's shoes beside the bed – the student had fled barefooted. And *she* also saw the shoes and Maria Ilyinishna's eyes.

Before breakfast she went to the General's wife and said she must leave all of a sudden: started calmly lying that she had received a letter from her father – the news that her brother was seriously wounded in Manchuria – that her father, by reason of his widowerhood, was completely alone in such misfortune...

"Ah, how I understand you!" said the General's wife, who already knew everything from Maria Ilyinishna. "Well, what's to be done, go. Only send a telegram to Dr Krivtsov from the station for him to come at once and stay with us until we find another nurse..."

Then she knocked at the student's door and thrust a note upon him: "All's lost, I'm leaving. The old woman saw your shoes beside the bed. Remember me kindly."

At breakfast his aunt was just a little sad, but spoke with him as though nothing were wrong.

"Have you heard? The nurse is going away to her father's. He's alone and her brother is terribly wounded..."

"I've heard, Aunt. What a misfortune this war is, so much grief everywhere. And what was the matter with Uncle after all?"

"Ah, nothing serious, thank God. He's a dreadful hypochondriac. It seems to be the heart, but it's all because of the stomach..."

At three o'clock Antigone was driven away to the station by troika. Without raising his eyes, he said goodbye to her on the perron, as though having run out by chance to order a horse to be saddled. He was ready to cry out from despair. She waved a glove to him from the carriage, sitting no longer in a headscarf, but in a pretty little hat.

2nd October 1940

An Emerald

THE NOCTURNAL DARK-BLUE blackness of the sky, covered in quietly floating clouds, everywhere white, but beside the high moon pale blue. If you look closely, it isn't the clouds floating, it's the moon, and near it, together with it, a star's golden tear is shed: the moon glides away into the heights that have no end, and carries the star away with it, ever higher and higher.

She is sitting sideways on the ledge of a wide open window and, with her head leaning out, is looking up – her head is spinning a little from the movement of the sky. He is standing at her knees.

"What colour is it? I can't define it! Can you, Tolya?"

"The colour of what, Kisa?"

"Don't call me that, I've told you a thousand times already..."

"I obey, Ksenya Alexandrovna, ma'am."

"I'm talking about that sky between the clouds. What a marvellous colour! Both terrifying and marvellous. Now that is truly heavenly, there aren't any like that on earth. A sort of emerald."

"Since it's in the heavens, of course it's heavenly. Only why an emerald? And what's an emerald? I've never seen one in my life. You simply like the word."

"Yes. Well, I don't know – maybe not an emerald, but a ruby... Only such a one as is probably only found in paradise. And when you look at it all like this, how can you possibly not believe that there is a paradise, angels, the throne of God..."

"And golden pears on willows..."

"How spoilt you are, Tolya. Maria Sergeyevna's right in saying that the very worst girl is still better than any young man."

"Truth itself speaks with her lips, Kisa."

The dress she is wearing is cotton, speckled, the shoes cheap; her calves and knees are plump, girlish, her little round head with a small braid around it is so sweetly thrown back... He puts one hand on her knee, clasps her shoulders with the other, and half-jokingly kisses her slightly parted lips. She quietly frees herself, removes his hand from her knee.

"What is it? Are we offended?"

She presses the back of her head against the jamb of the window, and he sees that she is crying.

"But what's the matter?"

"Oh, leave me alone…"

"But what's happened?"

She whispers:

"Nothing…"

And jumping down from the window ledge, she runs away.

He shrugs his shoulders:

"Stupid to the point of saintliness!"

3rd October 1940

The Visitor

THE VISITOR RANG ONCE, twice – it was quiet on the other side of the door, no reply. He pressed the button again, ringing for a long time, insistently, demandingly – heavy running footsteps were heard – and a short wench, sturdy as a fish, all smelling of kitchen fumes, opened up and looked in bewilderment: dull hair, cheap turquoise earrings in thick earlobes, a Finnish face covered in ginger freckles, seemingly oily hands filled with blue-grey blood. The visitor fell upon her quickly, angrily and cheerfully:

"Why on earth don't you open up? Asleep, were you?"

"No, sir, you can't hear a thing in the kitchen, the stove's ever so noisy," she replied, continuing to gaze at him in confusion: he was thin, swarthy, with big teeth, a coarse black beard and piercing eyes; he had a grey silk-lined overcoat on his arm, and a grey hat tilted back off his forehead.

"We know all about your kitchen! You've probably got a fireman boyfriend sitting with you!"

"No, sir..."

"Well, there you are, then, just you watch out!"

As he spoke, he quickly glanced from the entrance hall into the sunlit drawing room, with its rich red velvet armchairs and, between the windows, a portrait of Beethoven with broad cheekbones.

"And who are you?"

"How do you mean?"

"The new cook?"

"Yes, sir..."

"Fekla? Fedosya?"

"No, sir... Sasha."

"And the master and mistress aren't at home, then?"

"The master's at the newspaper and the mistress has gone to Vasilyevsky Island... to that, what's it called? Sunday school."

"That's annoying. Well, never mind, I'll drop by again tomorrow. So, tell them, say: a frightening dark man came, Adam Adamych. Repeat what I said."

71

"Adam Adamych."

"Correct, my Flemish Eve. Make sure you remember. And for the time being, here's what..."

He looked around again briskly and threw his coat onto a stand beside a chest:

"Come over here, quickly."

"Why?"

"You'll see..."

And in one moment, with his hat on the back of his head, he toppled her onto the chest and threw the hem of her skirt up from her red woollen stockings and plump knees the colour of beetroot.

"Sir! I'll shout so the whole house can hear!"

"And I'll strangle you. Be quiet!"

"Sir! For God's sake... I'm a virgin!"

"That's no matter. Well, here we go!"

And a minute later he disappeared. Standing by the stove, she cried quietly in rapture, then began sobbing, and ever louder, and she sobbed for a long time until she got the hiccups, right up until lunch, until someone rang for her. It was the mistress, young, wearing a gold pince-nez, energetic, sure of herself and quick, who had arrived first. On entering, she immediately asked:

"Has anybody called?"

"Adam Adamych."

"Did he leave a message?"

"No, ma'am... Said he'd drop by again tomorrow."

"And why are you all tear-stained?"

"It's the onions..."

At night in the kitchen, which gleamed with cleanliness, with new paper scallops along the edges of the shelves and the red copper of the scrubbed saucepans, a lamp was burning on the table; it was very warm from the stove, which had not yet cooled down; there was a pleasant smell of the remains of the food in a sauce with bay leaves, and of nice everyday life. Having forgotten to extinguish the lamp, she was fast asleep behind her partition – as she had lain down, without undressing, so had she fallen asleep, in the sweet hope that Adam Adamych would come again tomorrow, that she would see his frightening eyes and that, God willing, the master and mistress would once more not be at home.

But in the morning he did not come. And at dinner the master said to the mistress:

"Do you know, Adam has left for Moscow. Blagosvetlov told me. He must have popped in yesterday to say goodbye."

3rd October 1940

Wolves

THE DARK OF A WARM AUGUST NIGHT, and the dim stars can barely be seen twinkling here and there in the cloudy sky. A soft road into the fields, rendered mute by deep dust, down which a chaise is driving with two youthful passengers: a young miss from a small estate and a grammar-school boy. Sullen flashes of summer lightning at times light up a pair of draught horses with tangled manes, running evenly in simple harness, and the peaked cap and shoulders of a lad in a hempen shirt on the box; they reveal for a moment the fields ahead, deserted after the hours of work, and a distant, sad little wood. In the village the evening before there had been noise, cries, the cowardly barking and yelping of dogs: with amazing audacity, when the people in the huts were still having supper, a wolf had killed a sheep in one of the yards and had all but carried it off – the men had leapt out in time with cudgels at the din from the dogs and had won it back, already dead, with its side ripped open. Now the young miss is chuckling nervously, lighting matches and throwing them into the darkness, crying merrily:

"I'm afraid of the wolves!"

The matches light up the elongated, rather coarse face of the youth and her excited, broad-cheekboned little face. She has a red scarf tied right around her head in the Little Russian way,* the open cut of her red cotton dress reveals her round, strong neck. Rocking along with the speeding chaise, she is burning matches and throwing them into the darkness as though not noticing the schoolboy embracing her and kissing her, now on the neck, now on the cheek, searching for her lips. She elbows him aside and, deliberately loudly and simply, having the lad on the box in mind, he says to her:

"Give the matches back. I'll have nothing to light a cigarette with."

"In a moment, in a moment!" she cries, and again a match flares up, then a flash of lightning, and the dark is still more densely blinding with its warm blackness, in which it constantly seems that the chaise is driving backwards. She finally yields to him with a long kiss on the lips, when suddenly, shaking them both with a jolt, the chaise seems to run into something – the lad reins the horses in sharply.

"Wolves!" he cries.

Their eyes are struck by the glow of a fire in the distance to the right. The chaise is standing opposite the little wood that was being revealed in the flashes of lightning. The glow has now turned the wood black, and the whole of it is shakily flickering, just as the whole field in front of it is flickering too in the murky red tremor from the flame that is greedily rushing through the sky, and that, in spite of the distance, seems to be blazing, with the shadows of smoke racing within it, just a kilometre from the chaise, and is becoming more hotly and menacingly furious, encompassing the horizon ever higher and wider – its heat already seems to be reaching their faces, their hands, and even the red transom of some burnt-out roof is visible above the blackness of the earth. And right by the wall of the wood there stand, crimsonly grey, three big wolves, and in their eyes there are flashes now of a pellucid green lustre, now a red one – transparent and bright, like the hot syrup of redcurrant jam. And the horses, with a loud snort, strike off suddenly at a wild gallop to the side, to the left, over the ploughed field, and the lad at the reins topples backwards, as the chaise, careering about with a banging and a crashing, hits against the tops of the furrows.

Somewhere above a gully the horses reared up once again, but she, jumping up, managed to tear the reins from the hands of the crazed lad. At this point she flew into the box with all her weight and cut her cheek open on something made of iron. And thus for the whole of her life there remained a slight scar in the corner of her lips, and whenever she was asked where it was from, she would smile with pleasure:

"The doings of days long gone!" she would say, remembering that summer long ago, the dry August days and the dark nights, threshing on the threshing floor, stacks of new, fragrant straw and the unshaven schoolboy with whom she lay in them in the evenings, gazing at the brightly transient arcs of falling stars. "Some wolves scared the horses and they bolted," she would say. "And I was hot-blooded and reckless, and threw myself to stop them…"

Those she was still to loved, as she did more than once in her life, said there was nothing sweeter than that scar, like a delicate, permanent smile.

7th October 1940

Calling Cards

IT WAS THE BEGINNING OF AUTUMN, and the steamboat *Goncharov* was running down the now empty Volga. Early cold spells had set in, and over the grey floods of the river's Asiatic expanse, from its eastern, already reddened banks, a freezing wind was blowing hard and fast against it, pulling on the flag at the stern, and on the hats, caps and clothes of those walking on the deck, wrinkling their faces, beating at their sleeves and skirts. The steamboat was accompanied both aimlessly and tediously by a single seagull – at times it would fly in an outward curve, banking on sharp wings, right behind the stern; at times it would slip away at an angle into the distance, off to the side, as if not knowing what to do with itself in this wilderness of the great river and the grey autumnal sky.

And the steamboat was almost empty – there was only an artel of peasants on the lower deck, while backwards and forwards on the upper one, meeting and parting, walked just three people: two from second class, who were both travelling to the same place somewhere and were inseparable, always strolling together, continually talking about something in a businesslike way, and like one another in their inconspicuousness, and a first-class passenger, a man of about thirty, a writer who had recently become famous, conspicuous in his not exactly sad, not exactly angry seriousness and in part in his appearance: he was tall, robust – he even stooped slightly, as some strong people do – well dressed and in his way handsome – a brown-haired man of that eastern Russian type that is sometimes encountered among Moscow's merchant folk of long standing; he was indeed one of those folk by origin, although he no longer had anything in common with them.

He walked on his own with a firm step, in expensive and sturdy footwear, in a black cheviot overcoat and a checked English cap, paced backwards and forwards, now against the wind, now with the wind, breathing that powerful air of the autumn and the Volga. He would reach the stern, stand at it, gazing at the river's grey ripples unfolding and racing along behind the steamboat, and, turning sharply, would again walk towards the bow, into the wind, bending his head in the puffed-out cap and listening to the rhythmic beating of the paddle-wheel blades, from which there streamed a glassy canvas of roaring water. At last he suddenly paused and gave a sullen smile: there had appeared, coming up out of the stairwell from the lower deck, from third class, a rather cheap black hat, and underneath it the hollow-cheeked, sweet face of the woman whose acquaintance he had made by chance the previous evening. He set off towards her with long strides. Coming up onto the deck completely, she set off awkwardly in his direction too, and also with a smile, chased along by the wind, all aslant because of it, holding on to her hat with a thin hand, and wearing a light little coat, beneath which could be seen slender legs.

"How did you sleep?" he said loudly and manfully while still on the move.

"Wonderfully!" she replied, immoderately cheerful. "I always sleep like a log…"

He retained her hand in his big one and looked into her eyes. She met his gaze with a joyful effort.

"Why did you sleep so long, my angel?" he said with familiarity. "Good people are already having lunch."

"Daydreaming all the time!" she answered in a brisk manner, quite at odds with her entire appearance.

"And what about?"

"All sorts of things!"

"Oh dear, watch out! 'Thus little children they do drown, whilst bathing in the summer weather, the Chechen's there across the river'."*

"And it's the Chechen that I'm waiting for!" she replied with the same cheerful briskness.

"Better let's go and have vodka and fish soup," he said, thinking: she probably doesn't even have the money to buy lunch.

She began stamping her feet coquettishly:

"Yes, yes, vodka, vodka! It's hellish cold!"

And they set off at a rapid pace for the first-class dining room, she in front, he behind her, already examining her with a certain greed.

He had thought about her in the night. The day before, he had started speaking to her by chance and made her acquaintance by the steamboat's side, as it had approached some high, black bank in the dusk, beneath which there was already a scattering of lights; he had then sat with her on deck, on a long bench running the length of the first-class cabins, beneath their windows with white slatted shutters, but had not sat for long and had regretted it in the night. To his surprise, he had realized in the night that he already wanted her. Why? Out of the habit of being attracted to chance and unknown travelling women while on the road? Now, sitting with her in the dining room, clinking glasses to the accompaniment of cold, unpressed caviar and a hot *kalach*,* he already knew why she attracted him so, and impatiently awaited the matter being brought to a conclusion. Because of the fact that all this – both the vodka and her familiarity – was in astonishing contradiction to her, he was inwardly getting more and more excited.

"Well then, another one each and that'll do!" he says.

"Quite right, that'll do," she replies, striking the same note. "But it's splendid vodka!"

Of course, she had touched him with the way she had become so confused the day before when he had told her his name, the way she had been stunned by this unexpected acquaintance with a famous writer – sensing and seeing that confusion was, as always, pleasant, it always disposes you favourably towards a woman, if she is not utterly plain and stupid; it immediately creates a certain intimacy between you and her, lends you boldness in your treatment of her and as though a certain right to her already. But it was not this alone that aroused him: he had apparently struck her as a man as well, while it was with all her poverty and simple-heartedness that she had touched him. He had already adopted an unceremonious way with female admirers, an easy and rapid transition from the first minutes of acquaintance with them to a freedom of manner, ostensibly artistic, and that affected simplicity of questioning: who are you? where from? married or not? He had asked questions like that the day before too – he had gazed into the dusk of the evening at the multicoloured lights on the buoys forming long reflections in the darkening water around the steamboat, at the campfires burning red on the rafts, he had sensed the smell of the smoke from them, thinking: "This needs to be remembered – straight away there seems to be the smell of fish soup in that smoke," and had asked:

"May I learn your name?"

She had quickly told him her first name and patronymic.

"Are you returning home from somewhere?"

"I've been in Sviyazhsk at my sister's. Her husband died suddenly, and she was left in a terrible situation, you see."

At first she had been so confused that she had kept on looking somewhere into the distance. Then she had started answering more boldly.

"And are *you* married too?"

She had begun grinning strangely:

"I am. And, alas, not for the first year..."

"Why 'alas'?"

"In my stupidity I hurried into it too early. You don't have time to look around before your life's gone by!"

"Oh, there's still a long way to go until then."

"Alas, not long! And I've still experienced nothing in life, nothing!"

"It's still not too late to experience things."

And at that point, with a grin, she had suddenly shaken her head:

"And I will!"

"And what is your husband? A civil servant?"

She had waved her hand:

"Oh, a very good and kind but unfortunately completely uninteresting man... The secretary of our District Land Board..."

"What a sweet, unfortunate woman," he had thought, and had taken out his cigarette case:

"Would you like a cigarette?"

"Very much!"

And she had clumsily, but courageously lit up, inhaling quickly, in a woman's way. And inside him once again pity for her had stirred, pity for her familiarity, and, together with the pity – tenderness, and a voluptuous desire to exploit her naivety and tardy inexperience, which, he had already sensed, would be sure to be combined with extreme boldness. Now, sitting in the dining room, he looked with impatience at her thin arms, at the faded and for that reason still more touching little face, at the abundant dark hair, done up any old how, which she kept on giving a shake, having taken off her black hat and thrown her little grey coat off her shoulders, off her fustian dress. He was moved and aroused by the frankness with which she had talked to him the day before about her family life, about her age, no longer young, and by the fact that now she had suddenly plucked up her courage and was doing and saying the very things that were so amazingly unsuited to her. She

80

had become slightly flushed from the vodka; even her pale lips had turned pink, and her eyes had filled with a sleepily mocking gleam.

"You know," she said suddenly, "there we were talking about dreams: do you know what I dreamt of most of all as a schoolgirl? Ordering myself calling cards! We'd become completely impoverished then, sold the remains of the estate and moved into town, and there was absolutely no one for me to give them to, but how I dreamt! It's dreadfully silly…"

He gritted his teeth and took her firmly by the hand, beneath the delicate skin of which all the bones could be felt, but, not understanding him at all, she herself, like an experienced seductress, raised it to his lips and looked at him languorously.

"Let's go to my cabin…"

"Let's… It really is stuffy somehow in here, full of smoke!"

And, giving her hair a shake, she picked up her hat.

He put his arms around her in the corridor. Proudly, voluptuously, she looked at him over her shoulder. With the hatred of passion and love he almost bit her on the cheek. Over her shoulder, she Bacchically presented her lips to him.

In the half-light of the cabin, with the slatted grille lowered at the window, hurrying to oblige him and make full and audacious use of all the unexpected happiness that had suddenly fallen to her lot with this handsome, strong and famous man, she at once unbuttoned and trampled on the dress that fell off her onto the floor, remaining, slim as a boy, in a light camisole, with bare shoulders and arms and white drawers, and he was agonizingly pierced by the innocence of it all.

"Shall I take everything off?" she asked in a whisper, utterly like a little girl.

"Everything, everything," he said, growing ever more gloomy.

She submissively and quickly stepped out of all the linen she had thrown down onto the floor, and remained entirely bare, grey-lilac, with that characteristic of a woman's body when it feels nervously cold, becomes taut and chill and gets covered in goosebumps, wearing nothing but cheap grey stockings with simple garters and cheap little black shoes, and she threw a triumphantly drunken glance at him, getting hold of her hair and taking the pins out of it. Turning cold, he watched her. In body she proved better, younger than might have been thought. Thin collarbones and ribs stood out in conformity with the thin face and slender shins. But the hips were even large. The belly, with a small, deep navel, was sunken, the prominent triangle of dark, beautiful hair beneath it corresponded with the abundance of dark hair on her head. She took the pins out, and the hair fell down thickly onto her thin back with its protruding vertebrae. She bent to pull up the slipping stockings – the small breasts with frozen, wrinkled brown nipples hung down like skinny little pears, delightful in their meagreness. And he made her experience that extreme shamelessness which so ill became her, and which for that reason so aroused him with pity, tenderness, passion... Between the slats of the grille at the window, jutting upwards at an angle, nothing could have been seen, but in rapturous horror she cast sidelong glances at them when she heard the sound of carefree voices and the footsteps of people passing along the deck right by the window, and this increased still more terribly the rapture of her depravity. Oh, how close by they were talking and walking – and it would never even have occurred to anyone what was going on a step away from them, in this white cabin!

Afterwards he laid her on the bunk like a dead woman. Gritting her teeth, she lay with closed eyes and already with mournful tranquillity on her face, pale now, and utterly youthful.

Just before evening, when the steamboat moored at the place where she needed to disembark, she stood beside him, quiet, with lowered eyelashes. He kissed her cold little hand with that love which remains somewhere in the heart all one's life, and she, without looking back, ran down the gangway into the rough crowd on the jetty.

5th October 1940

Zoyka and Valeria

IN THE WINTER Levitsky spent all his free time at the Danilevskys'
Moscow apartment, and in the summer he started visiting them at
their dacha in the pine forests along the Kazan road.

He had entered his fifth year as a student, he was twenty-four, but at the
Danilevskys' only the doctor himself referred to him as his "colleague",
while all the others called him Georges and Georgeik. By reason of solitude and susceptibility to love, he was continually becoming attached
to one house of his acquaintance or another, soon becoming one of the
family in it, a guest from one day to the next and even from dawn till
dusk if classes permitted – and now this was what he had become at the
Danilevskys'. And here not only the mistress of the house, but even the
children, the very plump Zoyka and the big-eared Grishka, treated him
like some distant and homeless relative. To all appearances he was very
straightforward and kind, obliging and taciturn, although he would
respond with great readiness to any word addressed to him.

Danilevsky's door was opened to patients by an elderly woman in
hospital dress, and they entered into a spacious hallway with rugs
spread on the floor, furnished with heavy, old furniture, and the woman
would put on spectacles, with pencil in hand would look sternly at
her diary, and to some she would appoint a day and hour of a future
surgery, while others she would lead through the high doors of the
waiting room, and there they would wait a long time for a summons
into the surgery next door, to a young assistant in a sugar-white coat
for questioning and examination – and only after that would they get
to Danilevsky himself, to his large surgery with a high bed by the rear
wall, onto which he would force some of them to climb and lie down,
in what fear turned into the most pitiful and awkward pose: everything
troubled the patients – not only the assistant and the woman in the
hallway, where, gleaming, the brass disk of the pendulum in the old
long-case clock went from side to side with deathly slowness, but also
all the grand order of this rich, spacious apartment, that temporizing
silence of the waiting room, where nobody dared even sigh more than

was necessary, and they all thought that this was some sort of utterly special, eternally lifeless apartment, and that Danilevsky himself, tall, thick-set, rather rude, was unlikely to smile even once a year. But they were mistaken: that residential part of the apartment, into which led double doors to the right from the hallway, was almost always noisy with guests, the samovar never left the table in the dining room, the housemaid ran around, adding to the table now cups and glasses, now little bowls of jam, now rusks and bread rolls, and even in surgery hours Danilevsky not infrequently ran over there on tiptoe through the hallway, and while the patients waited for him, thinking he was terribly busy with someone seriously ill, he sat, drank tea and talked about them to the guests: "Let 'em wait a bit, damn 'em!" One day, sitting like that and grinning, throwing glances at Levitsky, at his wiry thinness and the certain stoop of his body, at his slightly bowed legs and sunken stomach, at his freckled face, covered with fine skin, his hawkish eyes and ginger, tightly curling hair, Danilevsky said:

"Own up now, colleague: there is some Eastern blood in you, isn't there – Yiddish, for example, or Caucasian?"

Levitsky replied with his invariable readiness to give answers:

"Not at all, Nikolai Grigoryevich, there's no Yiddish. There is Polish, there is, maybe, your own Ukrainian blood – after all, there are Ukrainian Levitskys too – and I heard from Granddad that there's apparently Turkish too, but whether that's true, Allah alone knows."

And Danilevsky burst out laughing with pleasure:

"There you are, I guessed right after all! So be careful, ladies and girls, he's a Turk, and not at all as modest as you think. And as you know, he falls in love in the Turkish way too. Whose turn is it now, colleague? Who now is the lady of your true heart?"

"Darya Tadiyevna," Levitsky replied with a simple-hearted smile, quickly flooding with delicate fire – he often blushed and smiled like that.

Charmingly embarrassed too, so that even her currants of eyes seemed to disappear somewhere for an instant, was Darya Tadiyevna, nice-looking, with bluish down on her upper lip and along her cheeks, wearing a black silk bonnet after a bout of typhus, half-lying in an armchair.

"Well, it's no secret for anyone, and perfectly understandable," she said, "after all, there's Eastern blood in me too..."

And Grisha began yelling voluptuously: "Ah, hooked, you're hooked!" while Zoyka ran out into the next room and, cross-eyed, fell backwards on the run against the end of a couch.

In the winter Levitsky had, indeed, been secretly in love with Darya Tadiyevna, and before her had experienced certain feelings for Zoyka too. She was only fourteen, but she was already very developed physically, especially at the back, although her bare, blue-grey knees under a short Scottish skirt were still childishly delicate and rounded. A year before she had been removed from grammar school, and she had not been taught at home either – Danilevsky had found the beginnings of some brain disease in her – and she lived in carefree idleness, never getting bored. She was so affectionate with everyone that she even made them smack their lips. She was steep-browed, she had a naively joyous look in her unctuous blue eyes, as though she was always surprised at something, and always moist lips. For all the plumpness of her body, there was a graceful coquetry of movement about it. A red ribbon tied in her hair with its tints of walnut made her particularly seductive. She used to sit down freely on Levitsky's knees – as though innocently, childishly – and probably sensed what he was secretly experiencing, holding her plumpness, softness and weight and trying to keep his eyes off her bare knees under the little tartan skirt. Sometimes he could not contain himself, and he would kiss her on the cheek as if in jest, and she would close her eyes with a languorous and mocking smile. She had once whispered to him in strict confidence what she alone in all the world knew about her mother: her mother was in love with young Dr Titov! Her mother was forty, but after all, she was as slim as a girl, and terribly young-looking, and the two of them, both her mother and the doctor, were so good-looking and tall! Later Levitsky had become inattentive to her – Darya Tadiyevna had begun appearing in the house. Zoyka seemed to become even merrier, more carefree, but never took her eyes off either her or Levitsky; she would often fling herself with a cry to kiss her, but so hated her that when Darya fell ill with typhus, she awaited daily the joyous news from the hospital of her death. And then she awaited her departure – and the summer, when Levitsky, freed from classes, would begin visiting them at the dacha along the Kazan road where the Danilevskys were living in the summer for the third year now: in a certain way she was surreptitiously hunting him down.

And so the summer arrived, and he began coming every week for two or three days. But then soon Valeria Ostrogradskaya came to stay, her father's niece from Kharkov, whom neither Zoyka nor Grishka had ever seen before. Levitsky was sent to Moscow early in the morning to meet her at the Kursk Station, and he arrived from their station not on a bicycle, but sitting with her in the station cabman's chaise, tired, with sunken eyes, joyously excited. It was evident that he had fallen in love with her while still at the Kursk Station, and she was already treating him imperiously as he pulled her things out of the chaise. However, running up onto the porch to meet Zoyka's mother, she immediately forgot about him, and then did not notice him all day long. She seemed incomprehensible to Zoyka – sorting out her things in her room and afterwards sitting on the balcony at lunch, she would at times talk a very great deal, then unexpectedly fall silent, thinking her own thoughts. But she was a genuine Little Russian beauty! And Zoyka pestered her with unflagging persistence:

"And have you brought morocco ankle boots with you, and a woollen shawl to wear around your waist? Will you put them on? Will you let people call you Valyechka?"

But even without the Little Russian costume she was very good-looking: strong, well-formed, with thick, dark hair, velvety eyebrows which almost met, stern eyes the colour of black blood, a hot, dark flush on her tanned face, a bright gleam of teeth and full, cherry-red lips, above which she too had a barely visible little moustache, only not down, like Darya Tadiyevna had, but pretty little black hairs, just like the ones between her eyebrows. Her hands were small but also strong and evenly tanned, as if lightly smoked. And what shoulders! And on them, how transparent were the pink silk ribbons holding the camisole beneath her fine white blouse! Her skirt was quite short, perfectly simple, but it fitted her amazingly well. Zoyka was so enraptured that she was not even jealous over Levitsky, who stopped going away to Moscow and did not leave Valeria's side, happy that she had let him close to her, had also started calling him Georges, and was forever ordering him to do things. Thereafter the days became perfectly summery and hot, guests came more and more frequently from Moscow, and Zoyka noticed that Levitsky had been dismissed, and was sitting beside her mother more and more, helping her to prepare raspberries, and that Valeria had fallen in love with Dr Titov, with whom her mother was secretly in love. In general, something had happened to Valeria – when there were no guests, she stopped changing her smart blouses, as she had done before; she would sometimes go around from morning till evening in Zoyka's mother's peignoir, and she had a fastidious air. It was terribly intriguing: had she kissed Levitsky before falling in love with Dr Titov or not? Grishka swore he had seen her once before dinner walking with Levitsky down the avenue of fir trees after bathing, wrapped up in a towel like a turban, and how Levitsky, stumbling, had been dragging her wet sheet along, and saying something very, very rapidly, and how she had paused, and he had suddenly caught her by the shoulder and kissed her on the lips:

"I pressed up behind a fir tree and they didn't see me," said Grishka fervently with his eyes popping out, "but I saw everything. She was terribly pretty, only all red, it was still terribly hot, and, of course, she'd spent too long bathing, I mean, she always sits in the water and swims for two hours at a time – I spied on that too – naked she's simply a naiad, and he was talking and talking, really and truly like a Turk..."

Grishka swore it, but he liked inventing all sorts of silly things, and Zoyka both did and did not believe it.

On Saturdays and Sundays, the trains that came to their station from Moscow were crammed full of people, weekend guests of the dacha-dwellers, even in the morning. Sometimes there was that delightful rain through sunshine, when the green carriages were washed down by it and shone like new, the white clouds of smoke from the steam engine seemed especially soft, and the green tops of the pines, standing elegant and thick behind the train, drew circles unusually high in the bright sky. The new arrivals vied with each other to grab the cab men's chaises on the rutted hot sand behind the station, and drove with the joy of the dacha down the sandy roads in the cuttings of the forest under the ribbons of sky above them. The complete happiness of the dacha set in when in the forest, which endlessly hid the dry, slightly undulating land all around. Dacha-dwellers taking their Muscovite friends for a walk said that bears were the only thing lacking here, they declaimed, "Both of resin and wild strawb'rries smells the shady wood,"* and hallooed one another, enjoyed their summer well-being, their idleness and freedom of dress – kosovorotkas with embroidered hems worn outside of trousers, the long braids of coloured belts, peaked canvas caps: the odd Muscovite acquaintance, some professor or journal editor, bearded and wearing glasses, was not even immediately recognizable in such a *kosovorotka* and such a cap.

Amidst all this dacha happiness Levitsky was doubly unhappy. Feeling himself from morning till evening pitiful, deceived, superfluous, he suffered all the more for understanding very well how vulgar his unhappiness was. Day and night he had one and the same thought: why, why had she so quickly and pitilessly let him close to her, made him not quite her friend, not quite her slave, and then her lover, who had had to be content with the rare and always unexpected happiness of kisses alone, why had she sometimes been intimate with him, sometimes formal, and how had she had the cruelty so simply and so easily to cease even noticing him all of a sudden on the very first day of her acquaintance with Titov? He was burning up with shame over his brazen loitering on the estate too. Tomorrow he should disappear, flee in secret to Moscow, hide from everyone with this ignominious unhappiness of deceived dacha love, so evident even for the servants in the house! But at this thought he was so pierced by the recollection of the velvetiness of her cherry-red lips that he lost the power of his arms and legs. If he was sitting on the balcony alone and she by chance was passing, she would with excessive naturalness say something particularly insignificant to him as she went – "Now where ever can my aunt be? You haven't seen her?" – and he would hasten to answer her in the same tone, while ready to break into sobs with the pain. If at tea or lunch he threw glances at her in secret, she would become fastidiously absent-minded. Once, as she was passing, she saw Zoyka on his knees – what was that to do with her? But she suddenly flashed her eyes in fury and gave a ringing cry: "Don't you dare climb all over men's knees, you vile girl!" – and he was filled with rapture: it's jealousy, jealousy! But Zoyka seized every moment when somewhere in an empty room she could run up and grab him round the neck and start whispering, licking her lips and with shining eyes: "Darling, darling, darling!" Once she caught his lips so deftly with her moist mouth that for the whole day he could not recall her without a voluptuous shudder – and horror: what ever is the matter with me! How can I look Nikolai Grigoryevich and Klavdia Alexandrovna in the eye now!

The yard of the dacha, which resembled a country house, was a large one. To the right of the entrance stood an empty old stable with a hayloft added above it, then a long wing for the servants adjoining the kitchen, from behind which looked birches and limes, and to the left, on hard, hilly ground, old pines grew in lots of space, and on the grass between them there rose giant's strides and swings, and further on, right by the wall of the forest now, was a flat croquet lawn. The house, which was also large, stood just opposite the entrance, and behind it a large area was occupied by a mixture of forest and garden, with a sombrely majestic avenue of ancient firs going, in the midst of that mixture, from the rear balcony to the bathing place at the pond. And the master and mistress, alone or with guests, always sat on the front balcony, which ran into the house and was protected from the sun. That hot Sunday morning only the mistress and Levitsky were sitting on this balcony. The morning, as always when there were guests, seemed especially festive, and a lot of guests had come, and the housemaids, with their new dresses gleaming, were continually running through the yard from the kitchen into the house and from the house into the kitchen, where pressing work was going on towards lunch. Five people had come: a dark-faced, bilious writer, always excessively serious and stern, but a passionate lover of all sorts of games; a short-legged professor who looked like Socrates and who, at fifty, had just married his twenty-year-old pupil and had come with her, a slender little blonde; a small, very well-dressed lady nicknamed the Wasp for her height and thinness, her angriness and touchiness; and Titov, whom Danilevsky had nicknamed the insolent gentleman. Now all the guests, Valeria and Danilevsky himself were under the pines beside the forest, in their transparent shade – Danilevsky was smoking a cigar in an armchair, the children were busy on the giant's strides with the writer and the professor's wife, while the professor, Titov, Valeria and the Wasp were running about, hitting croquet balls with mallets, calling to one another, arguing, squabbling. And Levitsky and the mistress of the house were listening to them. Levitsky had wanted to go there too, but Valeria had banished him straight away: "Auntie's preparing cherries by herself, be so good as to go and help her!" He had smiled awkwardly, had stood for a little and watched how, with a mallet in her hands, she bent towards a croquet ball, how her tussore skirt hung over her taut calves in fine stockings of pale yellow silk, how plumply and heavily her breasts stretched her transparent blouse, beneath which could be seen the tanned flesh of her rounded shoulders, seeming pinkish from the pink straps of her camisole – and had ambled off to the balcony.

89

He was especially pitiful that morning, and the mistress of the house, equable, calm and clear as always, with her young-looking face and the gaze of her pure eyes, who was also listening with a secret pain in her heart to the voices underneath the pines, threw him the occasional sidelong glance.

"You just won't be able to get your hands clean now," she said, digging a gilded fork into a cherry with bloodied fingers, "and somehow, Georges, you always manage to make yourself particularly messy... Why are you still in your tunic, dear? It's hot, isn't it, you could perfectly well go around in just a shirt with a belt. And you haven't shaved for ten days..."

He knew that his sunken cheeks were covered with a growth of reddish stubble, that he had made his only white tunic terribly dirty with wear, that his student trousers were shiny and his shoes uncleaned, he knew how round-shouldered he was, sitting there with his narrow chest and sunken stomach, and, blushing, he replied:

"It's true, it's true, Klavdia Alexandrovna, I'm unshaven, like a runaway convict; in general I've let myself go completely, shamelessly exploiting your kindness – forgive me, for God's sake. I'll put myself in order this very day, all the more as it's high time I went to Moscow; I've so outstayed my welcome here already that everyone's sick of the sight of me. I've taken the firm decision to go tomorrow. A comrade is inviting me to visit him in Mogilyov – he writes that it's an amazingly picturesque town..."

And he bent still lower over the table, hearing Titov shouting imperiously at Valeria from the croquet:

"No, no, madam, that's against the rules! You don't know how to put your foot on the ball and you're hitting it with the mallet – that's your fault. But it's not done to roquet twice..."

At lunch it seemed to him that all those sitting at the table had moved inside him – were eating, talking, joking and chuckling inside him. After lunch everyone went to rest in the shade of the avenue of firs, thickly strewn with slippery conifer needles, and the housemaids dragged rugs and cushions there. He went through the hot yard towards the empty stable, climbed up the ladder on the wall to the semi-darkness of its loft, where there was old hay lying about, and collapsed into it, trying to make a decision; he began looking intently, lying on his stomach, at a fly which was sitting on the hay right in front of his eyes and, to begin with, quickly criss-crossing its front legs, as though washing – but then, unnaturally somehow, with an effort, it began kicking up the rear ones. Suddenly someone ran quickly into the loft, threw open and closed the door – and, turning round, in the light from the dormer window he saw Zoyka. She jumped towards him, sank into the hay and, gasping for breath, began whispering, lying on her stomach as well and looking him in the eyes as though in fright:

"Georgeik, darling, I have to tell you something – something you'll find terribly interesting, something remarkable!"

"What is it, Zoyechka?" he asked, raising himself a little.

"Well, you'll see! Only first give me a kiss for it – you have to!"

And she began kicking her legs in the hay, baring her plump thighs.

"Zoyechka," he began, made powerless by spiritual exhaustion to suppress the unhealthy tenderness inside him, "Zoyechka, you alone love me, and I love you very much too... But don't, don't..."

She began kicking her legs even more.

"Do, do, you have to!"

And her head fell onto his chest. He saw beneath the red ribbon the youthful shine of her walnut hair, sensed its smell and pressed his face against it. All of a sudden, quietly and piercingly, she cried "ow!" and grabbed hold of the back of her skirt.

He leapt up:

"What is it?"

Dropping her head into the hay, she began sobbing:

"Something's given me a terrible bite there... Take a look, take a look, quickly!"

And she tossed the skirt up onto her back, and pulled the drawers down from her plump body:

"What's there? Blood?"

"But there's absolutely nothing there, Zoyechka!"

"What do you mean, nothing?" she cried, breaking into sobs again. "Blow on it, blow on it, I'm in terrible pain!"

And after blowing, several times he greedily kissed the delicate cold of her backside's broad plumpness. She leapt up in mad rapture with her eyes and tears flashing:

"Fooled you, fooled you, fooled you! And in return for that, here's the terrible secret for you: Titov's dismissed her! Dismissed her completely! Grishka and I heard everything from behind the armchairs in the drawing room: they're walking along the balcony, we sat down on the floor behind the armchairs, and he says to her, terribly insultingly: 'Madam, I'm not one of those men that can be led by the nose. And, moreover, I don't love you. I'll come to love you if you merit it, but for the time being, no declarations.' Isn't it great? That's what she deserves!"

And, leaping up, she darted out of the door and down the ladder.

He followed her with his eyes:

"I'm a scoundrel for whom hanging's too good!" he said loudly, still tasting her body on his lips.

In the evening the estate was quiet, tranquillity set in, a sense of family life – the guests had left at six o'clock... The warm twilight, the medicinal smell of the limes in bloom behind the kitchen. The sweet smell of smoke and food from the kitchen, where dinner was being prepared. And the peaceful happiness of it all – the twilight, the smells – and the torment, still promising something, of her presence, of her existence beside him... the torment, tearing his soul apart, of love for her – and her merciless indifference, absence... Where was she? He went down from the front balcony, listening to the rhythmic shriek and creak, with intervals, of a swing under the pines, and went towards it – yes, it was her. He stopped, gazing at her flying expansively up and down, pulling the ropes ever tauter, striving to fly up to the uttermost height and pretending she had not noticed him. With a shriek of the rings, she flies horribly upwards, disappears in the branches and, as if shot and wounded, hurtles swiftly down, sinking low and with her skirt hem fluttering. Oh, to catch her! Catch and strangle, rape her!

"Valeria Andreyevna! Do be careful!"

As if not hearing, she goes at it still harder...

At dinner on the balcony under a hot, bright lamp, they laughed at the guests and argued about them. She laughed too, unnaturally and viciously, and ate curd cheese and sour cream greedily, again without a single glance in his direction. Zoyka alone was silent, and she kept looking sidelong at him with a gleam in her eyes, which knew something in common with him alone.

They all dispersed and went to bed early, and not a single light remained in the house. Everywhere became dark and dead. Slipping away unnoticed immediately after dinner to his room, the door of which opened onto the front balcony, he started shoving his bits of linen into his shoulder bag, thinking: I'll take the bicycle out nice and quiet, get on – and off to the station. I'll lie down on some sand somewhere in the forest beside the station until the first morning train... Although no, not like that. It'll come out looking like God knows what – ran away like a little boy, in the night, without saying goodbye to anyone! I must wait until tomorrow – and leave carefree, as if nothing were the matter: "Goodbye, dear Nikolai Grigoryevich, goodbye, dear Klavdia Alexandrovna! Thank you, thank you for everything! Yes, yes, to Mogilyov, an amazingly beautiful town, they say... Zoyechka, good luck, dear, grow up and have fun! Grisha, let me shake your 'honest' hand! Valeria Andreyevna, all the best, remember me kindly..." No, "remember me kindly"'s unnecessary, silly and tactless, as if sort of hinting at something...

Sensing there was not the slightest hope of falling asleep, he quietly descended from the balcony, deciding to go out onto the road to the station and give himself a hard time, to stride out for two or three kilometres. But in the yard he stopped: the warm dusk, the sweet quietness, the milky white of the sky from the countless little stars... He set off across the yard, stopped again, raised his head: the starriness receding upwards ever deeper and deeper, and there, a terrible sort of blue-black darkness, voids leading away somewhere... and peace, silence, an incomprehensible, great wilderness, the lifeless and aimless beauty of the world... the speechless, eternal religiosity of the night... and he was alone, face to face with it all, in the abyss between sky and earth... Inwardly, without words, he began praying for some kind of heavenly mercy, for someone's pity on him, sensing with bitter joy his union with the sky and already a certain deliverance from himself, from his body... Then, trying to retain these sensations within him, he looked at the house: the stars were reflected with flattened lustre in the black panes of the windows – and in the panes of her window... Was she sleeping, or lying in the dull numbness of ever the one thought of Titov? Yes, now it was her turn.

He went round the large house, ill-defined in the dusk, went towards the rear balcony, towards the clearing between it and the two rows, terrible in their nocturnal height and blackness, of motionless fir trees with their sharp tops in the stars. In the darkness under the firs were scattered the motionless little greenish-yellow lights of glow-worms. And something showed dimly white on the balcony... He paused, peering closely, and suddenly froze with fear and the surprise: there rang out from the balcony a soft and even expressionless voice:

"Why is it you're wandering about in the night?"

He started forward in astonishment and immediately made out that she was sprawling in a rocking chair, wearing the old, silvery shawl that all the Danilevskys' female guests threw over themselves in the evenings if they were staying for the night. In confusion he too asked:

"And why aren't you asleep?"

She did not reply, was silent for a moment, then got up and inaudibly came down to him, adjusting the slipping shawl with her shoulder:

"Let's take a walk…"

He set off after her, at first behind, then alongside, into the darkness of the avenue, which seemed as if it was concealing something in its gloomy immobility. What's this? He's with her again, alone together in this avenue at such an hour? And again this shawl, always slipping from her shoulders and pricking the tips of his fingers with its silk fibres when he put it right for her… Mastering a spasm in his throat, he uttered:

"Why do you torment me so terribly, to what end?"

She began shaking her head:

"I don't know. Be quiet."

He grew bold, raised his voice:

"Yes, why and to what end? To what end did you…"

She caught his hanging hand and gave it a squeeze:

"Be quiet…"

"Valya, I don't understand a thing…"

She cast his hand away and glanced to the left, at the fir tree at the end of the avenue with the triangle of its mantle wide and black:

"Do you remember this place? Here I kissed you for the first time. Kiss me here for the last time…"

And, passing quickly under the branches of the fir, she impulsively flung the shawl onto the ground.

"Come here to me!"

Immediately after the final moment she sharply and disgustedly pushed him away, and she remained lying as she was, only lowering her raised and outspread knees and dropping her arms alongside her body. He lay face down next to her with his cheek stuck to the conifer needles onto which his hot tears flowed. In the frozen quietness of the night and the forests, low over a dim field, the late moon showed red in the distance like a motionless slice of melon.

In his room, with eyes swollen from crying, he glanced at the clock and took fright: twenty to two! Hurrying and trying not to make a noise, he wheeled the bicycle down from the balcony, wheeled it quietly and quickly across the yard. Outside the gates he leapt up onto the saddle and, bending sharply, began working his legs furiously, bouncing over the sandy potholes of the cutting amidst the frequent blackness of tree trunks that flew upon him from both sides, letting through the light of the pre-dawn sky. "I'll be late!" And he worked his legs even more heatedly, wiping his sweaty brow with the crook of his arm: the express from Moscow flew by the station – without stopping – at two fifteen – he had only a few minutes left. Suddenly, in the dawn's half-light that still resembled twilight, he glimpsed at the end of the cutting the dark building of the station. There it was! He turned decisively down the road to the left, alongside the railway track, turned right onto the crossing, under the barrier, then left again, between the rails, and sped off, bumping over the sleepers, downhill towards the roaring steam engine with its blinding lights that was bursting upwards from the bottom of the slope.

13th October 1940

Tanya

S HE WAS IN SERVICE as a housemaid to a relative of his, Kazakova, a minor landowner; she was in her eighteenth year and was of no great height, which was particularly noticeable when, gently waggling her skirt and with her small breasts lifted slightly beneath her blouse, she went about bare-footed or, in winter, in felt boots; her simple little face was only pleasant-looking, while her grey, peasant's eyes were beautiful only by virtue of youth. At that distant time he expended himself particularly recklessly, led a nomadic life, had many chance amorous encounters and liaisons – and regarded the liaison with her as a chance one too...

* * *

She quickly became reconciled to the fateful, amazing thing that had somehow suddenly happened to her that autumn night; she cried for a few days, but with every day became more and more convinced that it was not a misfortune that had occurred, but good fortune, that he was becoming ever sweeter and dearer to her; at moments of intimacy, which soon began to be repeated more and more often, she already called him Petrusha and spoke of that night as of their shared, cherished past.

At first he both did and did not believe it:

"Is it really true you weren't pretending to be asleep then?"

Yet she only opened her eyes wide:

"But didn't you sense I was asleep, do you really not know how lads and lasses sleep?"

"If I'd known you were really asleep, I wouldn't have touched you for anything."

"Well, I didn't feel a thing, not a thing, almost till the very last minute! Only why did you take it into your head to come to me? You arrived here and didn't even give me a glance, it was only in the evening you asked: you must have been taken on recently, you're called Tanya, I think? And then what a long time you looked as if you were paying no attention. So were you pretending?"

He replied that of course he was pretending, but he was telling a lie: everything had turned out quite unexpectedly for him too.

He had spent the beginning of the autumn in the Crimea, and on the way to Moscow had dropped in on Kazakova, had lived for a couple of weeks in the soothing simplicity of her estate and the meagre days of the start of November, and had been on the point of leaving. That day, in farewell to the countryside, with a rifle over his shoulders and a hound, he went riding from morning till evening through empty fields and bare copses, found nothing, and returned to the estate tired and hungry, ate a pan of rissoles with sour cream at dinner, drank a carafe of vodka and several glasses of tea while Kazakova, as always, talked about her late husband and her two sons who worked in Oryol. At about ten o'clock the house, as always, was already dark, only one candle was burning in the study beyond the drawing room where he stayed whenever he came. As he went into the study, she was kneeling on his bedclothes on the ottoman with a candle in her hand, passing the burning candle over the log-built wall. On seeing him, she thrust the candle onto the nightstand and, jumping down, darted off.

"What's this?" he said in bewilderment. "Hang on, what were you doing here?"

"Burning a bedbug," she replied in a rapid whisper. "I started straightening the bedclothes for you, I look, and there's a bedbug on the wall..."

And she ran away laughing.

His eyes followed her, and without undressing, taking off only his boots, he lay down on the quilt on the ottoman, hoping still to have a smoke and a think about something – it was not his custom to go to sleep at ten o'clock – and immediately dropped off. He came to for a moment, worried through his sleep by the flickering flame of the candle, blew on it and dropped off again. And when he opened his eyes again, there outside the two windows into the yard and the light-filled side window into the garden was the autumnal moonlit night, empty and solitarily beautiful. He found his slippers in the gloom beside the ottoman and went into the hallway next to the study to go out onto the back porch – they had forgotten to leave him what he needed for the night. But the door out of the hallway proved to be padlocked from the outside, and he set off through the house, mysteriously lit from the yard, for the front porch. That way out was through the main hallway and a large, log-built lobby. In this hallway, opposite a tall window above an old locker was a partition wall, and behind it a room without windows where the housemaids always lived. The door in the partition wall was ajar, and it was dark beyond it. He lit a match and saw her sleeping. She was lying on her back on a wooden bed wearing just a nightshirt and a little fustian skirt – her small breasts were round under the nightshirt, her naked legs were bared to the knees, her right arm, thrown out towards the wall, and the face on the pillow seemed dead... The match went out. He stood for a while – then cautiously went towards the bed...

* * *

Going out through the dark lobby onto the porch, he thought feverishly:

"How strange, how unexpected! And surely she wasn't really asleep?"

He stood for a while on the porch, set off across the yard... And the night was a strange one somehow. The wide, empty yard, brightly lit by the high moon. Opposite, sheds, roofed with old, petrified straw – the cattle yard, the coach house, the stables. Behind their roofs, on the northern horizon, mysterious nocturnal clouds are slowly dispersing – dead mountains of snow. Overhead there are only light, white ones, and in them the high moon shedding tears like diamonds, continually emerging into patches of clear, dark blue, into the starry depths of the sky, and seeming to illumine the roofs and the yard still more brightly. And everything around is strange somehow in its nocturnal existence, disengaged from everything human, aimlessly radiant. And it is strange too, because it is as though he is seeing this whole nocturnal, moonlit, autumnal world for the first time...

He sat down beside the coach house on the footboard of the tarantass, bespattered with dried mud. There was an autumnal warmth, the smell of the autumnal garden, the night was majestic, impassive and benign, and it was uniting in a surprising way somehow with the feelings he had brought away from that unexpected union with a female creature still half a child...

She had begun sobbing quietly on coming to her senses, as if realizing only at that moment what had happened. Yet perhaps not as if, but

99

actually? Her whole body had yielded to him as though lifeless. First he had tried to wake her in a whisper: "Listen, don't be afraid…" She had not heard, or had pretended not to. He had cautiously kissed her hot cheek – she had not responded to the kiss at all, and he had thought she had silently given him her consent to all that might follow this. He had parted her legs, their delicate, ardent warmth – she had only sighed in her sleep, stretched weakly and thrown an arm up behind her head…

"And if there was no pretence?" he thought, getting up from the footboard and gazing at the night in agitation.

When she had begun sobbing, sweetly and mournfully, he had, with a feeling not only of animal gratitude for the unexpected happiness she had unconsciously granted him, but also of rapture, of love, started kissing her neck, her breast, all of which smelt ravishingly of something rural, maidenly. And she, while sobbing, had suddenly responded to him with an unconscious female impulse – tightly, and also as though gratefully, she had embraced him and pressed his head against her. Who he was, she, half-asleep, did not yet understand, but all the same – he was the one with whom, at a certain set point, she had been intended to unite for the first time in the most mysterious and blissfully mortal intimacy. That mutual intimacy had taken place and could not now be undone by anything in the world, and he had taken it away inside him for ever, and now this extraordinary night was accepting him into its inscrutable bright realm together with it, that intimacy.

How could he leave and then remember her only by chance, forget her dear, simple-hearted little voice, her now joyful, now sorrowful, but always loving, devoted eyes, how could he love others and attach to some of them much greater significance than to her!

* * *

She served at table the next day without raising her eyes. Kazakova asked:

"Why are you like this, Tanya?"

She replied submissively:

"I've got more than enough to grieve me, ma'am…"

When she had left the room, Kazakova said to him:

"Yes, of course, an orphan, no mother, her father a destitute, dissolute peasant…"

Just before evening, as she was setting up the samovar on the porch, he said to her when passing by:

"Don't you go thinking anything, I fell in love with you a long time ago. Give up crying and grieving, that won't help a thing..."

She replied quietly, shoving flaming kindling into the samovar:

"If you'd really fallen in love with me, it'd all be easier..."

Then she started glancing at him occasionally, as if timidly asking with her gaze: really?

One evening, when she went in to straighten his bed, he went up to her and put his arm round her shoulder. She glanced at him in fright and, blushing all over, whispered:

"Go away, for God's sake. The old woman might well come in..."

"What old woman?"

"The old housemaid, as if you don't know!"

"I'll come to you tonight..."

It was as if she had been scorched – to begin with, the old woman horrified her:

"Oh, what are you thinking of, what are you thinking of! I'll go mad with terror!"

"No, it's all right, don't be afraid – I won't come," he said hurriedly.

Now she was already working as before, quickly and solicitously, again she began rushing across the yard to the kitchen like a whirlwind, as she had rushed previously, and at times, seizing a convenient moment, she would surreptitiously throw at him glances that were already embarrassed and joyful. And then one day, in the morning, first thing, when he was still asleep, she was sent to town for some shopping. At dinner Kazakova said:

"What's to be done, I've sent the *starosta** and the workman off to the mill, there's no one to send to the station for Tanya. Maybe you'd go?"

Containing his joy, he answered with feigned carelessness:

"Why, I'll willingly go for a drive."

The old housemaid, who was serving the food, frowned.

"Why do you want to put the girl to shame for good, ma'am? What'll they start saying about her all over the village after this?"

"You go yourself, then," said Kazakova. "What, she's to come on foot from the station, is she?"

Around four, he rode out in the charabanc with the old, tall, black mare and, afraid of being late for the train, he drove her on hard beyond the village, bouncing along the greasy, hummocky road that had frozen a little and then turned damp – recent days had been wet, misty, and that day the mist was especially dense: even when he was driving through the village it had seemed that night was coming on, and in the huts smoky-red lights had already been visible, weird somehow beyond the blue-grey of the mist. Further on, amidst the fields, the darkness had become almost complete and already impenetrable because of the mist. There was a cold wind and damp gloom coming towards him. But the wind was not dispersing the mist, on the contrary, it was driving its cold, dark blue-grey smoke even more densely together, suffocating him with it, with its odorous dampness, and it seemed that beyond its impenetrability there was nothing – the end of the world and everything living. His peaked cap, knee-length jacket, eyelashes, moustache, everything was covered in the tiniest wet beads. The black mare hurtled onwards with a flourish, the charabanc, bouncing over the slippery hummocks, was hitting him in the chest. He grew adroit enough to light up – the sweet, fragrant, warm, human smoke of the cigarette merged with the primeval smell of the mist, the late autumn, the wet, bare fields. And everything was growing dark, everything was growing gloomy all around, above and below – the long neck of the horse, indistinctly dark, and its pricked ears had become almost invisible. And growing ever stronger was a feeling of closeness to the horse – the only living creature in this wilderness, in the deathly hostility of all that was to the right and to the left, ahead and behind, of all the unknown things that were so ominously hidden in this smoky dark, that flew upon him ever denser and blacker...

When he drove into the village by the station, he was gripped by the joy of habitation, the pitiful lights in the wretched little windows, their gentle comfort, and, at the station, everything about the place seemed another world completely, lively, cheerful, urban. And he had not had time to tether the horse, before the train with its light windows began flashing with a roar towards the station, covering everything with the sulphurous smell of coal. He ran into the station, feeling as though he were waiting for his young wife, and he immediately saw her, dressed for the town, come in through the doors opposite, following the station watchman, who was lugging two bags of shopping: the station building was dirty, it stank of the paraffin in the lamps that dimly lit it, but she was all radiant with excited eyes, with the youth of her face, stirred by the unusual journey, and the watchman was saying something to her politely. And suddenly her gaze met his and she even came to a halt in her perplexity: what's the matter, why is he here?

"Tanya," he said hurriedly, "hello, I've come for you, there was no one else to send..."

Had she ever had such a happy evening in her life? He came for me himself, and I've come from town, I'm dressed up and so pretty; he couldn't even have imagined it, always seeing me only in an old skirt and a poor cotton blouse; my face is like a milliner's under this white silk headscarf, I'm wearing a new, brown worsted dress under a thick cloth jacket, I've got white cotton stockings on and new calf-length boots with brass heels! All atremble inside, she began speaking to him in the sort of tone people use when out visiting and, lifting her hem a little, she set off after him with ladylike little steps, condescendingly marvelling: "Oh Lord, how slippery it is here, what dirty footprints the peasants have left!" Turning all cold with joyful terror, she lifted her dress high above her white calico underskirt so as to sit down on the skirt, not on the dress, and she got into the charabanc and sat down next to him as though she were his equal, drawing herself up awkwardly away from the bags at her feet.

In silence he set the horse moving and drove it into the icy dark of the night and the mist, past little lights, glimpsed here and there low down in huts, over the potholes of this torturous rural road in November, and she did not dare utter a word, horrified at his silence: was he, maybe, angry about something? He understood this and was deliberately silent. And suddenly, having driven out beyond the village and plunged now into total gloom, he brought the horse to a walk, took the reins into his left hand, and with his right gave her shoulders in the jacket, sprinkled with cold wet beads, a squeeze, mumbling and laughing:

"Tanya, Tanyechka..."

And she threw her whole body at him, pressed her silk headscarf, her gentle, glowing face, her eyelashes filled with hot tears up against his cheek. He found her lips, wet with the joyful tears, and, stopping the horse, for a long time could not tear himself away from them. Then, like a blind man, unable to see a thing in the mist and the gloom, he got out of the charabanc, threw his coat onto the ground and drew her towards him by the sleeve. Understanding everything at once, she immediately jumped down to him and, lifting her entire cherished costume, the new dress and the skirt, she groped her way down with quick solicitude onto the coat, giving up to him for ever not only the whole of her body, already his absolute property now, but the whole of her soul as well.

* * *

Again he put off his departure.

She knew it was for her sake; she saw how affectionate he was with her, how he already spoke as with an intimate, his secret friend in the house, and she stopped being afraid and quivering whenever he approached her, as she had quivered to begin with. He became calmer and more natural at moments of love – she quickly adjusted to him. She changed completely with the speed of which youth is capable, she became equable, carelessly happy, already called him Petrusha easily, and sometimes even pretended he was bothering her with his kisses: "Oh Lord, I just can't get rid of you! The moment he sees me alone – he's at me straight away!" – and this afforded her particular joy: that means he loves me, that means he's completely mine, if I can talk to him like that! And there was another happiness – expressing to him her jealousy, her right to him:

"Thank God there's no work at the barn, otherwise there'd be young girls about, and I'd show you for hanging around them!" she would say.

And, suddenly getting embarrassed, would add with a touching attempt at a smile:

"Aren't I enough for you on my own, then?"

Winter set in early. After the mists came a frosty north wind, it froze hard the greasy hummocks of the roads, turned the earth to stone, burned the last of the grass in the garden and the yard. Leaden white clouds started to appear, the noise of the totally denuded garden was restless and hasty, as though it were running away somewhere, and at night the white moon was forever diving into puffy storm clouds. The estate and the village seemed hopelessly poor and rough. Then light snow began to fall, whitening the frozen mud as if with castor sugar, and the estate and the fields that could be seen from it became greyish white and expansive. In the village the final work was being completed

– potatoes were being sorted over and tipped down into cellars for the winter, with the rotten ones being thrown aside. Once he went to take a walk through the village, donning a *poddyovka* with a fox-fur lining and pulling on a fur hat. The north wind blew his moustache about and stung his cheeks. Above everything hung the sullen sky, the greyish-white, sloping field beyond the little river seemed very close. In the village, on the earth beside the thresholds of the huts lay pieces of sacking with piles of potatoes. Sitting working on the sacking were married women and young girls, bundled up in hempen shawls, in men's torn jackets, battered felt boots, and with their faces and hands turned blue – he thought with horror: and under their skirt hems their legs are completely bare!

When he got home, she was standing in the hallway, wiping the boiling samovar with a cloth so as to carry it to the table, and she said at once in a low voice:

"I expect you've been to the village, the girls are sorting over the potatoes there... Well, you walk around, walk around, and try and find yourself the nicest one!"

And holding back her tears, she slipped out into the lobby.

Towards evening the snow fell thick as could be and, running past him through the reception hall, she glanced at him with irrepressible childish merriment and whispered teasingly:

"So, be doing a lot of walking now, will you? And this is only the start – the dogs are rolling around all over the yard – it's going to blow such a blizzard, you won't even poke your nose out of the house!"

"Lord," he thought, "how will I ever pluck up the courage to tell her I'm on the point of leaving!"

And he felt a passionate desire to be in Moscow as soon as possible. The frost, a snowstorm, on the square, opposite Iverskaya, pairs of grey horses with little jingling bells, on Tverskaya the electric light of the lamps up high in the swirling snow... In the Moscow Grand the chandeliers are sparkling, string music is spilling out, and now, throwing his snow-covered fur coat into the arms of the doormen, wiping his moustache, wet from the snow, with a handkerchief, he goes cheerfully, in his customary way, down the red carpet into the heated, crowded hall, into the sound of voices, into the smell of food and cigarettes, into the fussing of footmen and the all-embracing waves of strings, now dissolutely languorous, now stormily rollicking...

For the whole of dinner he could not raise his eyes to her carefree bustling, to her calmed face.

Late in the evening he put on felt boots, an old raccoon coat of the late Kazakov's, pulled on a hat and went out through the back porch into the blizzard – to get a breath of air, to take a look at it. But an entire snowdrift had already piled up under the roof of the porch, he stumbled in it and gathered up whole sleeves full of snow, further on it was pure hell, a rushing white fury. Wading with difficulty, he went around the house, reached the front porch and, stamping, shaking himself down, ran into the dark lobby, which was howling in the storm, then into the warm hallway, where a candle was burning on the locker. She leapt out bare-footed from behind the partition in that same little fustian skirt, and clasped her hands together:

"Lord! Where on earth have you been!"

He threw his fur coat and hat off onto the locker, sprinkling it with snow, and in a mad rapture of tenderness he grabbed her up in his arms. In that same rapture she tore herself free, grabbed a besom and began beating at his boots, which were white with snow, and pulling them from his feet.

"Lord, and masses of snow there too! You'll catch your death of cold!"

* * *

At times in the night, through his sleep, he would hear the monotonous noise of monotonous pressure on the house, then there would be a stormy swoop, sprinkling snow with a rattle against the shutters, shaking them – and then dying down, moving away with a soporific drone... The night seemed endless and sweet – the warmth of the bed, the warmth of the old house, alone in the white darkness of the streaming sea of snow...

In the morning he thought it was the wind of the night that was throwing the shutters wide open with a bang, hitting them against the walls – he opened his eyes – no, it was already light, and looking in from everywhere through the snow-caked windows was white, white whiteness, piled up to the very window ledges, and on the ceiling lay its white reflection. The storm was still droning and blowing, but quietly, already in the manner of the daytime. Visible opposite him from the

106

head of the ottoman were two windows with double, time-blackened frames and a pattern of small panes, the third, to the left of the bedhead, was whitest and lightest of all. On the ceiling is this white reflection, and in the corner, trembling, howling and occasionally banging, is the door of the stove, drawn in by the fire flaring up – how nice, he had been asleep, had heard nothing, while Tanya, Tanyechka, faithful and beloved, had opened up the shutters, then come in quietly in felt boots, all cold, with snow on her shoulders and head, which she had bundled up in a hempen headscarf, and, kneeling down, had got it going. And he had not had time to think about it before in she came, carrying a tray with tea, already without the headscarf. As she put the tray onto the little table by the bedhead, with a scarcely perceptible smile she glanced into his eyes, which had a morning-time clarity and an air of surprise, coming straight from sleep:

"How is it you've slept so late?"

"What's the time then?"

She looked at the watch on the table and did not answer at once – even now she couldn't make out what the time was straight away:

"Ten... Ten minutes to nine..."

Glancing at the door, he pulled her towards him by the skirt. She declined, pushing his hand away:

"It's quite impossible, everyone's awake..."

"Oh, for one minute!"

"The old woman'll come in..."

"No one'll come in – for one minute!"

"Oh, the trouble you cause me!"

Quickly taking her woollen-stockinged legs, one after the other, out of the felt boots, she lay down, looking round at the door... Ah, that peasant smell of her head, her breath, the apple cold of her cheek! He began whispering angrily:

"Again you're kissing with your lips pressed together! When will I break you of it?"

"I'm not a young lady... Wait, I'll lie down a bit lower... Well, be quick, I'm scared to death."

And they stared one another in the eye – intently and senselessly, waiting.

"Petrusha..."

"Be quiet. Why do you always talk at these times?"

"But when am I then to have a talk with you, if not at these times? I won't press my lips together any more... Swear that you've got no one in Moscow..."

"Don't squeeze my neck like that."

"No one in your life will love you like this. Now, you fell in love with me, and it was as if I fell in love with myself too, I just dote on myself... But if you abandon me..."

Slipping out with a hot face under the roof of the back porch into the blizzard, she stood there, squatted down for an instant, then hurled herself into the swirls of white to reach the front porch, sinking in deeper than her bare knees.

The hallway smelt of the samovar. The old housemaid, sitting on the locker under the tall, snow-covered window, was supping from a saucer and, without tearing herself away from it, gave her a dirty look:

"Where've you been? You're all covered in snow."

"I was taking Pyotr Nikolayevich his tea."

"Taking it to him in the servants' room, were you? We know all about your tea."

"If you know, then good luck to you. Is the mistress up?"

"She's remembered! Up before you were."

"You're always in a temper!"

And with a happy sigh, she went behind the partition to get her cup, and there she started singing, barely audibly:

When I go into the garden,
Into the garden green,
Into the garden green to walk,
My own true love to see...

* * *

In the afternoon, sitting in the study with a book, listening to ever the same noise, first lessening, then menacingly growing around the house, which was sinking more and more into snow in the midst of the milky whiteness sweeping in from all directions, he thought: when it dies down, I'll leave.

In the evening he found a moment to tell her to come to him later on in the night, when the house was most sound asleep – for the whole night, until morning. She shook her head, had a think and said: all right. It was really frightening, but all the sweeter.

He felt the same as well. And he was stirred too by pity for her: she didn't even know it was their last night!

In the night he would now fall asleep, now wake up in alarm: would she dare to come? The darkness of the house, the noise around the darkness, the shutters shaking, the constant howling in the stove... Suddenly he came to in terror: he had not heard – it was impossible to hear her, given that criminal caution with which she made her way through the house in the dense darkness – he had not heard, but had sensed that, invisible, she was already standing by the ottoman. He reached out his arms. She silently dived under the blanket to him. He could hear her heart beating, feel her frozen bare feet, and he whispered the most ardent words he could possibly find and utter.

They lay like that for a long time, chest to chest, kissing with such force that it hurt their teeth. She remembered he had bid her not to press her mouth shut and, trying to please, she opened it wide like a baby jackdaw:

"You've probably not slept at all?"

She answered in a joyful whisper:

"Not a minute. I was waiting all the time..."

After groping on the table for matches, he lit a candle. She gasped in terror:

"Petrusha, what have you done? Now if the old woman wakes up and sees the light..."

"To hell with her," he said, gazing at her flushed little face. "To hell with her, I want to see you..."

He held her and did not take his eyes off her. She whispered:

"I'm scared – why are you looking at me like that?"

"Because there's no one on earth prettier than you. This head, with this little braid around it, like a young Venus..."

Her eyes shone with laughter, with happiness:

"Who's this Vinus?"

"There used to be this... And this little nightshirt..."

"Well, you buy me a calico one... You really must love me a lot!"

"I don't love you a bit. And again you smell – is it of quails, or is it dry hemp?..."

"Why is it you like that? And you were saying *I* always talk at these times... but now... you're talking yourself..."

She began pressing him tighter and tighter against her, she wanted to say something else but was no longer able to...

Afterwards he put out the light and lay for a long time in silence, smoking and thinking: but I do have to tell her anyway, it's terrible, but I have to. And he began, barely audibly:

"Tanyechka..."

"What?" she asked, just as mysteriously.

"I have to leave, you know..."

She even sat up:

"When?"

"Soon, I'm afraid... very soon... I've got pressing business..."

She fell onto the pillow:

"O Lord!"

His business of some sort, somewhere there, in some Moscow or other, inspired in her something akin to awe. But how could she part with him, after all, for the sake of this business? And she fell silent, quickly and helplessly racking her brains for a way out of this insoluble horror. There was no way out. She wanted to cry: "Take me with you!" But she did not dare – was that really possible?

"I can't stay here for ever..."

She listened and agreed: no, no...

"I can't take you with me..."

Suddenly, in despair, she uttered:

"Why not?"

He thought quickly: "Yes, why not, why not?" And hastily replied:

"I have no home, Tanya, all my life I've been travelling from place to place... In Moscow I live in rented rooms... And I'm never getting married to anyone..."

"Why not?"

"Because I was just born that way."

"And you're never getting married to anyone?"

"Not to anyone, ever! And I give you my word of honour, honest to God, it's essential for me, very important and pressing business. I'll come back without fail for Christmas!"

She pressed her head against him, she lay for a while, dripping warm tears onto his hands, and whispered:

"Well, I'll be going... It'll soon start getting light..."

And she got up and began making the sign of the cross over him in the darkness:

"May the Queen of Heaven preserve you, may the Mother of God preserve you!"

Running into her room behind the partition, she sat down on the bed and, pressing her hands to her breast and licking the tears from her lips, to the accompaniment of the humming of the snowstorm in the lobby, she began whispering:

"Lord and Father! Queen of Heaven! O Lord, let it not abate, if only for a day or two more!"

* * *

Two days later he left – the abating swirls of snow were still rushing through the yard, but he could not protract her secret torment and his own any more, and he did not give in to Kazakova's attempts to persuade him to wait at least until the following day.

Both the house and the estate as a whole became empty, died. And of imagining Moscow and him in it, his life there, his business of some sort, there was no possibility whatsoever.

* * *

He did not come for Christmas. What days they were! In what a torment of unresolved expectation, in what pitiful pretence to herself, as if there were no expectation at all, did the time pass from morning till evening! And for the whole of Christmas-tide she went about in her very best clothes – the same dress and the same calf-length boots she had worn when he met her then, in the autumn, at the station, on that unforgettable evening.

At Epiphany she believed avidly for some reason that at any moment from down the hill there would appear a peasant's sledge, which he would have hired at the station, not having posted a letter for horses to be sent out for him, and she did not get up off the locker in the hallway for the whole day, gazing into the yard until her eyes hurt. The house was empty – Kazakova had gone off to visit neighbours, the old woman had had dinner in the servants' room and sat there after dinner too, enjoying some spiteful talk with the cook. And she did not even go and have dinner, saying she had a stomach ache...

But then the evening started drawing in. She glanced once more at the empty yard with its glittering crust of ice on the snow and got up, saying to herself firmly: that's it, I don't need anyone any more, and I don't want to wait for anything! – and, dressed up, she set off at a stroll through the reception hall, through the drawing room, in the light of the wintry, yellow sunset from the windows, and began singing loudly and carelessly – with the relief of a life that was settled:

When I go into the garden,
Into the garden green,
Into the garden green to walk,
My own true love to see...

And just at the words about her true love she entered the study, saw his empty ottoman, the empty armchair beside the writing desk, where he had once sat with a book in his hands, and she fell into the armchair with her head on the desk, sobbing and crying: "Queen of Heaven, send me death!"

* * *

He came in February – when she had already completely buried inside her any hope of seeing him even once more in her life.

And it was as if all there had been before returned.

He was staggered when he saw her – she had grown so thin and become all faded, so timid and sad were her eyes. She too was staggered for the first moment: he seemed to her to be different somehow too, older, a stranger, and even unpleasant – his moustache seemed to have got bigger, his voice rougher, his laughter and conversation while he was taking his things off in the hallway were excessively loud and unnatural, she felt awkward about looking him in the eye... But each tried to conceal all this from the other, and soon everything carried on, seemingly the way it had been before.

Then a terrible time began to approach again – the time of his new departure. He swore to her on an icon that he would come for Holy Week, and then that would be for the whole summer. She believed him, but she thought: "And what will happen in the summer? Again the same as now?" This now was no longer enough for her – she needed either completely, completely what had been before, and not a repetition, or else an inseparable life with him, without partings, without new agonies, without the shame of vain expectations. But she tried to drive this thought from her, tried to imagine all the happiness of the summer, when there would be so much freedom for them everywhere... – in the night and in the day, in the garden, in the fields, in the barn, and he would be beside her for a long, long time...

* * *

On the eve of his new departure it was a night already on the verge of spring, light and windy. Behind the house the garden was agitated, and constantly audible from it, carried by the wind, was the angry, helpless, abrupt barking of the dogs over the pit amidst the fir trees: imprisoned there was a vixen which had been caught in a trap and brought to the mistress's yard by Kazakova's forester.

He lay on his back on the ottoman with his eyes shut. She was next to him, on her side with the palm of her hand beneath her sad little head. Both were silent. Finally she whispered:

"Petrusha, are you asleep?"

He opened his eyes and looked into the light dusk of the room, illumined from the left by the golden light from the side window:

"No. What is it?"

"You don't love me any more, you know, you ruined me for nothing," she said calmly.

"Why ever for nothing? Don't be silly."

"You'll be to blame. Where will I go now?"

"And why do you have to go anywhere?"

"Here you are again, again leaving for that Moscow of yours, and what on earth am I going to do here by myself?"

"Why, just the same as you did before. And then – I told you for sure, didn't I? – in Holy Week I'll come back for the whole summer."

"Yes, maybe you will come too... Only you didn't say such things to me before: 'And why do you have to go anywhere?' You used to really love me, said you'd not seen anyone prettier than me. And was I like this then?"

113

No, you weren't, he thought. She had changed dreadfully. Even her body had become feebler somehow, all her bones could be felt.

"My time's past," she said. "I used to slip in to you – and I'd be both scared to death and pleased – well, the old woman's gone to sleep, thank Heaven. But I'm not even scared of her now…"

He shrugged his shoulders:

"I don't understand you. Give me the cigarettes from the table…"

She handed them to him. He lit up:

"I don't understand what's wrong with you. You're simply unwell."

"And I suppose that's why I've stopped being dear to you. And what illness have I got?"

"You don't understand me. I'm saying you're unwell mentally. Because just think, please: what is it that's happened, where have you got the idea that I don't love you any more? And why do you keep repeating one and the same thing: used to, used to…"

She did not reply. The window was shining, there was the noise of the garden, the abrupt barking could be heard, angry, hopeless, plaintive… She slipped gently off the ottoman and, pressing her sleeve to her eyes, with her head jerking, she went softly in her woollen stockings towards the doors into the drawing room. He called her quietly and sternly:

"Tanya."

She turned and answered barely audibly:

"What do you want?"

"Come here to me."

"Why?"

"Come, I say."

She went up to him obediently with her head bent down so he would not see that the whole of her face was covered in tears.

"Well, what do you want?"

"Sit down and don't cry. Give me a kiss – well?"

He sat up, and she sat down next to him and embraced him, sobbing quietly. "My God, what ever am I to do?" he thought in despair. "Again these warm childish tears on a child's hot face… She doesn't even suspect all the strength of my love for her! But what can I do? Take her away with me? Where? To what sort of life? And what will come of it? Tying myself down, ruining myself for ever?" And he began whispering quickly, feeling his own tears too tickling his nose and lips.

"Tanyechka, my joy, don't cry, listen: I'll come in the spring for the whole summer, and you and I really will go 'into the garden green' – I've heard that little song of yours and I'll never forget it – we'll drive into the forest in the charabanc – remember how we drove in the charabanc from the station?"

"No one will let me go with you, darling!" she whispered bitterly, shaking her head on his chest, using this endearment for the first time. "And you won't drive anywhere with me..."

But in her voice he could already hear timid joy, hope.

"I will, I will, Tanyechka! And don't you dare speak to me like a servant again. And don't you dare cry..."

He put his arm under her woollen-stockinged legs and sat her down, ever so light, on his knees:

"Well, say: 'Petrusha, I love you very much!'"

She repeated it dully, hiccupping from her tears:

"I love you very much..."

This was in February of the terrible year of 1917. He was in the countryside then for the last time in his life.

22nd October 1940

In Paris

WHEN HE WAS WEARING A HAT – walking along the street or standing in a Metro carriage – and his close-cut reddish hair could not be seen to be turning sharply silver, going by the freshness of his thin, shaved face and the upright bearing of his thin, tall figure in the long waterproof overcoat that he wore both summer and winter, he might have been given no more than forty. Only his light eyes looked out with dry sadness, and he spoke and held himself like a man who had experienced a lot in life. At one time he had rented a farm in Provence, had heard a lot of caustic Provençal jokes, and in Paris he sometimes liked to insert them with a grin into his always concise speech. Many knew that while still in Constantinople he had been abandoned by his wife and had lived since then with a constant wound in his soul. He never revealed the secrets of that wound to anyone, but he sometimes unwittingly hinted at it – he would joke carelessly if the conversation touched upon women:

"*Rien n'est plus difficile que de reconnaître un bon melon et une femme de bien.*"*

One day, on a damp Paris evening in late autumn, he dropped by to have dinner in a small Russian eating house on one of the dark side streets near Rue Passy. As an annex to the eating house there was something in the manner of a grocer's shop – he unconsciously stopped in front of its broad window, behind which on the window sill could be seen pink conical bottles of rowan-berry vodka and yellow cube-shaped ones of sweetgrass vodka, a dish of dried-up fried patties, a dish of rissoles that had turned grey, a box of halva, a box of sprats; further on – the counter, covered with hors d'œuvres, and, behind the counter, the shopkeeper, with an inimical Russian face. It was light inside the shop, and he was drawn to that light from the dark side street with its cold and seemingly greasy roadway. He went in, bowed to the shopkeeper and went through into the still empty, dimly lit room adjoining the shop, where tables covered with paper showed up white. There he unhurriedly hung his grey hat and long coat on the horns of the coat stand, sat down at a table in the very furthest corner and, absent-mindedly rubbing his hands with their ginger, hairy wrists, began reading the endless list of hors d'œuvres and main dishes on a greasy card, partly typed, partly written in lilac ink that had run. Suddenly his corner was illuminated, and he saw approaching him in a neutrally polite way a woman of about thirty with black hair parted in the middle and black eyes, wearing an embroidered white apron and a black dress.

"*Bonsoir, monsieur,*" she said in a pleasant voice.

She seemed to him so good-looking that he grew embarrassed and replied awkwardly:

"*Bonsoir*... But you're Russian, aren't you?"

"Yes. I'm sorry, I've got into the habit of speaking to customers in French."

"Do you have a lot of French people, then?"

"Quite a lot, and all of them are sure to ask for sweetgrass vodka, pancakes, even borsch. Have you already chosen something?"

"No, there's so much here... You suggest something yourself."

She started running through the list in a pre-learnt tone:

"Today we have naval cabbage soup, rissoles Cossack-style... you can have a veal chop or, if you wish, a Karsky kebab..."

"Splendid. Be so kind as to bring me the cabbage soup and the rissoles."

She lifted up the notepad hanging from her belt and made a note on it with a stub of pencil. Her hands were very white and noble in form, her dress well worn, but evidently from a good house.

"Will you have a drop of vodka?"

"Gladly, the damp outside is terrible."

"What would you like to go with it? There's wonderful herring from the Danube, red caviar, which we had in not long ago, lightly pickled Korkun cucumbers..."

He glanced at her again: the embroidered white apron on the black dress was very pretty, protruding prettily beneath it were the breasts of a strong young woman... her full lips were not made up, but fresh, there was simply a coiled black plait on her head, but the skin of her white hand was well looked after, the nails shiny and slightly pink – evidently a manicure...

"What would I like to go with it?" he said, smiling. "If you'll permit me, just herring with hot potatoes."

"And what wine would you like?"

"Red. The ordinary wine – what you always serve here."

She made a note on the pad and moved a carafe of water from the next table onto his. He shook his head:

"No, *merci*, I never drink either water or wine with water in it. *L'eau gâte le vin comme la charrette le chemin et la femme – l'âme.*"*

"You do have a high opinion of us!" she replied indifferently, and went to fetch the vodka and the herring. His eyes followed in her wake, watching the way she held herself, the way her black dress swayed as she walked... Yes, politeness and indifference, all the habits and movements of a modest and worthy office girl. But good, expensive shoes. Where from? There's probably an elderly, well-to-do *"ami"*...*

He had not been as animated as he was this evening for a long time, thanks to her, and this last thought aroused in him a certain irritation. Yes, from year to year, from day to day, you secretly await only one thing – a happy amorous encounter – you live, in essence, only for the hope of that encounter – and all in vain...

The next day he came again and sat down at his table. She was busy at first, taking two Frenchmen's order and repeating it out loud as she noted it down on the pad:

"*Caviar rouge, salade russe... Deux chachlyks...*"*

Then she left the room, came back, and went up to him with an easy smile, already as to an acquaintance:

"Good evening. It's nice that you liked it here."

He cheerfully rose a little from his seat:

"Your good health. I liked it very much. What should I call you?"

"Olga Alexandrovna. And you, may I ask?"

"Nikolai Platonych."

They shook hands with one another, and she lifted up her notepad:

"Today we have wonderful *rassolnik*.* We have a remarkable chef, he worked on Grand Duke Alexander Mikhailovich's* yacht."

"Splendid, if it's to be *rassolnik*, then so be it... And have you worked here long?"

"This is my third month."

"And before that where?"

"Before that I was a sales assistant in Printemps."

"I suppose you lost your job because of staff cuts?"

"Yes, I wouldn't have left of my own free will."

He thought with pleasure: "It's not a matter of an '*ami*' then," and asked:

"Are you married?"

"Yes."

"And what does your husband do?"

"He works in Yugoslavia. A former participant in the White movement. You too, probably?"

"Yes, I took part in both the Great and the Civil War."

"It's obvious at once. And probably a general," she said, smiling.

"A former one. Now I've been commissioned to write histories of the wars by various foreign publishing houses... How is it that you're by yourself?"

"I just am..."

On the third evening he asked:

"Do you like the *cinéma*?"

Putting a bowl of borsch on the table, she replied:

"It can sometimes be interesting."

"Well, there's a remarkable sort of film on at the Cinéma Étoile at the moment, they say. Would you like to go and watch it with me? You do, of course, have days off?"

"*Merci*. I'm free on Mondays."

"Well, then we'll go on Monday. What's today? Saturday? So the day after tomorrow. Does that suit?"

"Yes, it does. You evidently won't be coming tomorrow?"

"No, I'm going out of town to see acquaintances. And why do you ask?"

"I don't know... It's strange, but I've already grown accustomed to you somehow."

He glanced at her gratefully and blushed:

"And I to you. You know, there are so few happy encounters on earth..."

And he hastened to change the subject:

"So the day after tomorrow. Where are we to meet? Where do you live?"

"By the Metro Motte-Picquet."

"You see how convenient – a direct journey to the Étoile. I'll be waiting for you there at the exit from the Metro at exactly eight thirty."

"*Merci*."

He bowed jokily:

"*C'est moi qui vous remercie.** Put the children to bed," he said, smiling, to find out whether she had a child, "and come."

"That's property I haven't got, thank God," she replied, and smoothly took away his plates.

He was both touched and frowning while going home. "I've already grown accustomed to you…" Yes, perhaps this actually is the long-awaited happy encounter. Only it's too late, too late. *Le bon Dieu envoie toujours des culottes à ceux qui n'ont pas de derrière…**

On Monday evening it was raining, the hazy sky over Paris was a dull red. Hoping to have supper with her on Montparnasse, he did not eat dinner, but dropped into a café on Chaussée de la Muette, ate a ham sandwich, drank a glass of beer and, lighting a cigarette, got into a taxi. He stopped the driver by the entrance to the Metro Étoile and got out onto the pavement into the rain – the fat driver with crimson cheeks trustingly waited for him. The smell of the bathhouse wafted from the Metro, people came up the stairs thick and black, opening up their umbrellas as they walked, and beside him a newspaper vendor cried out abruptly in a low, duck-like quack the names of the evening editions. All of a sudden she appeared in the ascending crowd. He moved joyfully to meet her:

"Olga Alexandrovna…"

Smartly and fashionably dressed, she raised her black-lined eyes to him freely, not the way she did in the eating house, and with a ladylike movement she gave him her hand, on which there hung an umbrella, gathering up the hem of her long evening dress with the other – he was even more pleased: "An evening dress – so she thought we'd go on somewhere after the *cinéma* too," and he turned back the edge of her glove and kissed the wrist of her white hand.

"Poor thing, were you waiting long?"

"No, I've only just arrived. Quick, let's go to the taxi…"

And with an excitement he had not experienced for a long time he followed her into the semi-darkness of the carriage, which smelt of damp cloth. At a turn, the carriage lurched violently, its interior was lit up for an instant by a streetlamp, and he involuntarily supported her by the waist, sensed the smell of powder from her cheek, caught sight of her big knees beneath the black evening dress, the gleam of a black eye and her full lips in red lipstick: a completely different woman was sitting beside him now.

In the dark auditorium, gazing at the radiant whiteness of the screen, across which, with a droning buzz, spread-eagled aeroplanes flew obliquely and fell in the clouds, they exchanged quiet remarks:

"Do you live alone or with a girlfriend?"

"Alone. It's dreadful, really. It's a clean little hotel, warm, but you know, it's one of the ones you can drop into for the night or for a few hours with a girl... The fifth floor, no lift, of course, the red carpet on the stairs ends at the third floor... At night in the rain it's terribly depressing. If you open the window, there's not a soul anywhere, it's a completely dead city, God knows where down below there's a single streetlight in the rain... And you're a bachelor, of course, and live in a hotel too?"

"I have a small apartment in Passy. I live alone too. A Parisian of long standing. At one time I lived in Provence, rented a farm, wanted to withdraw from everyone and everything, live by the labour of my hands – and couldn't endure that labour. I took on a Cossack to help – he turned out to be a drunkard, a gloomy fellow, terrible when tight – I got chickens, rabbits – and they'd die, one day the mule almost bit me to death – a really vicious, clever animal... And the main thing was the utter loneliness. My wife left me while still in Constantinople."

"Are you joking?"

"Not a bit. A very commonplace story. *Qui se marie par amour a bonnes nuits et mauvais jours.** But I didn't even have very many of either the one or the other. She left me in the second year of our marriage."

"And where is she now?"

"I don't know..."

She was silent for a long time. Some imitator of Chaplin was running foolishly around the screen on splayed feet, in absurdly huge down-at-heel shoes, and with a bowler hat on the tilt.

"Yes, you must be very lonely," she said.

"Yes. But still, one must bear it. *Patience – médecine des pauvres.**

"V~   *médecine.*"

'ess. To the extent," he said, grinning, "that sometimes
\ a peep inside *Illustrated Russia* – there's a section
', where they print something akin to marriage and
its: 'Bored Russian girl from Latvia would like to
ensitive Russian Parisian, who should please send

122

photograph... Serious auburn-haired lady, not modern, but attractive, widow with nine-year-old son, seeks correspondence with serious aim with sober gentleman no younger than forty, materially provided for by driving or some other work, who likes family comforts. Cultured ways not essential...' I understand her completely – they're not essential."

"But surely you have friends, acquaintances?"

"No friends. And acquaintanceships are poor comfort."

"And who does your housekeeping?"

"My housekeeping is modest. I brew my own coffee, I also get breakfast myself. Towards evening the *femme de ménage** comes."

"Poor thing!" she said, giving his hand a squeeze.

And they sat like that for a long time, hand in hand, united by the gloom, the closeness of their seats, pretending to be looking at the screen, to which the light from the cubicle in the rear wall passed above their heads in a smoky, chalky-bluish strip. The imitator of Chaplin, whose battered bowler hat had come away from his head in horror, was flying furiously towards a telegraph pole in the wreckage of an antediluvian motorcar with a smoking samovar chimney. The loudspeaker roared musically in a range of voices, and from below, from the pit of the auditorium, smoky from cigarettes – they were sitting in the balcony – there thundered, together with applause, desperately joyous laughter. He leant towards her:

"You know what? Let's go on somewhere, Montparnasse, for example – it's terribly dull here and there's no air to breathe..."

She nodded her head and began putting on her gloves.

Climbing once more into the semi-darkness of a carriage and gazing at the windows sparkling in the rain and constantly flaring up with multicoloured diamonds from the streetlights and the play – now of blood, now of mercury – of advertisements in the blackness on high, he again turned back the edge of her glove and gave her hand a protracted kiss. She looked at him with eyes that were also sparkling strangely, their lashes large and coal black, and with loving sadness she reached her face, her full lips with the sweet taste of lipstick, towards him.

In the Café Coupole they began with oysters and Anjou, then they ordered partridges and red Bordeaux. Over the coffee with yellow Chartreuse they were both slightly tipsy. They had smoked a lot, and the ashtray was full of her blood-stained cigarette ends. In the middle of the conversation he looked at her flushed face and thought she was quite the beauty.

"But tell the truth," she said, removing crumbs of tobacco in little pinches from the tip of her tongue, "you have had encounters over these years, haven't you?"

"I have. But you can guess what kind. Night hotels... And you?"

She paused:

"There was one very difficult episode... No, I don't want to talk about that. A wretch of a boy, in essence a *souteneur*... But how did you and your wife part?"

"Shamefully. There was a wretch of a boy as well, a handsome young Greek, extremely wealthy. And in a month or two there wasn't a trace left of the pure, touching little girl who had simply worshipped the White Army, all of us. She started having supper with him in the most expensive dive in Pera, receiving gigantic baskets of flowers from him... 'I don't understand, can you really feel jealous of him and me? You're busy all day, I have fun with him, to me he's simply a sweet boy and nothing more...' A sweet boy! And she herself was twenty. It wasn't easy to forget her – the former, Yekaterinodar her..."

When the bill was brought, she looked it over carefully and told him to give no more than ten per cent for the service. After that it seemed even stranger to both of them to be parting in half an hour.

"Let's go to my place," he said dolefully. "We can sit and talk some more..."

"Yes, yes," she replied, getting up, taking his arm and pressing it against her.

The night driver, a Russian, drove them to a lonely side street, to the entrance of a tall building, beside which, in the metallic light of a gas streetlamp, the rain was sprinkling onto a tin rubbish bin. They went into the illuminated vestibule, then into the cramped lift, and they were slowly drawn upwards, embracing and quietly kissing. He managed to get the key into the lock of his door before the electric light went out, and he led her into the hallway, then into the small dining room, where only one bulb lit up miserably in the chandelier. Their faces were already tired. He suggested drinking some more wine.

"No, my dear," she said, "I can't drink any more."

He began persuading:

"We'll have just one glass of white each, I've got an excellent Pouilly standing outside the window."

"You have a drink, dear, but I'll go and get undressed and have a wash. And to bed, to bed. We're not children, I think you knew very well that since I'd agreed to come to your place... And in general, why should we part with one another?"

He could not reply from agitation, he silently took her into the bedroom, put the light on in there and in the bathroom, the door into which was open from the bedroom. Here the bulbs burned brightly, and everywhere there was warmth coming from the heating, while in the meantime the rain was beating rapidly and steadily on the roof. She immediately started pulling the long dress off over her head.

He left the room, drank two glasses, one after another, of icy, bitter wine, and could not restrain himself, but again went into the bedroom. In the bedroom, in the large mirror on the opposite wall, the lighted bathroom was brightly reflected. She was standing with her back to him, completely naked, white, strong, bent over the washbasin, washing her neck and breasts.

"You can't come in here!" she said and, throwing on a bathrobe, but without covering her ripe breasts, her strong white stomach and her taut white hips, she came up to him and embraced him like a wife. And he embraced her like a wife too, the whole of her cool body, kissing her still moist chest, which smelt of toilet soap, her eyes and lips, from which she had already wiped the make-up...

Two days later, giving up her job, she moved in with him.

One day in the winter he persuaded her to take a safe in her own name in Crédit Lyonnais and to put into it everything he earned:

"Precautions never do any harm," he said. "*L'amour fait danser les ânes*,* and I feel just as if I'm twenty. But who knows what might happen..."

On the third day of Easter he died in a Metro carriage – reading the newspaper, he suddenly threw his head against the back of the seat and his eyes rolled...

As she was returning in mourning from the cemetery, it was a nice spring day, spring clouds were floating here and there in the soft Parisian sky, and everything spoke of life that was youthful, eternal – and of hers, that was finished.

At home she began tidying the apartment. In the corridor, in the cupboard, she saw his old summer greatcoat, grey with a red lining. She took it off the hanger, pressed it to her face and, as she did so, sat down on the floor, her whole body jerking with sobs, and cried out, begging someone for mercy.

26th October 1940

Galya Ganskaya

A N ARTIST AND AN EX-SAILOR were sitting on the terrace of a Parisian café. It was April, and the artist was in raptures about how beautiful Paris was in the spring and how charming the Parisiennes were in their first spring costumes.

"Yet in my golden age Paris in the spring was, of course, even more beautiful," he was saying. "And not only because I was young – Paris itself was completely different. Just think: not a single car. And as if Paris lived then the way it does now!"

"Well, for some reason spring in Odessa has come to mind for me," said the sailor. "You, as a native of Odessa, know even better than I do all its utterly special charm – that mixture of the already hot sun and the still wintry freshness of the sea, the bright sky and the spring clouds out at sea. And on days like this, the spring smartness of the women on Deribasovskaya Street…"

The artist, puffing at his pipe, called: *"Garçon, un demi!"** and turned back to him animatedly:

"I'm sorry, I interrupted you. Imagine – talking about Paris, I was thinking about Odessa too. You're absolutely right – spring in Odessa really is something special. Only my memories of Parisian springs and the Odessa ones are always inseparable somehow, they used to alternate for me – I mean, you know how often I came to Paris in the spring in those days… You remember Galya Ganskaya? You saw her somewhere and told me you'd never met a girl more charming. Don't you remember? But it's all the same. Just now, starting to talk about Paris as it was then, I was thinking specifically of her too, and of that spring in Odessa when she came to my studio for the first time. Every one of us probably has some particularly dear amorous memory or some particularly grave amorous sin. Well, and Galya is, I think, my most splendid memory and my gravest, although, God is my witness, nonetheless involuntary sin. It's such an ancient business now I can tell you about it with complete frankness…

"I knew her when I was still an adolescent. She grew up, without a

127

mother, with her father, whom her mother had left long before. He was a very well-to-do man, but by profession an unsuccessful artist, an amateur, as they say, but such a passionate one that, other than painting, he was interested in nothing in the world, and he did nothing all his life except stand at an easel and pack his house – he had an estate at Otrada – full of pictures old and new, buying up everything he liked, everywhere, wherever he could. He was a very handsome man, burly, tall, with a wonderful bronze beard, half Polish, half Ukrainian, with the ways of a grand gentleman, proud and with a refined politeness, inwardly very reserved, but who pretended to be a very open man, especially with us: at one time we, the young artists of Odessa, all visited him in a gang every Sunday for about two years in succession, and he always greeted us with open arms, behaved with us, for all the difference in our years, in a totally comradely way, talked about painting endlessly and entertained us lavishly. Galya was then about thirteen or fourteen, and we were enraptured with her, only, of course, as a little girl: uncommonly sweet, playful and gracious she was, a little face with light-brown ringlets like an angel's down her cheeks, but so coquettish that her father said to us one day when she'd run into his studio for some reason, whispered something in his ear and immediately slipped out:

"'Dear oh dear, what sort of a girl have I got growing up, my friends! I'm afraid for her!'

"Then, with the rudeness of youth, we somehow all at once and to a man, as though we'd arranged it, gave up visiting him, we were fed up with something about Otrada – probably his incessant conversations about art and about how he'd finally discovered another remarkable secret about how one should paint. It was just at that time I spent two springs in Paris, imagined myself to be a second Maupassant where matters of love were concerned and, returning to Odessa, went about like the most vulgar fop: a top hat, a pea-green knee-length overcoat, cream gloves, semi-patent-leather ankle boots with buttons, an amazing cane – and add to that wavy whiskers, also in imitation of Maupassant, and a treatment of women that was utterly vile in its irresponsibility. And so I'm walking once down Deribasovskaya on a wonderful day in April, I cross Preobrazhenskaya, and on the corner, beside Liebmann's coffee house, I suddenly meet with Galya. Do you remember the five-storey corner building where that coffee house was – on the corner of

Preobrazhenskaya and Cathedral Square, renowned for the fact that in spring, on sunny days, its ledges were for some reason always packed with starlings and their twittering? Extraordinarily sweet and cheerful it was. And so imagine: it's spring, everywhere a multitude of smartly dressed, carefree and affable people, these starlings pouring out their unceasing twittering like some sort of sunny rain – and Galya. And no longer an adolescent, an angel, but an amazingly good-looking, slim girl, all in new clothes, light grey, springlike. The little face beneath the grey hat is half-hidden by an ash-grey veil, and through it shine eyes of aquamarine. Well, of course, exclamations, questions and reproaches: how you all forgot Papa, how long it is since you visited us! Ah yes, I say, so long that you've had time to grow up. Straight away I bought her a small bunch of violets from a ragamuffin of a girl – she, with a quick smile of gratitude in her eyes, immediately, as all women are supposed to, thrusts it up to her face. 'Would you like to sit down, would you like some chocolate?' – 'With pleasure.' She lifts the veil and drinks the chocolate, throwing festive glances and keeping on asking about Paris, and I keep on gazing at her. 'Papa works from morning till evening, so do *you* work a lot, or are you forever falling for Parisiennes?' – 'No, I don't fall for them any more, I work, and I've painted several decent little things. Would you like to drop into my studio? You can, you're an artist's daughter after all, and I live just a stone's throw from here.' She was terribly pleased: 'Of course I can! And then I've never been inside a single studio, apart from Papa's!' She lowered the veil, grabbed her parasol, I take her by the arm, she hits me on the leg as we walk and laughs. 'Galya,' I say, 'I can call you Galya, can't I?' She answers quickly and seriously: you may. 'Galya, what's happened to you?' – 'What do you mean?' – 'You always were delightful, but now you're simply amazingly delightful!' Again she hits me on the leg and says, maybe joking, maybe serious: 'This is nothing, there's more to come!' You remember the dark, narrow staircase from the yard to my turret? Here she suddenly falls quiet, walks up, rustling her silk underskirt, and keeps looking back. She entered the studio even with a certain reverence, began in a whisper: how lovely and secretive you are here, what a terribly big couch! And how many pictures you've painted, and they're all of Paris... And she started going from picture to picture in quiet rapture, forcing herself to be even excessively unhurried and attentive. She looked her fill and gave a sigh: yes, how many beautiful things you've created! 'Would you like a glass of port and some biscuits?' – 'I don't know...' I took her parasol from her, threw it onto the couch, and took her hand in its white kid glove: may I kiss it? 'But I'm wearing a glove...' I unbuttoned the glove and kissed the start of the little palm. She lowers the veil, looks through it expressionlessly with her aquamarine eyes, and says quietly: well, it's time I was going. No, I say, first we'll sit for a little, I've not had a good look at you yet. I sat down and set her on my knees – you know that entrancing weightiness of women, even of the light ones? Enigmatically somehow, she asks me: do you find me attractive? I looked at the whole of her, looked at the violets, which she'd pinned to her nice new jacket, and even burst out laughing with tenderness: and you, I say, do you find these violets attractive? 'I don't understand.' – 'What's so hard to understand? Here you are, just exactly the same as these violets.' Dropping her eyes, she laughs: 'At our school, such comparisons of young ladies with various flowers were called hack work.' – 'That may be so, but how else can I put it?' – 'I don't know...' And she gives her smart, dangling legs a little swing, her child's lips are half open, gleaming... I raised the veil, bent her little head down and kissed her – she bent it down a little more. I went up her slippery, greenish silk stocking as far as the fastening on it, as far as the elastic, unfastened it, kissed the warm pink flesh of the start of the hip, then again the half-open mouth – she began giving my lips little bites..."

The sailor shook his head with a grin:

"*Vieux satyre!*"*

"Don't talk nonsense," said the artist. "Remembering all this is very painful for me."

"Well, all right, tell me what happened next."

"Next was my not seeing her for a whole year. One day, also in spring, I finally went to Otrada and was greeted by Gansky with such touching joy that I was burnt up with shame at how swinishly we had dropped him. He'd aged a lot, there was silver in his beard, but there was still that same animation in conversations about painting. He began showing me his new works with pride – huge golden swans flying over some blue dunes – he was trying, poor chap, not to fall behind the times. I lie through my teeth: wonderful, wonderful, you've taken a great step forward! He stays strong, but he's glowing like a boy. 'Well, I'm very glad, very glad, and now lunch!' – 'And where's your daughter?' – 'Gone into town. You won't recognize her! Not a little girl, but already a young lady, and the main thing is, completely, completely different: she's grown up, shot up like a poplar!' There's bad luck, I think, I'd actually come to visit the old man only because I'd had a terrible desire to see her, and now, as if on purpose, she was in town. I had lunch, kissed his soft, fragrant beard, made promises to be there without fail the next Sunday, left the house – and coming towards me it's her. She stopped joyously: is it you? What brings you here? You've been with Papa? Ah, how glad I am! – 'And I even more so,' I say, 'your Papa told me you can't even be recognized now, no longer a sapling, but a grown poplar – and it's absolutely true.' And it really was the case: as though not even a young lady, but a young woman. She's smiling, and twirling an open parasol on her shoulder. The parasol's white, lacy, her dress and large hat are white and lacy too, her hair to the side of the hat has the most delightful ginger tint, there's no longer the former naivety in her eyes, the little face has lengthened... 'Yes, I'm even a little taller than you.' I just shake my head: it's true, it's true... Let's take a stroll, I say, to the sea. 'Let's.' We set off down a lane between gardens, I can see she senses all the time that, while saying any old thing, I'm not taking my eyes off her. She walks along, elegantly swinging her shoulders, she's closed the parasol and she's holding her lace skirt with her left hand. We came out onto the cliff – a fresh wind began to blow. The gardens are already clothing themselves, delighting in the sun, while the sea is like a northern one, low, icy, rolling in in steep, green waves, covered in white horses, and sinking in the distance in blue-grey murk – in short, Pontus Euxinus.* We fall silent, stand looking, and seem to be waiting, and she's evidently thinking the same thing as I am – of how she had sat on my knees a year before. I took her by the waist and pressed the whole of her so hard against me that she bent back. I try to catch her lips – she attempts to free herself, twists her head, turns aside, and suddenly gives in, gives me them. And all this in silence – not a sound, not from me, not from her. Then suddenly she tore herself free and, adjusting her hat, said simply and with conviction:

"'Ah, what a good-for-nothing you are. What a good-for-nothing.'

"She turned and, without looking back, set off rapidly down the lane."

"And had there been anything between you that time in the studio, or not?" asked the sailor.

131

"Not all the way there hadn't. We'd done an awful lot of kissing, well, and all the rest, but then pity had taken hold of me: she'd got all flushed, like fire, all dishevelled, and I can see that, in an utterly childish way, she can no longer control herself – she's frightened, but she's dreadfully eager for this frightening thing as well. She'd pretended to be offended: well, don't, don't, if you don't want to, then don't... I'd started kissing her hands tenderly, and she'd calmed down..."

"But how on earth after that did you not see her for a whole year?"

"The devil knows. I was afraid I wouldn't take pity a second time."

"You were a bad Maupassant."

"Perhaps. But wait, just let me finish the story. I didn't see her for about another half a year. The summer was over, everyone had started returning from the dachas, although that was just the time to be staying at a dacha – that Bessarabian autumn is something divine in the tranquillity of the monotonous hot days, in the clarity of the air, in the beauty of the even blue of the sea and the dry yellow of the maize fields. I too had returned from the dacha, and one day I'm walking past Liebmann's again – and imagine, again she's coming towards me. She comes up to me as if nothing had happened, and starts chuckling, curling her mouth charmingly: 'What a fateful spot, Liebmann's again!'

"'Why is it you're so cheerful? I'm terribly glad to see you, but what's the matter with you?'

"'I don't know. After the seaside, I'm beside myself all the time with the pleasure of running around town. I've got a suntan and I've shot up some more, haven't I?'

"I look, and it's true, and the main thing is, such gaiety and freedom in her conversation, in her laughter and in her entire manner, as though she'd got married. And suddenly she says:

"'Do you still have port and biscuits?'

"'Yes.'

"'I want to see your studio again. May I?'

"'Good Lord! I'll say!'

"'Well, let's go, then. And quickly, quickly!'

"I caught her on the stairs, again she bent back, again began shaking her head, but without great resistance. I led her to the studio, kissing her upturned face. In the studio she started whispering mysteriously:

"'Don't listen, but this really is madness, you know... I'm out of my mind...'

"Yet she'd already pulled off her straw hat herself and thrown it into an armchair. Her gingery hair is drawn up onto the crown of her head and held with a vertical tortoiseshell comb, on her forehead is a curled fringe, her face bears a light, even tan, her eyes have a senselessly joyous look... I began undressing her any old how, she hurriedly began helping me. In a single moment I'd thrown the white silk blouse off her and, you understand, a mist simply fell at the sight of her pinkish body with the tan on her gleaming shoulders and the milky white of her breasts, lifted by her corset, with their prominent scarlet nipples, and then at the way she quickly pulled out of her fallen skirts, one after the other, her slim legs in little golden shoes, cream lace stockings and those, you know, loose, cambric knickers with a slit in the side, like they used to wear at that time. When I brutally grabbed her through that slit and toppled her onto the cushions of the couch, her eyes turned black and widened still more, her lips opened feverishly – I can see it all as if it were happening now, she was extraordinarily passionate... But we'll leave that. This is what happened after a couple of weeks, in the course of which she visited me almost every day. She runs in unexpectedly one morning, and straight from the threshold it's:

"'They say you're leaving for Italy in a few days?'

"'Yes. So what of it?'

"'But why didn't you say a word about it to me? Did you want to leave in secret?'

"'Heaven forfend. I was meaning to call this very day and tell you.'

"'In front of Papa? Why not tell me in private? No, you're not going anywhere!'

"I flared up in a foolish way:

"'Yes I am.'

"'No you're not.'

"'And I'm telling you I am.'

"'Is that your final word?'

"'It is. But you must understand that I'll be back in something like a month, a month and a half maximum. And in general, listen, Galya...'

"'I'm not Galya to you. I understand you now – I understand everything, everything! And if you began swearing to me this minute that you'd never ever go away anywhere, it's all the same to me now. That's no longer the point!'

"And, throwing open the door, she slammed it with all her might, and her heels started rapidly down the stairs. I wanted to rush after her, but restrained myself: no, let her come to her senses, I'll set off for Otrada in the evening, say I don't want to upset her, that I'm not going to Italy, and we'll make it up. But suddenly, at about five o'clock, in comes the artist Sinani, wild-eyed:

"'Do you know – Gansky's daughter has poisoned herself! Fatally! With something rare, the devil knows what, lightning quick, swiped something from her father – you remember, that old idiot showed us a whole cabinet of poisons, imagining he was Leonardo da Vinci.* What crazy people these damned Poles are, the men *and* the women! No one can comprehend what happened to her all of a sudden! The father says it's as if he's been struck by a bolt from the blue...'

"I wanted to shoot myself," the artist said quietly after a pause, filling his pipe. "I almost went out of my mind..."

28th October 1940

Heinrich

ON A FAIRY-TALE ICY EVENING with a lilac hoar frost in the gardens, the cab man Kasatkin was speeding Glebov in a high, narrow sledge down Tverskaya to the Loskutnaya Hotel – they had dropped into the Yeliseyevs' for fruit and wine.* It was still light over Moscow, the clear and transparent sky was turning green towards the west, the bays at the tops of the bell towers let the subtle light through, but below, in the grey-blue haze of the frost, it was already getting dark, and motionless and gentle shone the lights of the recently lit streetlamps.

At the entrance to the Loskutnaya, throwing back the wolf-skin travelling rug, Glebov ordered Kasatkin, who was besprinkled with snow dust, to come for him in an hour:

"You'll take me to the Brest Station."

"Yes, sir," replied Kasatkin. "You're going abroad then."

"I am."

Turning his tall, old trotting horse sharply, scraping the metal bindings of the sledge runners, Kasatkin gave his hat a disapproving nod:

"A willing horse needs no spur!"

The large and somewhat neglected vestibule, the spacious lift, and the boy with eyes of different tints and rust-coloured freckles, Vasya, who stood politely in his little tunic while the lift was drawn slowly upwards – it suddenly felt a shame to abandon all this, long familiar, customary. "And really, why am I going?" He looked at himself in the mirror: young, vigorous, wirily thoroughbred, eyes shining, hoar frost on his handsome moustache, well and lightly dressed... it was wonderful in Nice now, Heinrich was an excellent comrade... and the main thing was, it always seemed that somewhere there would be something especially lucky there, some encounter... you would put up somewhere or other on the way – who stayed here before you, what hung or lay in this wardrobe, whose are these women's hairpins forgotten in the bedside table? Again there would be the smell of gas, coffee and beer at the Vienna station, the labels on the bottles of Austrian and

Italian wines on the tables in the sunny restaurant car in the snows of Zemmering, the faces and clothes of European men and women filling the car for lunch... Then night-time, Italy... In the morning, along the route beside the sea towards Nice, there would now be the rides between stations in the clattering and smoking darkness of tunnels, with the lamps burning weakly in the ceiling of the compartment, now the stops, and some gentle and incessant ringing at the little stations covered in flowering roses beside the gulf, which languished in the hot sun like a fusion of precious stones... And he set off quickly down the carpets of Loskutnaya's warm corridors.

The room was warm and pleasant too. The sunset and the transparent concave sky were still shining into the windows. Everything was tidy, the suitcases were ready. And again he felt a little sad – it was a shame to abandon the familiar room and all of Moscow's winter life, and Nadya, and Lee...

Nadya was due to drop in and say goodbye at any moment. He hurriedly put the wine and fruits away in a suitcase, threw his overcoat and hat onto the couch behind the round table and immediately heard a rapid knocking at the door. Before he had had time to open it, she had come in and embraced him, all cold and gently fragrant, in a squirrel-skin coat and a squirrel-skin hat, in all the freshness of her sixteen years, the frost, her flushed little face and her clear green eyes.

"Are you going?"

"I am, Nadyusha..."

She sighed and dropped into an armchair, undoing her coat.

"You know, I was taken ill, thank God, during the night... Ah, how I'd love to see you to the station! Why won't you let me?"

"Nadyusha, you know for yourself it's not possible, I'm going to be seen off by people you don't know at all, you'll feel out of place, lonely..."

"And I think I'd give my life to go with you!"

"And how do I feel? But you know it's not possible..."

He sat down in the armchair close up against her, kissing her warm little neck, and felt her tears on his cheek.

"Nadyusha, what's all this?"

She lifted her face and, with an effort, smiled:

"No, no, I won't... I don't want to constrain you the way women do, you're a poet, freedom's essential for you."

"You're my clever girl," he said, touched by her seriousness and her childish profile – the purity, delicacy and hot flush of her cheek, the triangular cut of her half-parted lips, the questioning innocence of the raised, tear-soaked eyelash. "You're not like other women, you're a poetess yourself."

She stamped on the floor:

"Don't you dare speak to me about other women!"

And with dying eyes she began whispering in his ear, caressing him with her fur and breath:

"Just for a minute... We still can today..."

* * *

The entrance to the Brest Station shone in the blue darkness of the frosty night. Entering the booming station in the wake of the hurrying porter, he caught sight of Lee at once: slim, tall, in a straight, oily-black astrakhan fur coat and a large, black velvet beret, from under which black ringlets hung down her cheeks in long curls; she kept her hands inside a large astrakhan muff, and her black eyes looked at him angrily, terrifying in their magnificence.

"You're leaving after all, you good-for-nothing," she said indifferently, taking him by the arm and hurrying along with him in the wake of the porter in her high, grey overshoes. "Just you wait, you'll be sorry, you won't find another like me, you'll be left with your idiot of a poetess."

"That idiot is still just a child, Lee – you should be ashamed of thinking God knows what."

"Be quiet. I'm not an idiot. And if that 'God knows what' really is going on, I'll throw sulphuric acid over you."

From under the prepared train, lit from above by matt electric globes, there belched hotly hissing grey steam that smelt of rubber. The international coach stood out with its yellowish wooden facing. Inside, in its narrow, red-carpeted corridor, in the mottled sheen of the walls, upholstered in stamped leather, in the thick, granular glass panels in the doors, foreign parts were already there. The Polish carriage attendant in a brown uniform jacket opened the door into a small compartment, very hot, with tight bedding already prepared, and softly lit by a table lamp under a red silk shade.

"How lucky you are!" said Lee. "You've even got your own privy here. And who's next door? Maybe some bitch of a travelling companion?"

And she pulled at the door into the next compartment.

"No, this is locked. Well, your God's a lucky one. Kiss me quickly, it'll be the third bell soon…"

From the muff she pulled a hand, pale and bluish, refined and thin, with long, sharp fingernails, and, writhing, she embraced him impetuously, flashing her eyes immoderately, kissing and biting now his lips, now his cheeks, and whispering:

"I adore you, I adore you, you good-for-nothing!"

* * *

Outside the black window, big, orange sparks rushed backwards like a fiery witch, and there were glimpses of white snowy slopes lit up by the train and black thickets of pine forest, secretive and morose in their immobility and the mystery of their wintry nocturnal life. He closed the red-hot heater underneath the table, lowered the heavy blind onto the cold glass and knocked on the door beside the washbasin which connected his and the next compartment. The door opened inwards and, laughing, in came Heinrich, very tall, in a grey dress, with gingery-lemon hair dressed in a Greek style, delicate facial features like an Englishwoman's and lively, amber-brown eyes.

"Well then, have you said all your goodbyes? I heard everything. Best of all I liked the way she tried forcing her way into my compartment and called me a bitch."

"Are you starting to get jealous, Heinrich?"

"I'm not starting, but continuing. If she weren't so dangerous, I'd have demanded her complete dismissal long ago."

"And that's just the point, that she's dangerous, you try dismissing someone like that all at once! And then I do, after all, tolerate your Austrian, and the fact that the day after tomorrow you'll be sleeping with him."

"No, I won't be sleeping with him. You know very well that I'm going first and foremost to break up with him."

"You could have done that in writing. And could very well have gone direct with me."

She sighed and sat down, adjusting her hair with gleaming fingers, touching it softly and crossing her feet in their grey suede shoes with silver buckles.

"But my dear, I want to part with him in such a way as to have the opportunity of continuing to work with him. He's a calculating man and he'll accept an amicable break. Who will he find capable of supplying his journal with all the theatrical, literary and artistic scandals of Moscow and St Petersburg the way I do? Who will translate and place his brilliant novellas? Today's the fifteenth. So you'll be in Nice on the eighteenth, and I'll be there no later than the twentieth or the twenty-first. And that's enough about that – after all, you and I are first and foremost good friends and comrades."

"Comrades," he said, gazing joyfully at her delicate face, with scarlet, transparent colour on the cheeks. "Of course, I shall never have a better comrade than you, Heinrich. It's only with you that I always feel easy, free, that I can truly talk about everything as with a friend, but you know what the problem is? I'm falling in love with you more and more."

"And where were you yesterday, in the evening?"

"In the evening? At home."

"And with whom? Oh, who cares. But you were seen during the night in the Strelna, you were in some sort of large group in a private room with gypsies. Now that really is bad form – Styopas, Grushas, their fateful eyes…"

"And Viennese drunkards like Przybyszewski?"*

"They, my dear, are a thing of chance and not my field at all. Is she really as good-looking as they say, this Masha?"

"Neither is the gypsy thing my field, Heinrich. And Masha…"

"Come on, describe her to me."

"No, you're getting decidedly jealous, Yelena Heinrichovna. What is there to describe, have you never seen gypsies or something? Very thin, and not even good-looking – flat, tar-coloured hair, quite a coarse, coffee-coloured face, the whites of her eyes senseless and bluish, equine collarbones with a large, yellow sort of necklace, a flat stomach… it all looks very good, though, with a long silk dress the colour of golden onion skin. And you know, when she picks a shawl of old heavy silk up in her arms and, to the sound of tambourines, starts giving glimpses of her little shoes from under her hem, shaking her long silver earrings – it's simply a calamity! But let's go and eat."

She stood up with a little grin:

"Let's. You're incorrigible, my dear. But we'll make do with what God gives us. Look how nice we have it here. Two wonderful little rooms!"

"And one of them quite superfluous."

She threw a knitted Orenburg headscarf over her hair, he put on a travelling cap, and they set off swaying down the endless tunnels of the carriages, crossing clanking iron bridges in the cold, draughty concertinas with a scattering of snow dust in between them.

He returned alone – he had sat in the restaurant smoking while she had gone on ahead. When he returned, in the warm compartment he felt the happiness of a completely domestic night. She had thrown back the corner of the blanket and sheet on the bed, had got his nightclothes out, put the wine on the table and the pears in a box made out of laths, and she was standing in front of the mirror above the washbasin holding hairpins between her lips, with her bare arms lifted to her hair and her full breasts on display, already in just her shift, with bare legs and wearing slippers trimmed with polar fox. Her waist was slim, her hips of full weight, her ankles light and chiselled. He kissed her for a long time standing up, then they sat down on the bed and started drinking the hock, kissing again with lips cold from the wine. Feasting his eyes, he exposed her legs up as far as her belly, up to the ginger hair, their rounded largeness with the almond lustre of the knees.

"And Lee?" she said. "And Masha?"

* * *

In the night, lying beside her in the darkness, with light-hearted sadness he said:

"Ah, Heinrich, how I love such railway-carriage nights, this darkness in the speeding carriage, the lights of a station glimpsed behind the blind – and you, you, 'human women, the net for the enticement of man'! That 'net' is something truly inexpressible, divine and devilish, and when I write about this, try to express it, I'm accused of shamelessness, of low motives... Base spirits! It's well put in one old book: 'A writer has the same absolute right to boldness in his verbal depictions of love and its characters as has at all times been granted in that respect to painters and sculptors: only base spirits see baseness even in what is beautiful or terrible.'"

"And of course, Lee," asked Heinrich, "has small, sharp breasts that stick out in different directions? A sure sign of a hysterical woman."

"Yes."

"Is she stupid?"

"No... Actually, I don't know. Sometimes she seems to be very intelligent, sensible, straightforward, easy and cheerful, she grasps everything at the very first word, but sometimes she spouts such highfaluting, vulgar or vicious, bad-tempered nonsense that I sit and listen to her with the tension and vacancy of an idiot, like someone deaf and dumb... But you're getting on my nerves, asking about Lee."

"I'm getting on your nerves because I don't want to be a comrade to you any more."

"I don't want it any more either. And I say again: write to that Viennese scoundrel that you'll see him on the return journey, but now you're unwell, you need to have a holiday in Nice after influenza. And we'll stay together and go not to Nice, but somewhere in Italy..."

"And why not to Nice?"

"I don't know. I suddenly don't want to any more for some reason. The main thing is, we'll go together!"

"Darling, we've already talked about this. And why Italy? You were assuring me that you'd grown to hate Italy."

"Yes, that's true. I'm angry at it because of our aestheticizing numskulls. 'In Florence I like only the *trecento*...' Yet he himself was born in Belyevo, and in all his life has been in Florence for just one week. *Trecento, quattrocento...* And I grew to hate all those Fra Angelicos, Ghirlandaios, the *trecento*, *quattrocento* and even Beatrice and lean-faced Dante* in a woman's bonnet and a laurel wreath... Well, if not to Italy, then let's go somewhere in the Tyrol, to Switzerland, right into the mountains, to some little stone village in the midst of those granite devils, mottled with snow, poking up into the sky... Just imagine: the pungent, damp air, those barbaric stone huts, steep roofs, huddled beside a humpbacked stone bridge, beneath it the rapid roar of a milky-green stream, the clatter of the bells of a flock of sheep walking ever so tightly packed together, there too a chemist's and a shop selling alpenstocks, a little hotel, terribly warm, with branching deer antlers above the door, which seem as if specially carved out of pumice... in short, the bottom of a ravine, where for a thousand years this barbarity of the mountains, alien to the whole world, has been living, giving birth, marrying, burying, and where, high above it, some eternally white mountain has been gazing out for all time from behind the blocks of granite, like a giant dead angel... And what girls there are there, Heinrich! Taut, red-cheeked, in black bodices and red woollen stockings..."

"Oh, these poets!" she said with an affectionate yawn. "And again, girls, girls... No, it's cold in that little village, darling. And I don't want any more girls..."

* * *

In Warsaw, towards evening, when they were transferring to the Vienna Station, a wet wind was blowing against them and a cold rain falling in large but infrequent drops; the Lithuanian moustache of the wrinkled cabman was blown about as he sat on the box of the spacious carriage, angrily driving on his pair of horses, and the water flowed from his leather peaked cap, and the streets seemed provincial.

Raising the blind at dawn, he saw a plain, pale from the sparse snow, on which, here and there, could be seen the red of little brick houses. They stopped immediately after and stood for quite a time at a large station where, after Russia, everything seemed very small – the carriages on the tracks, the narrow rails, the iron posts of the streetlamps – and everywhere there were piles of black coal; a little soldier with a rifle, wearing a tall kepi the shape of a truncated cone and a short, mousy-blue greatcoat, was walking across the tracks from the locomotive depot; along the wooden planking beneath the windows walked a lanky, moustached man in a check jacket with a rabbit-fur collar and a green Tyrolean hat with a multicoloured feather at the back. Heinrich woke up and asked him in a whisper to lower the blind. He lowered it and lay down in her warmth beneath the blanket. She put her head on his shoulder and started to cry.

"Heinrich, what is it?" he said.

I don't know, darling," she replied quietly. "I often cry at dawn. You wake up, and suddenly you feel so sorry for yourself... In a few hours' time you'll leave, and I'll remain alone, I'll go to a café to wait for my Austrian... And in the evening – a café again, and a Hungarian orchestra, those violins that pain your soul..."

"Yes, yes, and the strident cymbals... That's what I'm saying: send the Austrian to the devil and on we'll go."

"No, darling, I can't. What am I going to live on if I quarrel with him? But I swear to you, there'll be nothing between me and him. You know, the last time I was leaving Vienna, he and I were already, as they say, sorting out our relationship – at night, in the street, underneath a gas lamp. And you can't imagine what hatred there was in his face! His face was pale green, olive, pistachio-coloured from the gas and the spite... But the main thing is, how *can* I now, after you, after this compartment, which has brought us so very close..."

"Listen, is that true?"

She pressed him up against herself and started kissing him so hard that he was gasping for breath.

"Heinrich, I don't recognize you."

"Nor I myself. But come, come to me."

"Wait..."

"No, no, this minute!"

"Just one word: tell me exactly – when will you be leaving Vienna?"

"This evening, this very evening!"

The train was already moving, and the spurs of the border guards were going softly past the door and ringing against the carpet.

* * *

And there was the Vienna station, and the smell of gas, coffee and beer, and Heinrich drove off, smartly dressed, with a sad smile, in an open landau drawn by a nervous, delicate European jade, with a red-nosed driver on the high box wearing a cape and a lacquered top hat, who took the blanket off the jade, then began bellowing and cracking a long whip when it started jerking its long, aristocratic, worn-out legs and ran askew with its short-cropped tail after a yellow tram. There was Zemmering and all the foreign festiveness of midday in the mountains, a hot left-hand window in the restaurant car, a little bunch of flowers, Apollinaris water and the red wine Feslau on the blindingly white table beside the window, and the blindingly white midday brilliance of the snowy peaks, rising in their solemnly joyous vestments up into the heavenly indigo of the sky within touching distance of the train, which wound along precipices above a narrow abyss, where the wintry shade, still of the morning, was coldly blue. There was a frosty, primordially chaste, pure evening, turning a deathly scarlet and blue towards

143

night-time, on some pass that was sinking with all its green fir trees in a great abundance of fresh, fluffy snow. Then there was a long wait in a dark gorge beside the Italian frontier, in the midst of a black Dantean hell of mountains and some sort of red, inflamed, smouldering light at the entrance to the smoke-blackened mouth of a tunnel. Then – everything was already completely different, unlike anything that had gone before: an old, peeling, pink Italian station, and the short-legged station soldiers with the pride of cockerels, and cockerels' feathers on their helmets, and instead of a buffet at the station, a solitary little boy lazily wheeling a barrow past the train, on which there were only oranges and fiascos. And thereafter comes the train's now free, ever accelerating race down and down, and from the Lombardy plain, dotted in the distance with the gentle lights of dear Italy, the wind beating ever softer, ever warmer out of the darkness into the open windows. And just before evening of the following, perfectly summery day – the station at Nice, the seasonal throng on its platforms…

In the blue dusk, when right as far as Cap d'Antibes, melting away like an ashen spectre in the west, there stretched in a curved diamond chain innumerable waterside lights, he stood in just a tailcoat on the balcony of his room in a hotel on the promenade, thinking of how it was minus twenty degrees in Moscow now, and expecting there would soon be a knock on his door, and he would be handed a telegram from Heinrich. Eating in the hotel dining room under gleaming chandeliers, in a crush of tailcoats and women's evening dresses, he again expected a boy in a blue waist-length uniform jacket and white knitted gloves to bring him deferentially at any moment a telegram on a tray; he absent-mindedly ate a thin soup with roots, drank red Bordeaux and waited; he drank coffee, smoked in the vestibule and waited again, becoming more and more agitated and surprised: what is the matter with me, since my very earliest youth I've not experienced anything like it! But there was still no telegram. There were glimpses of the shining lifts sliding up and down, boys ran back and forth, taking round cigarettes, cigars and evening newspapers, a string orchestra struck up from the stage – there was still no telegram, but it was already past ten o'clock, and the train from Vienna ought to bring her at twelve. After the coffee he drank five glasses of brandy and, feeling exhausted, disgusted, he took the lift to his room, looking maliciously at the boy in uniform: "Ah, what a scoundrel he'll grow into, this sly, obsequious wretch of a boy, already corrupted through and through! And who thinks up the foolish little hats and jackets for all these wretched boys, some blue, some brown, with epaulettes and piping!"

There was no telegram in the morning either. He rang, and a young footman in tails, a handsome Italian with the eyes of a gazelle, brought him coffee: "*Pas de lettres, monsieur, pas de télégrammes.*"* He stood in pyjamas beside the open door onto the balcony, squinting because of the sun and the sea's dancing golden needles, gazing at the promenade, at the dense crowd of strolling people, listening to the Italian singing that, swooning in happiness, reached him from below, from beneath the balcony, and he thought with enjoyment:

"Well, to hell with her. Everything's clear."

He went to Monte Carlo, spent a long time gambling, lost two hundred francs, returned, to kill time, in a cab – he was driving for almost three hours: clip-clop, clip-clop, swish! And an abrupt shot from the whip in the air... The hotel porter grinned joyously:

"*Pas de télégrammes, monsieur!*"

He dressed for dinner vacantly, constantly thinking one and the same thing.

"If there were suddenly a knock at the door now and she suddenly came in, hurrying, agitated, explaining on the move why she hadn't sent a telegram, why she hadn't arrived yesterday, I think I should die of happiness! I'd tell her that never in my life had I loved anyone in the world as much as her, that God would forgive me many things for such a love, would forgive even Nadya – take all of me, all of me, Heinrich! Yes, but Heinrich's now having dinner with her Austrian. Oh, what a thrill it would be to give her the most brutal slap in the face and crack his head open with the bottle of champagne they're drinking together now!"

After dinner he walked through the streets in the dense crowd, in the warm air, in the sweet stench of dirt-cheap Italian cigars, he came out onto the promenade, to the pitch blackness of the sea, gazed at the precious necklace of its black curve, disappearing sadly in the distance to the right, dropped into bars and drank continually, now brandy, now gin, whisky. On returning to the hotel, white as chalk, in a white tie, in a white waistcoat, in a top hat, he went up to the hotel porter with a pompous and offhand air, mumbling with lips growing numb:

"*Pas de télégrammes?*"

145

And the porter, pretending to notice nothing, replied with joyous alacrity:

"*Pas de télégrammes, monsieur!*"

He was so drunk that he fell asleep after throwing off only his top hat, overcoat and tails – he fell onto his back and at once flew giddily into bottomless darkness, bespeckled with fiery stars.

On the third day he fell sound asleep after lunch and, waking up, suddenly took a sober and firm look at all his pitiful and shameful behaviour. He ordered tea in his room and began clearing the things out of his wardrobe into suitcases, trying not to think of her any more and not to regret his senseless, spoilt trip. Just before evening he went down into the vestibule, ordered his bill to be prepared, set off at a calm pace for Thomas Cook's and took a ticket to Moscow via Venice on the evening train: I'll spend a day in Venice and at three o'clock in the morning, by the direct route, without any stops, home to the Loskutnaya Hotel... What's he like, this Austrian? Going by portraits and what Heinrich said, strapping, wiry, with a gloomy and decisive look – feigned, of course – on a face bent and crooked under a wide-brimmed hat... But why think about him! And who knows what else life might bring! Tomorrow – Venice. Again the singing and guitars of street singers on the embankment below the hotel – the sharp and unconcerned voice of a dark, bare-headed woman with a shawl on her shoulders stands out, as she sings the second part to the outpourings of a short-legged tenor in a beggar's hat, who seems like a dwarf from a height... a little old man in rags helping people into a gondola – the year before he had helped him in with a fiery-eyed Sicilian girl wearing swinging cut-glass earrings, with a yellow bunch of flowering mimosa in hair the colour of black olives... the smell of the festering water of the canal, the gondola, its inside funereally lacquered, with an indented, rapacious axe shape at the prow, the rocking of the gondola, and, standing high up in the stern, the young rower with a slender waist, belted with a red scarf, moving forwards monotonously as he leant on the long oar, with his left leg set classically back...

Evening was coming on, the pale evening sea lay calm and flat, a molten green mix with an opal gloss, above it the seagulls were straining with angry and piteous cries, sensing bad weather on the morrow, the hazily grey-blue west beyond Cap d'Antibes was murky, and in it stood the fading disc of the little sun, a blood orange. He gazed at it for a long time, crushed by an even, hopeless melancholy, then came to and set off briskly for his hotel. "*Journaux étrangers!*"* cried a newspaper seller running towards him, thrusting *The New Age* upon him as he ran. He sat down on a bench, and in the dying light of the sunset began absent-mindedly unfolding and looking through the still-fresh pages of the newspaper. And suddenly he leapt up, stunned and blinded as if by a magnesium explosion:

Vienna. 17th December. Today, in the Franzensring Restaurant, the well-known Austrian writer Arthur Schnitzler* killed with a revolver shot the Russian journalist and translator of many contemporary Austrian and German novelists who worked under the pseudonym "Heinrich".

10th November 1940

Natalie

1

THAT SUMMER I donned the peaked cap of a student for the first time and was happy, happy with the special happiness of the start of a young, free life which only comes at that period. I had grown up in a strict noble family in the country, and as a youth I dreamt fervently of love, was still pure in soul and body, blushed at the unrestrained conversations of my grammar-school comrades, and they would frown: "You should become a monk, Meschersky!" That summer I would no longer have blushed. Arriving home for the holidays, I decided that the time had come for me too to be like everyone else, to violate my purity, to seek love without romance and, on the strength of that decision and also a desire to show my blue cap band, I started visiting the neighbouring estates, relatives and acquaintances in search of amorous encounters. Thus I found myself on the estate of my uncle on my mother's side, a retired and long-widowed uhlan, Cherkasov, the father of an only daughter, my cousin Sonya...

I arrived late and was met inside the house by Sonya alone. When I leapt out of the tarantass and ran into the dark hallway, she emerged into it wearing a flannel dressing gown, holding a candle high in her left hand, she presented me with her cheek for a kiss, and said, shaking her head with her usual mockery:

"Ah, the young man who is always and everywhere late!"

"Well, but this time through no fault of his own at all," I replied. "It wasn't the young man that was late, but the train."

"Quiet, everyone's asleep. They were dying of impatience and expectation the whole evening, but in the end gave up on you. Papa went off to bed angry, calling you a featherbrain and Yefrem, who was evidently staying at the station until the morning train, an old fool. Natalie went off in a huff, the servants dispersed as well, I alone proved patient and faithful to you... Well, take off your things and we'll go and have supper."

I replied, admiring her blue eyes and raised arm, which was exposed right up to the shoulder:

"Thank you, dear friend. It's particularly pleasant for me to be assured of your fidelity now – you've become an absolute beauty, and I have the most serious designs upon you. What an arm, what a neck, and how seductive that soft dressing gown is, probably with nothing underneath it!"

She laughed:

"Almost nothing. But you've become quite all right too, and very much a grown-up. The lively gaze and the vulgar little black moustache... Only what has happened to you? In these two years that I haven't seen you, you've turned from a little boy, forever blushing out of shyness, into a very prepossessing cad. And that would have promised us many an amorous delight, as our grandmothers used to say, if it weren't for Natalie, with whom you'll fall in love to the grave straight away tomorrow morning."

"And who's Natalie?" I asked, following her into the dining room, lit by a bright hanging lamp and with its windows open to the blackness of the warm and quiet summer's night.

"She's Natasha Stankevich, my friend from school, who's come to stay with me. And now she really *is* a beauty, unlike me. Imagine: a delightful little head, so-called 'golden' hair and black eyes. And not eyes even, but black suns, to put it the Persian way. Enormous eyelashes, of course, and black as well, and the amazing golden colour of her face, shoulders and everything else."

"What else?" I asked, more and more delighted with the tone of our conversation.

"Tomorrow morning I'll be swimming with her – I advise you to steal into the bushes, then you'll see what. And a figure like a young nymph..."

On the table in the dining room there were cold cutlets, a piece of cheese and a bottle of red Crimean wine.

"Don't be angry, there's nothing else," she said, sitting down and pouring wine for me and for herself. "And there's no vodka. Well, God grant, we'll at least clink glasses of wine."

"And what should God grant in particular?"

"That I find a fiancé soon who's prepared to come 'into our yard'. I've already turned twenty, you know, and I can't possibly marry and go somewhere else: who ever would Papa be left with?"

"Well, God grant!"

And we clinked glasses and, after slowly draining the whole glass, with a strange grin she began gazing at me, at the way I worked with my fork, saying as though to herself:

"No, you're not bad, like a Georgian, and quite handsome; you really were very skinny and green in the face before. All in all you've changed a lot, become easy and pleasant. Only your eyes are shifty."

"That's because you're disturbing me with your charms. After all, you aren't entirely the same as you used to be either..."

And I examined her cheerfully. She was sitting on the other side of the table, the whole of her on the seat of the chair with one leg bent beneath her and one plump knee upon the other, rather sideways on to me; the even tan of her arm gleamed under the lamp, her lilac-blue, smiling eyes shone, and her thick soft hair, done up for the night into one big plait, was shot with reddish chestnut; the collar of her dressing gown had come open and revealed a round, tanned neck and the beginning of a growing bust, on which there also lay a triangle of suntan; on her left cheek she had a mole with a pretty curl of black hair.

"Well, and how's your papa?"

Still continuing to gaze with that same grin, she took a small silver cigarette case and a silver box of matches from her pocket and, with even a certain excessive deftness, she lit up, shifting on the hip that was pressed beneath her:

"Papa, thank God, is up to the mark. Upright and firm as before, taps around with a crutch, fluffs up his grey quiff, secretly dyes his moustache and whiskers with something brown, throws bold looks at Khristya... Only he shakes and rocks his head even more than before, more persistently. It looks as if he never agrees with anything," she said with a laugh. "Do you want a cigarette?"

I lit one, although I did not yet smoke at the time, and she again poured wine for me and for herself and looked into the darkness beyond the open window:

"Yes, for the moment, thank God, everything's fine. And it's a beautiful summer – and what a night, eh? Only the nightingales have already quietened down. And I really am very glad to see you. I sent for you to be fetched as early as six o'clock, I was afraid Yefrem, who's gone senile, would be late for the train. *I* was waiting for you most impatiently of all. And then I was even pleased that everyone had dispersed and you were late, and if you came, we'd sit for a while on our own. For some reason I did think you'd have changed a lot – with people like you that's the way it always is. And you know, it's such a pleasure – sitting alone in the whole house on a summer's night when you're waiting for someone from the train, and finally hearing they're coming, the bells are jangling, they're driving up to the porch..."

I took her hand across the table firmly and held it in my own, already feeling a thirst for the whole of her body. With cheerful tranquillity she was blowing smoke rings from her lips. I dropped her hand and said, as though joking:

"You talk about Natalie... No Natalie will compare with you... Incidentally, who is she, where's she from?"

"She's like us, from Voronezh, from a splendid family, once very rich but now simply destitute. They speak English and French in the house but there's nothing to eat... A very touching little girl, nice and slender, still fragile. A clever thing, only very reserved, you can't work out at once whether she's clever or stupid... These Stankeviches are near neighbours of your dearest cousin Alexei Meschersky, and Natalie says he seems to have started dropping in on them quite often and complaining about his bachelor life. But she doesn't like him. And then he's rich – people will think she's married for money, sacrificed herself for her parents."

"Right," I said. "But let's get back to business. Natalie, Natalie, but what about the romance between you and me?"

"Natalie won't interfere with our romance anyway," she replied. "You'll be mad with love for her, but you'll be kissing with me. You'll cry on my breast at her cruelty, and I'll comfort you."

"But you do know, don't you, that I've been in love with you for ages."

"Yes, but that was the usual infatuation with a cousin, wasn't it, and what's more, it was all just too clandestine, you were only ridiculous and boring then. But all right, I forgive you your former stupidity and I'm prepared to begin our romance straight away, tomorrow, in spite of Natalie. But for now, we're going to bed, I need to get up early tomorrow to deal with the housekeeping."

And she stood up, pulling the dressing gown together, picked up the almost burnt-out candle in the hall and led me to my room. And on the threshold of that room, rejoicing and wondering at the same thing I had been wondering and rejoicing at in my heart all supper – the oh so fortunate success for my amorous hopes that had suddenly fallen to my lot at the Cherkasovs' – I spent a long time greedily kissing her and pressing her against the door frame, while she closed her eyes duskily and let the dripping candle drop ever lower. Leaving me with her face crimson, she wagged a finger at me and said:

"Only watch out now: in front of everyone tomorrow, don't you dare devour me with 'passionate looks'! God forbid that Papa should notice anything. He's dreadfully scared of me, and I of him even more so. And I don't want Natalie to notice anything either. I'm very bashful, you know, please don't judge by the way I'm behaving with you. And if you don't carry out my order, I'll immediately begin to find you repugnant…"

I undressed and dropped into bed with my head in a spin, but I instantly fell into a sweet sleep, worn out with happiness and tiredness, not suspecting in the least what great unhappiness awaited me up ahead, nor that Sonya's jokes would turn out not to be jokes.

I subsequently remembered more than once, as a sinister sort of omen, that when I entered my room and struck a match to light a candle, a large bat softly flung itself in my direction. It flung itself so close to my face that even by the light of the match I could clearly see its loathsome, dark velvetiness and big-eared, snub-nosed, predatory, deathlike little snout, and then, quivering disgustingly and contorting itself, it dived into the blackness of the open window. But at the time I forgot about it straight away.

2

I saw Natalie for the first time the next morning only in passing: she suddenly slipped into the dining room from the hall, took a look – she had not yet done her hair and was wearing just a light dressing gown made of something orange – and, with a flash of that orange colour, the golden brightness of her hair and her black eyes, she vanished. At that moment I was alone in the dining room, I had just finished having coffee – the uhlan had finished earlier and left – and, having got up from the table, had by chance turned around…

I had woken up that morning quite early, in the still-complete silence of the entire house. There were so many rooms in the house

153

that I sometimes got them mixed up. I woke up in some remote room looking out onto a shady part of the garden, having had a good night's sleep; I washed with pleasure, dressed entirely in clean clothes – it was particularly pleasant to put on a new, red silk *kosovorotka* – made my wet black hair, cut the day before in Voronezh, look as nice as I could, went out into the corridor, turned into another one, and found myself in front of the door into the study, which at the same time was the uhlan's bedroom. Knowing he got up at about five o'clock in the summer, I knocked. No one replied, and I opened the door, glanced in, and satisfied myself with pleasure of the immutability of that old spacious room with a triple Italian window in imitation of hundred-year-old silver poplar: on the left was an entire wall of oak bookcases; in one spot between them there towered a mahogany clock with the brass disc of a motionless pendulum, in another there stood a whole heap of pipes with bead-decorated stems, and above them there hung a barometer; tucked into a third spot was a bureau from our grandfathers' times with the reddened green cloth of the lowered walnut top, and on the cloth there were pincers, hammers, nails and a brass spyglass; on the wall beside the door above a two-ton wooden couch was a whole gallery of faded portraits in oval frames; beneath the window were a writing desk and a deep armchair – the one and the other also of huge size; further to the right, above an extremely wide oak bed, was a picture covering the entire wall – a blackened, varnished background, puffs of swarthily smoke-coloured clouds and poetic greenish-blue trees scarcely visible against it, and in the foreground there shines, as if with petrified egg white, a plump, naked beauty, almost life-size, standing with her proud face half-turned towards the viewer, with all the bulges of her weighty spine, steep backside and the backs of her mighty legs, seductively concealing the nipple of a breast with the extended and splayed fingers of one hand, and the bottom of her belly, covered in creases of fat, with the other. Having looked it all over, I heard behind me the strong voice of the uhlan, approaching me with his crutch from the hallway:

"No, brother, you won't find me in the bedroom at this time. It's you, isn't it, that lies about in bed till three oaks."

I kissed his broad, wiry hand and asked:

"What oaks, uncle?"

"It's what the peasants say," he replied, shaking his grey quiff and looking me over with yellow eyes that were still penetrating and intelligent. "The sun's risen three oaks high, and you've still got your mug in the pillow, say the peasants. Well, let's go and have some coffee…"

"A wonderful old man, a wonderful house," I thought, following him into the dining room, into which, through the open windows, gazed the greenery of the morning garden and all the summer well-being of a rural estate. The old nanny, small and hunchbacked, waited at table; the uhlan drank strong tea with cream from a thick glass in a silver glass-holder, using a broad finger to hold the long, thin, twisted stem of an ancient, round, gold teaspoon in the glass, while I ate slice after slice of black bread and butter and kept on pouring myself refills from a hot, silver coffee pot; interested only in himself, the uhlan, without asking me about anything, talked about the neighbouring landowners, abusing and mocking them in every possible way, and I pretended I was listening, gazing at his moustache, his sideburns and the sizeable hairs on the end of his nose, while actually waiting so impatiently for Natalie and Sonya that I could not sit still: what is this Natalie like, and how will Sonya and I meet after what happened yesterday? I felt rapture and gratitude towards her, and thought wantonly of her and Natalie's bedrooms, about everything that is done in a woman's bedroom in the disorder of the morning… Maybe Sonya had after all told Natalie something of this love of ours that had started the day before? If so, then I felt something like love for Natalie, and not because she was supposed to be a beauty, but because she had already become Sonya's secret accomplice and mine – why should I not love the two of them? At any time now they would come in in all their morning freshness, they would see me, my Georgian good looks and red *kosovorotka*, they would start to talk, start to laugh, would sit down at the table, pouring prettily from this hot coffee pot – the young, morning appetite, young, morning excitement, the brilliance of eyes after a good sleep, a light coating of powder on cheeks that seemed to have grown younger still after sleep, and that laughter after every word, not entirely natural, and so all the more charming… And before lunch they would go through the garden to the river, would undress in the bathing hut, their naked bodies lit up from above by the blueness of the sky, and from below by the reflection of the transparent water… My imagination had always been vivid, and mentally I could see how Sonya and Natalie, holding onto the handrail of the ladder in the bathing hut, would awkwardly begin going down its steps, immersed in the water, wet, cold and slippery from the disgusting green velvet of the slime that had formed on them, how Sonya, throwing back her head of thick hair, would suddenly fall decisively onto the water, her raised breasts first – and, with the whole of her bluish, chalky body strangely visible in the water, would spread the crooked angles of her arms and legs in different directions, just like a frog...

"Well, until dinner time – you remember, don't you: dinner at twelve," said the uhlan, shaking his head negatively, and he stood up with his clean-shaven chin, with his brown moustache joined to similar sideburns, tall, agedly firm, in a roomy tussore suit and blunt-toed shoes, with a crutch in his broad hand which was covered in buckwheat, and he patted me on the shoulder and left at a rapid pace. And it was at this point, when I also got up to go out through the next room onto the balcony, that she slipped in, appeared fleetingly, and vanished, immediately striking me with joyous delight. I went out onto the balcony amazed – a beauty indeed! – and I stood there for a long time, as though gathering my thoughts. I had been waiting so impatiently for them to come to the dining room, but when I finally heard them in the dining room from the balcony, I suddenly ran down into the garden – I was seized by a sort of terror, perhaps before the two of them, with one of whom I already had a captivating secret, perhaps most of all before Natalie, before that instantaneousness with which she had dazzled me in her quickness half an hour before. I walked about for a while in the garden, which lay, like the whole estate, on low land by the river, and, finally overcoming myself, went in with assumed ingenuousness and met Sonya's cheerful boldness and a sweet joke from Natalie, who, with a smile, threw up at me from her black lashes the radiant blackness of her eyes, which was particularly striking with the colour of her hair:

"We've already seen one another!"

Then we stood on the balcony, leaning on the stone balustrade, sensing with the pleasure of summer how hot the sun was on our bare heads, and Natalie stood beside me, while Sonya, with her arm around Natalie and as though absent-mindedly gazing at something, kept singing with a grin: "Amidst a noisy ball, by chance..."* Then she straightened up:

"Well, now to bathing! Us first of all, then it'll be your turn..."

Natalie ran off for sheets, while Sonya delayed and whispered to me:

"From today, be so good as to pretend that you've fallen in love with Natalie. And beware, if it should turn out that you don't need to pretend."

And I almost replied with cheerful impudence that no, I didn't need to now, but, looking sidelong at the door, she added quietly:

"I'll come to you after dinner..."

When they returned, I went to the bathing place – first by a long avenue of silver birches, then amidst various old riverside trees, where there was a warm smell of river water and rooks were yelling in the treetops; I walked and again thought with two diametrically opposed feelings about Natalie and about Sonya, and about how I would be bathing in the same water in which they had just been bathing...

After dinner in the midst of all those happy, aimless, free and tranquil things that gazed through the open windows from the garden – the sky, the greenery, the sun – after a long dinner with cold summer soup, fried chickens and raspberries and cream, during which I was secretly dying from the presence of Natalie and from anticipation of the hour when the whole house would grow quiet for the period after dinner, and Sonya (who had come out to dinner with a dark-red velvety rose in her hair) would come running to me surreptitiously to continue what there had been the day before, but this time not hastily and any old how – after dinner I immediately went off to my room and, setting the slatted shutters ajar, began waiting for her, lying on the Turkish couch, listening to the hot quietness of the estate and the already languid afternoon singing of the birds in the garden, from which through the shutters came air sweet with flowers and grasses, and I wondered desperately: how on earth am I now to live in this duality – in secret rendezvous with Sonya and next to Natalie, just one thought of whom already enveloped me in such pure amorous delight and in a passionate longing to gaze at her with nothing but that joyous adoration with which, a little while before, I had gazed at her slender, inclined figure, and the sharp, girlish elbows on which, half-standing, she had leant on the sun-warmed old stone of the balustrade? Sonya, leaning alongside her and with an arm around her shoulder, had been in her frilled cambric peignoir like a young woman who had just got married, while she, in a gingham skirt and embroidered Little Russian blouse, beneath which could be divined all the youthful perfection of her figure, had seemed almost an adolescent. And that was where the supreme joy lay, that I did not even dare think of the possibility of kissing her with the same feelings with which I had the day before kissed Sonya! In the light and wide sleeve of the blouse, embroidered across the shoulders in red and blue, could be seen her slender arm, against the drily golden skin of which lay little gingery hairs – I had gazed and thought: what would I experience if I dared touch them with my lips! And, sensing my gaze, she had thrown up towards me the brilliant blackness of her eyes and the whole of her bright little head, encircled with the lash of quite a large plait. I had walked away and hurriedly lowered my eyes, having seen her legs through the hem of her skirt, which was translucent in the sun, and her slender, strong, thoroughbred ankles in grey transparent stockings...

Sonya, with the rose in her hair, opened and closed the door quickly, and quietly exclaimed: "What, you were asleep!" I leapt up – not at all, not at all, could I have been asleep! – and seized her hands. "Lock the door..." I rushed to the door, and she sat down on the couch, closing her eyes – "well, come here to me" – and we immediately lost all shame and reason. We scarcely uttered a word in those minutes, and she, in all the loveliness of her hot body, now allowed me to kiss her everywhere – but only to kiss her – and she closed her eyes ever more duskily and grew ever more flushed in the face. And again, when leaving and adjusting her hair, she warned in a whisper:

"And as regards Natalie, I repeat: beware of passing beyond pretence. My character's not at all as sweet as you might think!"

The rose was lying on the floor. I put it away in the desk, and by evening its dark-red velvet had become limp and lilac.

3

My life went on in an outwardly ordinary way, but inwardly I did not know a minute's peace, growing more and more attached to Sonya, to the sweet habit of exhaustingly passionate rendezvous with her by night – she came to me now only late in the evening, when the whole house had fallen asleep – and surreptitiously, ever more agonizingly and rapturously, watching Natalie, her every movement. Everything went on in the normal summer manner: meetings in the morning, bathing before dinner and dinner, then everyone resting in their own rooms, then the garden – they would be doing some embroidery, sitting in the avenue of birch trees and forcing me to read Goncharov out loud, or making jam in a shady clearing under the oak trees, not far from the house, to the right of the balcony; after four o'clock, tea in another shady clearing to the left, in the evening, walks or croquet in the wide yard in front of the house – Natalie and I against Sonya, or Sonya and Natalie against me – in the dusk, supper in the dining room... After supper the uhlan would go off to bed, but we would sit for a long time yet in the darkness on the balcony, Sonya and I joking and smoking, and Natalie in silence. Finally Sonya would say: "Well, bedtime!" and, after saying goodnight to them, I would go to my room and, with my hands growing cold, would await that cherished hour when the whole house became dark and so quiet that the constantly ticking thread of the pocket watch under the dying candle by my bedhead could be heard racing along and, horrified, I would keep on wondering: why had God punished me so, why had He given me two loves at once, so different and so passionate, such agonizing beauty in the adoration of Natalie, and such bodily rapture over Sonya. I sensed that at any time we would fail to sustain our incomplete intimacy and that then I would go completely mad from expectation of our nocturnal meetings and from the sensation of them the whole day afterwards, and all this alongside Natalie! Sonya was already jealous and would flare up sternly on occasion, but at the same time would say to me in private:

"I'm afraid that at the table and in front of Natalie we're not relaxed enough. I think Papa's beginning to notice something, Natalie too, and Nanny, of course, is already certain of our romance and is probably telling tales to Papa. Sit alone with Natalie in the garden a bit more, read her that unbearable thing *The Precipice*,* take her off for a walk sometimes in the evenings... It's awful, I notice how idiotically you stare at her, you know, and at times I feel hatred towards you, I'm ready to grab you by the hair in front of everyone, like some Odarka,* but then what can I do?"

Most awful of all was the fact that Natalie, as it seemed to me, had begun perhaps to suffer, perhaps to be indignant, to sense that there was some secret between me and Sonya. Taciturn to begin with, she was becoming ever more taciturn, and she played croquet or did her embroidery unnecessarily intently. We seemed to have got used to one another, had become good friends, but then once, sitting alone with her in the drawing room, where she was half-lying on a couch, leafing through some sheet music, I joked:

"I've heard, Natalie, that you and I may perhaps become relatives."

She glanced up at me sharply:

"How's that?"

"My cousin, Alexei Nikolayich Meschersky..."

She did not let me finish:

"Ah, so that's it! Your cousin, forgive me, that fatted giant, all overgrown with shiny, black hair, with the burr and the lush, red mouth... And who gave you the right to have such conversations with me?"

I took fright:

"Natalie, Natalie, why are you so stern with me? I can't even make a joke! Do forgive me," I said, taking her hand.

She did not take her hand away and said:

"I still don't understand... don't know you... But enough about that..."

So as not to see her agonizingly attractive white tennis shoes, tucked up at an angle on the couch, I rose and went out onto the balcony. A storm cloud was rising from beyond the garden, the air was growing dim, a soft summery rustling was spreading ever wider, moving closer through the garden, there was the sweet breath of rain-filled wind from the fields, and I was suddenly seized so sweetly, youthfully and freely by some unmotivated happiness, amenable to anything, that I cried:

"Natalie, come here for a minute!"

She came up to the threshold:

"What?"

"Take a breath – what a wind! What a joy everything could be!"

She paused.

"Yes."

"Natalie, how unfriendly you are with me! Do you have something against me?"

She shrugged a shoulder proudly:

"What can I have against you and why?"

In the evening, sprawling in wicker armchairs in the darkness on the balcony, all three of us were silent – the stars could only be glimpsed here and there in dark clouds, a limp wind was wafting weakly from the direction of the river, where the frogs were drowsily murmuring.

"It's going to rain, I'm feeling sleepy," said Sonya, stifling a yawn. "Nanny said the new moon had been born and for a week or so now it would be 'taking a wash'." And after a pause she added: "Natalie, what do you think about first love?"

Natalie responded from out of the darkness:

"I'm convinced of one thing: of the terrible distinction between the first love of a young man and a girl."

Sonya had a think:

"Well, girls can be different as well…"

And she got up decisively:

"No, bedtime, bedtime!"

"Well I'll drowse here for a little, I like the night," said Natalie.

Listening to Sonya's footsteps moving away, I whispered:

"You and I had bad words for some reason today!"

She replied:

"Yes, yes, we did have bad words…"

The next day we met seemingly calmly. There had been gentle rain in the night, but in the morning the weather improved, and after dinner it became dry and hot. Just before having tea at about four o'clock, while Sonya was doing domestic accounting of some sort in the uhlan's study, we sat in the avenue of birch trees and tried to continue reading *The Precipice* out loud. She was bent over some sewing, giving glimpses of her right arm, while I read and glanced from time to time with sweet pangs at her left arm, visible in her sleeve, at the little gingery hairs lying against it above the wrist and at similar ones where the nape of her neck turned into her shoulder, and I read ever more animatedly, without understanding a word. Finally I said:

"Well, you read for a bit now…"

She straightened up, and the points of her breasts appeared beneath her thin blouse; she put her sewing aside and, bending forwards again, dropping her strange and wonderful head down low and showing me the back of her head and the beginning of her shoulder, she put the book on her knees and began reading in a rapid and uncertain voice. I gazed at her arms, at her knees underneath the book, feeling faint from frenzied love for them and for the sound of her voice. In various parts of the late afternoon garden orioles were crying out on the wing, and high up opposite us, pressed against the trunk of a pine that grew alone amidst the birches in the avenue, there hung a reddish-grey woodpecker.

"Natalie, what an amazing colour your hair is! And your plait's a little darker, the colour of ripe maize…"

She continued to read.

"Natalie, a woodpecker, look!"

She glanced up:

"Yes, I've seen it before, I saw it today, and I saw it yesterday… Don't stop me reading."

I was silent for a while, then again:

"Look how like dried-up grey worms that is."

"What, where?"

I pointed to the bench between us, to a bird's dried lime dropping:

"Isn't it?"

And I took her hand and squeezed it, mumbling and laughing in happiness:

"Natalie, Natalie!"

She gazed at me quietly for a long time, then uttered:

"But you love Sonya!"

I blushed like a scoundrel caught out, but I disavowed Sonya with such fervent haste that she even parted her lips a little:

"Isn't it so?"

"It isn't, it isn't! I love her very much, but as a sister, I mean, we've known one another since childhood!"

4

The next day she did not emerge either in the morning or for dinner.

"Sonya, what's the matter with Natalie?" asked the uhlan, and Sonya replied with an unpleasant laugh:

"She's been lying all morning in her dressing gown with her hair uncombed, and it's clear from her face that she's been bawling her eyes out; she was brought coffee and didn't finish it… What's wrong? 'Headache.' Perhaps she's fallen in love!"

"Quite likely," said the uhlan cheerily, glancing at me with a hint of approval, but shaking his head in denial.

Natalie emerged only for evening tea, but she came onto the balcony easily and briskly, smiled at me cordially and as though a little guiltily, surprising me with her briskness, her smile and a certain new smartness: her hair was done up tightly, curled a little at the front and set in waves with tongs, her dress was a different one, made of something green, in one piece, very simple and very clever, especially the way it was taken in at the waist, her shoes were black, high-heeled – I gasped inwardly in new rapture. I was sitting on the balcony, looking through *The Historical Bulletin*, several volumes of which had been given me by the uhlan, when she suddenly appeared with that briskness and somewhat embarrassed cordiality:

"Good evening. Let's go and have tea. I'm at the samovar today. Sonya's unwell."

"What do you mean? First you, now her?"

"I simply had a headache in the morning. I'm ashamed to say that only now have I tidied myself up…"

"How amazing that green is with your eyes and hair!" I said. And I suddenly asked, blushing: "Did you believe me yesterday?"

She blushed too – delicately and scarlet – and turned away:

"Not at once, not entirely. Then I suddenly realized that I don't have any grounds for not believing you… and in essence, what ever have I got to do with you and Sonya's feelings? But let's go…"

Sonya too emerged for supper and found a moment to say to me:

"I've been taken ill. It always affects me very badly, I'm in bed for about five days. I could still come out today, but not tomorrow. Behave sensibly without me. I love you terribly and I'm dreadfully jealous."

"And will you really not even look in on me today?"

"You're stupid!"

This was both good fortune and ill fortune: five days of complete freedom with Natalie, and five days of not seeing Sonya in my room by night!

For about a week the house was run by Natalie, she was in charge of everything and went across the yard to the kitchen in a little white apron – I had never before seen her so businesslike, and it was clear that the role of deputy for Sonya and solicitous mistress of the house gave her great pleasure, and that she seemed to be resting from her secret attentiveness to the way Sonya and I talked and exchanged glances. All those days, experiencing at dinner first alarm as to whether everything was all right, and then contentment that everything *was* all right, and that the old cook and Khristya, the Ukrainian maid, were bringing things and serving them on time without irritating the uhlan, she would go off after dinner to Sonya's room, where I was not allowed, and stay with her until evening tea, and then after supper for the entire evening. She was obviously avoiding being alone with me, and I was at a loss, miserable and suffering in solitude. Why, having become friendly, was she avoiding me? Was she afraid of Sonya or of herself, of her feeling for me? And I passionately wanted to believe it was of herself, and I revelled in an ever strengthening dream: not for good was I tied to Sonya, not for good would I – nor Natalie either – be staying here, in a week or two I would have to be leaving anyway – and then there would be an end to my torment... I would find an excuse to go and get acquainted with the Stankeviches as soon as Natalie returned home... Leaving Sonya, what's more with a deception, with this secret dream of Natalie, with hope of her love and hand, would of course be very painful – was it just with passion alone that I kissed Sonya, didn't I love her too? – but what was I to do, sooner or later it couldn't be avoided all the same... And incessantly thinking thus, in incessant spiritual agitation, in expectation of something, I tried when meeting with Natalie to behave with as much restraint, as nicely as possible – to be patient, to be patient for the time being. I suffered, I was miserable – as if on purpose, rain fell for three days, running rhythmically, knocking on the roof like thousands of little paws, the house was dusky, the flies were asleep on the ceiling and on the lamp in the dining room – but I bore up, sometimes sitting for hours in the uhlan's study, listening to his various stories...

At first Sonya started coming out for an hour or two in her dressing gown with a languid smile at her weakness, she would lie down on the balcony in a linen armchair and, to my horror, speak to me capriciously and with immoderate tenderness, unabashed by the presence of Natalie:

"Sit beside me, Vitik, I'm in pain, I'm sad, tell me something funny... The moon really did take a wash, but now it seems to have finished; it's cleared up, and how sweet the flowers smell..."

Secretly becoming irritated, I replied:

"If there's a strong smell from the flowers, it'll be taking a wash again."

She hit me on the hand:

"Don't you dare argue with a sick woman!"

Finally she began coming out both for dinner and evening tea, but still pale, and ordering an armchair to be brought for her. Yet she was still not coming out for supper, nor onto the balcony after supper. And once, after evening tea, when she had gone off to her room and Khristya had taken the samovar from the table to the kitchen, Natalie said to me:

"Sonya's angry that I keep sitting with her and that you're always on your own. She's not yet fully recovered, and you miss her."

"I miss only you," I replied. "When you're not there."

She changed countenance, but got the better of herself and, with an effort, smiled:

"But we agreed not to quarrel any more... Better, listen to this: you've sat at home too long, go and take a walk until supper, and then I'll sit with you in the garden – the predictions about the moon haven't come true, thank God, and the night will be splendid..."

"Sonya feels sorry for me, but you? Not a bit?"

"I'm terribly sorry," she replied, and laughed awkwardly, putting the tea service onto a tray. "But Sonya's already well, thank God, soon you won't be missing her..."

At the words "and in the evening I'll sit with you" my heart had contracted sweetly and mysteriously, but I immediately thought: no! It's just simply a friendly word! I went to my room and lay for a long time gazing at the ceiling. Finally I got up, took my cap and someone's stick from the entrance hall, and unconsciously went out from the estate onto the broad highway which lay between it and the Ukrainian village a little above it on a bare hillock in the steppe. The highway led into the empty evening fields. It was hilly everywhere, but you could see a long way in the wide expanses. To the left of me lay the low ground by the river, beyond it, towards the horizon, fields that were also empty rose a little, and there the sun had just set and the afterglow was burning. Opposite it, to the right, the straight row of identical white huts of what looked like a deserted village showed red, and I looked miserably now at the afterglow, now at them. When I turned back, there was a wind wafting towards me, now warm, now almost hot, and the new moon was already shining in the sky, half of it gleaming and not boding well: the other half was visible too, like a transparent cobweb, and all together it was reminiscent of an acorn.

At supper – we had supper in the garden too on this occasion, it was too hot in the house – I said to the uhlan:

"What do you think of the weather, Uncle? It seems to me there'll be rain tomorrow."

"Why, my friend?"

"I've just been walking in the fields, thinking with sadness that I'll soon be leaving you…"

"Why's that?"

Natalie looked up at me suddenly too:

"You intend leaving?"

I affected a laugh:

"Well, I can't…"

The uhlan began shaking his head with particular energy, and on this occasion appropriately:

"Nonsense, nonsense! Your mother and father can put up with being separated from you perfectly well. I shan't let you go sooner than in two weeks. And she won't let you go either."

"I don't have any rights to Vitaly Petrovich," said Natalie.

I exclaimed plaintively:

"Uncle, forbid Natalie to call me that."

The uhlan slapped the palm of his hand on the table:

"I forbid it. And that's enough chattering about your departure. Now as regards the rain, you're right, it's quite possible that the weather will deteriorate again."

"It was just too clear and bright in the fields," I said. "And the moon's very clear, and it looks like an acorn, and the wind was blowing from the south. And there, you see, it's already clouding over."

The uhlan turned and looked into the garden, where the moonlight was now fading, now burning bright.

"You'll make a second Bruce,* Vitaly…"

After nine o'clock she came out onto the balcony where I was sitting waiting for her, thinking despondently: this is all nonsense, even if she does have any feelings for me, they're not at all serious, they're changeable, transient. The new moon was sparkling ever higher and brighter in the piles of cloud that were gathering more and more, smokily white, majestically packing the sky, and when its white half came out from behind them like a human face in profile, bright and deathly pale, everything was lit up, flooded with phosphoric light. Suddenly I looked around, sensing something: Natalie was standing on the threshold with her hands behind her back, gazing at me silently. I stood up and she asked indifferently:

"You're not asleep yet?"

"But you told me…"

"I'm sorry, I'm very tired today. Let's take a stroll down the avenue, and then I'll go to bed."

I followed after her, she paused on the balcony step, gazing at the treetops in the garden, from behind which the clouds were already rising in rain-filled billows, twitching and flashing with soundless lightning. Then she went in under the long, transparent awning of the avenue of birches into the mottled patches of light and shade. Drawing level with her, just to say something I said:

"How magically the birches shine in the distance. There's nothing stranger or more beautiful than the interior of a wood on a moonlit night and that white, silky lustre of birch trunks in its depths…"

She stopped, her eyes fixed upon me blackly in the dusk:

"Are you really leaving?"

"Yes, it's time."

"But why so immediately and quickly? I'm not hiding it: you astonished me just then, saying you were leaving."

"Natalie, may I come and introduce myself to your family when you return home?"

She remained silent. I took her hands and, going quite cold, kissed the right one.

"Natalie…"

"Yes, yes, I love you," she said, hurriedly and expressionlessly, and set off back towards the house. I went after her as though sleepwalking.

"Leave tomorrow," she said as she walked, without turning round. "I'll go back home in a few days' time."

5

On entering my room, I sat down on the couch without lighting the candles, and froze, became rooted to the spot at the terrible and wonderful thing that had so suddenly and unexpectedly happened in my life. I sat, having lost all sense of place and time. The room and the garden were already sunk in the darkness of the rain clouds, and in the garden, beyond the open windows, everything was rustling, trembling, and I was ever more frequently and brightly lit up by a quick, blue-green flame, which in that very same second disappeared. The quickness and strength of this thunderless light was increasing all the time, and then the room was suddenly lit up to an implausible degree of visibility, a rush of fresh wind came at me, and there was such a noise from the garden, as if it had been seized by horror: see that, the earth and sky are catching fire! I leapt up, with difficulty closed the windows, one after another, catching their frames and overcoming the wind that was tugging me about, and I went running on tiptoe through the dark corridors to the dining room: I would not have thought to have been bothered at that time about the open windows in the dining room and drawing room, where the storm could have broken the window panes, but I went running all the same, and even with great anxiety All the windows in the dining room and drawing room proved closed – I saw this in blue-green illumination, in the colour and brightness of which there was something truly unearthly, revealing itself everywhere at once, like quick eyes, making all the window frames huge and visible to the last transom, and then immediately drowning them in dense gloom, leaving for a second in one's dazzled vision a trace of something tinny and red. And when I went quickly into my own room, as though afraid that something might have happened there without me, an angry whisper was heard from the darkness:

"Where have you been? I'm scared, light a light quickly…"

I struck a match and saw Sonya sitting on the couch in just her nightshirt and with nothing but shoes on her feet.

"Or no, no, don't," she said hastily, "come here to me quickly, put your arms around me, I'm afraid…"

I sat down submissively and put my arms around her cold shoulders. She began whispering:

"Well, kiss me then, kiss me, take me completely, I've not been with you for a whole week!"

And she pushed herself and me firmly back onto the couch cushions.

At that same moment, in her dressing gown and with a candle in her hand, Natalie flung herself in at the threshold of the open doorway. She saw us at once, but all the same cried out unconsciously:

"Sonya, where are you? I'm terribly afraid…"

And immediately she disappeared. Sonya rushed after her.

6

A year later she married Meschersky. She was married in his village of Blagodatnoye in an empty church – we and other relatives and friends on his and on her sides did not receive invitations to the wedding. And the newly-weds did not make the usual visits after the wedding either, they left immediately for the Crimea.

In January of the following year, on Tatyana's Day,* there was a ball for Voronezh students in the Nobles' Assembly Rooms in Voronezh. Already a Moscow student, I was spending Christmas-tide at home, in the country, and that evening went to Voronezh. The train arrived all white, its smoke filled with the snow of a blizzard, and on the way from the station into town, as the cabman's sledge was carrying me to the Nobles' Hotel, the lights of the streetlamps could scarcely be glimpsed through the blizzard. But after the country, this urban blizzard and the urban lights were exciting, promising the imminent pleasure of going into a warm, even too warm a room of the old provincial hotel, asking for a samovar and starting to get changed, to get ready for the long night of the ball and the carousing of students until dawn. In the time that had passed since that terrible night at the Cherkasovs', and then since her marriage, I had gradually recovered – or in any event I had grown used to the condition of a man mentally ill, which is what I secretly was, and outwardly I lived like everybody else.

When I got there, the ball had only just begun, but the grand staircase and its landing were already filled with new arrivals, and from the main ballroom, from its musicians' gallery, a regimental band was drowning out, muffling everything, resounding sonorously in the mournfully exultant beats of a waltz. Still fresh from the frost, in my nice new full-dress uniform, which made me immoderately refined, excessively polite, as I forced my way in the crowd over the red carpet of the staircase, I went up onto the landing and entered the particularly dense and already hot crowd which was crammed together in front of the doors into the ballroom, and for some reason I began forcing my way further forward so insistently that I was probably taken for the master of ceremonies with pressing business in the ballroom. And I did finally force my way through, then stopped on the threshold, listening to the floods and peals of the orchestra just above my head, and gazing at the sparkling ripples of the chandeliers and the dozens of couples, flashing in great variety beneath them in the waltz – and then I suddenly drew back: one couple from that spinning crowd had stood out for me all of a sudden, flying ever closer to me among all the others in quick and nimble glissades. I recoiled, looking at how large and burly he was, somewhat stooped in his waltzing, all black with his shiny black hair and tailcoat, and light with that lightness which some bulky people surprise you with when dancing, and at how tall she was with her hair piled up high for the ball, in a white gown and elegant gold shoes, leaning back somewhat as she span around, with lowered eyes, and with her arm in a white elbow-length glove placed on his shoulder and bent in a way that made the arm look like the neck of a swan. For an instant her black eyelashes fluttered up straight at me, the blackness of her eyes sparkled very close by, but at that point he, with the application of a bulky man, sliding nimbly on his polished toes, turned her sharply, her lips parted slightly in a sigh on the turn, there was a flash of the silvery hem of her gown, and they set off back again, moving away in glissades. I squeezed through once more into the crowd on the landing, forced my way out of it and stood for a moment... Through the doors of the room that was opposite me at an angle and still completely empty and cool, two girl students in Little Russian costume could be seen standing idly waiting behind a champagne refreshment bar – a pretty blonde and a wiry, dark-faced Cossack beauty almost twice as tall as the other. I went in, and with a bow proffered a hundred-rouble note. Banging their heads together and laughing, they pulled a heavy bottle out from a bucket of ice under the bar and exchanged irresolute glances – there were no opened bottles yet. I went behind the bar and in a minute had dashingly popped the cork. Then I cheerfully offered them a glass – *Gaudeamus igitur*!* – and drank down the remainder, one glass after another, by myself. They looked at me at first with surprise, then with pity:

"Oh dear, but you're terribly pale as it is!"

I finished drinking and left at once. In the hotel I asked for a bottle of Caucasian brandy in my room and started drinking by the teacup in the hope that my heart would burst.

And another year and a half went by. And one day at the end of May, when I had again come home from Moscow, the messenger from the station brought a telegram from her in Blagodatnoye: "Alexei Nikolayevich died suddenly this morning from stroke." My father crossed himself and said:

"May he rest in peace. How awful. Forgive me, God, I never liked him, but it's awful just the same. I mean, he wasn't even forty yet. And

170

I'm awfully sorry for her – a widow at such an age, and with a babe in arms... I've never seen her – he was such a nice man that he never once brought her here to see me – but they say she's charming. So what's to be done now? Neither I nor Mama can travel more than a hundred and fifty kilometres at our age, of course – *you* must go..."

It was impossible to refuse – what grounds did I have for refusing? And I would not have been able to refuse in that semi-insanity into which I had suddenly been plunged once again by this unexpected news. I knew one thing: I would see her! The pretext for the meeting was terrible, but legitimate.

We sent a telegram in reply, and the next day, at the time of sundown in May, horses from Blagodatnoye conveyed me in half an hour from the station to the estate. Approaching it along a rise in the ground beside water meadows, I saw while still at a distance that on the west side of the house, facing towards the still-light sunset, all the windows in the reception hall were covered with shutters, and I quaked at the terrible thought: *he* lay behind them, and *she* was there too! In the courtyard, densely overgrown with young grass, the bells of two troikas belonging to some other people were rattling from time to time beside the coach house, but there was not a soul about, apart from the coachmen on the boxes – both the visitors and the servants were already standing inside the house for the office for the dead. Everywhere there was the quietness of sundown in the countryside in May, the springtime purity, freshness and newness of everything – of the air of the fields and the river, of that dense young grass in the courtyard, of the densely flowering garden that approached the house from the rear and the south side, but on the low front porch, by the wide-open doors into the lobby, upright against the wall leant the large, yellow-brocaded lid of a coffin. In the delicate chill of the evening air there was the strong smell of sweet pear blossom, its white denseness showing milky white in the south-eastern part of the garden against the flat and, because of that milkiness, matt horizon, where pink Jupiter alone was burning. And the youth, the beauty of it all, and the thought of her beauty and youth, and of her having once loved me, suddenly so tore my heart apart with grief, happiness and a need for love that, leaping out of the carriage by the porch, I felt myself to be as though before an abyss – how was I to step into this house, to see her face to face once more after three years apart, and already a widow, a mother! And nonetheless I went into the gloom and incense of that terrible hall, speckled with the yellow lights of candles, into the blackness of the people standing with those lights before the coffin, which was raised at an angle with its head towards the near corner, lit up from above by a large, red lamp before the gold rizas* of the icons, and from below by the flickering silver lustre of three tall church candles – I went in to the words and singing of the clergymen as they walked around the coffin censing and bowing, and immediately lowered my head so as not to see the yellow brocade on the coffin and the face of the dead man, and, most of all, afraid of seeing her. Someone handed me a lighted candle. I took it and started holding it, feeling the way that, trembling, it warmed and illumined my face, which was drawn with pallor, and I listened with dull submissiveness to those calls and the clanking of the censer, seeing from under my brows the solemn and sweet-smelling smoke floating up to the ceiling, and suddenly, lifting my face, I nonetheless saw her – in front of everyone, in mourning dress, with a candle in her hand lighting up her cheek and the goldenness of her hair – and, as if from an icon, I could no longer tear my eyes away from her. When all had fallen silent, and it had started to smell of snuffed candles, and everyone had begun to move cautiously and gone to kiss her hand, I waited to be the last to approach her. And having approached, I glanced with the horror of rapture at the monastic elegance of the black dress which made her especially chaste, at the pure, youthful beauty of her face, lashes and eyes, which dropped at the sight of me, I bowed ever so low, kissing her hand, in a barely audible voice said everything that had to be said in compliance with decorum and kinship, and asked permission to leave at once and spend the night in the garden, in the old rotunda in which I had slept when coming to Blagodatnoye when still a schoolboy – Meschersky's bedroom for hot summer nights had been there. She replied without raising her eyes:

"I'll give orders straight away for you to be taken there and supper served you."

In the morning, after the burial service and interment, I left without delay.

Saying goodbye, we again exchanged only a few words, and again did not look one another in the eye.

7

I completed my course, shortly afterwards lost my father and mother almost simultaneously, settled in the country, farmed and took up with an orphaned peasant girl, Gasha, who had grown up in our house and worked in my mother's rooms... Now, together with Ivan Lukich, our former house serf, an old man grey to the point of green and with big shoulder blades, she worked for me. Her appearance was in part still that of a child – small, thin, black-haired, with expressionless eyes the colour of soot, enigmatically taciturn, as though apathetic about everything, and so dark all over with her delicate skin that my father had once said: "That's probably what Hagar was like."* She was endlessly dear to me, I liked carrying her in my arms and kissing her; I thought: "This is all that's left to me in life!" And she seemed to understand what I was thinking. When she gave birth – to a small, black-haired boy – and stopped working, moving into my former nursery, I wanted to marry her. She replied:

"No, I don't need that, I'd only be ashamed in front of everyone, what sort of a lady am I! And what would you want it for? You'd stop loving me even quicker then. You need to go to Moscow, or else you'll get totally bored with me. And I won't get bored now," she said, gazing at the child, who was in her arms and sucking at her breast. "Go and live for your own pleasure, just remember one thing: if you fall in love with someone properly and have the idea of marrying, I won't delay for a minute, I'll drown myself along with him."

I looked at her – it was impossible not to believe her. I hung my head: yes, and you know, I was only twenty-six years old... Falling in love, marrying – that I could not even imagine, but Gasha's words had reminded me once more that my life was over.

In early spring I went abroad and spent about four months away. Returning home at the end of June via Moscow, this is what I thought: I'll spend the autumn in the country, and I'll go away somewhere again for the winter. On the way from Moscow to Tula I was calmly melancholy: here I am home again, but why? I remembered Natalie – and spread my hands: yes, that love "to the grave', which Sonya had mockingly foretold for me, does exist; only I had already got used to it, as somebody over the years gets used to the fact that, for example, he has had an arm or a leg cut off... And while sitting at the station in

Tula waiting to change trains, I sent a telegram: "Travelling past you from Moscow, will be at your station at 9 p.m., allow me to drop in, learn how you are."

She met me on the porch – behind her was a maid shining a lamp – and with a half-smile she reached out both her hands to me:

"I'm terribly glad!"

"Strange as it might seem, you've grown a little more," I said, kissing and touching them, already in torment. And I glanced at the whole of her in the light of the lamp, which the maid had raised a little and around the glass of which, in the soft air after rain, little pink moths were circling: the black eyes looked more firmly, more confidently now, she was already in the completely full bloom of young womanly beauty, elegant, modestly smart, in a dress of green tussore.

"Yes, I'm still growing," she replied, smiling sadly.

In the reception hall, in the front corner, there hung, as before, a large red icon lamp before old gold icons, only it was unlit. I hurried to look away from that corner and followed her through into the dining room. There on a shining tablecloth stood a kettle on a spirit lamp, and there shone a fine tea service. The maid brought cold veal, pickles, a carafe of vodka and a bottle of Lafitte. She took hold of the kettle:

"I don't eat supper, I'll just have some tea, but you have something to eat first... You've come from Moscow? Why? What is there to do there in the summer?"

"I'm returning from Paris."

"I say! And were you there long? Oh, if only I could go somewhere! But my little girl's still not yet four, you know... They say you're a keen farmer?"

I drank a glass of vodka without eating and asked permission to smoke.

"Oh, please do!"

I lit up and said:

"Natalie, there's no need for you to be genteelly courteous with me, don't pay me any particular attention. I've dropped in just to take a look at you and then disappear again. And don't feel any awkwardness – after all, everything that was is long forgotten and gone without return. You can't help but see that I'm dazzled by you again, but now you can't be at all inhibited by my admiration – it's unselfish and calm now..."

She lowered her head and eyelashes – it was impossible ever to get used to the wonderful contrast of the one and the other – and her face began slowly turning pink.

"It's absolutely certain," I said, growing pale, but in a strengthening voice, assuring myself that I was telling the truth. "Everything in the world passes, you know. As for my terrible guilt before you, I'm sure it became a matter of indifference to you long, long ago now, and much more understandable, forgivable than before: my guilt was, after all, not entirely of my own free will, and even at that time deserved leniency because of my extreme youth and the amazing combination of circumstances into which I fell. And then I've already been punished sufficiently for that guilt – by my complete ruin."

"Ruin?"

"Isn't it so, then? Even now don't you understand me, don't you know me, as you once said?"

She paused.

"I saw you at the ball in Voronezh… How young I still was then and how amazingly unhappy! Although can there ever be unhappy love?" she said, lifting her face and asking with the entire black expanse of her wide eyes and lashes. "Doesn't the most mournful music in the world give happiness? But tell me about yourself, surely you haven't settled in the countryside for ever?"

With an effort I asked:

"So you still loved me then?"

"Yes."

I fell silent, sensing that now my face was already burning like fire.

"Is it true, what I heard… that you have love, a child?"

"It's not love," I said. "Terrible pity, tenderness, but that's all."

"Tell me everything."

And I did tell her everything – even to the point of what Gasha had said to me, advising me to "go and live for my own pleasure". And I ended like this:

"Now you can see that I've been ruined in every possible way…"

"Enough!" she said, thinking some thought of her own. "You still have your whole life ahead of you. But marriage is, of course, impossible for you. She is, of course, one of those people who wouldn't even spare the child, let alone herself."

"It's not a matter of marriage," I said. "My God! Me marrying!"

She looked at me thoughtfully:

"No, no. And how strange. Your prediction came true – we did become relatives. Do you feel that you're, after all, my cousin now?"

And she placed her hand on mine:

"But you're awfully tired after the journey, you haven't so much as touched a thing. You look dreadful, that's enough conversation for today, go, a bed's been made up for you in the pavilion…"

I kissed her hand submissively, she summoned a maid, and with a lamp, although it was quite light from the moon hanging low behind the garden, the latter conducted me, at first by the main avenue, and then by a side one, into a spacious clearing, to that old rotunda with its wooden columns. And I sat down by the open window in the armchair beside the bed and started smoking, thinking: I was wrong to carry out this stupid, sudden action, I was wrong to come here and rely on my calm, my strength… The night was extraordinarily still, and it was already late. There must have been more light rain – the air had become even warmer, softer. And in delightful conformity with that unmoving warmth and stillness, in the distance, in various parts of the village, the first cockerels were protractedly and cautiously crowing. It was as if the light circle of the moon, hanging opposite the rotunda, behind the garden, had frozen in the one spot, as if it were gazing expectantly, shining among the distant trees and the nearby spreading apple trees, mixing its light with their shadows. Where the light spilt through, it was bright and glassy, but the shade was dappled and mysterious… And she, in something long, dark, silkily shiny, came up to the window, so mysteriously, inaudibly too…

Later on, the moon was already shining above the garden and looking straight into the rotunda, and we took it in turn to speak – she lying on the bed, I kneeling alongside and holding her hand.

"On that terrible night with the lightning I already loved just you alone, there was no longer any other passion inside me except the most ecstatic and pure passion for you."

"Yes, with time I understood everything. And nevertheless, whenever I suddenly recalled that lightning, immediately after memories of what had happened an hour before it in the avenue…"

"Nowhere in the world is there anyone like you. A little while ago, when I was looking at that green tussore and your knees beneath it, I felt I was prepared to die for one touch of it with my lips, just the tussore."

"Did you never, ever forget me in all these years?"

"Only the way you forget you're alive, breathing. And what you said was true: there is no unhappy love. Ah, that orange dressing gown of yours, and the whole of you, still almost a little girl, glimpsed fleetingly that morning, the first morning of my love for you! Then your arm in the sleeve of the Little Russian blouse. Then the inclination of your head as you were reading *The Precipice*, and I mumbled, 'Natalie, Natalie!'"

"Yes, yes."

"And then you at the ball – so tall and so terrible in your already womanly beauty – how I wanted to die that night in the rapture of my love and ruin! Then you with a candle in your hand, your mourning dress and your chastity as you wore it. It seemed to me that the candle by your face had become holy."

"And here you are with me again, and now for ever. But we'll rarely even see one another – how can I, your secret wife, become your lover, obvious to everyone?"

* * *

In December she died on Lake Geneva in premature labour.

4th April 1941

Part Three

Upon a Long-Familiar Street

ONE NIGHT IN PARIS in the spring I was walking along a boulevard in the twilight created by the dense, fresh greenery, beneath which the streetlamps had a metallic gleam, I was feeling light and young, and thinking:

Upon a long-familiar street
An ancient house I know,
It had a staircase, dark and steep,
A curtain at its window...

Wonderful lines! And how amazing that it all happened to me once too! Moscow, Presnya, lonely, snowy streets, a little wooden lower-middle-class house – and I, a student, some other I, in whose existence it's already hard to believe now...

A little light, mysterious,
Till midnight's hour shone out...

It shone out there too. And the blizzard swirled, and the wind blew the snow off the wooden roof and whisked it about like smoke, and there was a light from upstairs in the mezzanine, behind a red cotton curtain...

Ah, what a wondrous maiden fair
At night-time's cherished hour
Would meet me with her loosened hair
Within her own sweet bower...

There was that too. The daughter of some sexton in Serpukhov, who'd left her destitute family there and gone away to Moscow to study... And so I'd go up onto the little, wooden, snow-covered porch, tug on a ring of jangling wire that ran into the lobby, and in the lobby the bell

181

would give a tinny tinkle – and on the other side of the door footsteps would be heard running quickly down the steep wooden staircase, the door would open – and it would be her, her shawl and white blouse besprinkled by the wind, by the blizzard... I would rush to kiss her, putting my arms around her against the wind, and we would run upstairs, in the frosty cold and the darkness of the staircase to her little room, cold too, and miserably lit by a kerosene lamp... The red curtain at the window, a table beneath it with the lamp, by the wall an iron bed. I'd throw my greatcoat and cap down anywhere and take her onto my knees, sitting down on the bed, feeling her body, her bones through her skirt... There was no loosened hair, it was braided into quite a meagre, light-brown plait, there was a face typical of the common people, transparent from hunger, a peasant's eyes that were transparent too, lips of that gentleness you sometimes find in weak girls...

How ardently, not like a child,
Her lips so close to me,
She'd whisper, all atremble, wild:
"Now listen, come let's flee!"*

"Let's flee!" Where to, why, from whom? How delightful, that fervent, childish silliness: "let's flee!" There was no "let's flee" for us. There were those weak lips, the sweetest in the world, in eyes there were hot tears, brought on by an excess of happiness, there was the deep languor of youthful bodies, which made us lean our heads on one another's shoulders, and her lips were already burning as if in a fever as I unbuttoned her blouse and kissed her milky-white girlish breasts with their points hardening like unripened wild strawberries... Coming to, she would leap up, light the spirit lamp, warm up some weak tea, and we would drink it with white bread and red-rinded cheese, talking endlessly about our future, sensing the winter, the fresh cold being carried in under the curtain, listening to the snow being sprinkled on the window... "Upon a long familiar street an ancient house I know..." What else do I know? I remember seeing her off at the Kursk Station in the spring, hurrying along the platform with her willow basket and her red blanket strapped up in a bundle, running down a long train which was already prepared for departure, looking into the green carriages crammed full of people... I remember her finally clambering up into the doorway of one of them, and talking, saying goodbye and kissing one another's hands, promising her I'd come to Serpukhov in two weeks' time... I don't remember anything else. There *was* nothing else...

25 May 1944

A Riverside Inn

INSIDE THE PRAGUE the chandeliers were glittering, amidst the noise and chatter of dinner time a Portuguese string orchestra was playing, and there was not a single place free. I stood for a little, looking around, and was already meaning to leave when I caught sight of a military doctor I knew, who immediately invited me to his table in a bay beside a window, open to the warm spring night, to the Arbat with its ringing trams. We had dinner together, knocking back a fair amount of vodka and Kakhetian wine and talking about the recently convened State Duma, then asked for coffee. The doctor took out an old silver cigarette case, offered me his Asmolov "cannon"* and, lighting up, said:

"Yes, it's the Duma this, the Duma that... Shall we have some brandy? I'm feeling a bit sad."

I took this for a joke, as he was a tranquil and rather dry man by nature (strong and powerful in build, very well-suited to military uniform, stiffly ginger-haired, with silver on the temples), but he added seriously:

"Sad because of the spring, probably. With the approach of old age, and a dreamy, bachelor's one what's more, you become generally much more sensitive than in your youth. Can you sense the smell of poplars and the resonance of the trams' ringing? Incidentally, let's close the window, it's not very cosy," he said, getting up. "Ivan Stepanych, some Shustovsky..."

He was absent-mindedly silent while old Ivan Stepanych went to fetch the Shustovsky. When it was served, and we had each been poured a glass, he kept the bottle on the table and, gulping the brandy down from a hot cup too, continued:

"There's this as well – certain memories. The poet Bryusov* was in here just before you with some slim little lass who looked like a poor student; in his burring, nasally baying voice he shouted something distinct, sharp and angry at the head waiter, who'd come running up to him, evidently with apologies for the absence of free seats – space had probably been reserved on the telephone, but not kept – then he haughtily left. You know him well, but I'm acquainted with him a little too, I come across him in circles interested in old Russian icons – I'm interested in them too, and have been for a long time now, ever since the towns on the Volga where I once served for several years. And besides that, I've heard enough about him, about his affairs among other things, and so I think both you and I would have experienced identical feelings towards this girl, undoubtedly the latest in his line of admirers and victims. She was dreadfully touching, but also pitiful, looking in confusion and rapture first at the for her probably utterly unwonted brilliance of the restaurant, then at him, while he was barking out his declamation with his black eyes and eyelashes sparkling demonically. And it was this that brought back memories to me. I'll tell you one of them, evoked specifically by him, since the orchestra's leaving and we can sit quietly for a while..."

He was already flushed from the vodka, the wine and the brandy, the way that red-haired people always flush from drinking wine, but he poured us both another glass.

"I recalled," he began, "how some twenty years ago, a certain quite young military doctor – that is, to put it bluntly, I myself – was walking one day through the streets of a town on the Volga. Walking along doing nothing important, to drop some letter or other into a postbox, with that carefree well-being in my soul that a man sometimes experiences without any reason in good weather. And the weather then was, sure enough, beautiful, a quiet, dry, sunny evening at the beginning of September, when fallen leaves on the pavements rustle so pleasantly under your feet. And so, thinking about something or other, by chance I raise my eyes and see: walking in front of me at a rapid pace and as though preoccupied, is a very smart girl in a grey suit, in a prettily curved grey hat, with a grey parasol in a hand encased in an olive-green kid glove. I see her and sense that there's something about her that I like terribly, and apart from that it seems somewhat strange: why is she hurrying so, and where to? You might not have thought there was anything to be surprised about – people can have all sorts of urgent business. But all the same, for some reason it intrigues me. Unconsciously I quicken my own step too, almost catch up with her – and, it turns out, a good thing too. Ahead, on a corner, is a low, old church, and I can see she's heading straight towards it, although it's a weekday and an hour when there's not yet any service in the churches.

There, having run up onto the church porch, she opens the heavy door with difficulty, and again I go after her and, on entering, stop by the threshold. The church is empty and, not seeing me, with a quick, light step, evenly and elegantly she goes towards the ambo, crosses herself and lithely gets down on her knees, she throws back her head, dropping the parasol on the floor, presses her hands to her breast and gazes at the altar with, by the look of everything, that insistently imploring gaze with which people ask for God's help, either in great sorrow or in ardent desire for something. Through a narrow window with an iron grille to the left of me the yellowish evening light is shining, tranquil and as though age-old and pensive too, but ahead, in the vaulted and squat depths of the church, it's already twilight, there's only the flickering gold of the rizas, hammered with wonderful ancient crudeness, on the icons of the altar wall, and she, on her knees, doesn't take her eyes off them. The slender waist, the lyre shape of her backside, the heels of her light, delicate shoes with their toes pressed against the floor... Then several times she clasps a handkerchief to her eyes, quickly picks her parasol up from the floor as if resolved upon something, gets up lithely, runs towards the way out, suddenly sees my face – and I'm simply staggered by the beauty of the most terrible fright which has flashed all of a sudden in eyes shining with tears..."

In the next room the chandelier went out – the restaurant had already emptied – and the doctor glanced at the clock.

"No, it's not late yet," he said. "Only ten. You're not hurrying off anywhere? Well then, let's stay sitting a little longer and I'll finish telling you this quite strange story. Strange about it first and foremost was the fact that the same evening – that is, to be more precise, late that evening – I met her again. I suddenly took it into my head to go to a summer inn on the Volga where I'd been only two or three times over the entire summer, and then only to sit in the river air after a hot day in town. Why I went specifically on that already fresh evening, God knows: it was as if something was directing me. Of course, you could say that it was simply chance: the man went along, having nothing else to do, and there's nothing surprising in a new chance meeting. It stands to reason, it's all entirely true. But then why was there something else too, that is, the fact that I'd met her the devil knows where, and that suddenly those vague conjectures and premonitions of some kind that I'd experienced when first I saw her and the concentration, the mysterious, disturbing sort of purpose with which she'd been going to the church, and with which, in such tension and silence – that is, with that most important, most genuine something that there is in us – had there been praying to God for something, had proved justified? Arriving, and having forgotten about her completely, I sat alone and miserable for a long time in this riverside inn – very expensive, by the way, famous for the nocturnal binges of merchants that not infrequently cost thousands – and I swallowed Zhigulyovskoye beer from time to time without tasting it at all, remembering the Rhine and the Swiss lakes, where I'd been in the summer of the previous year, and thinking about how vulgar all provincial Russian places of out-of-town entertainment are, and in particular those on the Volga... Have you visited the towns along the Volga and inns of that sort on the water, on piles?"

I replied that I knew the Volga little and had not been in any floating restaurants there, but could easily imagine them.

"Well, of course," he said. "The Russian provinces are everywhere pretty much identical. There's only one thing there that's like nothing else – the Volga itself. From early spring and until the winter it's always and everywhere extraordinary, in any weather, and by day or by night regardless. At night, for example, you sit in such an inn, look out of the windows which make up three of its walls, and when on a summer's night they're all open to the air, you look straight into the darkness, into the blackness of the night, and somehow you get a particular sense of all that wild grandeur of the watery expanses beyond them: you see thousands of scattered multicoloured lights, you hear the splashing of rafts going by, the voices of the men on them, or on barges or *belyanas*,* as they call to and fro, their cries warning one another, the many-toned music of now booming, now low steamer hooters and, merging with them, the thirds of some little river steamboats, racing along swiftly, you remember all those brigandly and Tatar words – Balakhna, Vasil-Sursk, Cheboksary, Zhiguly, Batraky, Khvalynsk – and the terrible hordes of dockers on their jetties, then all the incomparable beauty of the old Volga churches – and all you can do is shake your head: how truly incomparable with anything is this Rus of ours! But if you look around – what exactly is it, this inn? A building on piles, a shed made of logs with windows in crude frames, filled with tables under white but dirty tablecloths with heavy, cheap cutlery, where the salt in the salt cellars is mixed with pepper and the napkins smell of grey soap; a plank platform, a cheap theatre stage – that is, for balalaika and accordion players and female harpists – lit along the back wall by kerosene lamps with blinding tin reflectors; flaxen-haired waiters, the owner from peasant stock with thick hair, with the little eyes of a bear – and how can all this be married up with the fact that a thousand roubles' worth of Mumm and Roederer is forever being drunk here in a night! Yet you know, all that is Rus too... But aren't you sick of me?"

"Heavens, no!" I said.

"Well, allow me to finish then. What I'm driving at with all this is what a smutty place I suddenly met her in again in all her pure, noble charm, and with what a companion! Towards midnight the inn began to come to life and fill up: they lit a huge and terribly hot lamp beneath the ceiling, the lamps around the walls and the little lamps on the wall behind the platform, an entire regiment of waiters emerged, and a crowd of guests poured in: of course, merchants' sons, clerks, contractors, steamer captains, a troupe of actors who were in the town on tour... contorting themselves in a depraved manner, the waiters began running around with trays, loud chatter and raucous laughter started up in the groups at the tables, tobacco smoke began floating around, out onto the platform to sit down in two rows along its sides came balalaika players in operatic peasants' shirts, nice clean puttees and nice new bast shoes, and behind them came a choir of well-rouged and powdered little tarts, who stood in a line with their hands clasped identically behind their backs, and who, with shrill voices and faces expressing nothing, joined in with the balalaikas as they started ringing away in a mournful, long-drawn-out song about some sad 'warrior', who had apparently returned from a long spell of Turkish captivity: 'Hi-is fa-a-amily they kne-ew him not, they asked the-e so-oldi-er who-o-o are you...' Then out with a huge accordion in his hands came some 'renowned Ivan Grachov', who sat down on a chair by the very edge of the platform and gave his thick, tow-coloured hair, loutishly parted down the middle, a shake: the brutish face of a floor-polisher, a yellow *kosovorotka*, embroidered along the high collar and hem with red silk, the braid of a red belt with the tassels dangling low, new boots with patent-leather tops... He gave his hair a shake, settled the three-row accordion with black-and-gold bellows on his raised knee, directed his blank eyes somewhere upwards, performed a devil-may-care run across the buttons – and began to make them growl and sing, bending, twisting and stretching the bellows like a thick snake, running across the buttons with the most amazing flourishes, and ever louder, more decisively and with more variations, then he jerked up his face, closed his eyes and broke into a feminine voice: 'I was strolling in the meadows, for to drive away my grief...'* And it was at that very moment I saw her, and of course she wasn't alone: I'd just then got up to summon a waiter and pay for the beer, and I simply let out a gasp: a door behind the platform opened from the outside and she appeared in some sort of khaki-coloured peaked cap, in a waterproof coat of the same colour with a belt – true, she was amazingly good-looking in all this, resembling a tall boy – and after her, holding her by the elbow, someone of no great height in a *poddyovka* and a nobleman's cap, dark-faced and already wrinkled, with black, restless eyes. And you understand, I simply went blind with rage, as they say! I recognized in him an acquaintance of mine, a landowner who'd squandered all his money, a drunkard, a libertine, a former lieutenant in the hussars who'd been expelled from his regiment, and, considering nothing, without thinking, I rushed forward between the tables so impetuously that I reached him and her almost at the entrance – Ivan Grachov was still crying: 'I was seeking pretty flowers for to send unto my love...' When I ran up to them, he, with a glance at me, managed to cry out cheerfully: 'Ah, Doctor, hello,' while she paled to a deathly shade of blue, but I pushed him away and whispered to her furiously: 'You in this tavern! At midnight, with a debauched drunkard, a card sharp, known to the whole district and town!' I grabbed her by the arm, threatening to maim him if she didn't get out of there with me that very minute. He was rooted to the spot – what could he do, knowing that with these hands I could break horseshoes! She turned and, bowing her head, set off towards the exit. I caught up with her under the first streetlamp on the cobbled embankment and took her by the arm – she didn't raise her head and didn't free her arm. After the second streetlamp, beside a bench, she stopped and, burying her head against me, began shaking with tears. I sat her down on the bench, holding on with one hand to her dear, slender, girlish hand, wet with tears, and putting my other arm around her shoulder. She was speaking incoherently: 'No, it's not true, it's not true, he's a good man... he's unhappy, but he's kind, generous, carefree...' I was silent – to object was useless. Then I hailed a passing cabman. She quietened down, and in silence we rode up into

190

the town. In the square she said quietly: 'Now let me go, I'll walk the rest of the way, I don't want you to know where I live,' and, suddenly kissing my hand, she slipped out and, without looking back, set off awkwardly at an angle across the square... I never saw her again, and I still don't know to this day who she was, what she was..."

When we had settled up, put on our things downstairs and gone out, the doctor went with me as far as the corner of the Arbat, and we paused to say goodbye. It was empty and quiet – until new animation towards midnight, until people left the theatres and suppers in restaurants, both in and out of town. The sky was black, the streetlamps' sparkle was pure under the young, pretty greenery on Prechistensky Boulevard, there was the soft smell of the spring rain which had dampened the roadways while we had been sitting in The Prague...

"But you know," said the doctor, looking around, "I was sorry later that I'd, so to speak, saved her. I've known other incidents of that kind too... But why, permit me to ask, did I interfere? Isn't it all the same what makes a person happy and how? Consequences? But they always exist just the same, don't they: I mean, cruel traces remain in your soul from everything – memories, that is, which are especially cruel and agonizing if you're remembering something happy... Well, goodbye, I was very glad to meet with you..."

27th October 1943

The Godmother

DACHAS IN PINE FORESTS outside Moscow. A shallow lake, bathing huts beside marshy banks.

One of the most expensive dachas not far from the lake: a house in the Swedish style. Beautiful old pines and bright flower beds in front of an extensive terrace.

The lady of the house is in a light, smart, lacy matinee coat all day, radiant with the beauty of a thirty-year-old woman of the merchant class and the tranquil contentment of summer life. Her husband leaves for the office in Moscow at nine in the morning and returns at six in the evening, strong, tired, hungry, and immediately goes to bathe before dinner, he undresses with relief in a bathing hut that has been heated up during the day, and he smells of healthy sweat, of a sturdy common man's body...

An evening at the end of June. The samovar has not yet been cleared away from the table on the terrace. The lady of the house is preparing berries for jam. A friend of her husband's, who has come to stay at the dacha for a few days, is smoking and looking at her sleek, round arms, bare to the elbow. (A connoisseur and collector of ancient Russian icons, an elegant man of wiry build with a small, trimmed moustache, with a lively gaze, dressed as for tennis.) He looks and says:

"Godmother, may I kiss your hand? I can't look at you in peace."

"My hands are covered in juice," and she holds up a shiny elbow.

Just touching it with his lips, he hesitantly says:

"Godmother..."

"What, godfather?"

"You know, there's this story: a man's heart went out of his hands and he said to his mind: goodbye!"

"How do you mean, his heart went out of his hands?"

"It's from Saadi, godmother. There was a Persian poet of that name."*

"I know. But what does 'his heart went out of his hands' mean?"

"It means that the man fell in love. The way I have with you."

193

"It seems as if you've said to your mind goodbye as well."

"Yes, godmother, I have."

She smiles absent-mindedly, as though occupied only with her own work.

"On which I congratulate you."

"I'm being serious."

"Good health."

"It's not good health, godmother, it's a very grave illness."

"You poor thing. You should get it seen to. And have you had it long?"

"I have, godmother. Do you know since when? Since the day when, out of the blue, you and I were godparents for the Savelyevs – I don't understand what possessed them to invite specifically you and me to be godparents... Do you remember what a blizzard there was that day and how you arrived all covered in snow, excited by the fast driving and the blizzard, how I myself took your sable coat off you, and you went into the reception hall in a modest, white silk dress, with a little pearl cross at your slightly open bosom, and later you held the child in your arms with your sleeves tucked up, and you stood with me by the font, gazing at me with an embarrassed sort of half-smile?... It was then that something secret began between us, some sort of sinful intimacy, our kinship, as it already seemed to be, and, because of that, a special lust."

*"Parlez pour vous."**

"And then we sat next to one another at lunch and I couldn't understand – was it the hyacinths on the table that smelt so wonderful, young and fresh, or was it you?... And it's since then that I've become ill. And I can be cured only by you."

She gave him a look from under her brows:

"Yes, I remember that day well. And as regards treatment, it's a shame Dmitry Nikolayevich is spending tonight in Moscow – he'd have recommended a genuine doctor to you straight away."

"And why is he spending the night in Moscow?"

"He said this morning, as he was leaving for the station, that they have a shareholders' meeting today before they go away. They're all going away – some to Kislovodsk, some abroad."

"But he could have come back on the twelve o'clock."

"And the farewell drinking session after the meeting at The Mauritania?"

At dinner he was sad and silent, but joked unexpectedly:

"Maybe I should push off to The Mauritania too on the ten o'clock, get completely plastered there and drink '*Bruderschaft*'* with the head waiter?"

She gave him a lengthy look:

"Push off and leave me alone in an empty house? So that's how you remember the hyacinths!"

And quietly, as if deep in thought, she placed her palm onto his hand as it lay on the table...

After one o'clock in the morning, wearing only a dressing gown, to the distinct ticking of the clock in the dining room, he stole from her bedroom through the dark, quiet house to his own room, in the twilight of which, through the windows that were open onto the garden balcony, there shone the distant, lifeless light of the sunset's afterglow, which did not go out the whole night long, and there came the smell of nocturnal sylvan freshness. He fell blissfully onto his back on the bed, groped on the bedside table for his matches and cigarette case, lit up greedily and closed his eyes, recalling the details of his unexpected good fortune.

In the morning, the dampness of gentle rain was wafting in through the windows, its drops were beating evenly on the balcony. He opened his eyes, sensed with delight the sweet simplicity of everyday life, thought: "I'll leave for Moscow today, and the day after tomorrow for the Tyrol or for Lake Garda," and fell asleep again.

Emerging for lunch, he kissed her hand deferentially and sat down at the table modestly, unfolding a napkin...

"Do forgive me," she said, trying to be as natural as possible: "only cold chicken and yoghurt. Sasha, bring some red wine, you've forgotten again..."

Then, without raising her eyes:

"Please leave today. Tell Dmitry Nikolayevich that you too felt a terrible urge to go to Kislovodsk. I'll be there in a couple of weeks, and I'll send him to his parents in the Crimea, they've got a marvellous dacha there in Miskhor... Thank you Sasha. You don't like yoghurt – do you want some cheese? Sasha, bring the cheese, please..."

"'And are you liking cheese, they asked the hypocrite,'"* he said, laughing awkwardly. "Godmother..."

"A fine godmother!"

He took her hand across the table and squeezed it, saying quietly: "Will you really come?"

She replied in a steady voice, looking at him with a slight smirk: "And what do you think? I'll deceive you?"

"How am I to thank you!"

And at once he thought: "And there, in those patent-leather boots, the riding habit and bowler hat, I'll probably conceive an immediate fierce hatred for her!"

25th September 1943

The Beginning

"WELL I, GENTLEMEN, fell in love for the first time, or, to be more accurate, lost my innocence, at about twelve. I was at grammar school then, and was travelling home from town into the country for the Christmas holidays, on one of those warm grey days that so often occur at Christmas-tide. The train was moving through pine forests under deep snow, I was childishly happy and calm, sensing this gentle winter's day, this snow and these pines, dreaming of the skis awaiting me at home, and I was sitting entirely on my own in the over-heated first-class part of an old-style mixed carriage comprised of just two sections, that is, of four red velvet couches with high backs – it was as if that velvet made it even hotter and stuffier – and four small couches of that same velvet beside the windows on the other side, with an aisle between them and the big ones. I spent more than an hour there, carefree, peaceful and alone. But at the second station from the town the door from the carriage entrance opened, there was a sudden pleasing smell of wintry air, and in came a porter with two suitcases in covers and a holdall of tartan material; behind him was a very pale, black-eyed young lady in a black satin bonnet and an astrakhan fur coat, and behind the lady a strapping gentleman with yellow, owlish eyes wearing a deerskin hat with the ear-flaps raised, felt boots to above the knees and a brilliant deerskin coat. I, of course, as a well-brought-up boy, immediately rose and moved from the big couch beside the door to the carriage entrance into the second section, but not onto another big couch, rather onto a small one beside a window, facing the first section, so as to have the opportunity to observe the newcomers – after all, children are just as attentively curious about new people as a dog is about unfamiliar dogs. And it was there, on that couch, that my innocence perished. When the porter had put the things onto the rack above the couch on which I had just been sitting, had said to the gentleman, who had thrust a paper rouble into his hand: "Safe journey, Your Highness!" and, with the train already moving, had run out of the carriage, the lady immediately lay down on her back on the couch under the rack with the back of her head on its velvet bolster, and the gentleman, awkwardly, with hands unaccustomed to any work, pulled the holdall down from the rack onto the couch opposite, tugged a little white pillow out of it and, without looking, handed it to her. She said quietly: "Thank you, my dear," and, pushing it under her head, closed her eyes, while he, after throwing his coat off onto the holdall, stood by the window between the small couches of his section and lit up a fat cigarette, diffusing its aromatic smell densely in the stuffy heat of the carriage. He stood at his full, powerful height, with the earflaps of his deerskin hat sticking up and, it seemed, with his eyes fixed on the pines racing backwards, while I at first kept my eyes fixed on him and felt only one thing: terrible hatred towards him for his having completely failed to notice my presence, his not once having even glanced at me, as though I hadn't been in the carriage at all – and, on the strength of that, for everything else as well: for his lordly calm, for his princely peasant's size, predatory round eyes, carelessly neglected chestnut moustache and beard, and even for his heavyweight and roomy brown suit, for his light, velvety felt boots, pulled up above the knees. But not even a minute had passed before I'd already forgotten about him: I suddenly remembered that deathly but beautiful pallor by which I'd been unconsciously struck at the entrance of the lady who was now lying on her back on the couch opposite me, I transferred my gaze to her, and no longer saw anything else besides her, her face and body until the next station, where I needed to get off. She sighed and lay more comfortably, a little lower down; without opening her eyes she flung open her fur coat, worn over a flannel dress; using her feet, she kicked her warm overshoes off her open suede shoes and onto the floor; she removed the silk bonnet from her head and dropped it down beside her – her black hair proved, to my great surprise, to be cut short like a boy's – then on the right and on the left she unhooked something from her grey silk stockings, raising her dress as far as the bare flesh between it and the stockings, and, adjusting the hem, dozed off: her heliotropic, femininely young lips with dark down above them opened a little, her face, pale to the point of transparent whiteness and with the black eyebrows and lashes very prominent upon it, lost all expression... The sleep of a woman you desire, who draws your whole being to her – you know what that is like! And so for the first time in my life I saw and felt it – until then I'd seen only the sleep of my sister, my mother – and I kept on looking, looking with unmoving eyes and a dry mouth at that boyishly feminine black head, at the motionless face, on the pure whiteness of which the fine black eyebrows and closed black lashes stood out so wonderfully, at the dark down above the parted lips, utterly agonizing in their attractiveness. I was already absorbing and coming to comprehend all there is that is indescribable in the recumbent female body, in the fullness of the hips and the slenderness of the ankles, and with terrifying vividness could still see in my mind that incomparable, delicate, feminine flesh colour which she had accidentally shown me while unhooking something from the stockings underneath her flannel dress. When the jolt of the train stopping in front of our station unexpectedly brought me round, I went staggering out of the carriage into the sweet wintry air. Beyond the wooden station building stood a troika sledge with a pair of greys in harness, their bells jangling, and waiting beside the sledge with a raccoon fur coat in his hands was our old coachman, who said to me in an unfriendly fashion:

"'Your Mummy said you must be sure to put it on...'

"And I obediently slipped into that coat of my grandfather's, smelling of fur and wintry freshness, with its huge, already yellow and long-haired collar, I sank into the soft and spacious sledge and, to the muffled, hollow muttering of the bells, began rocking down the deep and soundless road of snow in a cutting through the pines, closing my eyes and still overcome by what I had just experienced, thinking confused and sadly sweet thoughts about that alone – and not about all the nice things from before that awaited me at home along with the skis and the wolf cub, taken in the den of a she-wolf killed during a hunt in August, and now sitting in a pit in our garden, which even in the autumn, when I'd been home for two days for the Intercession, had already given off such a weird and wonderful stench of wild animal."

23rd October 1943

"The Oaklings"

I WAS THEN, MY FRIENDS, in only my twenty-third year – an affair, as you can see, of long ago, still in the days of Nicholas I of blessed memory – I'd just been promoted to the rank of cornet in the Guards and, in the winter of what was a memorable year for me, I'd been granted two weeks' leave on my family estates in Ryazan where, since the death of my father, my mother had lived alone, and, on arriving, I fell in a short time cruelly in love: I looked in one day on a long empty country seat of my grandfather's in a certain little village called Petrovskoye in the neighbourhood of our own house, and then on various pretexts I began looking in there more and more frequently. The Russian countryside is wild even now, in winter most of all, so what was it like in my day! Petrovskoye was wild like that too, with, on its outskirts, that empty country house called "The Oaklings", for at the entrance to it there grew several oak trees, in my time already ancient and mighty. Beneath those oaks stood an old crude hut, beyond the hut were some outbuildings, wrecked by time, and further on still were the wastelands of the felled orchard, covered with snow, and the ruin of the manor house with the dark voids of frameless windows. And it was in that hut beneath the oaks that I used to sit almost every day, jabbering all sorts of nonsense, ostensibly about estate management, to our village headman, Lavr, who lived in it, and even basely seeking his friendship, while surreptitiously casting mournful looks at his taciturn wife, Anfisa, who was more like a Spaniard than a simple Russian house serf, and was almost half the age of Lavr himself – a strapping peasant with a brick-coloured face covered in a dark-red beard, who might easily have become ataman of a gang of Murom robbers. In the morning I would read indiscriminately whatever came to hand, tinkle on the fortepiano, singing along languorously: "Oh when, my soul, you prayed either to perish or to love,"* then, after having dinner, I would go off until evening to "The Oaklings", irrespective of the burning winds and blizzards which flew to us untiringly from the Saratov steppes. Thus Christmas-tide passed, and the time for my return to duty approached, of which one day, with feigned naturalness,

I duly informed Lavr and Anfisa. Lavr remarked edifyingly on the fact that service to the Tsar, of course, came before everything, and then went out of the hut to fetch something, while Anfisa, who was sitting with sewing in her hands, suddenly lowered the sewing onto her knees, followed her husband with her Castilian eyes, and, as soon as the door had slammed behind him, flashed them at me with impetuous passion and said in a fervent whisper:

"Master, he'll be leaving for town tomorrow and staying overnight – come here to me and while away the evening in farewell. I've held back, but now I'll say it: parting with you will be bitter for me."

I, of course, was overwhelmed by such an admission, and only had time to nod my head to signify consent before Lavr came back into the hut.

After that, as you can understand, I didn't hope, in my inexpressible impatience, even to survive until the following evening, I didn't know what to do with myself, thinking only one thing: I would neglect my entire career, give up the regiment, remain for ever in the countryside, join my fate with her upon Lavr's death – and more of the like... "I mean, he's already old," I thought, regardless of the fact that Lavr wasn't yet even fifty, "he should die soon..." Finally the night passed – right through until morning I was first smoking a pipe, then drinking rum, without getting the least bit drunk, forever growing heated in my foolhardy dreams – the short winter's day passed too, it began to get dark, and outside there was a really severe snowstorm. How could I leave the house now, what could I tell my mother? I'm at a loss, don't know what to do, when suddenly I have a simple idea: I'll go in secret, that's all there is to it! I proclaimed myself indisposed, said I wouldn't be having any supper but would be going to bed, then as soon as my mother had finished eating and withdrawn to her room – the early winter's night had already come down – I dressed in great haste, ran to the stablemen's hut, ordered a light sledge to be harnessed up, and was off. Outside, not a thing could be seen in the white darkness of the blizzard, but the horse was familiar with the way, I let it go at random, and not half an hour had passed before the humming oaks above the cherished hut began showing black in that darkness, its window began shining through the snow. I tied the horse to an oak, threw a horse cloth over it and, beside myself, went through a snowdrift and into the dark lobby! I groped for the door of the hut, stepped over the threshold, and she, already dressed up, powdered, rouged, in the brightness and red smoke of a torch, is sitting on a bench by the table, which is covered with refreshments on a white tablecloth, and waiting for me, all eyes. Everything is indistinct and trembling in this brightness and the smoke, but even through them her eyes are visible – so wide are they and intent! In a holder on a post by the stove, above a tub of water a spill is crackling, dazzling with its quick, crimson flame, and dropping fiery sparks which hiss in the water; on the table there are plates of nuts and mint sweets, a bottle of fruit liqueur, two glasses; and she, by the table, with her back to the window, which is white with snow, is sitting in a lilac silk sarafan, a calico blouse with loose sleeves, a coral necklace – her little jet-black head of hair, which would have done any society beauty honour, is brushed smooth and parted in the middle, silver earrings hang in her ears... Catching sight of me, she leapt up, in an instant had thrown off my snow-covered hat and fox-fur *poddyovka*, and pushed me towards the bench – all as if in a frenzy, contrary to all my former ideas about her proud unassailability – then she flung herself onto my knees and embraced me, pressing her hot cheeks against my face...

"Why ever did you hold back," I say, "and wait until we were parting?"

She replies in desperation:

"Ah, what else could I do? My heart would be racing when you came, I could see your agony, but I'm strong and didn't give myself away! And where could I have confided in you? I mean, not for a minute was I one to one with you, and in front of him you couldn't confide even with a glance: he's sharp-eyed as an eagle, and if he noticed anything, he'd kill, he wouldn't hesitate!"

And again she embraces me, squeezes my timid hand, puts it on her knees... I can sense her body on my legs through the light sarafan and am no longer in control of myself, when suddenly she straightens her whole body, alert and wild, and leaps up, gazing at me with the eyes of the Pythia:*

"Do you hear?"

I listen – I can hear nothing except the noise of the snow beyond the wall – what is it? I ask.

"Someone's driven up! A horse neighed! It's him!"

And, running round the table and sitting down at it, overcoming her heavy breathing, she says loudly in an ordinary voice, pouring from the bottle with a shaking hand:

"Drink some liqueur, sir. You'll feel the cold when you go…"

And it was at that point he came in, all shaggy with snow, in a sheepskin "three-eared" cap and sheepskin coat, he took a look, said: "Hello, sir," painstakingly put the coat up on the shelf above the stove, took off the hat and shook it down, and, wiping his wet face and beard with the hem of his sheepskin jacket, began talking unhurriedly:

"Well, what weather! Somehow I struggled as far as Bolshiye Dvory – no, I'm thinking, you're done for, you won't make it – drove to a wayside inn, stood the mare under an awning out of the storm, gave her some fodder, and went into the hut myself for some cabbage soup – I'd turned up just at dinner time – and there I sat almost till evening. And then I'm thinking – ah, I'll head home, come what may, maybe God'll get me back again – I can't be doing with town, I can't be doing with business in such a nightmare! And here I am back again, thank God…"

We're silent, sitting rooted to the spot in the most terrible embarrassment, we understand that he'd understood everything at once, she doesn't raise her eyelashes, I look up at him occasionally… I must confess, he was picturesque! Big, broad-shouldered, with a green belt done up tight around his short sheepskin jacket with its coloured Tatar patterns, solidly shod in Kazan felt boots; his brick-coloured face is burning from the wind, his beard is glittering with the melting snow, his eyes with threatening intelligence… Going up to the spill-holder, he set light to a new spill, then sat down at the table, picked up the bottle with his thick fingers, poured, drained the glass, and said to one side:

"I really don't know, sir, how you'll get back now. But it's high time you were going, your horse is all covered in snow, it's standing all bent over… Don't be angry, now, that I won't come out to see you home – over the day I've had a really hard time of it, and I've not seen my wife all day either, and there's something I have to have a talk with her about…"

Without a word in reply I got up, put on my things and left…

And in the morning, at first light, there's a rider from Petrovskoye: in the night, Lavr had hanged his wife with his green belt on an iron hook in a door lintel, and in the morning had gone to Petrovskoye and announced to the men:

"Neighbours, I've had a calamity. My wife has hanged herself – her mind was obviously disturbed. I woke up at dawn, and she's already hanging all blue in the face, her head's dropped onto her chest. She'd got dressed up for some reason, and rouged – and she's hanging, just a bit short of the floor... Witness it, Christian men."

They looked at him and said:

"How about that, what a thing to have done to herself! But why is it, headman, the whole of your beard's been torn out in tufts, your whole face has been slashed to pieces from top to bottom by claws, and your eye's pouring blood? Tie him up, lads!"

He was beaten with lashes and sent to Siberia, to the mines.

30th October 1943

Miss Klara

THE GEORGIAN IRAKLY MELADZE, the son of a rich merchant in Vladikavkaz, who had come to St Petersburg on his father's business in January, was having dinner that evening at Palkin's. He was, as always, without any reason, quite gloomy in appearance; short, slightly stooped, lean and strong, with a low forehead overgrown almost down to the eyebrows with coarse, reddish hair, his face shaved and a dark-brick colour; he had a nose like a *yataghan*,* brown, sunken eyes, small, wiry hands with hairy wrists, fingernails sharp, strong and round; he wore a blue suit of excessively fashionable provincial cut, and a light-blue silk shirt with a long tie which was sometimes golden in tint, sometimes pearly. He was dining in a large, crowded hall to the accompaniment of a noisy string orchestra, feeling with pleasure that he was in the capital and in the midst of its rich winter life – shining outside the windows was the Nevsky of the evening time, and onto its lights, and onto its incessant and thickly pouring stream of trams, flying cabs and cabmen fell snow in large flakes, lilac from the lights. After drinking two glasses of orange-blossom vodka with an hors d'œuvre of fatty eel, he was intently eating a runny hotpot, but kept on casting glances at a mighty brunette who was dining at a table nearby and seemed to him the height of beauty and smartness: a gorgeous body, a high bust and steep hips, all fitted tightly into a black satin dress; on her broad shoulders was an ermine boa; on her jet hair a magnificently curved black hat; her black eyes with arching false lashes shone imperiously and independently, her thin, orange-painted lips were proudly compressed; her large face was white as chalk with powder... As he was finishing a wood grouse in sour cream, Meladze shook his head and beckoned a flunkey towards him with a bent finger, indicating her with his eyes:

"Tell me, please, who's she?"

The flunkey winked:

"Miss Klara."

"Let me have the bill quickly, please..."

She was already paying too, after elegantly drinking a cup of white coffee, and having paid and carefully counted the change, she unhurriedly rose and walked smoothly to the ladies' toilet. Going after her, he ran down the staircase, covered with a well-worn red carpet, to the exit onto the porch, he hastily put his coat on there in the doorman's room and started waiting for her on the porch in the thickly falling snow. She emerged with her head tilted imperiously, wearing a roomy seal-fur coat, with her hands held in a large ermine muff. He blocked her way and, bowing, removed his astrakhan hat:

"Please allow me to accompany you…"

She paused and looked at him in genteel surprise:

"It's a little naive on your part to address a lady you don't know with such a proposal."

He put his hat on and, offended, mumbled:

"Why naive? We could go to the theatre, then have some champagne…"

She shrugged her shoulders:

"What persistence! You're evidently a visitor from the provinces?"

He hastened to say that he had come from Vladikavkaz, that he and his father had a large commercial business there…

"So it's business in the daytime, but you're bored in solitude in the evening?"

"Very bored!"

As though she had thought something over, she said with affected carelessness:

"Well then, let's be bored together. If you want, come to my place, we can find some champagne there too. And then we'll have supper somewhere on the Islands. Only beware, all that won't come cheap for you."

"How much will it be?"

"At my place fifty. But on the Islands, of course, it'll cost more than fifty."

He gave a fastidious grimace:

"Please! That's not an issue."

The cab man, plastered in snow and continually smacking his lips in time with the horse's knocking against the front of the sledge, conveyed them quickly to house number 15 on Ligovka. On the fourth floor the weakly lit staircase went right up to a single door to a completely self-contained apartment. Both had been silent on the way – at first he had shouted excitedly, boasting about Vladikavkaz and of having put up at the Northern Hotel, in the most expensive room, on the ground floor, then he had suddenly fallen silent, holding on to her wet sealskin now by the waist, now by her broad backside, and he had already been in torment, thinking only of the latter; she had hidden her face from the snow with her muff. They climbed the stairs in silence too. She unlocked the door unhurriedly with a Yale key, lit up the whole apartment with electric light from the entrance hall, took off her fur coat and hat, shaking the snow off them, and he saw that her big hair, shot with a sort of raspberry colour, was brushed flat with a centre parting. Containing his impatience and now his anger at her slowness, and sensing how hot, stuffy and remote this solitary apartment was, he did try to be courteous all the same and, taking off his things, said:

"How cosy!"

She replied indifferently:

"But a little cramped. Every convenience, a gas cooker, a wonderful bathroom, but only two other rooms: the reception room and the bedroom..."

In the reception room, carpeted in beaver, with old, soft furniture and plush curtains at the doors and windows, a lamp on a tall stand burned brightly under a pink horn-shaped shade, and in the bedroom adjoining the reception room there could also be seen, beyond the door, the pink light of a lamp on a bedside table. She went through to the bedroom, having put a shell ashtray out for him on an occasional table covered with a velvet tablecloth, and she shut herself in for a long time. He grew more and more gloomy, smoking in an armchair beside the table, looking sidelong at Klever's *Winter Sunset*,* which hung above the couch, and at another wall, at a large portrait of an officer who had a greatcoat from Nicholas I's time thrown over his shoulders, at his half-whiskers. Finally the door from the bedroom opened:

"Well then, now we'll sit and have a chat," she said, coming out of it in a black dressing gown embroidered with golden dragons, and wearing pink, backless, satin slippers on unstockinged feet.

He glanced greedily at her bare heels, which looked like white turnips, and she, catching his glance, grinned, went somewhere through the entrance hall and returned with a bowl of pears in one hand and an opened champagne bottle in the other. "My favourite, pink," she said, and went away again; she brought two glasses, filled them to the brim with lightly fizzing pink wine, clinked glasses with him, took a sip and sat down on his knees, choosing one of the more yellow pears from the bowl and immediately taking a bite out of it. The wine was warm and sickly sweet, but in his excitement he drained the glass and, with wet lips, jerkily kissed her plump neck. She pressed a large palm smelling of Chypre eau de cologne to his mouth:

"Only no kisses. We're not schoolchildren. And put the money here, on the table."

Pulling his wallet from the inside pocket of his jacket and his watch from his waistcoat, she put the one and the other on the table and, while finishing the pear, spread her legs. He grew bold and threw open the dressing gown with its dragons on her large, full-breasted, white body with thick, black hair below the wide, undulating stomach. "She's already old," he thought, glancing at her porous, chalky face, thickly sprinkled with powder, at her cracked orange lips, at the ugly false eyelashes, at the wide, grey parting in the middle of the flat hair the colour of shoe polish, but already going completely berserk at the size and whiteness of that bare body, the round breasts, the red nipples of which were for some reason very small, and the soft backside that lay heavily on his knees. She gave him a painful smack on the hand and stood up, flaring her nostrils:

"Impatient as a little boy!" she said angrily. "Now we'll drink another glass each and then we'll go…"

And she took hold of the bottle proudly. But with eyes that had filled with blood, he threw his entire body at her and knocked her off her feet onto the floor, onto the beaver. She dropped the bottle and, narrowing her eyes, with all her might gave him a cruel slap in the face. He started moaning sweetly with his head bent down, protecting himself from any new blow, and he fell upon her, grabbing her bare backside with one hand and unbuttoning himself quickly with the other. She sank her teeth into his neck and, throwing her right knee up, struck him with it so terribly in the stomach that he flew under the table, but he leapt up immediately, caught the bottle up from the floor and, as she half-rose, cracked her on the head. With a hiccup she fell onto her back, throwing out her arms and opening her mouth wide – blood flowed from it thickly. He grabbed the watch and wallet from the table and dashed into the hall.

At midnight he was sitting in an express train, he was in Moscow at ten in the morning, and at one o'clock he boarded a train for Rostov at the Ryazan Station. After six in the evening the next day, by the buffet bar at the station in Rostov, he was arrested.

17th April 1944

Madrid

IN THE LATE EVENING, by the light of the moon, he was walking along Tverskoy Boulevard, and she was coming towards him at a stroll with her hands held in a small muff, nodding her little round astrakhan fur hat, which was tilted a little to one side, and humming something. On coming up to him, she stopped:

"D'you wanna share my company?"

He took a look: small, snub-nosed, with rather broad cheekbones, eyes shining in the nocturnal half-light, a nice smile, timid, her little voice pure in the quiet, in the frosty air...

"Why not? With pleasure."

"And how much will you pay?"

"A rouble for love, a rouble for pin money."

She thought about it.

"Do you live far away? If not, then I'll come, I'll still have time to walk for a bit after you."

"A stone's throw. Here on Tverskaya, the Madrid rooms."

"Ah, I know! I've been there half a dozen times. This card sharp took me there. Jewish, but terribly kind."

"I'm kind too."

"I thought so. You're nice, I liked you at once..."

"So let's go then."

On the way, continually throwing glances at her – an uncommonly sweet girl – he began asking her questions:

"Why is it you're alone?"

"I'm not alone, there's three of us always go out together: me, Mur and Anelya. We live together too. Only it's Saturday today, and they were picked up by shop assistants. But nobody'd picked me up the whole evening. I'm not picked up very much, they prefer the plump ones, or else they have to be like Anelya. She may be thin, but she's tall and cheeky. Drinks an awful lot and can sing like a gypsy. She and Mur can't stick men, they're in love with each other like I don't know what, they live like man and wife..."

"Right, right... Mur... And what's your name? Only don't lie, don't make something up."

"I'm Nina."

"There you go, lying. Tell the truth."

"Well, I'll tell you. Polya."

"You can't have been on the streets long?"

"I have, for a long time now, ever since the spring. But why keep on asking questions! Better give me a cigarette. You probably have really good ones, look what a raincoat and hat you're wearing!"

"I will when we arrive. Smoking in the cold's bad for you."

"Well, that's up to you, but we always smoke in the cold and no 'arm done. Now it's bad for Anelya, she's got consumption... Why are you clean-shaven? He was clean-shaven too..."

"Are you still on about the card sharp? He really has stuck in your memory!"

"I remember him even now. He's got consumption too, but smokes like I don't know what. Burning eyes, dry lips, sunken chest, sunken cheeks, dark..."

"And the wrists hairy, ugly..."

"That's right, that's right! Oh, do you know him?"

"Now then, how could I possibly know him?"

"Then he went away to Kiev. I went to see him off at the Bryansk Station, and he didn't know I was coming. I arrived, and the train had already started. I ran after the carriages, and he'd just put his head out of the window, he saw me and began waving, started shouting that he'd soon be back again and would bring me some chopped dried fruit from Kiev."

"And he hasn't come back?"

"No, he's probably been caught."

"And how did you find out he was a card sharp?"

"He said so himself. He had a lot of port to drink, got sad and told me. I'm a card sharp, he says, no different to a thief, but what can I do, I've got to keep the wolf from the door... And you're an actor, maybe?"

"Something of the sort. Well, here we are..."

Beyond the entrance door a little lamp was burning above the desk, but there was no one there. On a board on the wall hung the keys to the rooms. When he removed his, she whispered:

"How ever can you leave it? They'll rob you!"

He looked at her, becoming more and more cheerful:

"If they rob me, they'll go to Siberia. But what a delightful little face you have!"

She became embarrassed:

"You keep on making fun... For God's sake, let's go quick, after all, taking someone to your room so late isn't allowed, is it?..."

"It's all right, don't be afraid, I'll hide you under the bed. How old are you? Eighteen?"

"You're an odd one! You know everything! Nearly eighteen."

They went up a steep staircase, over a worn carpet, and turned into a narrow, weakly lit, very stuffy corridor; he stopped and put his key in a door, and she rose up on tiptoe and looked to see what number it was:

"Five! He was staying in number fifteen on the second floor..."

"If you say just one more word to me about him, I'll kill you."

Her lips wrinkled in a contented smile and, swaying a little, she went into the hallway of the lighted room, unbuttoning her little coat with an astrakhan fur collar as she went:

"You left and forgot to put the light out..."

"It doesn't matter. Where's your handkerchief?"

"What do you want it for?"

"You've gone red in the face, but your nose is cold all the same..."

She understood, hurriedly took the little ball of a handkerchief from the muff and wiped herself. He kissed her cold little cheek and gave her back a rub. She took off her hat, gave her hair a shake and, standing up, began pulling the overshoe off one of her feet. The overshoe would not yield and, almost falling over from the effort she had made, she grabbed hold of his shoulder and gave a ringing laugh:

"Oh dear, I almost went flying!"

He took the coat off her little black dress, which smelt of the material and her warm body, and he pushed her gently into the room, towards the couch:

"Sit down and give me your foot."

"No-no, I'll do it myself..."

"I'm telling you to sit down."

She sat down and stretched out her right leg. He went down on one knee and put the leg on the other one, while she bashfully pulled her hem down over her black stocking:

"What a man you are, honestly! They really are awfully tight…"

"Be quiet."

And quickly pulling off the overshoes, one after the other, together with her shoes, he threw the hem back from her leg, gave the bare flesh above her knee a firm kiss, and stood up with a red face:

"Listen, I wanted to treat you to some port first, but I can't, we'll have a drink later on."

"Why can't you?" she asked, standing on the rug with her little feet in nothing but stockings, touchingly reduced in height.

"A complete idiot! I can't wait – understood?"

"Shall I undress?"

"No, get dressed!"

And turning away, he went over to the window and hurriedly lit a cigarette. Beyond the double glazing, which was frozen over at the bottom, the streetlights shone palely in the moonlight, and the bells on the grey horses could be heard jangling as they rushed by up Tverskaya… A minute later she called to him:

"I'm already lying down."

He extinguished the light and, undressing any old how, he hurriedly lay down under the blanket with her. Trembling all over, she pressed up against him and whispered with a happy little laugh:

"Only for God's sake don't blow on my neck or I'll start shouting for the whole building to hear, I'm terribly ticklish…"

An hour or so later she was fast asleep. Lying next to her, he gazed into the semi-darkness, mixed with the dim light from the street, thinking with irresolvable bewilderment: how on earth can it be that she'll go off somewhere towards morning? Where? She lives with bitches of some sort above some laundry or other, she goes out with them every evening, as though to the office, to earn two roubles underneath some swine or other – and what childish unconcern, simple-hearted idiocy! I think I'll "start shouting for the whole building to hear" too, out of pity, when she gets ready to leave tomorrow…

"Polya," he said, sitting up and touching her bare shoulder.

She woke up in fright:

"Oh Heavens! Please forgive me, I fell asleep quite by accident… Righ' away, righ' away…"

"What, right away?"

"I'll get up and dress righ' away…"

216

"No-no, let's have supper. I'm not letting you go anywhere until the morning."

"What do you mean, what do you mean! What about the police?"

"Nonsense. And my Madeira's no worse than your card sharp's port."

"Why is it you keep on reproaching me with him?"

All of a sudden he put on the light, which shone harshly into her eyes, and she buried her head in the pillow. He pulled the blanket off her and began kissing the back of her head, and she started kicking her legs joyously:

"Oh dear, don't tickle!"

He brought a paper bag of apples and a bottle of Crimean Madeira from the window sill, took two glasses from the washstand, sat down on the bed again and said:

"There, eat and drink. Or else I'll kill you."

She took a good bite out of an apple and started eating, washing it down with Madeira and reasoning:

"What do you think? Maybe someone *will* kill me. That's the way our business is. You go Heaven knows where, with Heaven knows who, and he's either drunk or crazy, he throws himself at you and strangles you, or knifes you... But what a warm room you have! You sit all naked and it's still warm. Is this Madeira? I do like it! How can you compare it with port – that always smells of cork."

"Well, not always."

"No, honestly, it does, even if you pay two roubles for a bottle, it's all one."

"Well, let me pour you some more. Let's clink glasses, drink and kiss. Down in one, down in one."

She drank, and in such haste that she choked and began coughing, and, laughing, let her head fall onto his chest. He lifted her head and kissed her wet, delicately compressed little lips.

"And will you come to the station to see me off?"

She opened her mouth wide in surprise:

"Are you going away too? Where? When?"

"To St Petersburg. But not for a while yet."

"Well, thank God! I'm only going to come to you now. D'you want that?"

"I do. Just to me alone. You hear?"

"I won't go to anyone, not for any money."

"That's right! And now – sleep."

"I need to go somewhere for a minute…"

"Here, in the bedside cupboard."

"I'm ashamed in full view. Put the light out for a minute…"

"I'll put it out completely. It's past two o'clock."

In bed she lay on his arm, all pressed up against him again – but quietly now, affectionately – and he began talking:

"Tomorrow you and I will have lunch together…"

She lifted her head animatedly:

"Where? I was at the Tower once, it's past the Triumphal Arch, so cheap they're simply giving it away, and the amount they give you – it's impossible to eat it all!"

"Well, we'll see where. And then you'll go home so that your bitches don't think you've been killed – and I've got things to do too – but come back here to me by seven, and we'll go and have dinner at Patrikeyev's, you'll like it there – there's an orchestrion, balalaika players…"

"And then to the Eldorado – yes? There's a wonderful film on there now, *The Fugitive Corpse*."*

"Splendid. But now – sleep."

"Righ' away, righ' away… No, Mur's not a bitch, she's terribly unfortunate. I'd have been done for without her."

"How's that?"

"She's Dad's cousin."

"So?"

"My dad was a coupler at the goods station in Serpukhov, he had his chest crushed there on the buffers, and Mum had died while I was still small, so I was left alone in all the world, and I came to her in Moscow – but it turns out she's not been working as a chambermaid in rooms for a long time already. I was given her address at the address bureau, and I came to her at the Smolensk Market by cab with my basket. I look, and she's living with this Anelya and going out with her in the evenings to the boulevards… Well, and she let me stay with her, and then persuaded me to go out as well…"

"And you say you'd have been done for without her."

"And where ever would I have gone alone in Moscow? Of course, she's ruined me, but did she wish me any evil? There's no point even talking about it. Maybe, God grant, I'll find some job in rooms too, only *I* certainly won't give the job up, and certainly won't let anyone near me, the tips will be enough for me, and with all found too. Now if it was here, in your Madrid! What could be better!"

"I'll have a think about it. Maybe I will fix you up somewhere with such a job."

"I'd bow down at your feet!"

"To make the idyll absolutely complete…"

"What?"

"No, nothing, I'm only half awake… Sleep."

"Righ' away, righ' away. I just got caught up thinking about things some'ow…"

26th April 1944

A Second Pot of Coffee

S HE IS BOTH HIS MODEL and his lover, and his housekeeper too – she
lives with him at his studio on Znamenka: yellow-haired, short, but
well-proportioned, still very young, nice-looking, affectionate. He is
painting her in the mornings now as "A Bather": on a small platform, as
though beside a stream in a forest, undecided about entering the water,
from which big-eyed frogs should be looking, she stands completely
naked, her body developed in the way the common people's are, covering the golden hair down below with a hand. After working for an hour
or so, he leans back from the easel, looks at the canvas first one way, then
another, narrows his eyes and says absent-mindedly:

"Well, this is a stop. Heat up a second pot of coffee."

She heaves a sigh of relief and, treading bare-footed over the mats,
she runs into the corner of the studio to the gas stove. He is scraping
something from the canvas with a slender knife, the little stove hisses,
giving off a sour smell from its green burners and the fragrant smell of
coffee, and she fills the whole studio with song in a carefree, resonant
voice:

"A little cloud slept, a little cloud of gold...
On the bre-east of a gi-i-iant cra-ag..."*

And, turning her head, she says joyfully:

"It was the artist Yartsev* that taught me that. Did you used to know
him?"

"I knew him a little. A lanky sort."

"That's him."

"He was a gifted chap, but pretty much of a dimwit. He died, I think,
didn't he?"

"He did, he did. Drank himself to it. No, he was kind. I lived with
him for a year, like with you. He took my virginity too, at only the
second sitting. Suddenly leapt up from the easel, dropped his palette
and brushes, and knocked me off my feet onto a carpet. I was so

221

frightened I couldn't even cry out. I grabbed hold of his jacket at the chest, but it was no use! Mad, merry eyes... As if he'd stuck me with a knife."

"Yes, yes, you've told me before. A good chap. And you loved him all the same?"

"Of course I did. I was really scared of him. He'd do me violence when he was drunk, the Lord save us. I'm saying nothing, and he says: 'Katka, shut up!'"

"Nice man!"

"Drunk. His shouting fills the studio: 'Katka, shut up!' And I've been quiet for a long time as it is. Then he goes and bursts into: "A little cloud slept..." And carries on at once with different words: "A little cow slept, a little cow, not old" – that means me. You could die laughing! And again – crash with his foot on the floor: 'Katka, shut up!'"

"Nice man. But hang on, I've forgotten: wasn't it some uncle of yours that brought you to Moscow?"

"It was, it was my uncle. I was left an orphan in my sixteenth year, and he went and brought me. That was to my other uncle, to his cab man's inn. I did the washing-up there, washed their linen for them, then my aunt took it into her head to sell me to a brothel. And she would have done, but God saved me. Once towards morning Shalyapin and Korovin* came from the Strelna to take a hair of the dog, saw me lugging a boiling twelve-litre samovar to the counter with Rodka the waiter, and started shouting and roaring with laughter: 'Good morning, Katyenka! We want *you* to be sure to serve us, and not that son of a bitch of a waiter!' I mean, how did they guess my name was Katya? Uncle was already awake, he came out yawning, knits his brows – she's not intended for that work, he says, she can't serve you. And Shalyapin just bellows: 'I'll leave you to rot in Siberia, I'll put you in irons – obey my order!' At that point Uncle got scared at once – I was scared to death too, wanted to dig my heels in – but Uncle hisses: 'Go and serve them, or else I'll flay you alive later on, those are the most famous men in all Moscow.' And so I went, and Korovin looked me over, gave me ten roubles and told me to come to him the next day – he'd taken it into his head to paint me, gave me his address. I came, but he'd already changed his mind about painting me, and sent me to Dr Gouloushev,* he was terribly friendly with all the artists, he examined drunks and corpses for the police and painted a bit too. Well, it was him started passing me around, he told me not to go back to the inn, and so I stayed with just the one dress."

"That is, what do you mean by passing around?"

"This. Around studios. At first I posed fully clothed, in a yellow scarf, and always for women artists, Kuvshinnikova, Chekhov's sister* – to tell the truth, she was no good at our business at all, a dillytant – then I found myself with Malyavin himself:* he sat me down naked on my feet, on my heels, with my back to him, with a shirt over my head, as though I was putting it on, and painted me. My back and backside turned out really well, powerful modelling, only he spoilt things with the heels and soles, twisted them around underneath my backside absolutely horribly…"

"Well, Katka, shut up. Second bell. Let's have the pot of coffee."

"Oh, Heavens, too much talking! Here it is, here it is…"

30th April 1944

Iron Coat

"No, I'm not a monk, my cassock and skullcap signify only the fact that I'm God's sinful servant, a wandering pilgrim already in a sixth decade of roaming on dry land and water. By birth I'm from far away, from the north. Russia there is remote, ancient, there are forests and marshes with lakes, settlements are rare. There are many beasts, the birds are without number, you can see the big-eared eagle owl – it sits in a black fir tree, its amber eye goggling. There's the big-nosed elk, there's the splendid deer – its crying and calling to its mate rings out in the woods... Winters are snowy and long, the wandering wolf comes right up to the windows. And in summer the big-pawed bear sways and staggers through the forests, the wood demon whistles, halloos, plays on the pipes in the wilds; in the night, drowned women are white like mist on the lakes, they lie naked on the banks, tempting a man to fornication, insatiable lechery; and there's no small number of unfortunates who do nothing but practise that lechery, spending the night with them and sleeping in the daytime, they burn in fevers, abandoning all other worldly cares... There isn't a single power in the world stronger than lust – whether in a man or in a reptile, in a beast, in a bird, but most of all in a bear and in a wood demon!

"We call that bear Iron Coat, and the wood demon – simply the Forest. And they love women, both the one and the other, to fierce sweetness. A married woman, or even a maiden, may go into the woods for firewood, or for berries – and before you know it, she's with child: she cries and repents – I was overpowered, she says, by the Forest. While another complains of the bear: Iron Coat ran into me, like, and engaged in fornication with me – how could I have escaped from him! I see him coming towards me, I prostrated myself, and he came up and sniffed at me, wondering if I was dead, folded back my gown and undergarment, crushed me... Only, to tell the truth, they're not infrequently being devious: it sometimes happens, even with maidens, that they themselves entice him, they fall to the ground face down and, as they're falling, bare themselves too, as though by accident. And then there's this; it's hard for a woman to resist, whether before a bear or a wood demon, and she doesn't think in advance that as a result in subsequent times she'll be possessed and have fits. The bear – he's both a beast and not one, and it's not for nothing our people believe he can talk, only doesn't want to. So you can understand how enticing it is for the female soul to have such a terrible coition! And as for the wood demon, it goes without saying – he's even more terrible and voluptuous. I can't assert anything about him, God's spared me from seeing him, but those who have seen him, they say in his shirt and trousers and the rest of his appearance he's like a peasant tar-stirrer, yet his blood, though, is blue, which is why he's dark of face; he's shaggy-legged, and can cast no shadow either in sunlight or in moonlight; catching sight of a man passing by on a forest path, he'll stoop down that very minute and be off at such a lick, a squirrel won't catch him! But not when meeting a woman: not only is he not afraid of her, but, knowing that she herself is at this moment seized by terror and lust, he dances up to her like a goat and takes her in merriment, in a frenzy: she falls to the ground face down, as before the bear, and he throws off the trousers from his hairy legs, falls on her from behind, tickles her nakedness, cackles, snorts and so inflames her that, already unconscious, she's overcome beneath him – some have told of it themselves...

"I'm leading up to myself with all this. I set off as a lonely pilgrim for the whole of my life by reason of the untold calamity that befell me at my very dawn. My parents married me to a splendid girl from a wealthy and old, honest peasant household, who was even younger than me and of wondrous charm: a transparent little face, whiter than the first snow, azure eyes like holy maidens have... But then, on the very first night of our marriage, she threw herself out of my embrace and onto the floor below the icons in the bedchamber, saying to me: 'Will you really dare take my body beneath a holy icon case and unctuous icon lamps? I took the marriage wreath with you not of my own volition and cannot be your spouse, as I must withdraw to a hermitage and convent in order to take another wreath, to be dead to the world for my cruel sins.' I answer her: you've clearly fallen into madness, whatever cruel sin can there be on your soul at your innocent age! And she says to me: 'The Mother of God alone knows of that, and to her, when I confessed, I made my vow to be pure.' And at that point, more than anything because of her resistance and other such terrible words – and beneath the sacred objects too – unbridled passion so brutalized me that I revelled in her right there on that spot, on the floor, no matter how she resisted with her weak powers and prayers and sobbing, and I realized only afterwards that she'd already lost her virginity when I'd had her, without thinking, though, of how and to whom she'd lost it. Being in my cups, I fell sound asleep that very minute. But she, in just her undergarment, fled from the bedchamber into the forest, and there by her wedding girdle hanged herself. And when they found her there, they saw this: sitting on the snow by her slender bare feet, with his head lowered, was a great bear. And, like the deer, for three days and three nights afterwards I filled the forests all around with my crying and calling, which could no longer reach her on earth."

1st May 1944

A Cold Autumn

I N JUNE THAT YEAR he was a guest on our estate – he was always considered one of the family: his late father had been a friend and neighbour
of my father. On 15th June Ferdinand was killed* in Sarajevo. On the
morning of the 16th the newspapers were brought from the post office.
With a Moscow evening paper in his hand, my father came out of his
study into the dining room, where Mama, he and I were still sitting at
the tea table, and said:

"Well, my friends, it's war! The Austrian Crown Prince has been
killed in Sarajevo. It's war!"

On Peter's Day* a lot of people descended on us – it was my father's
name day – and at dinner he was declared my fiancé. But on 19th July,
Germany declared war on Russia...

In September he came to see us for just twenty-four hours – to say
goodbye before leaving for the front (everyone thought then that the
war would soon end, and our wedding had been postponed until the
spring). And so our farewell evening arrived. After supper the samovar
was brought, as usual, and looking at the windows that had misted
over because of its steam, my father said:

"It's an amazingly early cold autumn!"

We sat quietly that evening, just occasionally exchanging insignificant,
exaggeratedly calm words, concealing our secret thoughts and feelings.
And it was with feigned naturalness that Father had spoken of the
autumn. I went up to the balcony door and wiped the glass with a
handkerchief: in the garden, in the black sky, pure, icy stars were
glittering clearly and sharply. Father was lying back in an armchair
smoking, gazing absent-mindedly at the hot lamp that hung above
the table, and under its light Mama, wearing glasses, was diligently
mending a little silk pouch – we knew what it was, and it was both
touching and horrible. Father asked:

"So you nevertheless want to go in the morning, and not after lunch?"

"Yes, if you'll allow me, in the morning," he replied. "It's very sad,
but I've not yet finished making arrangements about the house."

Father gave a little sigh:

"Well, as you wish, my dear. Only in that case it's time for bed for Mama and me, we want to be sure to see you off tomorrow…"

Mama stood up and made the sign of the cross over her future son, and he bent over her hand, and then over Father's. Left alone, we stayed in the dining room a little longer – I took it into my head to play patience, while he walked from corner to corner in silence, and then asked:

"Do you want to go for a little walk?"

My heart was becoming heavier and heavier, and I responded with indifference:

"Very well…"

Putting on his things in the hall, he continued thinking about something, and with a sweet smile recalled some lines of Fet:

"Oh, what an extremely cold autumn!
To put on your housecoat is wise…"

"I don't have a housecoat," I said. "How does it carry on?"
"I don't remember. Like this, I think:

Oh see – through the black of the pine trees,
It looks like a fire on the rise…" *

"What fire?"

"The moon rising, of course. There's a sort of rural, autumnal delight in those lines. 'To put on your housecoat is wise…' Our grandfathers' and grandmothers' times… Oh, my God, my God!"

"What is it?"

"Nothing, darling. I do feel sad, you know. Sad and happy. I love you very, very much…"

After putting on our things, we went through the dining room onto the balcony and down into the garden. At first it was so dark that I held on to his sleeve. Then in the lightening sky black branches began to be revealed, sprinkled with stars that shone like minerals. Pausing, he turned around towards the house:

"Look at how the windows of the house shine in a very particular way, autumnally. As long as I'm alive, I shall remember this evening for ever…"

I looked, and he put his arms around me in my Swiss cloak. I drew my downy scarf back from my face, and bent my head back slightly for him to kiss me. He kissed me, then looked me in the face:

"How your eyes are shining," he said. "You're not cold? The air's quite wintry. If I'm killed, you won't forget me immediately, will you?"

I thought: "And what if he really is killed? And will I actually forget him after a certain time – everything gets forgotten in the end, doesn't it?" And I replied hastily, frightened by my thought:

"Don't talk like that! I won't survive your death!"

After a pause he slowly uttered:

"Well then, if I'm killed, I'll wait for you there. You live, be happy in the world, and then come to me."

I began crying bitterly...

In the morning he left. Mama put that fateful pouch she had been mending in the evening around his neck – in it was a little gold icon which her father and grandfather had worn in war – and we all made the sign of the cross over him with a sort of impulsive despair. Gazing after him, we stood for a while on the porch in that torpor which is always there when you see someone off before a long separation, feeling only the amazing incompatibility between ourselves and the joyous, sunny morning that surrounded us, glittering with rime on the grass. After a while we went into the emptied house. I set off through the rooms, my hands clasped behind my back, not knowing what to do with myself now, nor whether I should burst out sobbing, or singing at the top of my voice...

He was killed – what a strange word! – a month later in Galicia. And now thirty whole years have passed since that time. And many, many things have been lived through during those years, which seem so long when you think about them carefully, when you pick over in your memory all the magical, unintelligible things, incomprehensible both for the mind and the heart, that are called the past. In the spring of 1918, when neither my father nor my mother was alive any more, I was living in Moscow, in a basement, with a tradeswoman from the Smolensk Market who was forever mocking me: "Well, Your Majesty, how would your riches be?" I was engaged in trade as well, selling, as many were selling then, some of the things I had left – now some ring or other, now a crucifix, now a moth-eaten fur collar – to soldiers in Caucasian fur hats and unbuttoned greatcoats, and it was there, trading on the corner of the Arbat and the Market, that I met a man of rare, fine spirit, a middle-aged, retired military man, whom I shortly married and with whom in April I left for Yekaterinodar. We were almost two weeks travelling there with his nephew, a boy of about seventeen, who was also stealing through to the Volunteers* – I as a peasant woman in bast shoes, he in a worn, homespun Cossack coat with a growth of black beard streaked with grey – and we spent more than two years on the Don and in the Kuban. In winter, in a hurricane, we sailed from Novorossiisk for Turkey with an innumerable crowd of other refugees, and on the way, at sea, my husband died of typhus. After that I had only three people dear to me left in the world: my husband's nephew, his young wife and their little girl, a child of seven months. But the nephew and his wife sailed away too after a certain time to the Crimea, to Wrangel,* leaving the child in my hands. And it was there that they went missing. But I continued to live in Constantinople for a long time, making a living for myself and the child by really hard unskilled labour. And then, like many, where didn't I roam with her! Bulgaria, Serbia, Czechia, Belgium, Paris, Nice... The girl grew up long ago and stayed in Paris; she had become completely French, very pretty and utterly indifferent to me; she worked in a chocolate shop beside the Madeleine, using her well-groomed little hands with silver nails to wrap boxes in satin paper and tie them with golden strings – while I lived, and still *do* live in Nice, as before, any way I can. I was in Nice for the first time in 1912 – and could I have thought in those happy days what it would one day become for me!

And thus I survived his death, having once precipitately said that I would not survive it. But, recalling all that I have lived through since then, I always ask myself: yes, and what has there been in my life after all? And I answer myself: only that cold autumn evening. Did it really once happen? And after all, it did. And that is all there has been in my life – the rest is an unwanted dream. And I believe, I fervently believe: somewhere there he is waiting for me – with the same love and youth as on that evening. "You live, be happy in the world, and then come to me..." I have lived, have been happy, and now I shall soon be coming.

3rd May 1944

232

The Steamer Saratov

IN THE DUSK OUTSIDE THE WINDOW was the noise of a brief May shower. The pockmarked batman who was drinking tea in the kitchen by the light of a tin lamp looked at the clock ticking on the wall, stood up and, awkwardly, trying not to let his new boots squeak, went through into the dark study and up to the ottoman:

"Your Honour, it's gone nine..."

He opened his eyes in fright:

"What? Gone nine? It can't have..."

Both windows were open to the street, remote, all gardens – through the windows came the smell of the freshness of spring damp and poplars. He had that sharpness of smell that people sometimes do after deep, youthful sleep, he sensed those smells and briskly threw his legs down off the ottoman:

"Light the light and go and get a cab quickly. Find me a fast one..."

And he went to get washed and changed, he poured cold water over his head, put on eau de cologne, and combed his short, curly hair, then glanced in the mirror once more: his face was fresh, his eyes shone; from one until six he had been lunching with a large party of officers, at home he had fallen into that instantaneous sleep you fall into after several hours of incessant drinking, smoking, laughter and chatter, yet he now felt excellent. In the hall the batman handed him his sabre, cap and light summer greatcoat and threw open the door onto the porch – and leaping up lightly into the cab, he cried somewhat hoarsely:

"Drive on, lively now! A rouble for your tip!"

Under the dense, oily greenery of the trees could be glimpsed the clear lustre of the streetlamps, the smell of the wet poplars was both fresh and heady, the horse rushed along, striking red sparks with its shoes. Everything was splendid: the greenery, the streetlamps, the imminent rendezvous and the taste of the cigarette he contrived to light while flying along. And everything merged into one: a happy feeling of readiness for absolutely anything. Is it the vodka, the Benedictine, the Turkish coffee? Nonsense, it's simply the spring, and everything's excellent...

The door was opened by a small and, to look at, very wanton maid on slender, wobbly high heels. Quickly throwing off his greatcoat and unbuckling his sabre, he tossed his cap onto the mirror table, fluffed his hair up a little and, with his spurs ringing, went into a small room made cramped by the excess of boudoir furniture. And straight away she too came in, wobbling a little as well on backless high-heeled shoes, and with her bare heels pink – long and undulating, in a tight housecoat that was mottled like a grey snake, with hanging sleeves slit up to the shoulder. Long too were her somewhat slanting eyes. In a long, pale hand was a smoking cigarette in a long amber cigarette holder.

Kissing her left hand, he clicked his heels together:

"Forgive me, for God's sake, I was delayed through no fault of my own…"

She looked from the height of her stature at the wet gloss of his short, tightly curling hair, at his shining eyes, and she sensed his winey smell:

"A fault long known…"

And she sat down on a silk pouffe, putting her left hand under the elbow of her right arm, holding the raised cigarette up high, crossing her legs and opening the side slit of the housecoat to above the knee. He sat down opposite on a silk canapé, pulling his cigarette case out from a trouser pocket:

"You see, what happened…"

"I see, I see…"

He lit up quickly and deftly, waved the burning match about and threw it into an ashtray on the oriental table beside the pouffe, settling down more comfortably and gazing with his usual immoderate rapture at her bare knee in the slit of the housecoat:

"Well, splendid, if you don't want to listen, you don't have to… This evening's programme: do you want to go to the Merchants' Garden? There's some 'Japanese night' on there today – you know, those lanterns, geishas on the stage, 'I won first prize for beauty…'"

She shook her head:

"No programmes. I'm staying at home today."

"As you wish. That's not a bad thing either."

Her eyes ran over the room:

"My dear, this is our last rendezvous."

He was cheerfully amazed:

"That is, how do you mean, last?"

"Just that."

His eyes began to sparkle still more cheerfully:

"Permit me, permit me, this is amusing!"

"I'm not being in the least amusing."

"Splendid. But nonetheless, I'd be interested to know what this dream's supposed to mean?* Wha's the 'itch all on a su'en, as our sergeant major says."

"What sergeant majors say is of little interest to me. And to tell the truth, I don't quite understand why you're so cheerful."

"I'm cheerful, as always, when I see you."

"That's very sweet, but on this occasion not entirely appropriate."

"But really, the devil take it, I don't understand a thing all the same. What's happened?"

"What has happened is what I should have told you about a long time ago. I'm going back to him. Our splitting up was a mistake."

"Mamma mia! Are you being serious?"

"Absolutely serious. I was criminally at fault before him. But he's prepared to forgive and forget everything."

"Wha-at magnanimity!"

"Stop playing the fool. I was already seeing him in Lent…"

"That is, in secret from me, and continuing…"

"Continuing what? I understand, but all the same… I was seeing him – and, it stands to reason, secretly, not wishing to cause you suffering – and it was then that I realized that I'd never stopped loving him."

He narrowed his eyes, chewing on the filter of his cigarette:

"That is to say, his money?"

"He's no richer than you. And what's the money of either of you to me! If I wanted—"

"Forgive me, only cocottes talk like that."

"And what am I, if not a cocotte? Do I live on my own money and not on yours?"

In the clipped speech of an officer he muttered:

"When there's love, the money has no significance."

"But I love him, don't I?"

"And so I, then, was just a temporary toy, an amusement to counter boredom and one of your profitable keepers?"

"You know very well you were far from an amusement or a toy. And yes, I'm a kept woman, but it's nonetheless vile to remind me of it."

"Take care on the bends! Choose your expressions well, as the French say!"

"I advise you to stick to that rule as well. In a word…"

He stood up and felt a new wave of that readiness for anything with which he had been dashing along in the cab, he walked around the room, collecting his thoughts, still not believing the absurdity, the unexpectedness that had suddenly destroyed all his joyful hopes for that evening, he kicked aside a yellow-haired doll in a red sarafan which was lying on a rug and sat down again on the canapé, gazing at her fixedly:

"I'll ask again: this isn't all a joke?"

Closing her eyes, she gave a wave with the cigarette which had gone out long before.

He fell into thought, lit another cigarette, and again began chewing the filter, saying distinctly:

"And what, do you think I'll give up these arms and legs of yours to him just like that, that he'll be kissing this knee here that I was kissing just yesterday?"

She raised her eyebrows:

"You know, my dear, I'm not an object, after all, that can be given up or not given up. And what right have you…"

He hurriedly put the cigarette down in the ashtray and, bending, took out of the back pocket of his trousers a slippery, small, weighty Browning, and rocked it on the palm of his hand:

"This is my right."

She looked askance with a bored smile:

"I'm not a lover of melodramas."

And raised her voice dispassionately:

"Sonya, give Pavel Sergeyevich his greatcoat."

"Wha-at?"

"Nothing. You're drunk. Go away."

"Is that your last word?"

"It is."

And she rose, adjusting the slit over her leg. He stepped towards her with joyful decisiveness:

"Mind it doesn't indeed become your last!"

"Drunken actor!" she said fastidiously and, straightening her hair at the back with her long fingers, she set off out of the room. He seized her so firmly by her bared forearm that she bent backwards and, turning quickly, with eyes that slanted even more, she aimed a blow at him. Dodging deftly, with a sarcastic grimace, he fired.

In December of that same year the Volunteer Fleet's steamer *Saratov* was in the Indian Ocean on its way to Vladivostok.* Under a hot awning stretched out on the forecastle, in the motionless sultry heat, in the hot half-light, in the brilliance of the mirrored reflections from the water, prisoners sat or lay on the deck, stripped to the waist with half-shaved, ugly heads, wearing trousers of white canvas, with the rings of shackles on the ankles above their bare feet. Like all of them, he too was stripped to the waist, his thin body brown with sunburn. Only half of his head, too, was dark with short-cropped hair, the coarse hairs on his long unshaven, thin cheeks were redly black and his eyes glistened feverishly. Leaning on the handrail, he stared at the densely blue waves, flying down below in humps along the high wall of the ship's side, and from time to time he spat into them.

16th May 1944

The Raven

M Y FATHER LOOKED LIKE A RAVEN. This occurred to me when I was still a boy: one day I saw a picture in *The Cornfield*, a cliff of some sort, and on it Napoleon with his white belly and buckskin breeches in short black boots, and suddenly I burst out laughing with joy, remembering the pictures in Bogdanov's *Polar Travels* – Napoleon seemed to me so like a penguin – and then I thought sadly: and Papa's like a raven...

My father held a very prominent official post in our province's main town, and this spoilt him still more: I think that even in the society of bureaucrats to which he belonged, there was not a man more difficult, more sullen, taciturn and coldly cruel in his sluggish words and deeds. Short, portly, a little stooping, coarsely black-haired, dark, with his long, clean-shaven face and big nose, he really was an absolute raven – especially when he was in his black tailcoat at our governor's wife's charity evenings and stood, stooping and sturdy, beside some kiosk in the form of a Russian peasant's hut, turning his big raven's head, looking askance with his shining raven's eyes at those dancing, at those coming up to the kiosk, and at the boyar's wife too, who, with an enchanting smile, was handing out coupes of yellow, cheap champagne from the kiosk with a large diamond-studded hand – a strapping lady in brocade and a peasant's headdress with a nose so pinky-white with powder that it seemed artificial. Father was long widowed, he only had the two of us children – my little sister Lilya and I – and our spacious official apartment on the first floor of one of the official buildings, which had its facades looking out onto the boulevard, filled with poplars between the cathedral and the main street, shone coldly and emptily with its huge, mirror-clean rooms. Fortunately, I lived for more than half the year in Moscow, studying at Katkov's Lycée,* and came home only for Christmas-tide and the summer holidays. That year, however, I was met at home by something completely unexpected.

In the spring of that year I graduated from the Lycée and, arriving from Moscow, I was simply staggered: it was as if the sun had suddenly begun shining in our apartment, formerly so dead – the whole of it was illuminated by the presence of the youthful, light-footed girl who had just replaced eight-year-old Lilya's nanny, a lanky, flat-chested old woman who had looked like a medieval wooden statue of some saint. A poor girl, the daughter of one of my father's minor subordinates, she was endlessly happy in those days at having found herself such a good position immediately after school, and then also at my arrival, the appearance in the house of someone of her own age. But how fearful she was, how timid in front of my father at our prim dinners, continually watching anxiously over black-eyed Lilya, taciturn too, yet abrupt not only in every one of her movements, but even in her taciturnity, as though she were constantly waiting for something, and forever turning her little black head back and forth in a way that was somehow defiant! My father had become unrecognizable at dinner: he did not throw severe glances at old Gury, who brought him his food wearing knitted gloves, but kept on talking – sluggishly, but talking – speaking, of course, only to her, addressing her with great formality by her first name and patronymic – "my dear Yelena Nikolayevna" – and he even tried to joke and grin. But she was so embarrassed that she would reply with only a piteous smile, with spots of scarlet appearing on her refined and delicate face – the face of a slim, blond-haired girl in a light white blouse with its armpits dark from her hot, youthful sweat, and beneath which were the outlines of her small breasts. She did not even dare raise her eyes to me at dinner: here I was even more terrifying for her than my father. But the more she tried not to see me, the colder were my father's sidelong looks in my direction: not only he, but I too, understood, sensed, that behind this torturous trying not to see me, but rather to listen to my father and keep an eye on the cross and fidgety, albeit also taciturn Lilya, there was concealed a completely different fear – the joyous fear of our shared happiness at being beside one another. In the evenings my father had always had tea while busy with something else, and previously he had been served his large, gold-rimmed cup at his desk in his study: now he had tea with us, in the dining room, and she sat at the samovar – Lilya was already asleep at that hour. He would emerge from the study in a long and loose-fitting double-breasted jacket with a red lining, settle down in his armchair and reach his cup out to her. She would fill it to the brim, as he liked, pass it to him with a trembling hand, pour for me and herself and, lowering her eyelashes, do some needlework; and he would unhurriedly say – something very strange:

"Blondes, my dear Yelena Nikolayevna, are suited either by black or crimson... Now your face would be very much suited by a dress of black satin with a jagged standing collar à la Mary, Queen of Scots, studded with small diamonds... or a medieval dress of crimson velvet with a little décolletage and a ruby crucifix... A coat of dark-blue Lyons velvet and a Venetian beret would suit you too... It's all dreams, of course," he would say, grinning. "Your father gets only seventy-five roubles a month from us, and apart from you he has another five children, each smaller than the next – and so most likely you'll have to live your whole life through in poverty. But then again: what's wrong with dreams? They enliven you, impart strength and hope. And then isn't it sometimes the case that certain dreams suddenly do come true? Rarely, it stands to reason, very rarely, but they do... I mean, didn't a cook at the station in Kursk recently win two hundred thousand with a lottery ticket – a simple cook!"

She tried to pretend that she took all of this as pleasant jokes, she forced herself to glance at him, to smile, while I, as though not even hearing anything, played Napoleon patience. And once he went even further – he suddenly said, nodding in my direction:

"This young man here probably dreams as well: you know, Daddy'll be dead in a little while and there'll be no end to the gold! And there will indeed be no end to it, because there'll be no beginning either. It stands to reason, Daddy does have something – for example, a little estate of a thousand hectares of black earth in Samara Province – only it's unlikely his little son will inherit it, he doesn't really favour Daddy with his love very much and, as far as I can see, he'll turn out a first-class spendthrift..."

This last conversation was the evening before Peter's Day – which was most memorable for me. In the morning of that day Father left for the cathedral, and from the cathedral for the home of the governor, who was celebrating his name day. On working days he never had lunch at home anyway, and so that day too the three of us had lunch together, and towards the end of the lunch, when cherry blancmange was served instead of her favourite pastry straws, Lilya began shouting shrilly at Gury and banging her fists on the table; she hurled her plate down on the floor, started shaking her head, and choked on her angry sobs. We somehow dragged her to her room – she kicked out and bit our hands – and begged her to calm down, promising to punish the cook severely, and she finally quietened down and fell asleep. How much timid tenderness there was for us just in that alone – in our combined efforts in dragging her along and in continually touching one another's hands! The rain was making a noise outside, lightning flashed at times in the darkening rooms and the thunder made the window panes shake.

"It's the thunderstorm that's had this effect on her," she whispered joyously when we had gone out into the corridor, and then suddenly she pricked up her ears:

"Oh, there's a fire somewhere!"

We ran into the dining room and threw open a window – the fire brigade was rushing past us along the boulevard with a clatter. Fast, torrential rain was pouring onto the poplars – the thunderstorm had already finished, as though the rain had extinguished it – and amid the clatter of the long, rushing cart, with the bronze helmets of the firemen standing on it, the hoses and ladders, amid the ringing of the shaft-bow bells above the manes of the black cart horses, which, with a crashing of horseshoes, sped the cart at a gallop over the cobbled roadway, gently, devilishly playfully, the horn of the bugler was singing in warning... Then ever so rapidly, the alarm began to be sounded on the bell tower of St John the Warrior in Lavy... We stood close beside one another at the window, through which came the fresh smell of water and the wet dust of the city, and we seemed only to be watching and listening with intent agitation. Then there was a glimpse of the final cart with some sort of huge red cistern on it, and my heart began beating harder, my forehead tightened, I took her hand, which hung lifelessly beside her hip, and gazed imploringly at her cheek, and she began to go pale, she parted her lips a little, lifted her breast in a sigh and, as though also imploringly, turned her eyes, bright and full of tears, towards me, while I seized her shoulder and for the first time in my life was overcome in the gentle cold of a girl's lips... After that there was not a single day without our hourly, seemingly chance meetings, now in the drawing room, now in the reception hall, now in a corridor, even in my father's study – he came home only towards evening – those short meetings and despairingly long kisses, insatiable and already intolerable in their irresolvability. And Father, sensing something, again stopped coming out into the dining room for evening tea, and again became taciturn and sullen. But we no longer paid him any attention, and she became calmer and more serious at dinner.

At the beginning of July Lilya fell ill after eating too many raspberries and lay recovering slowly in her room, constantly drawing fairy-tale towns with coloured pencils on large sheets of paper pinned to a board, and, like it or not, she did not leave her bedside, but sat embroidering a Little Russian blouse for herself – it was impossible to leave it: Lilya was demanding something every minute. And I was perishing in the empty, quiet house from a ceaseless, agonizing desire to see her, to kiss her and press her against me. I sat in my father's study, taking whatever came to hand from his library bookcases and making efforts to read. That is how I was sitting that time too, just before evening. And then suddenly there was the sound of her light and quick footsteps. I dropped the book and leapt up:

"What, has she gone to sleep?"

She waved a hand:

"Oh, no! You don't know – she can go two days without sleeping, and that's fine for her, as for all mad people! She drove me out to look for some yellow and orange pencils in her father's room…"

And bursting into tears, she came over and dropped her head onto my chest:

"My God, when will it ever end! Just tell him finally that you love me, that nothing in the world is going to part us anyway!"

And lifting her face, wet with tears, she embraced me impulsively and kissed me until she was out of breath. I pressed her whole body against me and drew her towards the couch – could I have considered or remembered anything at that moment? But on the threshold of the study a light coughing could already be heard: I glanced over her shoulder – my father was standing gazing at us. Then he turned and, hunched over, withdrew.

None of us emerged for dinner. In the evening Gury knocked on my door: "Your Daddy requests that you go and see him." I entered the study. He was sitting in an armchair in front of the desk and, without turning round, he began speaking:

"Tomorrow you'll leave for my village in Samara for the whole summer. In the autumn, go to Moscow or St Petersburg and find yourself work. If you dare to disobey, I'll disinherit you for good. But that's not all: straight away tomorrow I'll ask the Governor to deport you immediately to the village under guard. Now go, and don't show yourself in my sight any more. Money to pay for the journey and a certain amount of pocket money you'll receive via somebody else tomorrow morning. Towards the autumn I'll write to my village office for them to issue you with a certain sum for your initial living costs in the capitals. Don't have any hope at all of seeing her before your departure. That's all, my good man. Go."

That same evening I left for Yaroslavl Province, for the village of one of my Lycée comrades, and I stayed with him until the autumn. In the autumn, through the patronage of his father, I went to work in St Petersburg in the Ministry of Foreign Affairs, and I wrote to my father that I was renouncing for ever not only his inheritance, but also assistance of any kind. In the winter I learnt that, having left his post, he had also moved to St Petersburg – "with a delightful young wife", as I was told. And one evening, entering the stalls of the Maryinsky Theatre a few minutes before the curtain went up, I suddenly saw him and her. They were sitting in a box beside the stage, right by the barrier, on which lay a small mother-of-pearl opera glass. He, in tails, stooping, like a raven, was reading the programme carefully with one eye screwed up. She, holding herself easily and elegantly, with her blond hair piled up high, was looking around animatedly at the warm stalls, sparkling with chandeliers, filling up and softly humming, and at the evening dresses, tails and dress uniforms of the people entering the boxes. At her neck a ruby crucifix glittered with dark fire, her slender, but already rounded arms were bared, and a kind of peplos of crimson velvet was gripped at the left shoulder by a ruby clasp...

18th May 1944

The Camargue

S HE GOT ON AT a small station between Marseilles and Arles, passed down the carriage, wiggling the whole of her Spanish gypsy body, sat down by the window on a single-seat bench and, as if seeing no one, began shelling and gnawing roasted pistachios, from time to time lifting the hem of her black outer skirt and thrusting her hand into the pocket of her well-worn, white underskirt. The carriage, full of common people, was not made up of compartments, but was divided only by benches, and many of those sitting facing her just kept on staring at her.

Her lips moving over her white teeth were blue-grey, the bluish down on her upper lip thickened above the corners of her mouth. Her delicate, swarthily dark face, lit up by the brilliance of her teeth, was anciently savage. Her eyes, long, golden-brown and half-covered by swarthily brown lids, somehow gazed inside themselves – with a dull, primitive lassitude. From beneath the coarse silk of her jet-black hair, divided with a centre parting and falling in curling locks onto her low forehead, long silver earrings gleamed alongside her rounded neck. The faded light-blue shawl lying on her sloping shoulders was prettily tied at the breast. Her hands, wiry, Indian, with mummy-coloured fingers and lighter nails, kept on shelling more and more pistachios with simian quickness and dexterity. Finishing them, and sweeping the shells from her knees, she closed her eyes, crossed her legs and reclined against the back of the bench. Beneath her gathered black skirt, which gave a particularly feminine emphasis to the curve of her slender waist, her buttocks stood out in firm mounds, smoothly outlined. The thin, unstockinged foot, with its delicate tanned skin shining, was shod in a black cloth slipper and laced with differently coloured ribbons – blue and red...

Outside Arles she got off.

"*C'est une Camarguaise,*"* said my neighbour – for some reason very sadly, and following her with his eyes – a Provençal as mighty as an ox, with dark, ruddy skin covered in blood vessels.

23 May 1944

One Hundred Rupees

I SAW HER ONE MORNING in the courtyard of the hotel, the old Dutch house in the coco forests on the ocean shore where I lived in those days. And afterwards I saw her there every morning. She sprawled in a reed armchair in the light hot shade that fell from the building, a stone's throw from the veranda. His bare feet crunching over the gravel, a tall, yellow-faced, agonizingly narrow-eyed Malay, dressed in a white canvas jacket and trousers of the same kind, would bring her a tray with a cup of golden tea and set it down on a little table beside the armchair, would say something to her deferentially, without stirring his dry, tightly pursed lips, would bow and withdraw; and she would sprawl, and slowly flap her straw fan, rhythmically fluttering the black velvet of her astonishing eyelashes... To what species of earthly creations could she be assigned?

Her small body, tropically strong, had its coffee-coloured nakedness revealed at the breast, on the shoulders, on the arms and on the legs as far as the knees, while the torso and hips were somehow entwined with bright green cloth. Her small feet with red toenails peeped out between the red straps of varnished yellow-wood sandals. Her tar-black hair, piled up high, strangely failed to correspond in its coarseness with the delicacy of her childlike face. In the lobes of her small ears swung hollow gold rings. And improbably huge and magnificent were her black eyelashes – the like of those heavenly butterflies that flutter so magically on heavenly Indian flowers... Beauty, intelligence, stupidity – none of those words went with her at all, nor did anything human: she truly was as if from some other planet. The one thing that did suit her was speechlessness. And she sprawled and was silent, rhythmically fluttering the black velvet of her butterfly lashes, slowly flapping her fan...

Once, in the morning, when into the courtyard of the hotel ran the rickshaw with which I usually went into town, the Malay met me on the steps of the veranda and, with a bow, said quietly in English:

"One hundred rupees, sir."

24th May 1944

247

Vengeance

IN THE PENSION IN CANNES, where I had arrived at the end of August with the intention of bathing in the sea and painting from life, this strange woman drank coffee in the mornings and dined on her own with an invariably concentrated, gloomy air, as though seeing no one and nothing, and after her coffee she went off somewhere until almost the evening. I had been living in the pension for almost a week or so, and still looked at her from time to time with interest: thick black hair, a big black plait encircling her head, a strong body in a cretonne dress, red with black flowers, a pretty, rather coarse face – and that gloomy look... We were waited on by an Alsatian girl of about fifteen, but with large breasts and a broad backside, very plump, with an amazingly delicate and fresh plumpness, uncommonly stupid and nice, who at every word would blossom into fright and a smile; and so, encountering her one day in the corridor, I asked:

"*Dites, Odette, qui est cette dame?*"

She, prepared for both fright and a smile, raised her unctuous blue eyes to me:

"*Quelle dame, monsieur?*"

"*Mais la dame brune là-bas?*"

"*Quelle table, monsieur?*"

"*Numéro dix.*"

"*C'est une Russe, monsieur.*"

"*Et puis?*"

"*Je n'en sais rien, monsieur.*"

"*Est-elle chez vous depuis longtemps?*"

"*Depuis trois semaines, monsieur.*"

"*Toujours seule?*"

"*Non, monsieur, il y avait un monsieur...*"

"*Jeune, sportif?*"

"*Non, monsieur... Très pensif, nerveux...*"

"*Et il a disparu un jour?*"

"*Mais oui, monsieur.*"*

249

"Right, right!" I thought. "Some things make sense now. But where is it she disappears to in the mornings? Is she forever looking for him?"

The next day, soon after coffee, through the open window of my room I heard, as always, the crunch of shingle in the pension's little garden, and I took a glance – bare-headed, as always, beneath a parasol the same colour as her dress, she was going off somewhere at a rapid pace in red espadrilles. I grabbed my cane and boater and hurried after her. From our side street she turned into Boulevard Carnot, and I turned as well, hoping that in her constant state of concentration she would not turn around and would not sense me there. And so it was – she did not once turn around all the way to the station. She did not turn around at the station either, getting into a compartment of a third-class carriage. The train was going to Toulon and, just in case, I took a ticket as far as Saint-Raphaël and got into the next compartment. She was evidently not going far, but where? I leant out of the window at Napoule, at Théoule... Finally, leaning out for the minute's stop at Trayas, I saw she was already walking towards the exit from the station. I slipped out of the carriage and set off after her again, keeping, however, at a certain distance. Here I was obliged to walk for a long time – both round bends in the highway alongside cliffs above the sea, and along steep, stony paths through little pinewoods by which she shortened the route to the shore, to the little coves that indented the shore in this rocky and desolate area covered in woodland, this slope of the coastal mountains. Midday was approaching, it was hot, the air was still and thick with the smell of hot conifer needles, not a soul nor a sound anywhere – only the cicadas sawing and scraping – and the open sea to the south glittered and leapt with big silver stars... Finally she ran down a path towards a green cove between sanguine crags, threw her parasol onto the sand, quickly took off her shoes – all she had on her feet – and began undressing. I lay down on the stony slope below which she was undoing her gloomy-coloured dress, I gazed and thought that her swimming costume was probably just as sinister too. But there proved to be no costume at all beneath the dress – there was only a short pink vest. Throwing off the vest as well, suntanned brown all over, strong and sturdy, she set off over the pebbles towards the light, transparent water, her pretty ankles tensing, the steep halves of her backside twitching, the tan on her hips shining. She stood for a moment beside the water – its dazzle must have been making her squint – then she splashed about in it with her feet, squatted down, plunged in up to her shoulders and, turning, lay down on her stomach, stretched out her legs and pulled herself up towards the sandy beach, onto which she laid her elbows and her black head. In the distance the plain of the sea flickered, wide and free, with prickly silver, the enclosed cove and all its rocky cosiness was baked ever more hotly by the sun, and such quietness reigned in this torrid wilderness of cliffs and young southern woodland that from time to time the network of little glassy ripples could be heard running up onto the body lying face down below me, and then retreating from its glittering back, bifurcated backside and big, parted legs. Lying and glancing out from behind the rocks, I was becoming more and more disturbed by the sight of this magnificent nakedness, more and more forgetful of the absurdity and audacity of my action, and I raised myself a little, lighting a pipe in my agitation – and suddenly she too raised her head and stared up at me enquiringly, continuing, however, to lie as she had been lying. I stood up, not knowing what to do, what to say. She was the first to speak:

"I could hear somebody walking behind me all the way. Why did you come after me?"

I made up my mind to give a plain and simple answer:

"Forgive me, out of curiosity..."

She interrupted me:

"Yes, you're evidently inquisitive. Odette told me you'd been asking her questions about me, and I heard by chance that you were Russian and so wasn't surprised – all Russians are excessively inquisitive. But all the same, why did you come after me?"

"Still on the strength of that same inquisitiveness – professional, in particular..."

"Yes, I know, you're a painter."

"Yes, and you're very paintable. What's more, you were going off somewhere in the mornings every day, and that intrigued me – where, why? – you missed lunch, which people who are staying in pensions don't often do, and you always had a not entirely ordinary air too, you were concentrating on something. You're solitary, taciturn in your behaviour, as if you're concealing something within you... Well, and why didn't I leave as soon as you began undressing..."

"Well, that's easy to understand," she said.

And after a pause, she added:

"I'm coming out now. Turn away for a minute and then come here. You've got me interested as well."

"Not for anything will I turn away," I replied. "I'm an artist and we're not children."

She shrugged a shoulder:

"Well, all right, I don't care…"

And she rose to her full height, showing the whole of herself from the front in all her womanly strength, and she unhurriedly made her way across the shingle, threw her pink vest over her head, then uncovered her serious face from inside it and let it down over her wet body. I ran down to her and we took a seat next to one another.

"Besides the pipe, do you perhaps have cigarettes too?" she asked.

"I do."

"Give me one."

I did, and lit a match.

"Thank you."

And, inhaling, she began gazing into the distance, shifting her toes and not turning round; suddenly she said ironically:

"So I can still be found attractive?"

"I'll say!" I exclaimed. "A splendid body, wonderful hair and eyes… Only a really very unkind facial expression."

"That's because I am, indeed, occupied with a wicked idea."

"I thought so. You've recently parted with someone, someone's left you…"

"Not left, but dumped. Run away from me. I knew he was a hopeless case, but somehow I loved him. As it turned out, it was simply a scoundrel that I loved. I met him about a month and a half ago in Monte Carlo. I was gambling that evening at the casino. He was standing next to me, gambling as well, following the ball with crazy eyes, and he kept on winning – once he won, twice, three times, four… I kept winning as well, he saw it and suddenly said: 'That'll do! *Assez!*' and he turned to me: '*N'est-ce pas, madame?*'* Laughing, I replied: 'Yes, that'll do!' – 'Ah, you're Russian?' – 'As you see.' – 'Then let's go on the razzle!' I had a look at him – a very shabby man, but elegant in appearance… The rest isn't hard to guess."

"No, it isn't. You felt close over supper, talked endlessly, were amazed when the time came to part…"

"Absolutely correct. And we didn't part, and began squandering the winnings. Lived in Monte Carlo, in Turbie, in Nice, had lunch and dinner in bars on the road between Cannes and Nice – you probably know what that costs! – even stayed at one time in a hotel at Cap d'Antibes, pretending to be rich... But there was less and less money left, trips to Monte Carlo on our last coppers ended in failure... He started disappearing off somewhere and coming back again with money, though what he brought was trifling – a hundred francs or so, fifty... Then he sold my earrings and wedding ring somewhere – I was married once – my gold crucifix..."

"And, of course, he assured you he would be getting back some big debt from somewhere at any time, that he had distinguished and well-to-do friends and acquaintances."

"Yes, precisely so. Who he is, I don't know exactly even now, he avoided speaking clearly and in detail about his past life, and I was somehow inattentive to the fact. Well, the usual past of many émigrés: St Petersburg, service in a brilliant regiment, then the war, revolution, Constantinople... In Paris, thanks to his former connections, he was allegedly getting himself fixed up, and could always do so very nicely, but for the time being – Monte Carlo, or else the permanent possibility, as he said, of short-term borrowing from some titled friends in Nice... I was already becoming despondent, falling into despair, but he only grinned: 'Don't worry, rely on me, I've already taken several *démarches** in Paris, of what kind specifically – that, as they say, is no matter for a woman to worry her head over...'"

"Right, right..."

"Right what?"

And she suddenly turned towards me, her eyes flashing, throwing the cigarette, which had gone out, a long way away:

"All this amuses you?"

I grabbed her hand and gave it a squeeze:

"You should be ashamed of yourself! You know, I'll paint you as Medusa* or Nemesis!"

"Is that the goddess of vengeance?"

"Yes, and a very angry one."

She grinned sadly:

"Nemesis! What sort of Nemesis am I! No, you're a good man... Give me another cigarette. He taught me to smoke... Taught me everything!"

And lighting up, she again began looking into the distance.

"I forgot to tell you as well how surprised I was when I saw where you come to bathe – an entire expedition every day, and to what end? Now I understand: you're seeking solitude."

"Yes…"

The heat of the sun flowed ever thicker, the cicadas on the hot, fragrant pines sawed and scraped ever more insistently and furiously – I sensed how burning hot her black hair, exposed shoulders and legs must be, and said:

"Let's move into the shade, it really is baking, and then finish telling me your sad story."

She came to:

"Yes, let's…"

And we walked around the semicircle of the cove and sat down in light and sultry shade below red crags. I took her hand again and kept it in my own. She failed to notice.

"What is there to finish telling?" she said. "Somehow I no longer want to recall this truly very sad and shameful story. You probably think that I'm an habitual kept woman of one swindler after another. Nothing of the kind. My past's the most ordinary too. My husband was in the Volunteer Army, first with Denikin,* then with Wrangel, and when we rolled up in Paris he became a driver, of course, but he started drinking, and took to it so heavily that he lost his work and turned into a genuine down-and-out. I couldn't possibly have continued living with him any more. I last saw him on Montparnasse, by the doors of the Dominique – you know that little Russian restaurant, of course? Night-time, rain, and he's in down-at-heel shoes, standing around in puddles, he runs up to passers-by, bent double, reaches out his hand for a tip, awkwardly helps, or, to put it better, hinders the people driving up and climbing out of their taxis… I stood for a while, looked at him, went up to him. He recognized me and got frightened, embarrassed – you can't imagine what a splendid, kind, tactful man he is! He stands looking at me in bewilderment: 'Masha, is it you?' He's little, ragged, unshaven, all overgrown with ginger stubble, wet, trembling with cold… I gave him everything I had in my handbag, he grabbed my hand with his own wet, icy little hand, began kissing it and shaking with tears. But what on earth could I do? Only send him a hundred or two hundred francs two or three times a month – I have a milliner's studio in Paris, and I earn quite a decent amount. And I came here to have a holiday, to do some bathing – and so… I'll be leaving for Paris in a few days. To meet with him, give him a slap in the face and the like is a very silly dream, and do you know when I realized it properly? Only now, thanks to you. I started telling the story and realized it…"

"But all the same, how did he come to run away?"

"Ah, that's the whole point, that it really was very low. We'd taken up residence in that very same little pension where you and I have found ourselves neighbours – this was after the hotel at Cap d'Antibes – and one evening we went out, only about ten days ago, to have tea at the casino. Well, of course, there was music, several couples dancing – I was simply no longer able to see it all without repulsion, I'd seen enough! – however, I'm sitting eating the pastries he orders for me and for himself, and he's all the time laughing, strangely somehow – look, look, he says about the musicians, real monkeys, the way they stamp their feet and pull faces! Then he opens up an empty cigarette case, calls a chasseur and orders him to bring some English cigarettes, he brings them, and he absent-mindedly says *merci*, I'll pay you after tea, then gazes at his fingernails and says to me: 'What dreadful hands! I'll go and wash them…' He gets up and goes…"

"And doesn't come back again."

"No. And I sit and wait. I wait ten minutes, twenty, half an hour, an hour… Can you imagine it?"

"I can."

I could imagine it very clearly: they sit at the tea table, looking in silence, thinking in different ways about their loathsome situation… Beyond the panes of the large windows the sky is drawing towards evening, and there is the gloss, the calm of the sea and the darkening fronds of the palms are hanging there; the musicians, as if inanimate, are stamping their feet on the floor, blowing into their instruments, beating on metal cymbals, the men shuffling and swaying in time with them are pressing against their ladies, as though pushing them towards a clearly defined objective. A chap in leggings and some semblance of a green dress uniform doffs his cap deferentially and hands him a packet of High Life…

"Well and so? You're sitting…"

"I'm sitting, feeling that I'm done for. The musicians have gone, the room has emptied, the electric light has come on…"

"The windows have turned blue…"

"Yes, and all the time I can't get up from my seat: what am I to do, how am I to escape? In my handbag there's only six francs and some loose change!"

"And he had, indeed, gone to the lavatory, done what he needed to there, thinking about his cheating life, then he'd done himself up and run on tiptoe down the corridors to the other exit and slipped out into the street… Good God, think who it was you loved! Look for him, take revenge on him? What for? You're not a little girl, you should have seen what he was and the situation you were in. Why on earth did you continue that life, dreadful in every sense?"

She was silent, then twitched a shoulder:

"Who was it I loved? I don't know. There was, as they say, a need for love, which I've never really experienced… As a man, he gave me nothing, and couldn't have, he'd already lost his manly capabilities long before… Should I have seen what he was and the situation I was in? Of course, I should have, but I didn't want to see, to think – for the first time in my life I was living that sort of life, that celebration of vice, all its pleasures, I was living in a kind of delusion. Why did I want to meet him somewhere and somehow take revenge on him? Again a delusion, an *idée fixe*. Did I not sense that, apart from a vile and pitiful scene, I couldn't achieve anything? But you say: what for? Well, for the fact that it's thanks to him, after all, that I fell so low, lived that cheating life, and most of all, for the horror, the shame that I experienced that evening at the casino when he ran away out of the toilet! When, beside myself, I told some sort of lie at the casino's cash desk, trying to extricate myself, imploring them to take my handbag as security until the next day – and when they wouldn't take it, and scornfully let me off paying for the tea and the pastries, and the English cigarettes! I sent a telegram to Paris, two days later received a thousand francs, went to the casino – they took the money there without looking at me, even gave me a receipt… Oh, my dear, I'm no Medusa, I'm simply a woman, and, what's more, a very sensitive, lonely, unhappy one, but don't get me wrong – even a chicken has a heart, you know! I've simply been ill all these days since that damned evening. And it was simply God Himself that sent you to me, I've suddenly come to my senses somehow… Let go of my hand, it's time to get dressed, there'll be the train from Saint-Raphaël soon…"

"To hell with it," I said. "Better look around at these red cliffs, the green cove, the gnarled pines, listen to that heavenly scraping. We'll come here together from now on. Yes?"

"Yes."

"And we'll leave for Paris together too."

"Yes."

"And what happens thereafter isn't worth thinking about."

"No, no."

"May I kiss your hand?"

"Yes, yes…"

3rd June 1944

The Swing

O N A SUMMER'S EVENING he was sitting in the drawing room tinkling on the fortepiano, when he heard her footsteps on the balcony, struck the keys wildly and started shouting and singing out of tune:

"I envy not the gods and stars,
I envy not the regal tsars
When languid eyes do I remark,
A slender figure, plaits so dark!"*

She came in wearing a blue sarafan, with two long, dark plaits down her back, a coral necklace, and her blue eyes smiling in her suntanned face:
"Is that all about me? And the aria is of your own composition?"
"Yes!"
And again he struck and shouted:
"I envy not the gods and stars..."
"My, what an ear you've got!"
"But then I am a renowned painter. And as handsome as Leonid Andreyev. I've come to see you to your cost!"
"He's frightening, but I'm not afraid, said Tolstoy of your Andreyev."*
"We'll see, we'll see!"
"And what about Granddad's crutch?"
"Granddad, hero of Sebastopol* though he might be, is only menacing in appearance. We'll run away, get married, then throw ourselves at his feet – he'll burst into tears and forgive us..."
In the twilight, before supper, when aromatic rissoles and onions were being fried in the kitchen and the air was freshening in the dewy park, they stood opposite one another, flying on the swing at the end of the avenue of trees, with the rings screeching and the wind blowing, puffing out the hem of her skirt. Pulling on the ropes and adding to the swinging of the board, he made frightening eyes, and she, red in the face, watched fixedly, senselessly and joyously.

"Halloo! There's the first star and the new moon, and the sky above the lake is ever so green – look, painter, what a slim little sickle! Moon, moon, golden horns...* Oh dear, we're going to fall!"

Flying down from a height and jumping off onto the ground, they sat down on the board, gazing at one another and trying to contain their agitated breathing.

"Well, then? I told you!"

"Told me what?"

"You're already in love with me."

"Perhaps... Hang on, they're calling us to supper... Halloo, we're coming, we're coming!"

"Wait a minute. The first star, the new moon, the green sky, the smell of the dew, the smell from the kitchen – doubtless my favourite rissoles in sour cream again! – and blue eyes and a beautiful, happy face..."

"Yes, I don't think there'll ever in my life be an evening happier than this..."

"Dante said of Beatrice: 'In her eyes is the beginning of love, and the end is in the lips.'* And so?" he said, taking her hand.

She closed her eyes, bending towards him with her head lowered. He put an arm around her shoulders with their soft plaits and lifted her face:

"Is the end in the lips?"

"Yes..."

As they walked up the avenue, he looked where he was putting his feet:

"What are we to do now? Go to Granddad, fall to our knees and ask for his blessing? But what sort of a husband am I?"

"No, no, anything but that."

"Well, what then?"

"I don't know. Let there just be what there is... It won't get any better."

10th April 1945

Pure Monday*

THE GREY WINTER'S DAY in Moscow was darkening, the gas was light-ing up coldly in the streetlamps, the windows of the shops were warmly lit – and Moscow's evening life, freeing itself from the busi-ness of the day, was heating up: thicker and faster raced the cab men's sledges, more heavily thundered the overcrowded diving trams – in the twilight, green stars could already be seen sprinkling from the wires with a hiss – more animated was the haste of the dull black passers-by along the snowy pavements. Every evening at this hour I was sped by my coachman's extending trotter from the Red Gates to the Church of Christ the Saviour: she lived opposite; each evening I took her to dinner at the Prague, the Hermitage, the Metropole, after dinner to theatres, concerts, and then to the Yar, the Strelna... How it was all going to end, I did not know and tried not to think, I tried not to think it through: it was useless – just as was talking to her about it, for she had deflected conver-sations about our future once and for all; she was enigmatic, incompre-hensible to me, and our relationship was a strange one too – we were still not fully intimate – and all this kept me in endless unresolved tension, in agonizing expectation – and at the same time I was ineffably happy with every hour spent beside her.

She was a student for some reason on women's courses; she attended quite rarely, but did attend. I asked her once: "Why?" She shrugged a shoulder: "Why does anything get done in the world? Do we really understand anything about our actions? Besides, I'm interested in history..." She lived alone – her widower father, an enlightened man from a distinguished merchant family, lived in retirement in Tver, and, like all such merchants, collected something. For the sake of the view of Moscow she rented a corner apartment on the fourth floor in a building opposite Christ the Saviour, only two rooms, but spacious and well-furnished ones. A lot of space in the first was taken by a wide Turkish couch, there was an expensive piano on which she was forever learning the slow, somnambularly beautiful opening of 'The Moonlight Sonata'* – just the opening alone – on the piano and on the looking-glass table bloomed showy flowers in cut-glass vases – on my orders she had fresh ones delivered every Saturday, and when I arrived on a Saturday evening, lying on the couch, above which for some reason hung a portrait of a bare-footed Tolstoy,* she would unhurriedly extend a hand for me to kiss, and absent-mindedly say "Thank you for the flowers..." I brought her boxes of chocolates, new books – Hofmannsthal, Schnitzler, Tetmayer,* Przybyszewski – and got still that same "thank you" and the extended warm hand, sometimes an order to sit down beside the couch without removing my coat. "It's not clear why," she would say thoughtfully, stroking my beaver collar, "but I don't think anything can be better than the smell of wintry air with which you go into a room from outdoors..." It looked as if she needed nothing: not the flowers, nor the books, nor the dinners, nor the theatres, nor the suppers out of town; although there were, nonetheless, some flowers she liked and some she did not, all the books that I brought her she always read, she would eat a whole box of chocolates in a day, at dinner and supper ate no less than me, being fond of open-topped pasties with burbot soup and pink hazel grouse in well-baked sour cream, and she would sometimes say: "I don't understand how people don't get fed up with having dinner and supper every day, all their lives" – yet she herself had both dinner and supper with a Muscovite's understanding of the matter. Her only obvious weakness was good clothing, velvet, silks, expensive fur...

We were both rich, healthy, young and so good-looking that in restaurants and at concerts people's gazes followed us. Being by birth from the province of Penza, I was then handsome, with, for some reason, southern, passionate good looks; I was even "indecently handsome", as I was once told by a renowned actor, a monstrously fat man, a great glutton and a clever fellow –"the devil knows who you are, some kind of Sicilian," he said sleepily – and my character was southern too, lively, constantly ready with a happy smile, a gentle joke. And she had a beauty that was somehow Indian, Persian: a swarthily amber face, magnificent hair, somewhat ominous in its dense blackness, eyebrows that gleamed softly like black sable fur, eyes as black as velvet coal; a captivating mouth with its velvety crimson lips was set off by dark down; when going out, she would most often put on a garnet-coloured velvet dress and similar shoes with gold buckles (whereas she went to her courses as a demure student and had lunch for thirty kopeks at a vegetarian canteen on the Arbat), and as much as I was inclined to garrulity, to simple-hearted cheerfulness, so was she most often taciturn: she was forever thinking about something, forever as though delving into something mentally; lying on the couch with a book in her hands, she would often lower it and gaze questioningly into space. I saw this when I sometimes dropped in on her in the daytime too, because for three or four days each month she would not leave home at all, she would lie and read, making me too sit down in the armchair beside the couch and read in silence.

"You're terribly talkative and restless," she said, "let me read to the end of the chapter..."

"If I weren't talkative and restless, perhaps I would never have got to know you," I replied, thus reminding her of our meeting: one day in December, having turned up at the Arts Group to a lecture by Andrei Bely,* who had sung it while running around and dancing on the stage, I had been fidgeting and chuckling so much that she, who had found herself by chance in the seat next to mine and had at first looked at me with a certain bewilderment, had finally burst out laughing as well, and I had turned to her merrily at once.

"Quite so," she said, "but be quiet for a little all the same, read something, have a smoke..."

"I can't be quiet! You can't imagine all the strength of my love for you! You don't love me!"

"I *can* imagine. And as for my love, you know very well that, apart from my father and you, I have no one in the world. In any event, you are my first and last. Is that too little for you? But enough about that. Reading's impossible with you here, let's have tea..."

And I would get up, boil the water in the electric kettle on the little table at the end of the couch, take cups and saucers from the walnut cabinet that stood in the corner behind the table, saying whatever came into my head:

"Have you finished reading *The Fiery Angel*?"*

"I've finished looking at it. It's so high flown I'm ashamed to read it."

"And why did you leave Shalyapin's concert all of a sudden yesterday?"

"He was excessively flamboyant. And then in general I don't like yellow-haired Rus."

"Everything displeases you!"

"Yes, a lot does..."

"A strange love!" I thought, and while the water was coming to the boil, I stood looking out of the window. The room smelt of flowers and was becoming associated for me with their smell; outside one window, low in the distance there lay the huge picture of the snowy, blue-grey Moscow beyond the river; out of the other, further to the left, a part of the Kremlin was visible, and opposite, excessively close somehow, the too new white hulk of Christ the Saviour, in the gold dome of which the jackdaws that eternally circled around it were reflected in bluish spots... "A strange city!" I said to myself, thinking about Hunters' Row, about Iverskaya, about St Basil's. "St Basil's – and the Saviour in the Forest, the Italian cathedrals – and there's something Kyrgyz about the points of the towers on the Kremlin walls..."

Arriving at twilight, I sometimes found her on the couch in nothing but a sable-trimmed silk caftan – "the legacy of my Astrakhan grandmother," she said – and I would sit beside her in the semi-darkness without lighting a light, kissing her hands, her feet and her body, which was astonishing in its smoothness... And she did not resist against a thing, but all in silence. I was continually seeking her hot lips – and she gave them, her breathing already spasmodic, but all in silence. And when she sensed that I no longer had the power to control myself, she would push me away, sit up and, without raising her voice, ask me to put on the light, then go off into the bedroom. I would put it on, sit down on the revolving stool beside the piano and gradually come to my senses, cooling after the hot intoxicant. A quarter of an hour later she would emerge from the bedroom dressed, ready to go out, calm and natural, as though nothing had happened beforehand:

"Where to today? The Metropole, perhaps?"

And again all evening we spoke about extraneous things. Soon after we became close, she said to me when I raised the subject of marriage:

"No, I'm not suited to being a wife. I'm not, I'm not..."

This did not make me lose hope – "we'll see!" I said to myself, in the hope of a change in her decision with time, and I did not raise the subject of marriage any more. Our incomplete intimacy seemed to me sometimes unbearable, but here too – what was left me but reliance on time? One day, sitting beside her in that evening darkness and quiet, I took my head in my hands:

"No, it's beyond my strength! And to what end, why do you have to torture me and yourself so cruelly?"

She remained silent.

"No, all the same, this isn't love, it isn't love..."

She responded evenly out of the darkness:

"Maybe. But who knows what love is?"

"I do, I know!" I exclaimed. "And I'm going to wait until you too find out what love, what happiness is!"

"Happiness, happiness... 'Our happiness, old pal, is like water in a dragnet: you pull on it – and it fills out, but you pull it out – and there's nothing there.'"

"What's that?"

"That's what Platon Karatayev said to Pierre."*

I waved a hand:

"Oh, to hell with it, that oriental wisdom!"

And again all evening I spoke only about the extraneous – the Arts Theatre's* new production, Andreyev's new story... Again it was simply enough for me that here I was, first sitting up close to her, gathering speed in a flying sledge, holding her in the smooth fur of her coat, and then entering a crowded restaurant dining room with her to the accompaniment of the march from *Aida*,* eating and drinking next to her, hearing her slow voice, gazing at the lips I had been kissing an hour before – yes, kissing, I said to myself, gazing at them in ecstatic gratitude, at the dark down above them, at the garnet-coloured velvet of her dress, at the slope of her shoulders and the oval of her breasts, smelling the slightly heady scent of her hair, thinking: "Moscow, Astrakhan, Persia, India!" In the out-of-town restaurants, towards the end of supper, when it was becoming noisier and noisier all around in the tobacco smoke, she, smoking and getting tipsy as well, sometimes led me into a private room and asked me to invite the gypsies in, and in they would come, deliberately noisy and boisterous: ahead of the choir, with a guitar on a blue ribbon over his shoulder, an old gypsy in a *kazakin** with galloons, with the unpleasant blue-grey face of a drowned man, with a head as bare as an iron ball, and behind him the female leader of the choir with a low forehead beneath a tar-black fringe... She listened to the songs with a languorous, strange smile... At three, at four o'clock in the morning I took her home, and on the porch, shutting my eyes in happiness, I kissed the wet fur of her collar and then, in a sort of ecstatic despair, I was flying to the Red Gates. And tomorrow and the day after tomorrow it will still be the same, I thought, still the same torment and still the same happiness... Oh well – happiness all the same, great happiness!

So passed January, February, Shrovetide came and went. On the Sunday of Forgiveness she ordered me to come to her after four o'clock in the afternoon. I arrived, and she met me already dressed, wearing a short astrakhan fur coat, an astrakhan fur hat and black felt overshoes.

"All black!" I said, going in, as always, joyously.

Her eyes were affectionate and quiet:

"It's already Pure Monday tomorrow, you know," she replied, taking her hand out of her astrakhan fur muff and giving it to me in a black kid glove. "'O Lord and Master of my life...'* Do you want to go to the New Maiden Convent?"

I was surprised, but hastened to say:

"Yes, I do!"

"Why always taverns and more taverns?" she added. "Now yesterday morning I was at the Rogozhskoye Cemetery."

I was even more surprised:

"At a cemetery? Why? Is that the renowned schismatics' one?"

"Yes, it's the schismatics'.* Pre-Petrine Rus! They were burying their archbishop. And just imagine: the coffin's an oak log, like in ancient times, the gold brocade looks like hammered metal, the face of the deceased is covered with a white communion cloth embroidered with a large black ornamental design – beauty and dread. And there are deacons by the coffin with images of angels – *ripidy*, and triple candlesticks – *trikiry*..."

"How do you know all this? *Ripidy*, *trikiry*!"

"It's just that you don't know me."

"I didn't know you were so religious."

"It's not being religious. I don't know what it is... But, for example, I do often go in the mornings or the evenings, when you're not dragging me around to restaurants, to the Kremlin cathedrals, yet you don't even suspect it... And so: the deacons – and what deacons! Peresvet and Oslyabya!* And in the two choirs, two sets of singers, all Peresvets as well: tall, mighty, all in long black caftans, singing, responding to one another – first one choir, then the other – and all in unison and not from sheet music, but from 'neumes'.* And the inside of the grave was lined with shiny fir branches, and outside there's the frost, sunshine, dazzling snow... But no, you don't understand it! Let's go..."

The evening was peaceful and sunny, with hoar frost on the trees; on the blood- and brick-red walls of the Convent the jackdaws, looking like nuns, were chattering in the quietness, the chimes kept on playing, thin and sad, in the bell tower. Crunching across the snow in the quietness, we entered the gates and went along snowy paths through the cemetery – the sun had only just gone down, it was still perfectly light, frost-covered boughs were wonderfully silhouetted like grey coral against the gold enamel of the sunset, and glimmering mysteriously around us were the tranquil, mournful lights of a scattering of inextinguishable icon lamps above the graves. I walked behind her and gazed with tenderness at her little track, at the tiny stars left on the snow by her new black overshoes – and sensing this, she suddenly turned around:

"Truly, how you do love me!" she said with quiet bewilderment, shaking her head.

We stood for a while beside the graves of Ertel and Chekhov.* Keeping her hands inside her lowered muff, she gazed for a long time at Chekhov's gravestone, then shrugged a shoulder:

"What a revolting mixture of the sugary Russian style and the Arts Theatre!"

It had begun to get dark, and it was freezing as we slowly walked out of the gates, beside which my Fyodor was obediently sitting on his box.

"Let's drive around a little more," she said, "then we'll go to Yegorov's to eat the last pancakes... Only not too quick, Fyodor – all right?"

"No, ma'am."

"Somewhere on Ordynka there's a house where Griboyedov used to live.* Let's go and look for it..."

And for some reason we went to Ordynka, drove for a long time down lanes of some sort amid gardens, and were in Griboyedov Lane, but who on earth could have shown us which house Griboyedov used to live in – there was not a single passer-by, and would Griboyedov have mattered to anyone? It had already been dark for a long time, and the lighted windows were pink behind the frost-covered trees...

"The Convent of Saints Martha and Mary is here too," she said.

I laughed:

"Again to a convent?"

"No, I was just saying…"

The lower floor of Yegorov's tavern in Hunters' Row was full of shaggy-haired, heavily clad cab men cutting up piles of pancakes with excessive amounts of butter and sour cream poured over them, and it was as steamy as a bathhouse. In the upper rooms, very warm as well with their low ceilings, old-fashioned merchants were washing down fiery pancakes and unpressed caviar with iced champagne. We went through into the second room where, in a corner, an icon lamp was burning in front of the black board of an icon of the Three-handed Madonna, and we sat down at a long table on a black leather couch… The down on her upper lip was covered in frost, the amber of her cheeks was slightly pink, the blackness of her iris had merged completely with the pupil – I could not tear my ecstatic eyes off her face. And taking a handkerchief out of her fragrant muff, she said:

"Splendid! Downstairs wild muzhiks, and here – pancakes and champagne, and a Three-handed Madonna. Three hands! I mean, this is India!* You're a gentleman, you can't understand all this Moscow business the way I can."

"I can, I can!" I replied. "And let's order a 'mightful' dinner!"

"What's that, 'mightful'?"

"It means mighty. How come you don't know that? 'The Speech of Gyurgi'…"

"How splendid! Gyurgi!"

"Yes, Prince Yuri Dolgoruky. 'The Speech of Gyurgi to Svyatoslav, Prince Seversky':* 'Come to me, brother, in Muscovy, and order a mightful dinner set out'."

"How splendid. And it's only in some northern monasteries that Rus still remains. And in church singing too. I went recently to the Conception Monastery – you can't imagine how wonderfully the canticles are sung there! And in the Miracle Monastery even better. I kept on going there in Holy Week last year. Ah, how splendid it was! Puddles everywhere, the air already mild, gentleness, sadness in my soul somehow, and all the time this sense of the Motherland, its antiquity… All the doors in the cathedral are open, the common people going in and coming out all day, services all day… Oh, I'll go away somewhere and enter a convent, the most remote one, in Vologda, Vyatsk!"

I wanted to say that in that case I would go away too, or would murder someone, so that I would be sent to Sakhalin, and I lit a cigarette, forgetting myself in my agitation, but a waiter in white trousers and a white shirt, belted with a raspberry-coloured braid, came up and deferentially reminded me:

"Excuse me, sir, smoking isn't allowed here..."

And immediately, being particularly obsequious, he started his patter:

"What would you like with your pancakes? Some home-made herb water? Some nice caviar, salmon? To go with the fish soup we have some uncommonly good sherry, and with the cod..."

"Some sherry with the cod too," she added, delighting me with the friendly loquacity that was not deserting her all evening. And I was listening absent-mindedly now to what she said next. But she spoke with a quiet light in her eyes:

"I love the Russian chronicles and Russian legends so much that I keep rereading the bits I especially like until I've learnt them off by heart. 'There was in the Russian land a town, Murom by name, and in it there ruled a devout prince, Pavel by name. And the Devil introduced a flying serpent to his wife for lechery. And this serpent would come to her in human essence, most beautiful...'"

Joking, I made frightened eyes:

"Oh dear, how awful!"

Without listening, she continued:

"That was the way God tested her. 'And when the time came for her virtuous demise, this Prince and Princess begged God to let them stand before Him in a single day. And they agreed to be buried in a single coffin. And they ordered two coffin beds to be hewn out in a single stone. And at one and the same time too, they clothed themselves in monastic garments...'"*

And again my absent-mindedness gave way to surprise and even alarm – what is the matter with her today?

And then on this evening, when I had taken her home not at all at the usual time, but before eleven o'clock, after saying goodbye to me on the porch, she suddenly detained me as I was already getting into the sledge:

"Wait. Come over tomorrow evening no earlier than ten. Tomorrow it's the Arts Theatre's actors' party."

"So what?" I asked. "Do you want to go to this actors' party?"

"Yes."

"But you said you didn't know anything more vulgar than these parties!"

"And I don't now either. And all the same I want to go."

Mentally I shook my head – all whims, Muscovite whims! – and responded heartily in English:

"All right!"

The next day, at ten o'clock in the evening, having gone up in the lift to her door, I opened it with my key, and did not immediately go in from the dark hallway: it was unusually light beyond it, everything was lit – the chandeliers, the candelabra on the sides of the mirror and the tall lamp beneath a light shade behind the head of the couch – and the piano was ringing out with the opening of 'The Moonlight Sonata', ever rising, ringing out ever more agonizingly, invitingly, the further it went, in its somnambularly blissful sadness. I shut the hall door with a bang – the sounds broke off, the rustling of a dress was heard. I went in – she was standing, erect and somewhat theatrical beside the piano, in a black velvet dress which made her slimmer, she was brilliant in its smartness, in the festive arrangement of her jet-black hair, in the swarthy amber of her bare arms and shoulders and the delicate, plump beginnings of her breasts, in the gleaming of the diamond earrings hanging down her lightly powdered cheeks, in the charcoal velvet of her eyes and the velvety purple of her lips. On her temples, black glossy locks curved down in coils towards her eyes, lending her the appearance of an oriental beauty from a traditional popular print.

"Now if I were a singer and sang on the stage," she said, gazing at my perplexed face, "I'd respond to applause with a friendly smile and slight bows to the right and to the left, upwards and to the stalls, and would imperceptibly but carefully push my train aside with my foot, so as not to step on it…"

At the party she smoked a lot and continually sipped champagne, looking intently at the actors who, with cheery cries and refrains, were imitating something ostensibly Parisian: at big Stanislavsky, with white hair and black eyebrows, and thickset Moskvin, with a pince-nez on his trough-like face, who, with deliberate seriousness and assiduity, both leant back and did a wild cancan to the raucous laughter of the audience. We were approached by Kachalov,* pale from drink, with a wine glass in his hand and much sweat on his forehead, onto which there hung a shock of his White Russian hair. Kachalov raised his glass and, gazing at her with affected gloomy greed, said in his deep actor's voice:

"Maiden Queen, Princess of Shamakha,* your health!"

And she smiled slowly and clinked glasses with him. He took her hand, drunkenly bent down to it and almost lost his footing. He righted himself and, gritting his teeth, glanced at me:

"And who's this handsome fellow? I hate him!"

Then a barrel organ began wheezing, whistling and thundering, jumping up and down and stamping in a polka – and flying and sliding up to us came little, smiling Sulerzhitsky,* who was eternally in a hurry; he bent over, imitating the gallantry of a shopkeeper, and hurriedly mumbled:

"Permit me to engage you for the *polka tremblant*..."

And smiling, she rose and, with a brief tapping of her foot, with her earrings, her blackness and her bare arms and shoulders gleaming, she deftly set off with him between the tables, accompanied by enraptured gazes and clapping, while he, with his head thrown back, cried like a goat:

"Let's go, let's go, come on quickly,
And I'll dance the polka with you!"

She rose to go, with her eyes half-closed, after two o'clock in the morning. When we had put our coats on, she looked at my beaver hat, stroked my beaver collar, and set off towards the exit, saying, perhaps as a joke, perhaps seriously:

"Handsome, of course. What Kachalov said was true... 'A serpent in human essence, most beautiful'..."

She was silent as we drove, inclining her head against the bright, moonlit blizzard flying towards us. The full moon was diving in clouds above the Kremlin – "a kind of luminous skull," she said. On the Spasskaya Tower the clock struck three – she also said:

"What an ancient sound, a thing of tin and cast iron. And in the same way, with the same sound, it struck three in the morning in the fifteenth century too. And the chimes in Florence are just the same, they reminded me of Moscow there..."

When Fyodor drew up by the porch, she ordered lifelessly:

"Let him go…"

Staggered – she had never allowed me up to her apartment at night – I said in perplexity:

"Fyodor, I'll return on foot…"

And in silence we were drawn up in the lift and went into the nocturnal warmth and quiet of the apartment with the tapping of little mallets in the radiators. I helped her off with her fur coat, slippery with snow, and she threw her wet downy shawl off her hair into my arms and went quickly into the bedroom with her silk underskirt rustling. I took off my things, and with my heart stopping, as if above an abyss, I sat down on the Turkish couch. Her footsteps could be heard beyond the open doors of the illuminated bedroom, and also the way she pulled her dress off over her head, catching it on her hairpins… I got up and approached the doors: she was standing with her back to me in front of the cheval glass wearing nothing but swansdown slippers, brushing out with a tortoiseshell comb the black threads of the long hair hanging down beside her face.

"And he was always saying I didn't think about him enough," she said, tossing the comb onto the dressing table, and, throwing her hair behind her back, she turned towards me: "No, I was…"

At dawn I felt her moving. I opened my eyes – she was staring at me. I raised myself a little from the warmth of the bed and her body, and she leant towards me, saying quietly and evenly:

"I'm leaving this evening for Tver. Whether it's for long, God alone knows…"

And she pressed her cheek against mine – I could feel her wet eyelash blinking:

"I'll write everything down as soon as I arrive. I'll write everything about the future. I'm sorry, leave me now, I'm very tired…"

And she lay down on the pillow.

I dressed cautiously, timidly kissed her hair, and went on tiptoe out onto the staircase, which was already lightening with a pale light. I went on foot over the young, sticky snow – the blizzard was over now, all was calm, and it was already possible to see a long way down the streets, and there was the smell both of snow and from the bakeries. I walked as far as the Iverskaya Chapel, the interior of which was glowing hotly and shining with whole bonfires of candles, I knelt down in the crowd of old women and beggars on the trampled snow, and took off my hat... Someone touched me on the shoulder – I looked: a very unfortunate little old woman was gazing at me and pulling a face from tears of pity:

"Ah, don't grieve, don't grieve so! It's a sin, a sin!"

The letter I received two weeks or so later was short – a gentle but firm request not to expect her any more, not to try and find or see her: "I shan't return to Moscow, for the time being I'm going to become a novice, and later I may decide to take the veil... God grant you the strength not to reply to me – it's no use extending and increasing our torment..."

I carried out her request. And I disappeared for a long time in the filthiest taverns, taking to drink and sinking lower and lower in every possible way. Then I began, little by little, to set myself to rights – indifferently, hopelessly... Almost two years passed after that Pure Monday...

In 1914, approaching New Year, there was a quiet, sunny evening just like that unforgettable one. I left the house, took a cab and drove to the Kremlin. There I went into the empty Archangel Cathedral and stood for a long time in its gloom without praying, gazing at the feeble glimmering of the old gold of the iconostasis and the tombstones of the Muscovite Tsars – I stood as though waiting for something in that special quietness of an empty church, when you are afraid even to sigh in it. Leaving the cathedral, I ordered the cab man to go to Ordynka, and I rode at a walk, as then, down dark lanes among gardens, with the windows lit beneath the trees, drove down Griboyedov Lane – and kept on crying and crying...

On Ordynka I stopped the cab man by the gates of the Convent of Sts Martha and Mary: there in the courtyard were the black shapes of carriages, the open doors of the small, illuminated church could be seen, and from the doors carried the mournful and emotional singing of a female choir. For some reason I felt a desire to go inside without fail. The yardman by the gates blocked my path, begging gently, imploringly:

"You can't, sir, you can't!"

"What do you mean, I can't? I can't go into the church?"

"You can, sir, of course you can – only for God's sake, I beg you, don't go, Grand Duchess Yel'zavet' Fyod'rovna and Grand Duke 'Mitry Pa'lych* are there now..."

I thrust a rouble upon him – he heaved a grief-stricken sigh and let me pass. But no sooner had I entered the courtyard than icons and banners appeared, as they were carried out from the church, and behind them the Grand Duchess in something long and white, thin-faced, wearing a white veil with an embroidered gold cross on the forehead, tall, walking slowly, devoutly, with eyes lowered, with a large candle in her hand, and behind her stretched just as white a line of singing nuns or nurses, with the lights of candles by their faces – I do not know who they were or where they were going. For some reason I looked at them very carefully. And then one of those walking in the middle suddenly raised her head, which was covered with a white veil, and, blocking out the candle with her hand, she directed the gaze of her dark eyes into the darkness, as though straight at me... What could she have seen in the darkness, how could she have sensed my presence? I turned away and quietly went out of the gates.

12th May 1944

The Chapel

A HOT SUMMER'S DAY, in the fields, behind the garden of an old country estate, a long-neglected graveyard – hummocks covered in tall flowers and grasses and a solitary, ramshackle, brick-built chapel, all wildly overgrown with flowers and grasses, nettles and alliums. Children from the estate, squatting beside the chapel, are looking in with sharp eyes through a long and narrow broken window at ground level. Nothing can be seen there, there's only a cold draught coming from it. Everywhere else it's light and hot, but there it's dark and cold: there in iron boxes lie granddads and grannies of some sort, and some man who shot himself too. It's all very interesting and amazing: we here have the sunshine, flowers, grasses, flies, bumblebees and butterflies, we can play and run about, it's scary for us, yet fun too, squatting down, but they're always lying there in the darkness, like at night-time, in thick and cold iron boxes; the granddads and grannies are all old, but the man is still young…

"But why did he shoot himself?"

"He was very much in love, and when very much in love, they always shoot themselves…"

In the blue sea of the sky, there are beautiful white clouds in places like islands, and the warm wind from the fields bears the sweet scent of flowering rye. And the hotter and more joyously the sun burns, the colder the draught from the dark, from the window.

2nd July 1944

Note on the Text

This translation of *Dark Avenues* has been made from the last Russian edition published in Bunin's lifetime, *Temnye allei* (Paris, 1946). Bunin continued to work on the stories in the years leading up to his death, but there is no definitive text incorporating all the amendments he might have made to them in any subsequent edition. It is known, however, that he did intend to add two stories to the selection published in 1946, and these are represented here in the Appendix. The translations have again been made from the last Russian edition published in the writer's lifetime, *Vesnoi, v ludee. Roza Ierikhona* (New York, 1953), pp. 13–18 and 24–32.

Notes

p. 5, *tarantass*: A large, springless carriage.

p. 5, *Nicholas I's… Alexander II*: Russian Emperors of the nineteenth century: Nicholas I (*b*.1796) ruled 1825–55 and was succeeded by his son Alexander II (*b*.1818), who ruled until his assassination in 1881.

p. 7, *Thou shalt remember… away*: "Because thou shalt forget thy misery, and remember it as waters that pass away." Job 11:16.

p. 9, *All round… dark limes stood*: A slightly inaccurate quotation from the poem 'An Ordinary Tale' (1842) by Nikolai Platonovich Ogaryov (1813–77): "all round" should be "nearby".

p. 12, *Narzan*: Mineral water from the Caucasus.

p. 17, *red corners*: The name given to the corner of a room where the icons hang.

p. 18, *Hear my prayer… my fathers were*: Psalms 39:12 (slightly inaccurate: the phrase "on the earth" has been added).

p. 18, *Say unto God… thy works*: Psalms 66:3.

p. 18, *He that dwelleth… trample under foot*: Psalms 91:1, 13.

p. 18, *For every beast… on a thousand hills*: Psalms 50:10 (slightly inaccurate: the word "his" replacing "mine").

p. 19 *Tiger-Euphrates*: The Russian word for the river Tigris is the same as the word for "tiger".

p. 21, *Howls the cold wind… the highway*: A slightly inaccurate quotation from a poem by Alexei Fyodorovich Merzlyakov (1778–1830),

"Black of brow and black of eye" (1803), set to music by D.N. Kashin (1769–1841).

p. 21, *in the time of the great Tsarina*: Catherine the Great (1729–96) ruled Russia after her husband, Peter III, was deposed and killed in 1762.

p. 22, *Love's fires rage... all round the globe*: The closing lines of the poem 'If young women, mistresses' (published 1781) by Alexander Petrovich Sumarokov (1717–77).

p. 25, *kosovorotka and poddyovka*: A Russian peasant-style shirt fastened at the side and a light, tight-fitting, long-waisted coat respectively.

p. 32, *Shor's concert*: David Solomonovich Shor (1867–1942), pianist and Professor at the Moscow Conservatoire.

p. 37, *in Baty's time*: Baty Khan (1205–55) was the grandson of Genghis Khan and, like him, leader of the Golden Horde.

p. 42, *Requiem æternam... luceat eis*: From the Requiem Mass: "Eternal rest grant unto them, O Lord, and let perpetual light shine upon them" (Latin).

p. 42, *Alexei Mikhailovich*: Born in 1629, the second Romanov Tsar ruled Russia from 1645 until his death in 1676.

p. 46, *the Stroganov School of Painting*: The School was founded in 1825 by Baron Sergei Grigoryevich Stroganov (1794–1882), and was known after 1860 as the Stroganov School for Technical Drawing, specializing in teaching the applied and decorative arts.

p. 52, *The Cornfield*: A popular weekly illustrated journal published by A.F. Marx between 1870 and 1918.

p. 54, *Amata... nulla*: From Poem 8 by Gaius Valerius Catullus (c.84–c.54 BC): "She who was loved by me as none will ever be loved" (Latin).

p. 57, *Along the Roadway*: A well-known Russian folk song.

p. 59, *a new book by Averchenko*: Arkady Timofeyevich Averchenko (1881–1925), a Russian humorist, author of short stories, plays and pamphlets.

p. 60, *my Antigone... like Oedipus:* In Greek myth, Antigone was the daughter of Oedipus, King of Thebes, who blinded himself after unwittingly killing his own father; the faithful daughter accompanied him into exile.

p. 60, *my uncle, the most honest fellow*: The opening line of the novel in verse *Eugene Onegin* (1823–31) by Alexander Sergeyevich Pushkin

(1799–1837), where the eponymous hero is thinking of the dull life awaiting him as he travels to his sick uncle's rural estate.

p. 61, *Alexander*: This could be Alexander II or his son, Alexander III (1845–94), who ruled Russia after his father's assassination in 1881.

p. 62, *the Russo-Japanese War*: The Russo-Japanese War of 1904–05.

p. 62, *the white and red wines of Prince Golitsyn*: Prince Lev Sergeyevich Golitsyn (1845–1915) owned a fine winery in the Crimea.

p. 64, *Maupassant… Octave Mirbeau*: Guy de Maupassant (1850–93), French novelist and short story writer; Octave Mirbeau (1850–1917), radical French journalist, novelist and dramatist.

p. 75, *the Little Russian way*: Little Russia is a now archaic alternative name for Ukraine.

p. 78, *Thus little children… across the river*: An inaccurate quotation from the 'Circassian Song' in Alexander Pushkin's narrative poem *A Prisoner in the Caucasus* (1822).

p. 79, *kalach*: A round, white, wheatmeal loaf.

p. 87, *Both of resin… the shady wood*: From the poem 'Ilya Muromets' (1871) by Alexei Konstantinovich Tolstoy (1817–75).

p. 101, *starosta*: A village headman.

p. 117, *Rien n'est… une femme de bien*: "Nothing is more difficult than recognizing a good melon and a good woman" (French).

p. 119, *L'eau gâte… l'âme*: "Water spoils wine as the cart does the road and woman does the soul" (French).

p. 119, *ami*: "Lover" (French).

p. 119, *Caviar rouge… chachlyks*: "Red caviar, Russian salad… Two shashliks…" (French).

p. 119, *rassolnik*: A soup with pickled cucumbers.

p. 119, *Grand Duke Alexander Mikhailovich's*: A grandson (1866–1933) of Nicholas I who made a career in the Russian navy.

p. 121, *C'est moi… remercie*: "It's I who must thank you" (French).

p. 121, *Le bon Dieu… pas de derrière*: "The good Lord always sends breeches to those who have no backside…" (French).

p. 122, *Qui se marie… mauvais jours*: "He who marries for love has good nights and bad days" (French).

p. 122 *Patience… des pauvres*: "Patience – the medicine of the poor" (French).

p. 123, *femme de ménage*: "Charwoman" (French).

p. 125, *L'amour... les ânes*: "Love makes the asses dance" (French).

p. 127, *Garçon, un demi*: "Waiter, a glass of beer!" (French).

p. 130, *Vieux satyre*: "You old satyr!" (French).

p. 131, *Pontus Euxinus*: The Latin name for the Black Sea.

p. 134, *Leonardo da Vinci*: The great Renaissance artist (1452–1519) also had for his time a remarkable knowledge of the sciences.

p. 135, *the Yeliseyevs' for fruit and wine*: The Yeliseyev brothers had an exclusive food shop on Tverskaya Street.

p. 139, *Przybyszewski*: Stanislaw Przybyszewski (1868–1927), a Polish novelist, dramatist and critic of the Naturalist school who struggled with alcoholism, but was not a long-term resident of Vienna.

p. 141, *Trecento, quattrocento... Fra Angelicos, Ghirlandaios... Beatrice and dry-faced Dante*: *Trecento* and *quattrocento* are the Italian terms for the fourteenth and fifteenth centuries with particular reference to their artistic life, representatives of which in Florence were Fra Angelico, real name Guido di Pietri, monastic name Giovanni da Fiesole, (1387–1455) and Domenico Ghirlandaio (1449–94). Beatrice was the muse of Florence's Dante Alighieri (1265–1321).

p. 145, *Pas de lettres... télégrammes*: "No letters, sir, no telegrams" (French).

p. 147, *Journaux étrangers*: "Foreign newspapers!" (French).

p. 147, *Arthur Schnitzler*: Austrian novelist and dramatist (1862–1931) whose works reveal a particular interest in human sexuality.

p. 156, *Amidst a noisy ball, by chance*: The poem by Alexei Konstantinovich Tolstoy (1851) was set to music by Pyotr Ilyich Tchaikovsky (1840–93).

p. 159, *Goncharov... The Precipice*: The 1869 novel by Ivan Goncharov (1812–91).

p. 159, *Odarka*: The shrewish wife of Ivan Karas, hero of the opera *A Zaporozhian Cossack beyond the Danube* (1863) by Semyon Stepanovich Gulak-Artemovsky (1813–73).

p. 166, *a second Bruce*: James Bruce (1670–1735) was one of the many foreigners invited to Russia by Peter the Great for their scientific and technical skills, and became the author of a much reprinted *Calendar* (1709).

p. 169, *Tatyana's Day*: The 12th of January in the Old Style Russian calendar.

p. 170, *Gaudeamus igitur*: "Let us therefore rejoice" (Latin), the opening words of a drinking song popular among students throughout Europe, 'De brevitate vitæ' – 'On the Brevity of Life'.

p. 172, *rizas*: The ornamental, usually silver plates covering icons, with holes shaped to allow faces and other features to be visible.

p. 173, *what Hagar was like*: In Genesis, Hagar was the Egyptian handmaiden of Sarah, the wife of Abraham, who became Abraham's concubine and mother of Ishmael when Sarah was unable to conceive a child; when Sarah bore Isaac, Hagar and Ishmael were driven out into the wilderness.

p. 182, *Upon a long-familiar street... come let's flee!*: The slightly inaccurate quotations are from a poem entitled 'The Recluse' (1846) by Yakov Petrovich Polonsky (1819–98).

p. 185, *Asmolov "cannon"*: Asmolov and Co. were manufacturers of tobacco products and accessories.

p. 185, *The poet Bryusov*: Valery Yakovlevich Bryusov (1873–1924) was a leading Symbolist poet and novelist.

p. 188, *belyanas*: Large, flat-bottomed river boats of crude construction used for transportation on the Volga.

p. 190, *I was strolling... away my grief*: A popular song based on the poem 'Forget-me-nots' (1796) by Prince Grigory Alexandrovich Khovansky (1767–96).

p. 193, *Saadi... a Persian poet of that name*: Saadi was the assumed name of Sheikh Muslih Addin (*c.*1184–*c.*1291), whose considerable literary output includes works in a variety of genres.

p. 194, *Parlez pour vous*: "Speak for yourself" (French).

p. 195, *Bruderschaft*: "To brotherhood" (German).

p. 195, *And are you liking... the hypocrite*: The first line of Kozma Prutkov's 'Epigram No. 1' (1854); Prutkov was the pen name used by Alexei Konstantinovich Tolstoy and the brothers Zhemchuzhnikov, Alexei (1821–1908) and Vladimir Mikhailovich (1830–84), for their humorous, satirical writing. The epigram – which concludes: "'I am,' the man replied, 'I'm finding taste in it.'" – was the work of Tolstoy.

p. 201, *Oh when, my soul... or to love*: The opening lines of 'Elegy' (1821 or 1822) by Anton Antonovich Delvig (1798–1831), which was set to music by both M. Yakovlev and A. Dargomyzhsky.

p. 203, *the Pythia*: The priestess at the sanctuary of Apollo at Delphi, who would fall into a trance and utter delirious broken phrases to be interpreted subsequently by the priest.

p. 207, *yataghan*: A long, curved Turkish dagger without a guard.

p. 209, *Klever's Winter Sunset*: Yuli Yulyevich Klever (1850–1924) was a landscape artist with a tendency to paint similar scenes, such as sunsets, repeatedly.

p. 221, *A little cloud... gi-i-iant cra-ag*: The poem 'A Crag' (1841) by Mikhail Yuryevich Lermontov (1814–41) has been set to music by a host of Russian composers, including Dargomyzhsky, Rimsky-Korsakov, Balakirev and Rubinstein.

p. 221, *the artist Yartsev*: Grigory Fyodorovich Yartsev (1858–1918).

p. 222, *Shalyapin and Korovin*: The great bass Fyodor Ivanovich Shalyapin (often spelt Chaliapin, 1873–1938) and the Russian Impressionist painter Konstantin Alexeyevich Korovin (1861–1939).

p. 222, *Dr Goloushev*: The journalist, literary and theatre critic S.S. Goloushev (1855–1920), who wrote under the pen name "Glagol".

p. 223, *Kuvshinnikova, Chekhov's sister*: Sofia Petrovna Kuvshinnikova (1847–1907), and Maria Pavlovna Chekhova (1863–1957), the younger sister of the writer Anton Pavlovich Chekhov (1860–1904).

p. 223, *Malyavin himself*: Filipp Andreyevich Malyavin (1869–1940).

p. 229, *On 15th June Ferdinand was killed*: The date of the shooting of Archduke Franz Ferdinand is given according to the Old Style (Julian) Russian calendar, 28th June in the Gregorian calendar used elsewhere in Europe.

p. 229, *Peter's Day*: The Feast Day of Saints Peter and Paul, celebrated on 29th June in the Old Style Russian calendar.

p. 230, *Oh, what an extremely cold... fire on the rise*: A slightly inaccurate quotation of the opening stanza of an untitled poem of 1847 by Afanasy Afanasyevich Fet (1820–92), in which the pines are described as "slumbering" rather than black.

p. 232, *the Volunteers*: The Volunteer Army began forming under Mikhail Vasilyevich Alexeyev (1857–1918) in southern Russia and Ukraine in late 1917 and fought against the Bolsheviks until early in 1920.

p. 232, *Wrangel*: Baron Pyotr Nikolayevich Wrangel (1870–1928) was one of the leaders of the anti-Bolshevik forces in southern Russia and Ukraine, and took overall command from April 1920 until finally abandoning the Crimea in November of the same year.

p. 235, *what this dream's supposed to mean*: A misquotation that entered the language from Alexander Pushkin's verse fairy tale of 1825 *The Bridegroom*.

p. 237, *the Volunteer Fleet's steamer… on its way to Vladivostok*: The Russian Volunteer Fleet was founded in St Petersburg in 1878 and began sailings from Odessa to Vladivostok in 1880.

p. 239, *Katkov's Lycée*: The Lycée, officially named in honour of the eldest son of Alexander II, Nikolai, who died as a child in 1863, was founded by Mikhail Nikiforovich Katkov (1818–87) in 1867 and opened in the following year.

p. 245, *C'est une Camarguaise*: "She's from the Camargue" (French).

p. 249, *Dites, Odette… oui, monsieur:* "Tell me, Odette, who is that lady?"; "What lady, sir?"; "Why, the brunette over there."; "Which table, sir?"; "Number ten."; "She's a Russian, sir."; "And what else?"; "I don't know anything, sir."; "Has she been here with you a long time?"; "Three weeks, sir."; "By herself all the time?"; "No, sir, there was a gentleman…"; "Young, sporty?"; "No, sir… Very pensive, nervy…"; "And one day he disappeared?"; "Why, yes, sir." (French).

p. 252, *Assez!… N'est-ce pas, madame*: "Enough!… Isn't it, madam?" (French).

p. 253, *démarches*: "Steps" (French).

p. 253, *I'll paint you as Medusa*: In Greek mythology, Medusa was the only mortal one of the three monstrous Gorgons, at whom men could not look without turning to stone.

p. 254, *Denikin*: Anton Ivanovich Denikin (1872–1947), leader of the anti-Bolshevik Volunteer Army from April 1918 until April 1920.

p. 259, *I envy not the gods… plaits so dark*: A slightly inaccurate version of part of Alexander Pushkin's poem of 1825 'From the Portuguese'.

p. 259, *Leonid Andreyev… Tolstoy… Andreyev*: Leonid Nikolayevich Andreyev (1871–1919) became an extremely popular writer, particularly of short stories, but Leo Nikolayevich Tolstoy (1828–1910) was inconsistent in his response to his works, and his comments on Andreyev's desire to shock are recorded by more than one of their contemporaries.

p. 259, *Sebastopol*: The siege of Sebastopol was one of the major arenas of conflict in the Crimean War (1853–56).

p. 260, *Moon, moon, golden horns*: A phrase used in incantations.

p. 260, *Dante said of Beatrice... is in the lips*: The reference is to an explanatory passage from part XIX of Dante's *The New Life* (*c*.1283–93): "The second part is divided in two: for in the one I speak of her eyes, which are the source of love; in the second I speak of her mouth, which is love's end."

p. 261, *Pure Monday*: The first Monday in Lent after the feasting and merriment of Shrovetide.

p. 261, *'The Moonlight Sonata'*: Beethoven's 1801 piano sonata No. 14.

p. 262, *a bare-footed Tolstoy*: Leo Tolstoy adopted the dress and aspects of the lifestyle of the peasants on his estate and was regularly depicted in this mode by contemporary artists.

p. 262, *Hofmannsthal... Tetmayer*: Hugo von Hofmannsthal (1874–1929), an Austrian writer influenced by the Symbolist movement; Kazimierz Tetmayer (1865–1940), a Polish writer known for the candid nature of his love poetry; added to Schnitzler and Przybyszewski, with their modernist concerns, they indicate a bold body of reading.

p. 263, *the Arts Group... Andrei Bely*: The Arts Group was one of Moscow's many literary and artistic circles of the early twentieth century – Bunin was himself a member. Andrei Bely was the pen name of Boris Nikolayevich Bugayev (1880–1934), one of the leading figures in the Russian Symbolist movement.

p. 263, *The Fiery Angel*: A historical novel of 1907 by Valery Bryusov.

p. 265, *Platon Karatayev said to Pierre*: In Leo Tolstoy's *War and Peace* (1865–69), it is the peasant Karatayev who helps Pierre Bezukhov to find the good in life through simplicity and naturalness.

p. 265, *the Arts Theatre's*: The Moscow Arts Theatre was founded in 1898 and its early history was particularly notable for its staging of the plays of Anton Chekhov.

p. 265, *Aida*: Giuseppe Verdi's opera of 1871.

p. 265, *kazakin*: A short, straight caftan with a high collar.

p. 266, *O Lord and Master of my life*: The Prayer of the Righteous Ephrem, used in Lent.

p. 266, *the schismatics'*: The schism in the Russian Orthodox Church in the seventeenth century led to the formation of various heretical sects, whose members were referred to generally as Old Believers or schismatics. Persecution had not prevented them from flourishing into the twentieth century.

p. 266, *Peresvet and Oslyabya*: Alexander Peresvet (*d*.1380) and Rodion Oslyabya (*d*.1398) were both monks of the Trinity-St Sergiy Monastery and participants in the Russian victory at the Battle of Kulikovo, fought against the Mongols in 1380.

p. 267, *neumes*: In early musical notation, signs giving a rough indication of a rise or fall in pitch.

p. 267, *the graves of Ertel and Chekhov*: Alexander Ivanovich Ertel (1855–1908) was a writer close to the Populist movement. The monument on Chekhov's grave is the work of Leonid Mikhailovich Brailovsky (*c*.1863–1937) and was erected in 1907.

p. 267, *Somewhere on Ordynka... Griboyedov used to live*: Alexander Sergeyevich Griboyedov (1795–1829), diplomat and writer, most notably of the play *The Misfortune of Intelligence* (1822–24), often visited his uncle here as a child, but the house was destroyed in the fire of 1812.

p. 268, *the Three-handed Madonna... this is India*: St John of Damascus (*c*.675–*c*.753) is reputed to have suffered the punishment of having a hand cut off, but to have found it had miraculously grown back on the wrist. In gratitude, he painted a third hand on an icon of the Virgin, thus starting a tradition reminiscent of the depictions of Shiva with four hands.

p. 268, *Prince Yuri Dolgoruky... Svyatoslav, Prince Seversky*: Yuri Vladimirovich Dolgoruky (*c*.1099–1157), Grand Prince of Kiev, founded Moscow, according to tradition, in 1147, when he received his second cousin, Svyatoslav Olegovich of Novgorod-Seversky, in the newly fortified settlement.

p. 269, *There was in the Russian land... in monastic garments*: The fragments are from *The Tale of Pyotr and Fevronia of Murom*, dating probably from the late fifteenth century; in the first part Prince Pyotr delivers his brother and sister-in-law from the seductive serpent, and in the second he is cured of the resultant sickness by the tranquil maiden Fevronia, whom he subsequently marries. It is Pyotr and Fevronia who die together, having first become a monk and a nun.

p. 270, *Stanislavsky... Moskvin... Kachalov*: Konstantin Sergeyevich Stanislavsky, real name Alexeyev, (1865–1938), Ivan Mikhailovich Moskvin (1874–1946) and Vasily Ivanovich Kachalov, real name Shverubovich, (1875–1948), were all actors in the Moscow Arts Theatre.

p. 271, *Princess of Shamakha*: There was such a figure in the Caucasus in the eighteenth century, but the name is best known through Alexander Pushkin's use of it for the beautiful princess in *The Tale of the Golden Cockerel* (1834).

p. 271, *Sulerzhitsky*: Lev Antonovich Sulerzhitsky (1872–1916), writer and artist, and from 1905 a director and teacher at the Moscow Arts Theatre.

p. 273, *Grand Duchess Yel'zavet' Fyod'rovna and Grand Duke 'Mitry Pa'lych*: Grand Duchess Yelizaveta Fyodorovna (1864–1918), a grand-daughter of Queen Victoria and sister of the Empress Alexandra, was married to Grand Duke Sergei Alexandrovich, who was Governor of Moscow when assassinated in 1905, and she founded the community of Saints Martha and Mary, becoming its abbess, in 1909. Grand Duke Dmitry Pavlovich (1891–1941) was a grandson of Emperor Alexander II; his mother died in childbirth and he was raised by his aunt, Yelizaveta Fyodorovna. He is mainly remembered for his involvement in the death of Grigory Rasputin; his aunt was canonized in Russia in 1992 for her good works and subsequent martyrdom at the hands of the Bolsheviks.

Extra Material

on

Ivan Bunin's

Dark Avenues

Ivan Bunin's Life

Ivan Alexeyevich Bunin was born in the city of Voronezh, in south-western Russia, on 10th October 1870. His father Alexei Nikolayevich, a landowner with property in the Oryol and Tula Provinces, was a descendant of an aristocratic family, known since the fifteenth century. A gifted but impractical man, who was prone to occasional bouts of drinking and gambling, he lost all of his estates, one after another, and ended up destitute when Bunin was already a young man. Alexei and his wife Lyudmila Alexandrovna (née Chubarova, also an aristocrat) had nine children, four of whom survived infancy. Bunin had two older brothers, Yuli and Yevgeny, and a younger sister called Maria.

In an attempt to break Alexei's bad habits and to reduce living expenses, in 1874 the family moved from Voronezh to their estate in Butyrki in the Elets region of the Oryol Province, some 130 km north of Voronezh. This is where Bunin remained until 1881, tutored privately by Nikolai Osipovich Romashkov, a talented amateur artist and musician, who had studied at the Lazarev Institute of Oriental Languages in Moscow and at Moscow University. Under Romashkov's influence, Bunin contemplated becoming an artist too. Romashkov taught his pupil to read and write using Russian translations of Homer's *Odyssey* and Cervantes's *Don Quixote*. One of the first books Bunin read – an anthology of English poetry from Chaucer to Tennyson, in Russian translation, edited by Nikolai Gerbel (*Angliiskie poety v biografiiakh i obraztsakh*, 1875) – inspired him to become a poet. Spending a great deal of time outdoors, and in close contact with servants and peasants, fostered Bunin's love of nature and detailed knowledge of rural life.

In August 1881, Bunin entered a school in Elets, where he had to stay, mostly in rented accommodation, for four and a half years, going back to Butyrki for vacations (and, from spring 1883, to the village of Ozerki in the same region, where the family relocated to take possession of an inheritance). Bunin was not a particularly diligent student: he had to repeat his third year because he had failed maths, and was permanently excluded in March 1886 for non-attendance. He preferred to study at home with his brother Yuli, a member of the Populist "Black Repartition" group, who was taken into custody in September 1884 for revolutionary activity and eventually sentenced to a three-year detention at his parents' estate in 1885.

Early Writings and Publications While in Ozerki, in 1886–87 Bunin wrote his first novel, *Attraction (Uvlechenie)*, and the first part of the long poem *Pyotr Rogachev* (an imitation of Pushkin's *Eugene Onegin*) – but these did not appear in print in Bunin's lifetime. His first publication, in the St Petersburg weekly *Rodina (Motherland)* of 22nd February 1887, was a poem commemorating the untimely death of Semyon Nadson, a fashionable civic poet. Bunin must have been embarrassed by the rather clichéd rhetoric of the piece, because he later claimed that he had made his literary debut with a poem called 'The Village Beggar' (in *Rodina*, 17th May 1887), an emotive snapshot of an old vagabond. In the course of 1888, more of Bunin's poems came out in the St Petersburg literary monthly *Knizhki "Nedeli"* (Book Supplements to *The Weekly*), run by Liberal Populists. His contributions to various periodicals led to a job offer as a staff writer and copy editor at the regional newspaper *Orlovskii vestnik (The Oryol Herald)*, which he accepted in the autumn of 1889. Subsequently, *Orlovskii vestnik* issued Bunin's first book (a collection of poems written in 1887–91) and printed a number of his stories (most notably 'Small Landowners' in 1891, a series of satirical sketches of Gogolesque types in and around Elets, with Romashkov serving as a model for the character of Yakov Matveyev). However, Bunin engaged in fiction writing in earnest only in Poltava, where he moved in late August 1892, following his brother Yuli, to become a local administration employee.

Varvara Pashchenko Bunin came to Poltava with Varvara Paschenko, the daughter of an Elets physician. They met when she was a proofreader for *Orlovskii vestnik*, and lived as an unmarried couple, against the will of her parents who feared that Bunin would not be capable of earning a stable income. In Poltava, Bunin worked as a librarian and a statistician and contributed regularly to the newspaper *Poltavskie gubernskie vedomosti* (*The Poltava Regional News*) – as well as, occasionally, to the periodicals in the capital, including prestigious magazines such as *Vestnik Evropy* (*The European Herald*) and *Russkoe bogatstvo* (*The Russian Wealth*). He also joined the Tolstoyans and tried to disseminate the output of their publishing house Posrednik (The Intermediary). He was arrested for doing so without a licence, and sentenced to three months' imprisonment, but was amnestied before he could serve the time, following the death of Alexander III in October 1894 and Nicholas II's accession to the throne. Bunin's ambivalent view of the Tolstoyans is reflected in his later story 'At the Summer House' (1896). That same year, Paschenko ended her turbulent relationship with Bunin, to marry his wealthy friend Arseny Bibikov. In January 1895, Bunin left Poltava for St Petersburg and Moscow to pursue the career of a freelance writer.

On arrival, Bunin became acquainted with representatives *Literary Recognition* of the four most important Russian literary generations, such as the doyen of the Russian realist school Dmitry Grigorovich, the Populist novelists Nikolai Zlatovratsky and Alexander Ertel, as well as Anton Chekhov and the Symbolist poets Konstantin Balmont and Valery Bryusov. Although Bunin strove to maintain independence and impartiality, and did not wish to join any literary camp in particular, he felt more attracted by the classical Russian tradition than by its decadent modernist counterpart (although in 1901 he did bring out his *Falling Leaves* (*Listopad*) poetry collection in the Symbolist publishing house Skorpion). In St Petersburg Bunin published a collection of short stories, *To the End of the World* (*Na krai sveta*, 1897), the title piece describing Ukrainian peasant settlers on their way to the Russian Far East; in Moscow, yet another book of poetry, entitled *Under the Open Sky* (*Pod otkrytym nebom*, 1898); and in 1896 in Oryol, as a supplement to *Orlovskii vestnik*, his translation of *The Song of Hiawatha* by Henry Wadsworth Longfellow, awarded a Pushkin Prize by the Russian Academy of Sciences in 1903. Bunin had taught himself English and, among other things, also translated Byron's *Cain* and Tennyson's 'Godiva' – which, together with Bunin's 1903–07 collections of original poetry, received yet another Pushkin Prize in 1909.

Bunin became a member of the "Wednesday" literary circle, founded in 1898 by the author Nikolai Teleshov, with Zlatovratsky, Chekhov, Alexander Kuprin, Leonid Andreyev and other distinguished authors as its associates. The same year saw the foundation of the publishing cooperative Znanie (Knowledge) – closely linked to Maxim Gorky, whom Bunin met through Chekhov in 1899 – which produced the first five volumes of the first edition of Bunin's collected works (1902–09). In this period, Bunin was invited to undertake several editorial commissions: in 1904–05, he oversaw publications of fiction and poetry in the *Pravda* (*Truth*) magazine, but left its editorial board because of his rift with the Social Democrats on it; in 1907, he was briefly involved in the editing of the *Zemlia* (*Earth*) anthologies; and in 1909, he worked as a literary editor on the magazine *Severnoe siianie* (*Northern Lights*). Meanwhile, his reputation had grown to such an extent that in autumn 1909 he was elected one of the twelve honorary members of the Russian Academy of Sciences in the belles-lettres category. In his capacity as an honorary academician, Bunin was asked to appraise fiction and poetry submitted for the Academy's annual competitions, and his negative peer review of four books of poetry by the modernist Sergei Gorodetsky earned Bunin the Academy's golden Pushkin medal for 1911. In 1912, Bunin became an honorary member of the Society of Lovers of Russian Literature (affiliated to Moscow University); he also acted as the Society's sometime Deputy Chair and temporary Chair. On 27th–29th October 1912, the twenty-fifth anniversary of Bunin's literary activity was celebrated at a number of special ceremonies in Moscow, and in 1915, his complete works in six volumes were issued by the publisher Adolf Marx.

Travels and First Marriage Throughout these years of literary endeavour and success, Bunin always found time to travel widely. In autumn 1888 Yuli left Ozerki for the city of Kharkov in Ukraine to take up a job as a statistician. Early the next year, Bunin visited him there, and then went on to the Crimean peninsular to see the cities of Yalta and Sebastopol, thus making his first long-distance trip. From then on, Bunin tried to use every opportunity to travel, the further the better; a sedentary lifestyle had never been quite for him, especially in his younger years. His attempt to settle down in Odessa (a large port on the Black Sea) and marry, on 23rd September 1898, Anna Tsakni

– the daughter of the publisher of the newspaper *Iuzhnoe obozrenie* (*Southern Review*), which Bunin wrote for – ended in a separation in early March 1900. Bunin and Tsakni had a son, Nikolai, who was born in August 1900 and died in January 1905 of complications caused by scarlet fever and measles.

This failed marriage led to a period of increased travel. In October and November 1900, Bunin went abroad for the first time, with his friend Vladimir Kurovsky, an artist and custodian of the Odessa Art Museum. They visited Germany, France, Austria and Switzerland. In April 1903, Bunin went to Istanbul, which led to a lifelong fascination with the city (afterwards, Bunin returned to it at least twelve more times). From late December 1903 to early February 1904, he travelled through France and Italy in the company of the playwright Sergei Naidyonov. Four months later, Bunin toured the Caucasus and in July 1905 he went to Finland (then part of the Russian Empire).

In November 1905 Bunin began a relationship with his fu- *Second Marriage* ture second wife, Vera Nikolayevna Muromtseva, a graduate of the Science Faculty of the Higher Courses for Women in Moscow and the niece of a State Duma chairman. They started living together soon afterwards, but married only in November 1922 in Paris (as Bunin's divorce from Tsakni was finalized on 20th June 1922). She accompanied him on his travels, which were again frequent and far-ranging. In April and May 1907, Bunin and Muromtseva journeyed to Egypt, Syria and Palestine, via Turkey and Greece – a trip that few Russians at the time ever considered making (it was described in the Temple of the Sun cycle of stories, 1907–11). Then, in March and April 1909, Bunin and Muromtseva went to Italy (via Austria), spending much of their time on the Italian island of Capri, later described in Bunin's story 'The Gentleman from San Francisco' (1915), and between March and May 1910, they went to Algiers and Tunisia – via Austria, Italy, France, Greece and Turkey – and paid a visit to the Sahara desert. Between December 1910 and April 1911, the couple returned to Egypt, and from there journeyed to Ceylon. They even contemplated going from Ceylon to Japan, but ran out of time and money. Bunin's diary of the voyage along the Suez canal and across the Red Sea and the Indian ocean was published in 1925–26 under the title 'The Waters Are Many'; in addition, Ceylon

293

served as a background for his 1914 story 'Brothers', and one of its ancient capitals, Anuradhapura, was depicted in the 1924 story 'The City of the King of Kings'.

Bunin's journeys to remote exotic destinations assisted him in acquiring an enhanced awareness of Muslim, Jewish and Buddhist traditions, uncommon in a Russian intellectual with a strong Orthodox Christian background. Examples of this insight can be found for instance in his poems 'Mohammed in Exile' (1906), 'Torah' (1914) and the short stories 'Gautami' (1919) and 'The Night of Renunciation' (1921). Between November 1911 and March 1914, Bunin and Muromtseva returned to Italy several times (mostly to Capri), and visited Germany, Austria, Switzerland and Greece on their way from and to Russia. Bunin also went on a Black Sea voyage with his brother Yuli in summer 1913, stopping in Batumi, Trabzon, Istanbul and Constanta, and then proceeding to Bucharest, Iasi and Chisinau – Bunin later used a Bessarabian setting for his 1916 story 'A Song about a Noble Brigand'. A year later, the brothers made a trip along the Volga river, from Saratov to Yaroslavl. They were in Samara when the news about the assassination of Archduke Franz Ferdinand in Sarajevo reached them.

First World War,
Russian Revolution and
Emigration

After war was declared, Bunin spent three months doing little else besides reading newspapers in a state of shock. On 28th September 1914, the *Russkoe slovo* (*Russian Word*) periodical published his protest against German atrocities, written on behalf of Russian authors, actors and artists. In it, Bunin claimed that German soldiers were reminding mankind that "the ancient beast inside the human being is alive and strong, and even the nations that are leading the advance of civilization can easily give evil will a free rein and become like the half-naked hordes of their ancestors, who crushed the legacy of the classical world under their heavy feet fifteen centuries ago". However, the war did not make Bunin a chauvinist ascribing good and evil qualities to particular nations; on the contrary, he believed that the epoch ushered in by the war might well be dominated by a killer of indeterminate (or any) nationality, capable of executing defenceless people for no reason and without remorse – this is illustrated by the character of Adam Sokolovich in his 1916 story 'Loopy Ears', openly polemical against Dostoevsky's *Crime and Punishment* and its repentant murderer Raskolnikov. The ensuing February and October 1917 revolutions confirmed Bunin's worst fears, harboured at least since the 1905–07 Russian civil unrest, which he witnessed in Odessa (the Jewish pogroms in September and October 1905), Moscow (the December 1905 uprising) and in the countryside (where, in June 1906, peasants set on fire the estates of Bunin's brother Yevgeny and cousin Sofia Pusheshnikova).

Bunin was in Moscow when the February 1917 revolution took place. Although a man of moderate left-wing persuasions and by no means a monarchist, Bunin dismissed the Provisional Government as a "travesty". In early April 1917, he ended his long-term friendship with Gorky over his proximity to the Bolsheviks, whose coup d'état forced the Bunins out of Moscow. On 21st May 1918, they left for Odessa, which at the time belonged to the independent Ukrainian State, with Hetman Pavlo Skoropadsky as its head. They arrived on 3rd June, via Orsha, Minsk, Gomel and Kiev, and remained in Odessa for almost twenty months, surviving the rule of the Ukrainian Directorate in November and December 1918, the French occupation from December 1918 to April 1919, the Bolshevik regime of April to August 1919 and the White (Volunteer) Army administration of August 1919 to early 1920. In his diary *Cursed Days* (*Okaiannye dni*, 1936), covering life in Bolshevik-controlled Moscow and Odessa, Bunin noted: "Our children and grandchildren won't be able even to imagine the Russia that we once (only yesterday) lived in – Russia with all its might, complexity, wealth and happiness, which we neither appreciated nor understood". In Odessa, Bunin contributed to local periodicals, such as *Odesskie novosti* (*Odessa News*), *Odesskii listok* (*Odessa Sheet*) and *Nashe slovo* (*Our Word*), as well as co-editing the newspaper *Iuzhnoe slovo* (*Word of the South*), set up by the Volunteer Army. On 26th January 1920, facing the danger of yet another Bolshevik takeover, Bunin (who had by now become an accomplished anti-Communist) and Muromtseva left Russia for good. Their journey to Istanbul on the Sparta steamship is described in the story 'The End' (1921).

The couple settled in France, arriving there on 28th March 1920, via Sofia and Belgrade. From 1923, a pattern was established, according to which the Bunins tended to spend the winter months in Paris, and spring, summer and autumn at various villas on the French Riviera, most frequently in the town of Grasse. Bunin's royalties for translations into foreign languages and for publications in the Russian émigré press

– e.g. the Parisian newspapers *Poslednie novosti* (*The Latest News*), *Vozrozhdenie* (*Revival*) and *Rossiia i slavianstvo* (*Russia and the Slavic World*) – augmented by a grant from the Czechoslovakian government (disbursed in 1924–28), allowed him not only to lead a modestly independent life, but also to take under his wing a number of young aspiring Russian authors, who were often invited to stay for lengthy periods of time under one roof with the Bunins. Of these authors, Galina Kuznetsova was Bunin's lover between 1926 and 1934 (when she left him for the singer Margarita Stepun), and Leonid Zurov eventually inherited Bunin's intellectual property rights and archive.

Bunin's attitude to Russia differed from that of a typical émigré by avoiding cheap sentimentality and futile vindictiveness. In his story 'Eternal Spring' (1923), Bunin depicted pre-revolutionary Russia as a remote museum-like past, a return to which was neither possible nor desirable. Perhaps he was aided in this attitude by being something of a citizen of the world, who only feels at home when he is on the move. Even as a stateless person, Bunin managed to go abroad (e.g. to Wiesbaden from July to September 1921 and to London in February 1925), undeterred by significant visa problems. In his new poetry and fiction, Russian history and culture remained only one of many different themes. Still, his magnum opus, the loosely autobiographical novel *Arsenyev's Life* (*Zhizn' Arsen'eva*, written between 1927 and 1938 and first published in full in 1952), focused on a meticulous recreation of everyday existence in provincial Russia in the 1870s–90s.

In 1933, after years of vigorous campaigning behind the scenes, Bunin received the Nobel Prize for Literature, "for the strict artistry with which he has carried on the classical Russian traditions in prose writing" (the Swedish Academy's decision of 9th November). He was the first Russian to achieve this distinction. In December that year, accompanied by both Muromtseva and Kuznetsova, he travelled to Stockholm to the award ceremony. A large proportion of the prize money, around 120,000 French francs, was given away by Bunin to various charitable causes in support of Russian émigré circles. In 1934–39, the Berlin-based Petropolis publishing house issued a revised edition of Bunin's collected works in Russian, in twelve volumes. On publishing business, and to give a series of public readings (at which he excelled as a gifted orator), Bunin visited Brussels, London, Czechoslovakia, Germany, Italy, Yugoslavia, Lithuania,

Latvia and Estonia between 1935 and 1938. However, the life of a minor celebrity was not devoid of humiliating moments. Bunin was briefly detained by the German border guards in Lindau on 27th October 1936 for overstaying his visa (see the note "Russian Exile's Protest: Alleged Brutality at German Customs" in *The Times* of 3rd November 1936).

From September 1939 until May 1945, the Bunins had to remain in Grasse uninterruptedly. In these years of isolation and despair, Bunin wrote his finest short stories, which comprised the 1946 *Dark Avenues* (*Temnye allei*) collection. Although living in poverty, he firmly declined invitations to contribute to the collaborationist press, and gave shelter to Jews (e.g. the essayist Alexander Bakhrakh and the pianist Alexander Lieberman) who were hiding from the Nazis. After the war, the Bunins returned to Paris. Bunin's deteriorating health (he suffered from emphysema and underwent prostate surgery on 4th September 1950) and difficult financial circumstances (in 1949–51, he even accepted a monthly allowance of 10,000 francs from the millionaire and philanthropist Solomon Atran) did not present much opportunity for travel, although he allowed himself several stays in a Russian guesthouse in Juan-les-Pins between 1947 and 1949. The seventy-fifth and the eightieth anniversary of Bunin's birth were used to collect donations for his financial support. He rejected Soviet attempts to lure him back to Russia (partly prompted by the friend and author Alexei Tolstoy's letter to Stalin of 17th June 1941 about Bunin's miserable existence in war-torn France), and stopped a collection of his works, in preparation by a state publishing house in Moscow, from publication, because he could not exercise control over its content. On the other hand, in late 1947 he left the Union of Russian Writers and Journalists in France (which he used to chair), after it had expelled those of its members who had taken Soviet passports in the aftermath of a 1946 Supreme Soviet decree returning citizenship rights to former subjects of the Russian Empire. As a result, he fell out with his old friend and sponsor Maria Tsetlina, whose late husband was an heir to the Wissotzky Tea company. Bunin's controversial *Memoirs* (*Vospominaniia*, 1950), which pulled no punches in challenging the reputations of famous Russians such as Gorky and the futurist poet Vladimir Mayakovsky, was his last completed large-scale project. He died on 8th November 1953, of pneumonia, while

The Second World War and the Final Years

working on a book called *About Chekhov* (*O Chekhove*), intended to commemorate the fiftieth anniversary of his death. Its unfinished manuscript, edited by Muromtseva and Zurov, appeared posthumously, in 1955.

Ivan Bunin's Works

Genre Bunin began his literary career as a poet specializing in rather detached sketches of characters and locations, memorable for either their typicality or exoticism. His poetic style, earning him a reputation of "the only significant poet of the Symbolist age who was not a Symbolist" (Georgette Donchin in *The Times Literary Supplement* of 10th May 1957), owes a great deal to realistic landscape and portrait painting. Bunin found it impossible to separate his poetry from his prose, regularly publishing both under the same book cover. His trademark "unnarrative" (D.S. Mirsky) atmospheric prose often reads like poetry – such as the story 'Antonov Apples' (*Antonovskie iabloki*, 1900) – in which the smell of apples evokes a picture of the disappearing lifestyle of landowners in the south-west of Russia, accompanied by striking images of nature in the autumn. In a conversation with his nephew Nikolai Pusheshnikov, Bunin admitted that, for him, the key to a successful story was "finding the right sound. As soon as I have found it, the rest practically writes itself... But I never write what I want the way I want it. I don't dare. I would prefer to avoid any form and ignore literary devices". Thus, Bunin felt obliged to make certain concessions to conventional public taste, and framed his momentary observations of human types, moods, events and nature scenes into various traditional generic structures. Many of his short stories are in fact poems in prose, and the prose genre most befitting his idiosyncratic manner is perhaps that of a diary (often reworked for publication). Still, even his more substantial prose pieces, such as the 25,000-word novella 'Dry Valley' (*Sukhodol*, 1911) – about the decline of a gentry family, told from a female servant's point of view – were called "poems" or "prose poems" by the critics, and it was Bunin's "lyrical prose style [that] provided a welcome contrast with the rather colourless naturalism of the most influential group of novelists in Russia" (R.D. Charques in *The Times Literary Supplement* of 7th March 1935).

Bunin's lyricism, however, does not translate into idealiza- *Subject Matter*
tion of his favourite subject, rural Russia, but rather offsets
its mercilessly truthful representation, frequently making it
appear even bleaker than it would have been otherwise. His
first large-size prose work, *The Village* (*Derevnia*, 1910), is
a good example of this. It is a story of two ageing peasant
brothers, Tikhon and Kuzma, an owner and a manager of an
estate tellingly named Durnovka (derived from a Russian word
for "bad" or "evil"). The hard-working Tikhon, preoccupied
almost solely with material gain, and the dreamer Kuzma,
an epigone poet without a stable occupation, epitomize two
extremes of the Russian national character. Durnovka is not
easy to manage, because its inhabitants – personified by the
needy peasant Sery and his son Deniska – are lazy drunks,
indulging in domestic violence and wanton unruliness,
and living in conditions of "almost incredible ignorance,
hate, poverty, dirt, cruelty, idleness, supineness" (Harold
Hannyngton Child in *The Times Literary Supplement* of
25th October 1923). Neither of the brothers has anybody
to bequeath Durnovka to, and they decide to sell it and to
move to a nearby town. *The Village* – a symbol of Russia in
its entirety, displaying Chekhov's influence in its descriptions
of the steppe and a cherry orchard – was not intended "as
an indictment of the peasant class. No class depicted in the
book has any redeeming feature, and the whole picture of pre-
revolutionary provincial life is painted in the blackest possible
tones" (Georgette Donchin).

Bunin's perception of the West hardly provides any alternative. The Tolstoyan theme of the uselessness of material
wealth in the face of looming death, obvious in *The Village*,
is developed further in 'The Gentleman from San Francisco',
Bunin's most famous short story, written with "the intensity
of an apocalyptic vision of the horror and falsity of modern
civilization" (John Middleton Murry in *The Times Literary
Supplement* of 20th April 1922). In the story, Western
civilization is symbolized by an ocean liner, suggestively called
Atlantis, which conveys a holidaying American millionaire
and his family from the United States to Europe, and shortly
afterwards carries his corpse in the opposite direction (he dies
suddenly of a heart attack). The stokers in the engine room
are endlessly toiling to ensure that the well-to-do passengers upstairs can enjoy a life of exquisite luxury, and the

unswerving progress of this sophisticated piece of machinery is supervised by a captain who looks like a heathen idol. It is hard not to become "fascinated by this grandiose vision of the magnificence, the immense technical accomplishment of the setting man has made for himself, and by this ruthless vision of the shrivelled, inhuman, unclean thing that cowers within it", wrote *The Times* of 17th May 1922.

Bunin's concept of the East does not offer much consolation either. Thus, denizens of the lost Paradise – the island of Ceylon (now Sri Lanka) – succumb too easily to the fatal temptation of pursuing sensual pleasures, which should have been renounced in compliance with Buddhist teachings. For this, Bunin partly blames the corrupting influence of the exploitative West (see for example the young rickshaw man in 'Brothers', who commits suicide because his beloved becomes a rich Westerner's concubine). However, his insufficiently profound knowledge of both Eastern and Western ways appears to let him down on more than one occasion and undermine the value of the didactic message of his tales. ("Was ever an American citizen on board a liner in the Mediterranean seen to wear a silk top hat, patent-leather shoes and spats? And if in Ceylon the English officers drive the rickshaw men till they 'hear the death rattle in their throats', then a great number of people must have conspired together to misrepresent to us the facts of life upon that island," noted Cyril Bentham Falls in *The Times Literary Supplement* of 6th March 1924.) In this context, it is hardly surprising that John Middleton Murry said of Bunin: "If his West is a nightmare, his East is a dream – and we are left to wander uneasily between the two." Besides, it has to be admitted that Bunin's East, with its abject poverty, idolization of deities and oppressively hot summer nights, looks too much like Russia at times (see the 1916 story 'The Compatriot'). This might be partly explained by Bunin's conviction, acquired after travelling far and wide, that people are similar wherever one goes. The jobless, alcoholic sea captain in the story 'Chang's Dreams' (*Sny Changa*, 1916) seems to express Bunin's own pessimistic view of human nature when he says: "I've been across the entire globe. Life is the same everywhere!... People have neither God, nor conscience, nor any practical goal in life, nor love, nor friendship, nor honesty – not even simple pity".

Arsenyev's Life

Yet, perhaps paradoxically, Bunin's works continue to display his appreciation of every moment of his existence – no matter how dark – and his gratitude for being able to observe, remember and portray anything remarkable – even seemingly insignificant occurrences, which might never be repeated and are therefore uniquely precious. A selection of such moments, united by one life span, forms the basis of his longest work, the autobiographical novel *Arsenyev's Life* (the first four parts of which were translated into English in 1933 as *The Well of Days*). In it, Bunin's memory is cast back to the times of his childhood and youth, to follow the pattern established in Russia by Leo Tolstoy's 1852–56 autobiographical trilogy *Childhood, Boyhood, Youth*. The first part tells Arsenyev's story from his birth on a family estate to his first year at school in the nearest town; the second ends with his decision to leave the school while in his fifth year and remain on the estate; the third describes the loss of his virginity at the age of seventeen and an affair with a young married peasant woman; and the fourth his departure from the family estate for Kharkov, his travels through the south of Russia and, when in Oryol, his acquaintance with a woman called Lika (a character loosely modelled on Varvara Paschenko), who will soon become his lover and companion. The narrative pace is deliberately slow, bringing together what appears to be a series of brilliantly executed miniature paintings (Bunin himself compared his creative method to an old photographic album). Although Arsenyev's life is not particularly eventful, the reader is amply compensated for the paucity of action by "the magical freshness and fullness of the feelings and emotions of youth [that] are blended throughout with a special poetical sense for landscape and great depth of passionate receptivity" (Edward Garnett in *The Manchester Guardian* of 7th April 1933). The fourth part concludes with the depiction of a funeral train at the Oryol railway station, carrying the body of the Grand Duke Nikolai Nikolayevich Sr, who died in the Crimea in 1891. His son, Nikolai Nikolayevich Jr, is portrayed coming off the train, but the next scene, as if in a cinematic "flash forward", suddenly describes Nikolai Nikolayevich Jr himself lying in state in Antibes (Bunin visited his villa there shortly before the funeral). The death of this last undisputed heir to the Russian throne in 1929, quite out of place in a family chronicle set in the 1870s–90s, symbolizes the death of old Russia (to which *Arsenyev's Life* serves as an epitaph), and also gives the reader an early indication of more tragedies to come, including Lika's untimely demise in the fifth part of the novel (written much later and dealing, *inter alia*, with Arsenyev's attempts to find his own voice as an author).

In a review of *The Well of Days*, dated 21st March 1933, a London *Times* critic claimed that the book was "shadowed by the sense of mortality which is almost always present in Ivan Bunin's work". It appears that in *Arsenyev's Life*, Bunin feels nostalgic about the Russia of his youth not so much because the Bolsheviks have taken over the country and have changed it beyond recognition, but because his detailed memories of it, which he carries inside him, are bound to disappear when he dies.

The Liberation of Tolstoy It was this apprehension of mortality that Bunin tried to come to terms with in his next, non-fictional book *The Liberation of Tolstoy* (*Osvobozhdenie Tolstogo*, 1937). Bunin had held Tolstoy in the highest esteem long before they met in January 1894, owing a considerable debt of gratitude to him as an artist (for instance, 'Chang's Dreams', told from a dog's point of view, was undoubtedly inspired by Tolstoy's 'Kholstomer: The Story of a Horse', and 'The Gentleman from San Francisco' by 'The Death of Ivan Ilyich'). For Bunin, Tolstoy was in the same league as Buddha and King Solomon (see his 1925 story 'The Night', also known as 'Cicadas'), and is portrayed by him as a religious teacher who offers people advice on how to cope with death. According to Bunin, Tolstoy teaches that death is a liberation from the constraints of time and space, a return to an eternity which is full of love. By making this claim, Bunin polemicizes against alternative views of Tolstoy, including those of the Italian author Delfino Cinelli, the Russian émigré author Mark Aldanov, the lawyer, politician and diplomat Vasily Maklakov (1869–1957) – and Lenin. Quotations from their works are interspersed with Bunin's and others' personal reminiscences of Tolstoy. The book as a whole is framed by the repetition of phrases (such as, "I lived with Leo Nikolayevich for forty-eight years and I still couldn't understand what he was like", a comment made by Tolstoy's widow Sofia) and episodes (such as Tolstoy asking the zoologist Sergei Usov how long a person can survive if bitten by a mad dog), which function much as rhymes in a poem do, holding the structure together. Bunin's understanding of Tolstoy seems to have been determined, first and foremost, by his own concern with mortality, which throws into sharper relief an admiration of all the things life can offer, including love in all its manifestations.

Already in his 1924 novella 'Mitya's Love' (*Mitina liubov'*) — about a student who shoots himself because he cheated on his sweetheart, an aspiring actress, with a married peasant girl, while the actress, in an unrelated chain of events, left him for the headmaster of her drama school, a notorious womanizer — Bunin's "two principal motifs, love and death, the two most wonderful and incomprehensible things in life, meet and intermingle, and are woven into a fabric of unforgettable beauty" (Gleb Struve in *The Observer* of 25th February 1934). *Dark Avenues*

The interaction of these two motifs provided a common ground for most of his stories forming the cycle *Dark Avenues* (*Temnye allei*), written in 1937–45 and published, in different combinations, in the US in 1943 and in France in 1946. Bunin compared this book with Boccaccio's *Decameron*, because it was created at the height of the Nazi plague "to escape to a different world, where there was no bloodshed and people were not burned alive" (Vera Bunina), but also presumably because it is a veritable encyclopaedia of heterosexual relationships, complete with fatal attractions, love at first sight, unforgettable one-night stands, lightning-fast seduction of under-age children and even rape. The book's title refers to a popular garden feature on Russian estates – a setting for many of the stories – but also brings to mind the configuration of female genitalia. In his letter to the satirist Nadezhda Teffi of 23rd February 1944, Bunin stated, however, that the content of the stories "is not at all frivolous, but tragic... and all the stories in the book are only about love, about its 'dark' and, more often than not, gloomy and sinister avenues".

The title story – about a chance encounter between two old lovers, an army officer and an ex-serf, who suddenly reveals that, many years after he left her, she still harbours deep feelings for him – explains that the expression "dark avenues" has been borrowed from an 1842 poem by Nikolai Ogaryov (1813–77) called 'An Ordinary Tale' (*Obyknovennaia povest'*), in praise of first love (although the two young lovers mentioned in it later go their separate ways). It is true that some stories in the collection may appear either ordinary, or perhaps romantically clichéd, if summarized in terms of their plot alone. There are also stories that would not be out of place in a soap opera. Examples include a wronged husband coming to the Caucasus to look for his wife, who eloped there with her lover, and killing himself when he does not find her ('The Caucasus'); a Georgian man spending a night with a prostitute and killing her accidentally in a fit of passion ('Miss Klara'); an artist's daughter's teenage infatuation with another artist, leading to her suicide ('Galya Ganskaya'); and a woman returning to her old flame after a loveless marriage but dying shortly afterwards, when giving premature birth ('Natalie'). There are also tales of an irresistible passion that bridges the social and the human-animal divides. In 'Tanya', an aristocrat and a servant girl find that their feelings for one another are very serious, only to be separated for ever by the Russian Revolution (this story has invited comparisons between *Dark Avenues* and *Lady Chatterley's Lover* by D.H. Lawrence). In 'Iron Coat', a woman has had sexual intercourse with a bear (this story was apparently influenced by Prosper Mérimée's 'Lokis', 1869).

Dark Avenues could have easily turned out both trite and shockingly lewd. However, Bunin's mastery of language and characterization ensured that he successfully avoided the pitfalls of banality and vulgarity and struck a perfect balance between innocence and eroticism (irrespective of the criticism levelled at him that his upper- and middle-class female characters behave as if they were immoral members of the Young Communist League). As Robin Raleigh-King wrote of *Dark Avenues* in *The Times Literary Supplement* of 6th May 1949, Bunin "pinpoints the essential moments and details of a lifetime with such acid sharpness and such skill that for a moment the real world appears pallid by comparison... 'In Paris', the story of an elderly exile from Russia meeting a charming Russian woman in Paris, is an excellent example of the author's power to infuse nobility, breadth of vision and eternal significance into what might have been an ordinary love affair."

Not only does *Dark Avenues* offer a rare variety of types and situations, but every story in it is written in its own rhythm and style, 'Pure Monday' – about a woman torn between a man she loves and her urge to become a nun – being one of Bunin's best. And, in the words of Robin Raleigh-King, "the dominant note of nearly all these stories is one of regret – regret that life recedes like a tide, regret that one must stand alone on the desolate beach, regret that a human being is only capable of living one full cycle before he dies."

Bunin's *Memoirs*, his last completed book, is a collection *Memoirs* of reminiscences written in 1927–50 and structured as a musical composition, with the opening 'Autobiographical Notes' providing an overture of sorts to introduce various themes, which are elaborated upon in the ensuing sections on the musicians Sergei Rachmaninov and Fyodor Shalyapin, the artist Ilya Repin, the authors Jerome K. Jerome, Chekhov, Leo and Alexei Tolstoy, Alexander Kuprin, Prince Peter of Oldenburg and others. Bunin's memoirs are decidedly literary, filled with quotations from fiction, poetry and literary criticism of diverse provenance, as well as occasional fragments from personal correspondence and reference sources. Some quotations function as leitmotifs, used more than once in the narration (such as those from Maximilian Voloshin's 1906 poem 'The Angel of Vengeance' and Gorky's 1906 essay 'The City of the Yellow Devil'). Bunin's characterization of people he knew is largely affected by his rather conservative aesthetics, in the tradition of classical Russian realism, exemplified by Leo Tolstoy and Chekhov (whose spiritual heir Bunin believed himself to be). His biased view of Gorky, Vladimir Mayakovsky and Alexander Blok "that makes him incapable of perceiving their merit as writers" (R.D. Charques in *The Times Literary Supplement* of 6th April 1951), stems from his conviction that it was their loss of touch with reality, manifested in their modernist writings, that brought them to the Bolshevik camp. The almost forgotten Alexander Ertel seems to embody Bunin's ideal of a man, being both a gifted author and a successful estate manager (i.e. happily embracing a fantasy world and a businesslike attitude); a philanthropist who avoided the extremes of Tolstoyanism and revolutionism; and a self-made man who stayed away from the excesses of larger-than-life characters such as Kuprin and Shalyapin. Yet, as R.D. Charques points out, "the best pages in the book are those on Chekhov", and it was to commemorate the fiftieth anniversary of Chekhov's death that Bunin set to work on his new book *About Chekhov*, which remained unfinished.

The first section of *About Chekhov*, prepared for pub- *About Chekhov* lication in 1955 by Vera Bunina and Zurov, consists of biographical information on Chekhov, Bunin's memories of him (Bunin knew Chekhov's family and was a regular guest in the Chekhov household) and a section on Chekhov's romantic involvement with the author Lydia Avilova. Avilova's letters to

305

the Bunins, written when she was in Czechoslovakia in 1922–24, are also included in the book (just as reminiscences of Leo Tolstoy by the Bunins' friend Ekaterina Lopatina became part of *The Liberation of Tolstoy*). The second section consists of quotations from Chekhov's letters and Bunin's marginalia on the studies of Chekhov's art by the émigré scholar Pyotr Bitsilli and the Soviet critic Vladimir Ermilov, and on a collection of reminiscences about Chekhov with contributions from Teleshov, Gorky, Kuprin and others. In terms of an overarching concept, not much can be gleaned from this compilation of assorted fragments, but it is precisely the book's fragmentary nature that encapsulates the spirit of Bunin's persistent endeavour to capture fleeting impressions and images.

Film Adaptations

John Middleton Murry compared Bunin's art to that of a "cinema where the camera is old-fashioned; [the pictures] jump and flicker, they alternate between brilliancy and dullness, and they are sometimes tiring to the eyes". Although this is hardly a compliment, there are indeed certain pictorial qualities in Bunin's works, comparable to a collection of eye-catching stills. Bunin liked cinema (incidentally, the news about the award of the Nobel Prize arrived when he was at the pictures), and in 1938 he even planned to write a film script about Leo Tolstoy's life, in collaboration with Mark Aldanov and Tolstoy's daughter Tatyana. However, it was not until the times of perestroika that Bunin started attracting filmmakers' attention on a fairly regular basis. Unfortunately, not all the Bunin film adaptations reached a wide audience. The eponymous full-length film version of his story 'The Eternal Spring' (which includes several of his other stories, such as 'Rusya' and 'The Caucasus' from *Dark Avenues*, as well as 'Dry Valley'), directed by Vladimir Tolkachikov at the Belarusfilm studios in 1989, was banned after the first public screening. In 1994, a sixteen-minute student short *The Cricket*, based on a 1911 story of the same name, about a harness-maker's son freezing to death in the woods, was made at the All-Russia State Institute for Filmmakers by the director Alexander Panov, but did not receive a commercial release. The same year, however, saw the release of an eighty-minute-long TV film *Initiation to Love* (*Posviashchenie v liubov'*) – an adaptation of the stories 'A Cold Autumn', 'Rusya' and 'The Swing' from the *Dark Avenues* collection – directed by Lev Tsutsulkovsky at the Lentelefilm studios.

Stories from *Dark Avenues* have proved to be the most popular choice for film adaptations. In 1995, at the Vremya studios, the director Boris Yashin turned the stories 'Natalie', 'Tanya' and 'In Paris' into a feature film called *The Mescherskys* (*Meshcherskie*). In the same year, a Polish-Belorussian co-production brought out yet another film version of 'Natalie', entitled *The Summer of Love* (*Lato milosci*, directed by Feliks Falk). In 1999, a modern version of the stories 'Pure Monday' and 'The Chapel', under the title of *Pure Monday*, was filmed as an All-Russia State Institute for Filmmakers graduation project by the first-time director Marina Migunova. In 2000, Bunin himself became the subject of the biopic *His Wife's Diary* (*Dnevnik ego zheny*, directed by Alexei Uchitel at the Rok and Lenfilm studios). The film focuses on the complicated relationship between Bunin, his wife Vera, Galina Kuznetsova and Margarita Stepun. Regardless of its controversial nature, it has made Bunin a member of an exclusive group of Russian writers of exceptional standing, such as Lomonosov, Pushkin, Lermontov, Dostoevsky and Leo Tolstoy, whose lives have been deemed worthy of a feature film.

– Andrei Rogatchevski, 2008

Select Bibliography

Standard Edition
There is still no standard edition of *Dark Avenues*. A complex history of the various (in some instances, yet unpublished) versions of its constituent parts has been related in Hella Reese's *Ein Meisterwerk im Zwielicht: Ivan Bunins narrative Kurzprosaverknüpfung* Temnye allei *zwischen Akzeptanz und Ablehnung: eine Genrestudie* (München: Sagner, 2003).

Biographies and Additional Background Material in Russian:
Bunina, Vera, *Zhizn' Bunina: 1870–1906* (The Life of Bunin; Paris, [s.n.], 1958)
Kuznetsova, Galina, *Grasskii dnevnik* (The Grasse Diary; Washington: Victor Kamkin, 1967)
Grin, Militsa (ed.), *Ustami Buninykh* (As Spoken by the Bunins; Frankfurt/Main: Posev, 1977–82; in 3 vols)

Bakhrakh, Alexander, *Bunin v khalate* (Bunin in a Dressing Gown; Bayville: Tovarishchestvo zarubezhnykh pisatelei, 1979)

Burlaka, D.K. (ed.), *I.A. Bunin: Pro et contra: Lichnost i tvorchestvo Ivana Bunina v otsenke russkikh i zarubezhnykh myslitelei i issledovatelei: Antologiia* (St Petersburg: Izdatel'stvo Russkogo Khristianskogo gumanitarnogo instituta, 2001)

Baboreko, Alexander, *Bunin: Zhizneopisanie* (The Life of Bunin; Moscow: Molodaia gvardiia, 2004)

Biographies and Additional Background Material in English:

Heywood, Anthony J., *Catalogue of the I.A. Bunin, V.N. Bunina, L.F. Zurov and E.M. Lopatina Collections* (Leeds: Leeds University Press, 2000)

Kryzytski, Serge, *The Works of Ivan Bunin* (The Hague: Mouton, 1971)

Woodward, James B., *Ivan Bunin: A Study of His Fiction* (Chapel Hill: University of North Carolina Press, 1980)

Connolly, Julian W., *Ivan Bunin* (Boston, MA: Twayne Publishers, 1982)

Marullo, Thomas Gaiton, (ed.), *Ivan Bunin: Russian Requiem, 1885–1920: A Portrait from Letters, Diaries and Fiction* (Chicago: Ivan R. Dee, 1993)

Marullo, Thomas Gaiton, (ed.), *Ivan Bunin: From the Other Shore, 1920–1933: A Portrait from Letters, Diaries and Fiction* (Chicago: Ivan R. Dee, 1995)

Marullo, Thomas Gaiton, (ed.), *Ivan Bunin: The Twilight of Emigré Russia, 1934–1953: A Portrait from Letters, Diaries and Memoirs* (Chicago: Ivan R. Dee, 2002)

Zweers, Alexander F., *The Narratology of the Autobiography: An Analysis of the Literary Devices Employed in Ivan Bunin's* The Life of Arsen'ev (New York: Peter Lang, 1997)

Appendix

In Spring, in Judaea

"THOSE DISTANT DAYS in Judaea that left me lame, a cripple, for the rest of my life, were in the happiest time of my youth," said the tall, elegant man with a yellowish face, shining brown eyes and short, tightly curled silvery hair, who always walked with a crutch because of a left leg that did not bend at the knee. "I was then taking part in a small expedition which had as its aim the study of the eastern shores of the Dead Sea, the legendary sites of Sodom and Gomorrah, and I was living in Jerusalem, waiting for my companions, who had been delayed in Constantinople, and paying visits to one of the Bedouin camps on the road to Jericho, to Sheikh Ayid, who had been recommended to me by archaeologists in Jerusalem, and who had undertaken to provide all the necessary equipment for our expedition and to lead it in person. I went to him for the first time to negotiate with a guide, the next day he came to me in Jerusalem himself; then I started going to his camp by myself, having bought from him a wonderful filly to ride – I even started going excessively often... It was spring, Judaea was awash with the joyous brilliance of the sun, and the Song of Songs would come to mind: 'The winter is past, the flowers appear on the earth, the time of the singing of birds is come, and the voice of the turtle is heard, and the vines with the tender grape give a good smell...'* There, on that ancient path to Jericho, in the stony Judaean desert, everything was, as always, dead, wild, bare, the torrid heat and the sands were dazzling. But even there, in those radiant spring days, everything seemed to me endlessly joyous, happy: I was then in the East for the first time, I saw a completely new world before me, and in that world, something extraordinary – Ayid's niece.

"The Judaean desert is an entire country, descending steadily right as far as the Jordan valley: hills and passes, now stony, now sandy, in places overgrown with coarse vegetation, inhabited only by snakes and quails, sunk in eternal silence. In winter, as everywhere in Judaea, it pours with rain there, and icy winds blow; in spring, summer and autumn there is the same sepulchral tranquillity, monotony, but there is the intense heat from the sun, the sleep from the sun. In depressions where wells are to be found, the traces of Bedouin camps can be seen: the ash of campfires, stones piled in circles or squares on which tents are secured... But the camp to which I went, where the sheikh was Ayid, presented a picture like this: a wide, sandy gully between hills, and in it a small gathering of tents made of black felt, flat, rectangular and quite gloomy in their blackness against the yellowness of the sands. As I was arriving I would constantly see little smouldering heaps of pressed dung in front of some of the tents, and amidst the tents, cramped conditions: everywhere there were dogs, horses, mules, goats – to this day I don't understand how and where they all got fed – a multitude of bare, dark-skinned, curly-haired children; women and men, some looking like gypsies, others like Negroes, although not thick-lipped... And it was strange to see how warmly, in spite of the heat, the men were dressed: an indigo shirt down to the knees, a wadded jacket, and on top an abaya, that is, a very long and heavy, broad-shouldered chlamys made of two-toned wool, striped in two colours – black and white; on their heads a keffiyeh – a yellow headscarf with red stripes, spread out over the shoulders, hanging down by the cheeks, and gathered twice at the crown by a similarly two-toned, two-coloured woollen braid. All this presented a complete contrast to the women's clothing: the women have indigo headscarves thrown over their heads, their faces are exposed, and on their bodies is a long indigo shirt with pointed sleeves falling almost to the ground; the men wear crude shoes with iron pieces attached to the soles, the women go bare-footed, and all have wonderful feet, flexible and so suntanned as to be quite like coal. The men smoke pipes, the women too...

"When I arrived at the camp for the second time, without a guide, I was received already as a friend. Ayid's tent, which had its flaps raised for entry, was the most spacious, and inside it I found a whole collection of elderly Bedouins sitting around its black felt walls. Ayid had come out to meet me and performed a bow and the placing of the right hand to the lips and the forehead. On entering the tent in front of him, I waited for him to sit down on the rug in the middle of the tent, and then did what he had done for me upon meeting me, what is always required – the same bow and placing of the right hand to the lips and the forehead – and I did it several times, reflecting the number of seated people; then I sat down beside Ayid and, seated, did the same thing again; I was, of course, answered in the same way. Only the host and I spoke – briefly and slowly: it was custom too that required it to be this way, and I was not then very well versed in conversational Arabic either – the others smoked and remained silent. But meanwhile, outside the tent, refreshments were being prepared for me and the guests. Usually Bedouins eat *khibiz* – flat maize cakes – and boiled millet with goat's milk... But the essential refreshment for a guest is *kharuf*: a sheep which they roast in a hole dug in the sand by heaping layers of smouldering pressed dung upon it. After the sheep they give you coffee, but always without sugar. And so everyone sat and ate as though nothing were out of the ordinary, although in the shade of the felt tent it was hellishly hot and stuffy, and looking out of its wide-open flaps was simply terrifying: the sands in the distance were glittering so, they seemed to be melting before your eyes. After every word the sheikh would say to me: *khavádzha*, sir, and I to him: most esteemed sheikh *bédavi* (that is, son of the desert, Bedouin)... Incidentally, do you know what Jordan is called in Arabic? Quite simply: Shariyat, which all in all means watering place.

"Ayid was about fifty, short, broad in the bone, thin and very strong; his face was a baked brick, his eyes – transparent, grey, piercing; a copper beard streaked with grey, coarse, small, trimmed, and a similarly trimmed moustache – Bedouins always trim the one and the other; he was shod, like everyone, in thick, metal-soled shoes. When he visited me in Jerusalem there was a dagger at his belt and a long rifle in his hands.

"I saw his niece that very day when I already sat in his tent 'as a friend': she walked past the tent, holding herself erect, carrying a small can of water on her head and supporting it with her right hand. I don't know how old she was, I think no more than eighteen, but I subsequently learnt one thing – four years earlier she had been married, and in that same year had been widowed, without having had children, and she had moved into her uncle's tent, being an orphan and very poor. 'Return, return, O Shulamite!'* I thought. (After all, the Shulamite probably looked like her: 'I am black and beautiful, O ye maidens of Jerusalem.')* And, passing by the tent, she turned her head slightly and cast her eyes over me: those eyes were extraordinarily dark, mysterious, the face almost black, the lips lilac, large – at that moment I was struck more than anything by them... But by them alone? I was struck by everything: the amazing arm, bared to the shoulder, holding the can on her head, the slow, sinuous movements of the body beneath the long indigo shirt, the full breasts lifting that shirt... And it just had to happen that soon after that I met her in Jerusalem by the Jaffa Gate! She was walking towards me in a crowd, and on this occasion was carrying something wrapped up in canvas on her head. On seeing me, she paused. I rushed over to her:

"'You recognized me?'

"She patted me lightly on the shoulder with her free hand and smiled:

"'I did, *khavádzha*.'

"'What's that you're carrying?'

"'I'm carrying goat's cheese.'

"'To whom?'

"'To everyone.'

"'To sell, you mean? Then bring it to me.'

"'Where?'

"'Just over here, to the hotel...'

"I was living right by the Jaffa Gate, in a tall, narrow building joined to other buildings on the left side of the small square from which runs the stepped Street of King David – a dark passage, covered here by pieces of canvas, there by ancient stone vaults, between equally ancient workshops and shops. And she set off in front of me without any shyness up the steep and cramped stone stairway of this building, leaning back slightly, easily tensing her undulating body, holding the round of cheese in canvas on her head under its indigo headscarf with her right arm so bared that the dense black hair of her armpit could be seen. At one turn of the stairway she paused: there, deep down below outside the narrow window, could be seen the ancient Waterhole of the Prophet Ezekiel, the greenish water of which lay, as in a well, in a square formed by the unbroken walls of neighbouring buildings with gratings at their little windows – the very water in which Bathsheba, the wife of Uriah, had bathed and captivated King David with her nakedness.* Pausing, she looked out of the window and, turning, glanced at me in joyful surprise with her amazing eyes. I could not restrain myself and kissed her bare forearm – she glanced at me enquiringly: kisses are not customary among the Bedouins. Entering my room, she put her package onto the table and reached out to me the palm of her right hand. I put a few copper coins into her palm, then, cold with excitement, I took out a gold sovereign and showed her. She understood and lowered her lashes, bowed her head submissively and covered her eyes with the inner bend of her elbow, and she lay down on her back on the bed, slowly baring her sun-smoked legs and jerking her belly up and down in invitation...

"'When will you bring cheese again?' I asked, seeing her out onto the stairway an hour later.

"She gave her head a light shake:

"'Soon is not possible.'

"And she showed me five fingers: five days.

"A week or two later, when I was leaving Ayid's and had already ridden quite a long way off, behind me there was the crack of a gunshot – and a bullet struck a rock in front of me with such force that the rock began giving off smoke. I roused my horse to a gallop, bending low to the saddle – there was the crack of a second shot, and something lashed me hard below the knee of my left leg. I galloped all the way to Jerusalem, looking down at my boot, over which the frothing blood was pouring... I wonder to this day how Ayid could have missed twice. I wonder too at how he could have found out it was I who had bought the goat's cheese from her.

1946

A Place for the Night

I T HAPPENED in a remote mountainous area in the south of Spain.
It was a June night, and the small full moon was at its zenith, but its
light, slightly pinkish, as it sometimes is on hot nights after the brief
daytime downpours that are so common at the time the lilies are in
flower, nonetheless lit the passes of the low mountains, covered in low-
growing southern forests, so brightly that the eye could make them out
clearly right up to the horizons.

A narrow valley ran between these passes to the north. And in the
shadow from their heights on the one side, in the deathly quiet of this
desolate night, there was the monotonous noise of a mountain stream
and the mysterious, continual floating of fireflies, *lucciole*, regularly
going out and regularly flaring up, now like amethyst, now like topaz.
The heights opposite receded from the valley, and along the low ground
below them lay an ancient stony road. And on it, on that low ground,
just as ancient seemed the little stone town, into which, at this already
quite late hour, at walking pace on a bay stallion which was lame in
the right foreleg, there rode a tall Moroccan in a wide white woollen
burnous and a Moroccan fez.

The little town seemed dead, abandoned. And that is what it was.
The Moroccan at first rode down a shady street between the stone
shells of houses with yawning black voids in place of windows and
with gardens run wild behind them. But then he rode out onto a
light square, on which there was a long waterhole with an awning,
a church with a blue statue of the Madonna above the portal, a few
still-inhabited houses, and ahead, by the way out, an inn. There, on
the lower floor, the small windows were lit up, and the Moroccan, who
was already dozing, came to and pulled the reins taut, which made the
limping horse start to drum more briskly over the bumpy stones of the
square.

At this drumming, out onto the threshold of the inn there stepped an
emaciated little old woman, who could have been taken for a beggar,
and there leapt a round-faced girl of about fifteen with a fringe on

her forehead, with espadrilles on otherwise bare feet, and in a light little dress the colour of a faded glycinia, and there rose a huge black dog with a smooth coat and short ears standing on end, which had been lying beside the threshold. The Moroccan dismounted by the threshold, and at once the dog moved forwards with its eyes flashing, baring its fearsome white teeth as if in loathing. The Moroccan waved his whip, but the girl forestalled him:

"Negra!" she cried in fright in a ringing voice. "What's wrong with you?"

And dropping its head, the dog slowly walked away and lay down facing the wall of the building.

The Moroccan gave a greeting in bad Spanish and began asking if there was a blacksmith in the town – the horse's hoof needed to be looked at the next day – where the horse could be put for the night, and whether any fodder could be found for it, and for him some sort of supper. The girl looked with lively curiosity at his great height and small, very swarthy face, eaten away by smallpox, and threw wary sidelong glances at the black dog, which was lying quietly, but as though offended, while the old woman, hard of hearing, replied hurriedly in a raucous voice: there was a blacksmith, the hired hand was asleep in the cattle yard next to the house, but she would wake him up straight away and let him have some fodder for the horse – and as far as food was concerned, the guest must forgive them: they could fry up egg and pork fat, but from supper only a few cold beans and some vegetable ragout remained... And half an hour later, having dealt with the horse with the help of the hired hand, an eternally drunk old man, the Moroccan was already sitting at the table in the kitchen, eating greedily and greedily drinking yellowish white wine.

The inn building was old. Its lower floor was divided into two halves by a long lobby, at the end of which was a steep staircase to the upper floor: to the left was a spacious, low-ceilinged room with plank beds for the common people, to the right was a similarly spacious, low-ceilinged kitchen which also served as a dining room, with its ceiling and walls all densely blackened by smoke, with small windows, very deep because of the very thick walls, a hearth in the far corner, crude, bare tables, and benches, slippery with age, beside them, and an uneven stone floor. A kerosene lamp burned in the room, hanging down from the ceiling on a blackened iron chain, and there was the smell of stoking and burnt pork fat – the old woman had kindled the fire in the hearth, heated up the already sour ragout, and was frying eggs for the guest while he ate the cold beans dressed with vinegar and green olive oil. He had not taken his things off, had not removed his burnous, and he sat with his feet set wide apart, in thick leather shoes, above which, gathered tightly at the ankle, were wide trousers of the same white wool. And the girl, helping the old woman and waiting on him, kept taking fright at his quick, sudden glances at her, at the bluish whites of his eyes, which stood out on the dry and pockmarked, dark, thin-lipped face. She, at least, found him terrifying. Very tall, he was broad because of the burnous, and all the smaller did his head in the fez seem. Around the corners of his upper lip curled coarse dark hairs. Similar ones curled in places on his chin as well. His head was thrown slightly back, which made his large Adam's apple particularly prominent under his olive skin. On his slender, almost black fingers, silver rings showed up white. He ate, drank and was silent all the time.

When, having heated up the ragout and fried the eggs, the old woman sat down exhausted on a bench beside the extinguished hearth and asked him raucously where he was from and where he was going, he tossed her just one throaty phrase in reply:

"Far away."

Having finished the ragout and the eggs, he waved the already empty wine jug – there had been a lot of red pepper in the ragout – the old woman nodded her head to the girl, and when the latter, grabbing the jug, flashed through the open door out of the kitchen into the dark lobby, where fireflies were floating slowly and flaring up fantastically, he took a packet of cigarettes from out of his bosom and tossed out, still just as tersely:

"Granddaughter?"

"My niece, an orphan," the old woman began shouting, and started off on the story of how she had so loved her late brother, the girl's father, that for his sake she had remained a spinster, that this inn had belonged to him, that his wife had died already twelve years before, and he himself eight, and he had left everything to her, the old woman, for her lifetime, and that business had become very bad in this completely deserted little town...

Drawing on a cigarette, the Moroccan listened absent-mindedly, thinking some thoughts of his own. The girl ran in with a full jug and, glancing at her, he drew so hard on the cigarette stub that he burnt the tips of his sharp, black fingers; he hurriedly lit up a new cigarette and, addressing the old woman, whose deafness he had already noticed, said distinctly:

"It will be very nice for me if your niece pours me some wine herself."

"That's not her business," snapped the old woman, who passed easily from garrulity to abrupt terseness, and she began shouting angrily:

"It's already late, drink up your wine and go to bed, she's going to make up a bed for you now in the upper room."

The girl flashed her eyes animatedly and, without waiting for the order, slipped out once more and quickly started stomping up the stairs.

"And where do you both sleep?" the Moroccan asked, moving the fez back slightly from his sweaty forehead. "Upstairs too?"

The old woman shouted that it was too hot there in the summer, and when there were no guests – and there were hardly ever any now! – they slept in the other lower half of the building – over there, opposite – and she pointed towards the lobby, and again started off on complaints about bad business, and about everything having become very dear, and it being for that reason necessary, like it or not, to charge people passing through a lot...

"I'll be leaving early tomorrow," said the Moroccan, clearly no longer listening to her. "And in the morning you'll give me only coffee. So you can tot up right now how much I owe, and I'll settle up with you straight away. Let's just see where my small change is," he added, and he took out from under his burnous a soft red leather pouch, undid it, stretched out the strap which pulled its opening tight, spilt a little pile of gold coins onto the table, and pretended he was counting them carefully, while the old woman even half-rose from the bench beside the hearth, gazing at the coins round-eyed.

Upstairs it was dark and very hot. The girl opened the door into the stuffy, burning darkness, in which there was the sharp gleam of the cracks in the shutters, closed outside the two windows, which were just as small as those downstairs; she swerved deftly in the darkness past the round table in the middle of the room, opened a window, and, with a push, threw the shutters wide open to the shining moonlit night, to the huge bright sky with its occasional stars. It became easier to breathe, and the stream in the valley became audible. The girl leant out of the window to glance at the moon, which, still very high, was not visible from the room, and then she glanced down: down below, with its face lifted and gazing at her, stood the dog, which five years or so before had come running into the inn from somewhere as a stray puppy, had grown up before her eyes and become attached to her with that devotion of which only dogs are capable.

"Negra," said the girl in a whisper, "why aren't you asleep?"

The dog let out a weak yelp, shook its head upwards, and darted towards the open door into the lobby.

"Go back, go back!" the girl ordered in a hasty whisper. "Back to your place!"

The dog stopped and lifted its face again, its eyes flashing red fire.

"What do you want?" the girl, who always spoke to it as if with a person, began affectionately. "Why aren't you asleep, silly? Is it the moon that's worrying you so?"

As if wanting to make some reply, the dog again reached its face up, again gave a quiet yelp. The girl shrugged a shoulder. For her too the dog was the dearest, even the only dear creature in the world, whose feelings and thoughts almost always seemed comprehensible to her. But what the dog wanted to express now, what was worrying it at the moment, she did not understand, and for that reason she only wagged a finger sternly and ordered again in a whisper of feigned anger:

"Back to your place, Negra! Go to sleep!"

The dog lay down, and the girl stood by the window a little longer thinking about it... It was possible it was worried by this terrifying Moroccan. It almost always met the inn's guests calmly and paid no attention even to those who in appearance seemed like bandits or convicts. But it was nonetheless the case that at times for some reason it would throw itself at some people like a mad thing, barking thunderously, and then just she alone could restrain it. Though there could have been another reason too for its worry, its irritability – this hot night with its full moon, so dazzling, and without the slightest movement of the air. Perfectly audible in the extraordinary quietness of this night were the noise of the stream in the valley and the stamping of the hoofs of the goat that lived in the cattle yard, when something – maybe the inn's old mule, maybe the Moroccan's stallion – suddenly kicked it with a thud, and it began bleating so loudly and disgustingly that this devilish bleating seemed to have resounded all over the world. And the girl leapt back cheerfully from the window, opened the other one, and threw open the shutters there too. The twilight of the room became even lighter. Besides the table, there stood in it, by the wall to the right of the entrance with their heads towards the wall, three wide beds, covered only with rough sheets. The girl threw back the sheet on the bed nearest the entrance and adjusted the bedhead, which was fantastically illuminated all of a sudden by a pellucid, delicate, pale-bluish light: it was a firefly that had landed on her fringe. She passed her hand over it, and the firefly, flickering and going out, began floating around the room. The girl started singing gently and ran out.

In the kitchen the Moroccan was standing drawn up to his full height with his back to her, and was saying something to the old woman, quietly, but insistently and irritably. The old woman was shaking her head negatively. The Moroccan jerked his shoulders upwards and turned to the girl coming in with such a malicious expression on his face that she recoiled.

"Is the bed ready?" he cried throatily.

"Everything's ready," the girl hurriedly replied.

"But I don't know where I'm to go. Take me."

"I'll take you myself," said the old woman angrily. "Follow me."

The girl listened to her stomping slowly up the steep stairs and to the Moroccan's shoes tapping after her, and then she went outside. The dog, which was lying by the threshold, leapt up at once, reared up and, trembling all over with joy and tenderness, licked her face.

"Go away, go away," the girl whispered, pushing it aside affectionately and sitting down on the threshold. The dog sat down too on its hind paws, and the girl put her arms around its neck, kissed it on the forehead and started rocking with it, listening to the heavy footsteps and the Moroccan's throaty voice in the upstairs room. He was saying something to the old woman more calmly now, but it was impossible to make out what it was. Finally he said loudly:

"Well, all right, all right! Only let her bring me some drinking water for the night."

And the steps of the old woman were heard coming carefully down the staircase.

The girl went to meet her in the lobby and said firmly:

"I heard what he said. No, I won't go to him. I'm afraid of him."

"Nonsense, nonsense!" shouted the old woman. "So do you think I'll go again myself with my legs, and in the dark as well, and up such a slippery staircase? And there's no reason at all to be afraid of him. He's just very stupid and hot-tempered, but he's kind. He kept telling me he felt sorry for you, that you were a poor girl and no one would marry you without a dowry. And it's true too, what sort of a dowry have you got? After all, we're completely ruined. Who stays with us now, apart from beggarly peasants!"

"And what was he getting so angry about when I came in?" asked the girl.

The old woman grew flustered.

"What, what!" she mumbled. "I told him not to interfere in other people's business... And so then he was offended..."

And she shouted angrily:

"Go on, quickly, get some water and take it to him. He promised to give you some sort of present in return. Go, I say!"

When the girl ran with a full jug through the open door of the upstairs room, the Moroccan was lying on the bed already completely undressed: in the bright, moonlit twilight his birdlike eyes were piercingly black, his small, closely cropped head was black, his long shirt was white and his big bare feet were sticking out. On the table in the middle of the room there shone a large revolver with a drum and a long barrel, and his outer clothing was heaped in a white mound on the bed next to his... It was all very frightening. The girl shoved the jug onto the table on the run, and darted headlong back again, but the Moroccan leapt up and caught her by the arm.

"Wait, wait," he said quickly, drawing her towards the bed, then sat down without releasing her arm and whispered: "Sit down beside me for a minute, sit down, sit down, listen... just listen..."

Stupefied, the girl obediently sat down. And he began hurriedly swearing he had fallen madly in love with her, that for one kiss from her he would give her ten gold coins... twenty coins... that he had a whole pouchful of them...

And pulling the red leather pouch out from under the bedhead, he stretched it open with shaking hands and tipped the gold out onto the bed, mumbling:

"There, you see how many of them I have... You see?"

323

She shook her head desperately and leapt up from the bed. But again he caught her instantly and, stopping her mouth with his wiry, tenacious hand, he threw her onto the bed. She tore his hand away with furious strength and gave a shrill cry:

"Negra!"

He squeezed her mouth shut again, together with her nose, and with his other hand began trying to catch her bared legs, with which, kicking out, she was hitting him painfully in the stomach – but at the same moment he heard the barking of the dog, which was tearing up the staircase like a whirlwind. Leaping to his feet, he grabbed the revolver from the table, but did not have time even to catch hold of the trigger, as he was instantly knocked off his feet to the floor. Protecting his face from the jaws of the dog, which was stretched out on top of him and scalding him with its fiery canine breath, he gave a jerk, threw up his chin – and the dog, with a mortal grip, ripped out his throat.

23rd March 1949

Notes to the Appendix

p. 313, *The winter is past... give a good smell*: The incomplete quotation is from Solomon 2:11–13.

p. 315, *Return, return, O Shulamite*: Solomon 6:13.

p. 315, *I am black... maidens of Jerusalem*: An inaccurate quotation from Solomon 1:5.

p. 316, *Bathsheba... with her nakedness*: See 2 Samuel 11:2.

'Dark Avenues' in the Original Russian

В холодное осеннее ненастье, на одной из больших тульских дорог, залитой дождями и изрезанной многими черными колеями, к длинной избе, в одной связи которой была казенная почтовая станция, а в другой частная горница, где можно было отдохнуть или переночевать, пообедать или спросить самовар, подкатил закиданный грязью тарантас с полуподнятым верхом, тройка довольно простых лошадей с подвязанными от слякоти хвостами. На козлах тарантаса сидел крепкий мужик в туго подпоясанном армяке, серьезный и темноликий, с редкой смоляной бородой, похожий на старинного разбойника, а в тарантасе стройный старик военный в большом картузе и в николаевской серой шинели с бобровым стоячим воротником, еще чернобровый, но с белыми усами, которые соединялись с такими же бакенбардами; подбородок у него был пробрит и вся наружность имела то сходство с Александром II, которое столь распространено было среди военных в пору его царствования; взгляд был тоже вопрошающий, строгий и вместе с тем усталый.

Когда лошади стали, он выкинул из тарантаса ногу в военном сапоге с ровным голенищем и, придерживая руками в замшевых перчатках полы шинели, взбежал на крыльцо избы.

– Налево, ваше превосходительство, – грубо крикнул с козел кучер, и он, слегка нагнувшись на пороге от своего высокого роста, вошел в сенцы, потом в горницу налево.

В горнице было тепло, сухо и опрятно: новый золотистый образ в левом углу, под ним покрытый чистой суровой скатертью стол, за столом чисто вымытые лавки; кухонная печь, занимавшая дальний правый угол, ново белела мелом; ближе стояло нечто вроде тахты, покрытой пегими попонами, упиравшейся отвалом в бок печи; из-за печной заслонки сладко пахло щами – разварившейся капустой, говядиной и лавровым листом.

Приезжий сбросил на лавку шинель и оказался еще стройнее в одном мундире и в длинных сапогах, потом снял перчатки и картуз и с усталым видом провел бледной худой рукой по голове – седые волосы его с начесами на висках к углам глаз слегка курчавились, красивое удлиненное лицо с темными глазами хранило кое-где мелкие следы оспы. В горнице никого не было, и он неприязненно крикнул, приотворив дверь в сенцы:

– Эй, кто там!

Тотчас вслед за тем в горницу вошла темноволосая, тоже чернобровая и тоже еще красивая не по возрасту женщина, похожая на пожилую цыганку, с темным пушком на верхней губе и вдоль щек, легкая на ходу, но полная, с большими грудями под красной кофточкой, с треугольным, как у гусыни, животом под черной шерстяной юбкой.

– Добро пожаловать, ваше превосходительство, – сказала она. – Покушать изволите или самовар прикажете?

Приезжий мельком глянул на ее округлые плечи и на легкие ноги в красных поношенных татарских туфлях и отрывисто, невнимательно ответил:

– Самовар. Хозяйка тут или служишь?

– Хозяйка, ваше превосходительство.

– Сама, значит, держишь?

– Так точно. Сама.

– Что ж так? Вдова, что ли, что сама ведешь дело?

– Не вдова, ваше превосходительство, а надо же чем-нибудь жить. И хозяйствовать я люблю.

– Так, так. Это хорошо. И как чисто, приятно у тебя.

Женщина все время пытливо смотрела на него, слегка щурясь.

– И чистоту люблю, – ответила она. – Ведь при господах выросла, как не уметь прилично себя держать, Николай Алексеевич.

Он быстро выпрямился, раскрыл глаза и покраснел.

– Надежда! Ты? – сказал он торопливо.

– Я, Николай Алексеевич, – ответила она.

– Боже мой, Боже мой, – сказал он, садясь на лавку и в упор глядя на нее. – Кто бы мог подумать! Сколько лет мы не видались? Лет тридцать пять?

– Тридцать, Николай Алексеевич. Мне сейчас сорок восемь, а вам под шестьдесят, думаю?

– Вроде этого... Боже мой, как странно!

– Что странно, сударь?

– Но все, все... Как ты не понимаешь!

Усталость и рассеянность его исчезли, он встал и решительно заходил по горнице, глядя в пол. Потом остановился и, краснея сквозь седину, стал говорить:

– Ничего не знаю о тебе с тех самых пор. Как ты сюда попала? Почему не осталась при господах?

– Мне господа вскоре после вас вольную дали.

– А где жила потом?

– Долго рассказывать, сударь.

– Замужем, говоришь, не была?

– Нет, не была.

– Почему? При такой красоте, которую ты имела?

– Не могла я этого сделать.

– Отчего не могла? Что ты хочешь сказать?

– Что ж тут объяснять. Небось, помните, как я вас любила.

Он покраснел до слез и, нахмурясь, опять зашагал.

– Все проходит, мой друг, – забормотал он. – Любовь, молодость – все, все. История пошлая, обыкновенная. С годами все проходит. Как это сказано в книге Иова? "Как о воде протекшей будешь вспоминать".

– Что кому бог дает, Николай Алексеевич. Молодость у всякого проходит, а любовь – другое дело.

Он поднял голову и, остановясь, болезненно усмехнулся:

– Ведь не могла же ты любить меня весь век!

– Значит, могла. Сколько ни проходило времени, все одним жила. Знала, что давно вас нет прежнего, что для вас словно ничего и не было, а вот... Поздно теперь укорять, а ведь правда, очень бессердечно вы меня бросили, – сколько раз я хотела руки на себя наложить от обиды от одной, уж не говоря обо всем прочем. Ведь было время, Николай Алексеевич, когда я вас Николенькой звала, а вы меня – помните как? И все стихи мне изволили читать про всякие "темные аллеи", – прибавила она с недоброй улыбкой.

– Ах, как хороша ты была! – сказал он, качая головой. – Как горяча, как прекрасна! Какой стан, какие глаза! Помнишь, как на тебя все заглядывались?

– Помню, сударь. Были и вы отменно хороши. И ведь это вам отдала я свою красоту, свою горячку. Как же можно такое забыть.

– А! Все проходит. Все забывается.

329

– Все проходит, да не все забывается.

– Уходи, – сказал он, отворачиваясь и подходя к окну. – Уходи, пожалуйста.

И, вынув платок и прижав его к глазам, скороговоркой прибавил:

– Лишь бы Бог меня простил. А ты, видно, простила.

Она подошла к двери и приостановилась:

– Нет, Николай Алексеевич, не простила. Раз разговор наш коснулся до наших чувств, скажу прямо: простить я вас никогда не могла. Как не было у меня ничего дороже вас на свете в ту пору, так и потом не было. Оттого-то и простить мне вас нельзя. Ну, да что вспоминать, мертвых с погоста не носят.

– Да, да, не к чему, прикажи подавать лошадей, – ответил он, отходя от окна уже со строгим лицом. – Одно тебе скажу: никогда я не был счастлив в жизни, не думай, пожалуйста. Извини, что, может быть, задеваю твое самолюбие, но скажу откровенно, – жену я без памяти любил. А изменила, бросила меня еще оскорбительней, чем я тебя. Сына обожал, – пока рос, каких только надежд на него не возлагал! А вышел негодяй, мот, наглец, без сердца, без чести, без совести... Впрочем, все это тоже самая обыкновенная, пошлая история. Будь здорова, милый друг. Думаю, что и я потерял в тебе самое дорогое, что имел в жизни.

Она подошла и поцеловала у него руку, он поцеловал у нее.

– Прикажи подавать...

Когда поехали дальше, он хмуро думал: "Да, как прелестна была! Волшебно прекрасна!" Со стыдом вспоминал свои последние слова и то, что поцеловал у ней руку, и тотчас стыдился своего стыда. "Разве неправда, что она дала мне лучшие минуты жизни?"

К закату проглянуло бледное солнце. Кучер гнал рысцой, все меняя черные колеи, выбирая менее грязные и тоже что-то думал. Наконец сказал с серьезной грубостью:

– А она, ваше превосходительство, все глядела в окно, как мы уезжали. Верно, давно изволите знать ее?

– Давно, Клим.

– Баба – ума палата. И все, говорят, богатеет. Деньги в рост дает.

– Это ничего не значит.

– Как не значит! Кому ж не хочется получше пожить! Если с совестью давать, худого мало. И она, говорят, справедлива на это. Но крута! Не отдал вовремя – пеняй на себя.

– Да, да, пеняй на себя... Погоняй, пожалуйста, как бы не опоздать нам к поезду...

Низкое солнце желто светило на пустые поля, лошади ровно шлепали по лужам. Он глядел на мелькавшие подковы, сдвинув черные брови, и думал:

"Да, пеняй на себя. Да, конечно, лучшие минуты. И не лучшие, а истинно волшебные! "Кругом шиповник алый цвел, стояли темных лип аллеи..." Но, боже мой, что же было бы дальше? Что, если бы я не бросил ее? Какой вздор! Эта самая Надежда не содержательница постоялой горницы, а моя жена, хозяйка моего петербургского дома, мать моих детей?"

И, закрывая глаза, качал головой.

20 октября 1938

Acknowledgements

The Publisher wishes to thank Richard Davies of the Brotherton Library, Leeds University, for his advice and support, Neil Cornwell for his editorial help and Andrei Rogatchevski for his care and diligence in writing the extra material.

ONEWORLD CLASSICS

ONEWORLD CLASSICS aims to publish mainstream and lesser-known European classics in an innovative and striking way, while employing the highest editorial and production standards. By way of a unique approach the range offers much more, both visually and textually, than readers have come to expect from contemporary classics publishing.

✦

CHARLOTTE BRONTË: *Jane Eyre*

EMILY BRONTË: *Wuthering Heights*

ANTON CHEKHOV: *Sakhalin Island*
Translated by Brian Reeve

CHARLES DICKENS: *Great Expectations*

D.H. LAWRENCE: *The First Women in Love*

D.H. LAWRENCE: *The Second Lady Chatterley's Lover*

D.H. LAWRENCE: *Selected Letters*

JAMES HANLEY: *Boy*

JACK KEROUAC: *Beat Generation*

JANE AUSTEN: *Emma*

JANE AUSTEN: *Pride and Prejudice*

GIOVANNI BOCCACCIO: *Decameron*
Translated by J.G. Nichols

DANTE ALIGHIERI: *Rime*
Translated by Anthony Mortimer and J.G. Nichols

FYODOR DOSTOEVSKY: *The Humiliated and Insulted*
Translated by Ignat Avsey

FYODOR DOSTOEVSKY: *Winter Impressions*
Translated by Kyril Zinovieff

ÉMILE ZOLA: *Ladies' Delight*
Translated by April Fitzlyon

BOILEAU: *The Art of Poetry* and *Lutrin*
Translated by William Soames and John Ozell

CECCO ANGIOLIERI: *Sonnets*
Translated by C.H. Scott

LEO TOLSTOY: *Anna Karenina*
Translated by Kyril Zinovieff

STENDHAL: *The Life of Rossini*
Translated by Richard N. Coe

GIFT CLASSICS

HENRY MILLER: *The World of Sex*

JONATHAN SWIFT: *The Benefit of Farting*

ANONYMOUS: *Dirty Limericks*

NAPOLEON BONAPARTE: *Aphorisms*

ROBERT GRAVES: *The Future of Swearing*

CHARLES DICKENS: *The Life of Our Lord*

CALDER PUBLICATIONS

SINCE 1949, JOHN CALDER has published eighteen Nobel Prize winners and around fifteen hundred books. He has put into print many of the major French and European writers, almost single-handedly introducing modern literature into the English language. His commitment to literary excellence has influenced two generations of authors, readers, booksellers and publishers. We are delighted to keep John Calder's legacy alive and hope to honour his achievements by continuing his tradition of excellence into a new century.

ANTONIN ARTAUD: *The Theatre and Its Double*

LOUIS-FERDINAND CÉLINE: *Journey to the End of the Night*

MARGUERITE DURAS: *The Sailor from Gibraltar*

ERICH FRIED: *100 Poems without a Country*

EUGÈNE IONESCO: *Plays*

LUIGI PIRANDELLO: *Collected Plays*

RAYMOND QUENEAU: *Exercises in Style*

ALAIN ROBBE-GRILLET: *In the Labyrinth*

ALEXANDER TROCCHI: *Cain's Book*

To order any of our titles and for up-to-date information about our current and forthcoming publications, please visit our website on:

www.oneworldclassics.com